AMERICAN CHILDREN

Francesca Summers

CORGI BOOKS

AMBITION'S CHILDREN

A CORGI BOOK   0 552 13614 X

First publication in Great Britain

PRINTING HISTORY
Corgi edition published 1991

This book is set in 10/11pt Times
by Kestrel Data, Exeter

Corgi Books are published by Transworld Publishers Ltd., 61-63 Uxbridge Road, Ealing, London W5 5SA, in Australia by Transworld Publishers (Australia) Pty. Ltd., 15-23 Helles Avenue, Moorebank, NSW 2170, and in New Zealand by Transworld Publishers (N.Z.) Ltd., Cnr. Moselle and Waipareira Avenues, Henderson, Auckland.

Printed and bound in Great Britain by
Cox & Wyman Ltd, Reading

For my daughter, Lynn.

PROLOGUE

An air-raid was in progress over London when Sybil Jones abandoned her day-old twin daughters.

Clutching her worn tweed coat over her short nightdress, she moved through the hospital lobby with the shuffling steps of an old woman, and went out into the night.

No-one was there to stop her. Twenty minutes earlier, a bomb had fallen on the hospital's west wing. Enemy aircraft droned overhead and explosions were continuous. It was July 1940.

She walked towards the Underground. At three o'clock in the morning the streets were alive. Men and women wearing overalls and steel helmets hurried past her, seeking the injured. Fire-fighters were battling blazes in several houses, others were dousing incendaries. A darkened ambulance crept through the rubble towards the hospital.

A house near the Underground's entrance was on fire. She leant against a wall to rest and the flames illuminated her. A passer-by with the time or inclination to spare her a glance would have seen that her appearance belied her unsteady footsteps: she was only eighteen. Although her face was pale and exhausted, her eyes blazed with determination. By tomorrow, she intended to be a long way away.

She started down the steps into the Underground. Her legs were weak and rubbery and she clung to the railing for support. She was hardly aware of the all-clear until people began to climb up past her, anxious to find out if their homes were still intact. No-one took any notice of her and she did not ask anyone for help. On the platform of the Northern Line, she found a vacant place among the prone bodies of those who nightly sought shelter from the raids. She sat down on the ground, resting her back against the wall.

Inside the hospital, there was an atmosphere of controlled chaos. Fire-fighters ran to and from the burning west wing with hoses, axes and breathing equipment. Nurses were starting to move patients back into the wards from the basement shelters. They had carried out the routine many times. When the raid began, the bedridden had been secured on their mattresses with straps which lay permanently ready on each bed. They had been borne to the shelters and set in neat rows, like fish ready for canning. Now they were waiting to be returned, and those who were mobile were already on their way back to their beds.

Most of the cases were injuries caused by the war. The hospital's maternity ward was famous, but it had been evacuated to the country and only a skeleton service existed for the few women who insisted on staying in London to have their babies.

On this night, there were five new-born infants in the shelter. Three had been handed to their mothers and were feeding contentedly. The other two were still in their cots and each had a card tied to its right wrist. They were labelled Twin 1 and Twin 2.

One of them was mewling hungrily and a probationer picked it up. A senior nurse said irritably, 'Try to keep them quiet. Take them to the mother.'

'I can't find her, Sister. I've looked everywhere. Nobody has seen her.'

'Go and look again. Maybe she wandered into the wrong ward. Check the shelters.'

'I've already . . .'

'Go!'

'It is not possible, Sister, to mislay a patient during an air-raid!' Matron's mouth was tight and thin. 'What do you know about the girl?'

'She was brought in at about seven o'clock the night before last, Matron.' The sister allowed no trace of resentment to colour her voice. 'Her labour had started while she was on a train. Someone called an ambulance, and the babies were born around four o'clock. Twenty minutes between them. They're doing well.'

'I already know all that! What's her name?'

'She calls herself Sybil Jones.'

'Calls herself?'

'There's something odd . . . she didn't want anyone notified, refused to give an address. She wouldn't speak to the other women in the ward, nor to the nurses.'

'So the children are probably illegitimate. Do you think she's walked out on them?'

'It's possible, I suppose.'

'What kind of girl would desert her babies like that?'

The sister shrugged. 'Maybe Nurse Ferguson will find her . . .'

But Nurse Ferguson did not. 'She's gone, Matron. I even went through the kitchens . . .' Exhausted and emotional after the night's tumult, she sniffed.

'For Heaven's sake, Nurse, you hardly met the girl! Why are you snivelling?'

'I went to look at the babies again. They haven't even got names. No mother, no names. Just Twin 1 and Twin 2.' A tear overflowed.

During the weeks to come, others would weep over the deserted infants. Their mother never did.

Sybil Jones was in the front line of passengers waiting for the morning's first northbound train. She had not slept, and she ached all over. But she was no longer sharing her body with two babies and felt light and free.

Preceded by a rush of fetid air, the train pulled in and she stumbled aboard.

Three-quarters of an hour later she emerged into Heath Street, Hampstead, and stopped a man who was hurrying into the Tube. 'Church Row?'

Hardly pausing, he gestured across the road. 'Second right.'

Church Row was lined with houses and trees. The church was at the far end. No-one was about. She gritted her teeth against increasing weakness as she walked along, checking house-numbers. She found the address she wanted on the left, a narrow brick building with a fanlight above the door. She pressed its bell again and again.

A man opened the door. He was tall, and was wearing a dressing-gown. A woman was peering over his shoulder. They looked at her, thin-faced and trembling in her shabby coat. 'What the hell hour is this to come calling?' he snapped. 'What do you want?'

Her voice was little more than a whisper. 'I am Cybèle. Dominic said I should come to you.'

The woman gasped, then she said, 'Come in.'

PART ONE

1

The hotel's private banqueting-room was a blaze of lights. There were flowers on the tables and silver and glasses winked diamond pin-points, reflecting crystal chandeliers.

There were no spare seats, for this was a major social event, and scarcely an invitation had been refused. The glittering crowd was studded with well-known faces: actors and actresses, TV personalities, industrialists, best-selling authors, model-girls, publishers. The men were in dinner-jackets, the women were like chattering, highly coloured parrots in their silks and satins and laces. Those who had jewels were wearing them.

Lights and television cameras, which had been roaming the room, catching the celebrities with their mouths full, focused on a platform at one end. It was ten o'clock, the guests had been well-fed and wined, and the evening was about to reach its climax, its *raison d'être*.

Lord Sharpe of Foxfield, a small, ferret-faced newspaper magnate said to be among the richest men in Britain, thrust his way to the platform, attended by three minions. There was a burst of applause as he took his place at the microphone, then silence as he began to speak.

'Ladies and gentlemen, I am here tonight to announce the first winner of Britain's newest and, dare I say, most prestigious literary prize. I will remind you that it was provided for in the will of my friend and fellow-publisher Sir Joseph Harrington. His death was a great loss to the world of books, but his name will live on in the Harrington Book of the Year Award.

'A cheque for thirty thousand pounds will be presented annually to the author who has, in the opinion of the people who actually read books, produced the work, either of fiction or non-fiction, which they have most enjoyed during the preceding year. And I mean *enjoyed*. My committee and I have been – and will be – looking for books that entertain, rather than for Great Literature.' He capitalized the words contemptuously; his publications were not read for their literary content. 'Following announcements in my own newspapers and magazines, votes have been received from all over Britain during the past three months. Many titles were put forward, but one was outstanding, polling more than fifty per cent.'

Several authors, seated at different tables, were smiling bravely, hoping they could maintain their smiles when their suspicions that they had not won the prize were confirmed.

'Our winner is a lady already known to many of you, either personally or through her writing. I might say, known intimately, for her remarkable account of her own life is as frank an autobiography as any I, for one, have read. According to an eminent critic, it is "a ruthlessly honest book, written by an honestly ruthless woman." Be that as it may, it stacked up the highest sales figures of any British publication last year, appealing to men and women of all ages and classes. Foreign rights have been bought in France, Germany, Italy, Japan and Scandinavia, and its author is about to leave for the United States to promote the forthcoming American edition.

'She has written the story of a girl who started with nothing, and rose to become a major figure in the international fashion world, perhaps the most influential writer in her field; who founded a top-selling magazine regarded as a bible by everyone connected with fashion in Paris, London, Rome and New York; whose chain of boutiques has spread throughout Europe and made women in the nineties recognize that elegance is once again something more than a dirty word.

'But that doesn't begin to describe her life. For instance, her wartime bravery in France as a member of the Special Operations Executive, when she was still a teenager, earned her the red ribbon of the Légion d'Honneur. In her autobiography, she holds nothing back, from her extraordinary childhood, spent touring Europe with her mother, a failed

16

opera singer turned circus performer, to her decision to abandon her twins for adoption when they were twenty-four hours old. I won't go on. If any of you have not read her book, I urge you to do so.

'Now I will ask the winner of the first Harrington Book of the Year Award to come forward: Cybèle Meredith, author of *I am Cybèle*. Lady Meredith!'

A slender woman rose from her seat and moved to the platform, walking lightly as a young girl. His lordship kissed her on both cheeks and handed her an envelope with her name embossed on it in gold. Again, applause broke out.

At the press table well back in the hall, one member of the audience studied Cybèle Meredith with more than ordinary interest. He was a large young man, sitting hunched forward, his broad shoulders straining at the seams of his dinner-jacket. He had rough, dark hair and eyebrows that rose in circumflex peaks. There had been a sardonic twist to his mouth as he listened to the eulogy. His name was Christian Morel, and he was a freelance writer, covering the ceremony for a Paris magazine. Like his colleagues, he held a ball Pentel poised above a notebook; but he was not making notes.

She was not as he had imagined. In his mind, conditioned since childhood by his mother's obsessive hatred of this woman, he had seen a witchlike creature whose malice and lack of humanity must show in her face. Instead, she was, at sixty-eight, still strikingly beautiful. Her hair was a perfectly groomed silver halo, there was no sagging around the jaw-line. Her firm mouth was smiling, and blue almond-shaped eyes were sparkling. She was wearing an ankle-length dress in black chiffon, which floated over a figure-hugging petticoat. It was high-necked, with long, full sleeves, and her only jewellery was a rope of pearls. The Frenchman recognized that her understated chic made every other woman in the room look overdressed. There was no doubt in his mind that the effect was deliberate.

In a clear, bell-like voice, she thanked her host and the donors of the award, and her publishers, and the readers who

17

had enjoyed her book. It was more than she deserved, and she accepted in the humble certainty that far better writers had been unlucky this year. The platitudes fell over each other, but she managed to sound sincere, and her speech was mercifully short.

When it ended, she was ushered off the platform into a private room where the media waited to interview her. Christian Morel joined them, propping himself against a wall, tall enough to watch her over the surrounding crowd.

He took no part in the interviews and even now did not bother to make notes. At one point, attracted by his concentration, she looked up at him. Their eyes met and held for a moment, before she turned to another questioner.

The press conference ended and reporters and photographers were hustled out of the room as she faced the television cameras.

While his colleagues drifted back to their table, Morel waited for her in the passage. Twenty minutes later, the cameramen and TV interviewers emerged. She followed them, with Lord Sharpe. After a brief conversation, Morel heard her say, 'I've done my duty, Robert. Now I'm going home.'

'I'll take you.'

'No need.' She gestured to a man holding a chauffeur's cap who was waiting at the end of the passage. 'I have a car.'

As Sharpe turned back towards the banqueting-hall, Morel stepped forward. 'Lady Meredith . . .'

Her face hardened. 'No more interviews!'

'Not now, of course. But may I make an appointment to see you? Perhaps tomorrow?' He spoke in French.

She frowned, and said in the same language, 'Who are you?'

'Christian Morel. I've been commissioned by *France-Match* to prepare a feature about you and your work.'

She waved a dismissive hand. 'They must know everything there is to know about me already. And so will you if you read my book. I'm leaving for the United States the day after tomorrow, M. Morel. I have no time to see you.'

'I've read your book. It was – interesting.' His voice was

expressionless and the hesitation caught her attention. 'Your life has changed recently. I'm required to write about your occupations in your so-called retirement, your property in the Dordogne, your plans for the future, the effect publication of your autobiography has had.'

'I can give you that in a few words,' she said grimly. 'The destruction of my privacy.'

'But you asked for it, didn't you? You laid your life out for the world's inspection. What did you expect?'

She took a sharp, surprised breath and he awaited her anger. Instead, after glaring at him for a moment, she relaxed. 'You're impertinent, but you're right. I shouldn't complain – especially after tonight.' She glanced down at the envelope she held. 'I still haven't time for an interview. After the tour, I'm going straight to my house in France. I don't expect to be back in England for several months.'

'I know something about Le Bas-Fond, Madame, and how it's virtually run as a commune. You have no permanent paid staff apart from your manager, right?'

'That's well-known,' she said impatiently.

'And he depends for help on volunteers who come from all over the world and are prepared to work on the farm and in the vineyard for a few weeks or months at a time, in return for good company, a healthy outdoor life, as much wine and food as they like.'

She looked at him speculatively. 'You've done your home-work. And I believe I'm ahead of you. Are you volunteering?'

'If you'll allow me. I could spend a few weeks there, helping out, in return for your co-operation. It would give me a new angle on the life-style of Cybèle Meredith.' He smiled. 'And it sounds like fun.'

He had charm, she thought. He was good-looking, in-telligent, and clearly not awed by her. Also, she enjoyed the company of attractive young men.

As always, she wasted no time making up her mind, and said decisively, 'I'll expect to see you there when I get back in three weeks. I'll tell Charles McDonald to expect you.'

'McDonald? An Englishman?'

'Scots, I believe. Charles used to own Le Bas-Fond. When I bought it, he stayed on as manager. What you call the commune is his responsibility.'

Morel switched to English, which he spoke almost as fluently as his own language. 'I'll look forward to meeting him. Thank you, madame.'

She held out her hand and he bowed over it, then watched her walk briskly towards the waiting driver.

His smile went out like a light.

2

Even in the hired car taking her home, Cybèle did not allow herself to relax. She sat, ramrob straight, chin high, on show until she reached the sanctuary of her Eaton Square penthouse.

As she closed the door behind her, her spine began to curve and her shoulders slumped, thrusting her head forward like a pecking hen's. Her face settled into weary lines, adding years to her appearance. It didn't matter now. There was no-one to see that the woman who had been called 'ageless' was as vulnerable to the years as anyone else.

She kicked off her high-heeled shoes, padded across to the drinks cabinet and poured herself a stiff whisky. She would not risk losing a vestige of her control in public, so she drank nothing stronger than mineral water when she dined out, although there were times these days when she longed for alcoholic stimulation to help her through social occasions where the time seemed to pass increasingly slowly.

On the whole, this evening had produced its own stimulation, and she had enjoyed it, not least because of the gold-embossed envelope in her satin evening bag.

She let herself concertina into a deep armchair, not bothering, as she did in company, to sink slowly and gracefully. She had been conscious tonight of the arthritic ache in her left hip and had walked carefully to the platform so there would be no suggestion of a limp.

She took the cheque from its envelope. Thirty thousand pounds. She didn't need the money; what she already had would keep her in luxury for the rest of her life. But the Harrington prize was more than money. It was proof that she was not only functioning as well as ever, but was still able to take on new challenges. And win.

As she sipped the whisky, she looked around her sitting-room with the pleasure it never failed to inspire. It was her private monument to her achievements.

A long lease on the five-room apartment had cost her three-quarters of a million pounds even before London's real-estate values had exploded in the early eighties.

Furnishing it, she had deliberately avoided antiques, which had surprised a distinguished cameraman she had once allowed in to photograph it.

'There is nothing more ageing to a woman than living alone among old furniture,' she had informed him crisply. 'One tends to equate the age of the owner with her possessions. I am not yet ready to be classed as an antique.'

Instead, she had chosen modern, expensive sofas and chairs upholstered in off-white brocade and set them on an ivory carpet. There were no children in her life to sully their pallor. The walls were covered with satiny, self-striped cream paper. There was colour in her collection of vivid abstract paintings and needlepoint cushions, excitement in her Elisabeth Frink bird-sculptures and – her one concession to antiquity – two magnificent Persian prayer-rugs. There were always flowers and indoor trees, maintained and changed regularly by a specialist firm. The effect she had created was luxurious and youthful, enhanced by a wall of French windows leading on to a tiled terrace with a view across the rooftops of Chelsea and Belgravia.

Little Sybil Androwski had dreamed of such a room as she crouched in the leaking, creaking caravan in which she had spent most of her childhood, unable to sleep as her mother and stepfather made what passed for love in their heaving bunk. Cybèle Meredith had never stopped congratulating herself on having achieved it.

There was extra satisfaction tonight in the copy of her book which lay on the brass-framed, marble coffee-table in front of the sofa. Its dust-jacket was elegantly black and white, with her name in red type above a stylized fashion drawing. There was a large photograph of her on the back of the jacket.

She reached for it and turned the pages. As always, she read the words she had written as though they were those of a stranger. In fact, the character they portrayed was, in many ways, a stranger to her. Cybèle Meredith today bore little resemblance to the child who had lived in the circus caravan.

3

Extract from *I am Cybèle*, by Cybèle Meredith, Published by Keane and Thomas. £14.95

One of my earliest memories is of my mother's voice, soaring up through the guy-ropes and trapezes and platforms into the heights of the circus tent. She was billed as Etta, the Operatic Equestrienne, and she sang as she stood precariously on the back of a cantering horse.

Even as a child, I found her performance ridiculous. She sang extracts from operas, *Musetta's Waltz Song, Caro Nome, My Name is Mimi*, as she went round and round, the notes hiccuping to the thump of the old horse's hooves. With a singer's deep chest, she had heavy breasts which bounced more or less in time with the music. I hated watching her, and even more, I hated listening. Her voice had the ear-piercing quality of a train-whistle.

My father used to watch from beside the entrance to the ring, and sometimes he would cry at the ludicrous spectacle. This embarrassed me, and I was ashamed of him.

The audience thought she was as funny as any clown, and roared with laughter at the sight of that large woman in her vaguely Grecian robes, her hair bound with a gold fillet, murdering some of the world's most beautiful music on horse-back.

Once, she had been destined for a career in opera. She told me that the sheer volume of her voice had attracted much admiration. As a child, she had sung at a concert organized for charity in Brighton, and been described as a miniature Gracie Fields.

So how did this daughter of a Sussex shop-keeper find herself behaving like a performing monkey in a small circus in France? Quite simply, she had fallen in love, with the circus as well as a man.

At that time, after the First World War, touring circuses were common. They moved easily back and forth across borders and the Channel, and paused on the outskirts of towns and villages to set up their tents for half a dozen performances before moving on. They were polyglot, self-sufficient communities and it occurred to nobody that they should be censured for travelling with caged animals whose only taste of freedom was when they were allowed into the ring under their trainers' whips. The artistes ranged from Chinese acrobats to Cossack horsemen and Bulgarian strong men.

To my mother, the circus was Romance. From an early age, her yearly treat was a visit to whichever travelling show set up in Brighton. In adolescence she didn't dream of being carried off into the desert by Rudolf Valentino but of becoming an acrobat or a trapeze artist. But by the time she was fifteen, she weighed eleven stones, so the dream was unlikely to be fulfilled. Instead, her mother decided that she should be trained as an opera singer. *Her* dream was to see Etta as Brünnhilde on the stage at Covent Garden.

In the meantime, between her twice-weekly singing classes, she served behind the counter in the corner grocery shop which had been in her father's family for three generations.

She was nearly twenty, and Covent Garden had not yet beckoned, when Le Cirque Dando came to Brighton from

France. She bought tickets for each night of its two-week season.

The audiences were sparse, because the circus was small and unspectacular, but to her, every act created its own magic. The one she liked best was a group of aerialists who called themselves the Amazing Androwskis, four men and a girl, whose grace and beauty enchanted her.

She had already attended five performances when, one morning, a man came into the shop and asked in heavily accented English for paprika. She didn't know what he meant; in those days there was no great demand in Brighton for paprika.

The windows of the little shop were darkened by racks of tinned goods and piles of groceries. There were sacks of pulses and rice and other staples on the floor, from which she would measure amounts at demand into blue paper bags. At first she didn't see the customer clearly as he negotiated the hazards to reach the counter. Then, she told me dramatically, she almost fainted: it was one of the Androwskis, the handsomest: a muscular man with eyes that slanted up at the outer corners and straight dark hair brushed back from a strong, square face.

'I actually swayed, and everything went dark,' she said. 'He jumped over the counter, *jumped*, mind you, with one hand in a tray of currant buns, and caught me, because he thought I was going to fall. Only I didn't, I just lay in his arms, looking up at him and I told him there and then that I thought he was wonderful!'

Lajos Androwski apparently reciprocated and nobody who knew them ever doubted that he adored this big, awkward English girl whom he married a month after their meeting.

Her parents and her older brother, Teddy, did everything they could to put her off the foreigner. After Le Cirque Dando left Brighton she endured their bitter recriminations until she departed to join Lajos in Manchester, at the end of the circus's tour. They were married in Gretna Green and she went back to France with him. I was born in their caravan in 1922.

During my early years, I was happy to be a child of the

24

circus. My mother taught me to read and write and I learned to speak French and English with equal facility, plus reasonable German. My father, who came from generations of touring circus-performers, was a natural linguist and could make himself understood in most countries in Europe. He even had a smattering of Arabic and Chinese. His father had been Hungarian, his mother Italian and his forebears mixed a dozen nationalities.

He was an ebullient, friendly man who got on well with the rest of his troupe, which consisted of a Frenchman and his wife, a German and an English aerialist.

I don't know how good they really were. To Etta and to me they were magnificent, but if they had not been second-rate, I imagine they would not have been working in the impoverished Cirque Dando, with its old-fashioned acts, its mangy lions, its single elephant and a few ancient clowns.

Etta took no part in the performances. Had she been more slender and attractive, she might have postured on the ground, holding ropes and gesturing proudly at the stars. But even Lajos had to admit that she did not have the build of a showgirl. She didn't mind. It was enough for her to be allowed to travel with the circus. She looked after her husband and me, and cooked and kept our caravan spotlessly clean. Between times she practised singing, for Lajos claimed to love her voice and, like my grandmother, encouraged her to believe that one day she might become a diva.

I was seven when our lives changed.

At the end of a double somersault off the high trapeze, either Lajos or his catcher mistimed by a split second and he plunged down into the net. Instead of being held, he bounced uncontrollably off its edge and landed on the ground, a heap of smashed bones.

They tried to cobble him together, but for the rest of his life, he did not leave his wheelchair.

The circus could not afford to keep a non-productive family on the strength and we faced being thrown out of our cosy world with no means of support, except the hope that if she abased herself, my mother might be allowed to return to the

Brighton shop, which her brother had inherited. She and Lajos hated the idea, but there seemed no alternative.

It was Arnie Gold, the English member of the Amazing Androwskis, who came up with an idea.

Despite her size and weight, my father had amused himself – and her – by teaching Etta some simple balancing tricks on a broad-beamed white horse which belonged to the Cossack riders, but had been retired from active duty. She would never be good enough to perform in front of an audience, but it had made her feel more a part of the circus family.

Arnie was the son of a Jewish father, who had been a merchant of sorts in the East End of London, and had married an English unicyclist named Leda. He deserted her when their son was an infant, and she returned to the circus from which she had retired on marriage. Arnie had been trained as a trapeze artist from an early age. He had worked mainly in Britain until his mother's death, when he came to France and joined Lajos's act.

He was a sleek, agile young man with a beaked nose, pencil moustache and roving blue eyes, which had settled on my mother as soon as she married Lajos. He was forever coming to the caravan when my father was out, with the excuse that the only two English members of the troupe must stick together. My mother, while not encouraging him, enjoyed talking about the Old Country, and they took many a trip through England in memory, talking about the towns they had visited. She had been back there only once since her marriage, to show me off to her family, who had reluctantly forgiven her defection. Since then she had kept in intermittent touch with them, but there never seemed to be enough money to spare for another trip. The circus's main base was France, where we toured for most of the year, with an occasional season in Germany, Switzerland or Austria.

Arnie had often heard Etta sing, and one day, when she and Lajos were at their lowest ebb, wondering what on earth they were going to do, he came to the caravan.

'You got a voice to raise the roof, Etta,' he said. 'And you know how to stand up on that old horse. Why don't we see if you can put the two together into an act? Then Billy Dando might let you stay.'

That's how it started, but neither Lajos nor Etta had any suspicion that she was going to become a comedy turn. The circus's English owner and ringmaster, Billy Dando, agreed to give her a trial and she was a success from the first night, singing the *Bell Song* from *Lakmé*. When he heard the audience's howls of laughter, Billy took her on permanently and paid her what Lajos had been earning.

Each night, my father would wheel himself to a position where he could watch her, and that was when I saw him crying as the crowds good-naturedly hooted her ear-piercing voice and jeered at her appearance. Sometimes, when she slid heavily off her horse, there were tears in her eyes, too.

Lajos died when I was thirteen, of despair, I suspect. He had grown fat in his wheelchair, he was in constant pain and he couldn't bear the feeling that Etta's humiliation was his fault.

Six months later, for security, she married Arnie Gold, who was eleven years her junior.

If she had any thought that she might be able to retire from the ring, he soon disabused her. For one thing, he said he couldn't afford to maintain Lajos's daughter. For another, the Androwskis had broken up after my father's death. First the French couple left to join another circus, then the German went. Arnie had never found satisfactory replacements.

After his marriage to Etta, he decided to work up a double act. While she rode around the ring's perimeter, he clowned, galloping after her horse, tumbling, somersaulting, leaping up the animal's rump to get at her, miming hopeless passion. Occasionally as she hit a top note, he raised his voice in shrieking duet, making her appear even more foolish. She hated every moment of every performance, but she went on, year after year, enduring the audience's derision in order to maintain a stable home for me.

I disliked and distrusted Arnie, and I begged her to leave him and the circus, but she was too frightened of a future without security. She was a weak woman, and I despised her for it.

I suppose she and Lajos had made love in our caravan when I was a small child, but they had the good taste not to do it when I was present. Arnie had no such delicacy. He was a man of strong sexual urges and when he wanted Etta, he wanted her *now*. Night after night I would lie on my narrow mattress at the front of the caravan and hear them pounding the bunk a few yards away. I used to pull the blankets around my head to smother the noises.

Whenever I could, I sneaked away to the Cossacks or Billy Dando and his French wife, Lucille.

I was left much to myself and my education was neglected. As I grew older, I decided that I would have to educate myself, remembering that my father had often said: 'You must read, my darling! Read everything you can lay your hands on, because books are better teachers than people.' One of his regrets was that he had never been to school and to the end of his life he tried to make up for the lack by reading.

So I read, novels and history and biographies, in French and English and German. I read newspapers and learned about the world outside the circus. Reading became my escape from Arnie.

He tried to force me into the ring, but I was never interested in performing. Heights made me dizzy, and I steadfastly resisted his attempts to persuade me to learn to juggle or spin plates or balance on a wire or train animals. We had many rows and finally, for the sake of peace, I agreed to pull my weight by looking after my mother's wardrobe. As I designed and sewed costumes which I hoped would add some charm and dignity to her appearance, my interest in clothes was born.

Cybèle shut the book. Her time in the circus was history and seemed to bear no relevance to her life today. Yet it had formed her personality. If it hadn't been for Etta's marriage to Arnie, she might not have been so determined to pursue success and never allow herself to be in the position of her mother, dependent on a man she hated. If Etta had been

28

stronger, and left Arnie, everything might have been different.

She pushed herself up out of the chair, smiling. If everything *had* been different, she would not be here, thirty thousand pounds richer, about to be fêted in the United States, after which she would be able to return to her beautiful villa in France. And to Charles McDonald.

4

A red light on Suzy Leander's answering machine indicated that there were messages. She had been away from her Bayswater flat for two weeks, working in Morocco. The trip had not been particularly enjoyable, but neither was she as pleased as usual to be home, especially when she listened to the first message.

'I'll expect to hear from you the moment you get back, my dear.' Clive Corless was a problem she was going to have to face.

The second was from her agent: '*Vogue* has a job for you, Suze. Call me.'

Her mother and several friends had phoned, and finally, Clive again, this morning: 'The champagne and smoked salmon will be ready for you tonight, my dear.' She loathed his habit of calling her 'my dear'. 'Phone me immediately you come in.'

She had been sleeping with Clive for nearly a year. His pursuit of her, after they met at a charity ball where she was compèring a fashion show, had been relentless. He was in the Foreign Office and would certainly become an ambassador in a few years. A bulky, well tailored man, fifteen years her senior, he had a smooth skin that always looked freshly shaved and greying, crinkly hair he was terrified of losing. Eton and Oxford, then stints in embassies as he climbed the Foreign Office ladder, had varnished his personality to a high gloss.

She had enjoyed and been amused by his assiduous courtship for the first few months, but by now she was under no illusion as to the reason for it: he had simply decided that it was time he acquired a wife who would be an asset to him in whichever embassy his presence would eventually grace. He had checked up on her social and educational background. He had tested her ability as a hostess at dinner-parties in his Knightsbridge house. Although he expressed mild contempt for her choice of a career as a photographic model, he enjoyed the attention her looks received, which fed his considerable ego. Recently, he had indicated that she had passed his tests and was about to be honoured by a proposal of marriage.

Her trip to Morocco had put off the moment when she would tell him that she had no intention of becoming his ambassadress and that their affair was at an end.

She would not call him tonight, she decided. It was late, she was tired and she wanted to take a long bath and go to bed.

Before she unpacked, she turned on her TV to catch up with the news.

A face she knew filled the screen: Cybèle Meredith, with her aureole of silver hair, perfect skin and facial contours that had hardly aged since the one occasion when they had met eight years ago.

Suzy had been a frightened seventeen-year-old, on her first major photographic assignment for an up-market magazine, modelling sophisticated jewellery.

A woman had come into the studio, at first invisible behind the lights, and she heard a voice: 'That girl is totally unsuitable! Get her out!'

There was silence as she stood, strung around with diamonds, pitilessly lit by the huge lamps.

The woman came forward. Suzy was aware of a devastating elegance, an icy blue gaze as impersonal as if she were a piece of machinery.

She recognized the founder of the magazine which had commissioned the photographs: Cybèle Meredith was a well-known media face.

A finger flicked the diamond necklace she was wearing. 'Take it off, and get dressed.' Cybèle turned to the magazine's fashion-editor, who was hovering unhappily, aware that her job was in the balance. 'We are not a modelling school for gauche teenagers.'

At that, Suzy's volatile temper smothered her nervousness and humiliation. 'What the hell gives you the right to talk about me like that?' she said furiously. She pulled the necklace over her head, dropped it on the floor and marched off into the dressing-room. They had never met again, although since then Suzy had frequently modelled for Cybèle's magazine. In recent years she had achieved a quiet revenge by demanding from its editors a fee far in excess of her normal one, and such was her reputation that it was rarely questioned.

She sat on the end of her bed to watch the interview. It was being conducted by a dark-haired young woman with an aggressive manner which did nothing to disturb Cybèle's smiling serenity.

'Lady Meredith, you reveal that you abandoned your twins the day after they were born. Have you never felt that you would like to trace them?'

'Never.'

'I find that difficult to believe. I mean, even if you had no maternal feelings, surely normal curiosity . . . ? After all, you carried them for nine months, endured the pain of giving birth . . .'

'As I explain in my book, the father could have been either my step-father or a Nazi officer, neither of whom I cared for.' She spoke with no more emotion than if she were discussing the weather. 'I was eighteen and I wanted nothing to do with their offspring.'

'Wouldn't it be interesting to find out what happened to them?'

'Not to me.'

The interviewer persisted. 'In your book you don't give their date of birth. Exactly how old would they be now?'

'I deliberately didn't give the date because I suspected what might happen – and it already has. Since the book was published I've had several letters from people claiming that I am their mother.'

'What do you do with the letters?'

'I put them in the waste-paper basket.'

'You don't even say whether the twins were boys or girls. Don't you know?'

'Of course I do. I didn't say so for the same reason I've just given you.' There was a trace of irritation in her level tones. 'This episode in my life seems to have attracted more attention than it's worth. It all happened nearly half a century ago. There's no way I could identify those children, nor do I want to.'

'I'm afraid that's all we have time for, Lady Meredith. Once again, congratulations on winning the Harrington Award, and thank you for talking to me.'

'Thank *you*,' Cybèle smiled into the camera and the programme ended.

Suzy switched off the TV and sat for a moment, staring at the black square. Then she opened her suitcase and tumbled her clothes on to the bed. At the bottom, she found her copy of Cybèle Meredith's book. She had bought it at the airport book-stall on her way to Morocco but hadn't had a chance to read it. She turned it over and looked at the author's photograph on the back of the dust-jacket. There was a curious familiarity about the face which she had already noticed on the screen, but couldn't identify, a reminder of someone . . .

Her door-bell rang. Clive was outside. Without preamble, he said, 'I asked you to telephone as soon as you got back.'

She raised her eyebrows. 'Whatever happened to "Welcome home, Suzy. I hope you had a good trip"?'

He didn't smile. Clive didn't care for irony. 'My dear girl, I left messages on your machine. I've wasted the entire evening waiting for you. I only decided to call in on the off-chance on my way to the club. I really do think . . .'

'I've just arrived. The plane was an hour and a half late.'

'In that case, I suppose I must forgive you.' He kissed her, running a possessive hand down over her buttocks. 'Get your coat on. The car's outside and the night is young.'

She drew back. 'Clive, I'm tired. It's been a hectic couple of weeks. I need an early night.'

'Nonsense. Moët and smoked salmon await you. Let's go.'

Arrogance, she had long since decided, was one of his least attractive characteristics. 'No, Clive. Not tonight. Thank you.'

'Don't be absurd, my dear. I've kept myself free for you. A couple of glasses of champagne and you'll feel a new woman.'

'After the flight, I have champagne and smoked salmon coming out of my ears,' she snapped. 'What I want now is a bath, then bed. Alone.'

He looked down at her without expression, then he shrugged. 'Of course I must respect your wishes. But this is not what I expected.' He bowed. 'I'll say good night. Perhaps you'll phone me?'

'Yes. Good night, Clive.'

She watched him turn to the lift, with a touch of regret, knowing that this was the beginning of the end and that she would probably miss him at first. He was kind enough, and generous. An experienced lover. But he was also pompous, self-satisfied, and lacked any vestige of humour.

On her way back into her bedroom, she paused in front of a mirror. It was a habit, born of her job, to check her appearance frequently, though there were few flaws for even a close-up to record. Her colouring was spectacular: glowing, copper-coloured hair which was tied back in a careless pony-tail. Instead of the red-head's normal pale complexion and blue eyes, she had a golden-brown skin, which had been deepened by the North African sun. Her eyes were brown, under dark, curved brows, fringed by long thick lashes. She was tall, with a long neck and a slender, graceful body.

Without any vanity, she recognized her fortune in having been born with good looks, and she had capitalized on them until she had become one of Europe's highest-paid photographic models.

She looked at herself impersonally, and found no particular satisfaction in what she saw. I need a change, she thought. I am bored with being a bloody clothes-horse and flying around

33

the world with people who don't interest me, being used to sell clothes made for women with more money than sense. I want a new interest. A new man? Perhaps, but not yet. A chance to breathe first. Be myself. Somewhere under that colour-supplement exterior there might be an intelligence that has hardly been used. It's time it was dusted off and put to work.

Half an hour later, with the last of Morocco's dust washed off her body and out of her hair, she slid into bed and picked up Cybèle Meredith's book.

The decor of the Knightsbridge model agency was a symphony in pastel colours, as was its senior partner, in his pale blue suit and pink shirt with its rose-patterned tie and matching handkerchief. His hair was several shades blonder than when Suzy had last seen him. She had known Damien Bennett since she started modelling, and was fond of him.

'Darling Suze, super to have you back!' He kissed her and said briskly, 'Lots of lovely work, starting tomorrow . . .'

She held up her hand. 'Damien, listen. I'm not going to be available for a while. As of now.'

'Don't be silly! It's the height of the season. You can't go temperamental on me for at least a month.'

'I've already gone. I need a holiday.'

His voice became a falsetto. 'I don't believe this! You've just had two glorious weeks in exotic Morocco!'

'Fighting off a randy photographer who claimed he couldn't do his best work unless he slept with the model; avoiding fat Arabs who wanted to buy me for ten camels; modelling mink coats in hundred-degree temperatures; nursing a fashion editor with a bad case of gippy – or in this case, Marrakesh – tummy. It was no vacation. Sorry, love, I've made up my mind.'

'It's a man,' he said accusingly. 'You're going off with a man!'

'I'm going off *without* a man. That's the whole point.'

'A woman who is tired of men is tired of life, dear. What's the matter with you?'

34

She shrugged. 'I'm bored and I need a change. Damien, do you know Cybèle Meredith?'

'Has that woman been getting at you? Is that why . . . ?'

'Of course not. You do know her?'

'I wonder whether anyone really *knows* Cybèle, but she sometimes uses me as an extra man when she's short of one at a dinner-party. Why do you ask?'

'I've been reading her memoirs.'

'Amazing, aren't they? I mean, we'd thought she was *born* a lady. That poor old Mum with the big boobs pounding around the ring, singing her heart out . . .'

Again, Suzy stemmed the flow. 'What's she like? As a person?'

The pale gold eyebrows drew together. 'If she takes a fancy to you, she can charm a rabbit out of its burrow. I'm told that she's generous and caring towards people she respects. If she doesn't like you, or in any way suspects you might be her equal in wit, intelligence or looks, watch out. *You* should stay away from her, Suze – and that's meant as a compliment.'

'Where does she live?'

'She has a flat on the borders of Belgravia, but she's mostly in France these days. She has what she likes to call a farm in the Dordogne, not far from Bergerac.'

'Have you been there?'

'No, dear. And I don't know anyone who has. It's called Le Bas-Fond and it's her retreat from London's mad, mad, mad world. I believe she wrote her book there. Apparently there's a kind of commune on the property where young people can simply pitch up to work and lead a healthy life.' He made a face. 'Not my scene at all.'

'Doesn't sound like hers, either.'

'Oh, Cybèle's full of surprises. What's this all about?'

'Just curiosity.'

He looked at her narrowly. 'I'm not sure I believe that. However . . . are you serious about that holiday? What do you propose to do?'

'I haven't decided. Maybe take the car across the Channel and go where it points.'

'Alone, you say? I suppose I have to believe you. When will you be back?'

'Don't know that, either. I'll let you know.'

Half an hour later, she reached her mother's house in Pimlico.

Julia Leander was in her studio on the top floor. There was a half-finished illustration on her drawing-board.

'That's a lovely camel. Far nicer than the real thing,' Suzy remarked.

'It's not meant to look real. It's meant for kids to fall in love with. Its name's Clara. Anyhow, what do you know about camels?'

'More than I want to. They made me ride one in Morocco. It had yellow teeth, its breath stank, its stomach sounded like an erupting volcano and it had a foul temper.'

Julia laughed. 'What time did you get back last night?'

'About ten. But I read until three. Have you heard of Cybèle Meredith?'

'Who hasn't? And I recall that run-in you had with her years ago.'

'I was reading her autobiography. It's won some literary prize. She was on TV last night.'

'I didn't see her. I've never much liked the sound of her. By all accounts she's dedicated her life to the acquisition of power and money. Not my type.'

'Wouldn't you like to read the book? It might give you a new slant on her.'

Julia shrugged indifferently. 'Not particularly. I have plenty to read at the moment. If I want to later, I'll borrow your copy.'

There was a pause, then Suzy said abruptly, 'I'm thinking of going away for a while. I'm fed up with modelling and I've decided I need a holiday to work out my future.'

'I thought your future was pretty clear. What about Clive?'

'That's over. I'm telling him tonight.'

'Am I allowed to say I'm pleased? I never thought he was for you. A man who's still a bachelor in his forties . . . very hard to house-train at that age.'

'I'm going to take the car to France. Want to come?'

'Can't at the moment. I have too much work. Maybe later I could join you somewhere.' She glanced at her watch. 'Can you stay for lunch?'

'Yes, please.'

'I'll go down and tell Annie. She'll be delighted.'

Julia Leander was a successful illustrator of children's books. Rising fifty, looking younger, she had been a widow for twelve years. She lived alone, with a house-keeper who came in daily. If she was ever lonely, she didn't complain. She loved people and had a natural sympathy that attracted friends of all ages. Her firm body might be a few pounds overweight, but her lively, gamine face, which reflected every emotion, had good bones and her skin was hardly lined. She wore her dark hair short and straight, with a fringe. Below it, her eyes were brown with a slant that was almost oriental. She enjoyed good clothes, but hated shopping, so her wardrobe was a mish-mash of expensive garments, usually bought in a hurry, which she managed to combine with taste and originality.

Suzy watched her affectionately as she left the room, in a hurry, as usual. She was wearing brown suede boots with a long orange skirt made of rough linen, topped by a loose black shirt and a striped, multi-coloured poncho. The effect was eccentric and attractive.

When she had disappeared, Suzy went to a roll-top desk that stood in the corner of the studio. She reached into one of its pigeon-holes and drew out a pile of folded papers which were held together by a rubber band. Among them, she knew, was her birth certificate, her mother's marriage certificate and other family records. She found what she was looking for at the bottom of the pile: a small dog-eared rectangle of pink card, with a piece of tape attached to one corner. On it was scrawled in blue ink: 'Jones, Twin 1, 6lb. 2oz. 6/7/40, 3.55 a.m.'

She heard her mother coming up the stairs, slipped the card into her pocket and closed the desk.

'Annie says she can do ham omelettes and salad and

we have some good Brie,' Julia said.

'Lovely. Mother, do you ever wonder what happened to your twin?'

Julia picked up a pen and delicately outlined the camel's eye. 'What on earth makes you bring this up?'

'I read something recently about twins who were separated just after they were born.'

'Of course I wonder about her, and I'd love to find her.'

'Didn't you try once when I was a child? I've forgotten what happened.'

'Nothing happened. Gitta told me that I was adopted from a children's home in Ealing. I tried to find it, but it had been closed for years. And the hospital where I was born was destroyed, with all its records, during the V2 raids in 1944.'

'So all you've got is that label from the hospital?'

'Yes. The births are recorded at Somerset House . . . at least, twin girls *were* born in London on 6 July 1940. I assume one of them was me. The mother was a Sybil Jones. There was no father named.'

'Sybil Jones.' Suzy heard in her mind the first name pronounced in the French fashion. For a girl planning to desert her babies and therefore anxious to hide her identity, Jones would have been one of the first names to come to mind.

Realizing that Julia was looking at her enquiringly, she said, 'It must be an odd feeling, never having known your parents.'

'When you've lived with ignorance for nearly fifty years, you don't think about it. Gitta was all the mother I ever needed.' She hesitated. 'The strangeness isn't in not knowing my parents, it's the thought that I'm only half a person, and that somewhere in the world there's another half. I dream about her sometimes. We meet, and it's like seeing myself in a mirror. Curiously enough, she never seems to like me and for some reason she's always angry with me.' She moved towards the door and added, 'Though why she should be, I can't imagine. I wish her nothing but good, wherever she is. I hope she was as lucky in her adoptive mother as I was. Come, love, let's have a sherry before lunch and stop talking about the past. It's gone, and the future's much more interesting . . .'

But the past, after Suzy had left, refused to be dismissed.

Julia sat at her drawing-board, her eyes unfocused, her mind seeing a mirror-image of herself, staring back at her inimically, and once again she wondered why, when she dreamed about her twin, it was always as though they were enemies.

5

In an office overlooking the Kurfürstenstrasse, in West Berlin, a man sat behind a teak desk, spectacles pushed up on his head, his eyes fixed unseeingly on the opposite wall. His hands were resting on a pile of proofs. His rigidity was almost catatonic.

He was a neat man of medium height, with a shock of white hair and features that might have come off a Roman coin. At sixty-nine, his bright brown eyes were tired behind his thick glasses. His name was Klaus Fischer. Sitting as he was, a visitor would not have been aware of the twisted foot that had been shattered by a shell-splinter on the Eastern Front in 1943 and remained permanently crippled.

There was a knock on the door and his secretary came in with a sheaf of letters. He didn't acknowledge her. She put the letters in front of him, and said, 'Herr Fischer, is something wrong?'

He came to life. 'Nothing. You can go now, Kati. We've finished for the day.'

She looked at his desk. 'You've been reading the Meredith book? What do you think of it?' Ten years as his secretary gave her the right, she believed, to some familiarity, though, as she often told her colleagues, he was not an easy man to be friendly with: kind enough, but inclined to be over-formal and cold.

'Interesting. It is – interesting.' He spoke with an effort, unknowingly repeating the words which had been used in London by Christian Morel.

Acquisition of the German-language rights to the book had been hotly contested. Fischer, chairman of Ellmann Verlag, the old-established Berlin publishing company which won the contest, had been in the United States when his editorial director clinched the deal. Now the book was in proof and this had been his first chance to read it. Having discovered the author's identity, he wished they had never entered the fight.

'I can tell you didn't like it. I loved it,' Kati said defiantly, then added, 'Though I must say I find Lady Meredith frightening. Such ambition! To leave her babies like that . . . !' She shook her grey head. 'But to achieve what she did . . . it gives hope for all women, *ja*?'

That evening, alone in his office, Fischer typed a letter in English, which he spoke and wrote fluently.

'Dear Lady Meredith, I am so pleased that we will be including your distinguished autobiography in our Christmas list. I have one or two queries about some facts contained in the manuscript. Would it be possible for us to meet and discuss them? I will fly to London to see you, or anywhere else you care to nominate. I would be grateful for a reply as soon as possible.'

He paused before signing it. In her book she had referred to him only as 'the German'. Would she even remember his name? But Fischer was common enough, and when they had known each other, he had still been using the Christian name chosen by his parents.

When he had introduced himself with a heel-click as Adolf Fischer, she had remarked that Adolf was a joke name.

Shocked, he said, 'But the Führer . . .'

'He's a joke, too, isn't he? At least, he looks like one.' Amused by his expression, she had smiled and put a hand on his arm, 'Take no notice of me. Sometimes I say silly things I don't mean. If it is your name, I like it.'

By the time the war ended he, too, had come to dislike the

name and had decided that in future he would be known by his middle name, Klaus.

There was no reason why Cybèle Meredith should connect her Berlin publisher with the young soldier she had met in 1939.

6

The wasteland of the South Bronx lies across the Harlem River from Manhattan Island. Guidebooks which refer to the area delicately as being 'mainly inhabited by lower-income groups' give no hint of the extent of its dereliction, its resemblance to a bombed European city after the Second World War.

It was never beautiful, but until the sixties a former resident, probably one of the Blacks or Hispanics who dominated the population, might claim that it had been a good place to live. Then high city taxes forced the factories to move out, work became scarce, the jobless couldn't pay their rents. Bitter and vengeful, some of them torched their buildings before fleeing, and the blackened walls and charcoaled timbers were their memorial.

Great, decaying apartment blocks, twelve and fourteen storeys high, stood empty, their window-panes broken, leaving jagged glass slivers. Inside, the walls collapsed, the floors were covered with filth. Pavements crumbled and weeds grew up between the cracks. The roadways became a series of pot-holes. The City of New York had started a reclamation scheme, but rebuilding was slow.

In street after street, the only life to be seen was an occasional piece of human flotsam squatting against a wall, drinking from a bottle held in a brown paper bag.

But here and there, enclaves of apartment houses, shops and bars survived. To an outsider, they were scarcely less dispiriting than the desert that surrounded them, but behind the crumbling walls people who could afford nothing better existed in sometimes quiet, but more often noisy, desperation.

Two of them were Hank and Alice Lynam who had moved into two rooms at the top of one of the apartment houses. The house's owner was black. The other tenants, who lived two or three to a room, were black or Puerto Rican.

Hank Lynam was a huge man with a sagging gut that overhung his pants and small eyes set in a heavy, sullen face. He had been what he liked to describe as 'a white-collar, worker' – an assistant in a menswear shop. When he reached his early forties, it was discovered that he was diabetic, and that had been his excuse for giving up work. That, and the fact that he had recently married Alice Bukowsky, who was secretary to the shop's owner.

She was several years younger than Hank, a plump, brown-eyed woman with dark hair which was permed into shoulder-length waves. The youthful style made her look older than her years, but he thought she was very pretty. He was slimmer and better-looking then, and she made it clear that he attracted her, too.

She told him that she had lived with her English-born mother in Boston. After the mother's death she had moved to New York. She dressed neatly, was a good typist and could adopt an impressive English accent to order. Nathan Weitz, of Weitz's Menswear, had hired her at once.

Hank, divorced from his first wife, invited her to have a drink with him on her second day in the job. She accepted and after one evening he found himself in love.

Part of her charm for him was her mystery. She rarely talked about herself and even after they married he found out no more about her background than he had discovered on the day they met. All he did know was that she seemed to be a meek, smiling woman who was prepared to continue working indefinitely so their joint income would provide them with a comfortable living.

Their relationship began to change shortly after their marriage. Alice discovered that Hank was greedy, lazy and inclined to violence if crossed. He found that she was not as

42

biddable as she had appeared and sometimes revealed a vicious temper which she had been at pains to control before the wedding.

At first, they lived in Manhattan, but after he quit work, and rentals had begun to sky-rocket, her salary was not enough for them to maintain their apartment and keep Hank in the liquor to which he had grown accustomed. Even diabetes would not persuade him to give up drinking. He bitterly resented her habit of spending money on useless extravagances for herself, like a silk scarf, a piece of junk jewellery, a new watch. It didn't occur to him that she might not have come by them honestly.

While she was at work one day, he found the apartment in the Bronx, for which the rent was a pittance compared with what they had been paying. She was furious when she saw the rooms, mean in size and ingrained with dirt. But they had already been given notice from the other apartment, and there was no alternative. She told Hank the day after they moved in that it was a temporary arrangement, and they'd be leaving as soon as she could find somewhere else. Or she might even move out by herself and then what would he do?

What he did was slap her face and shout that he'd kill her if she tried to leave him. She grabbed a kitchen knife and slashed his left cheek.

As time passed, her determination to get out of the Bronx increased, and she had no intention of keeping Hank for the rest of her life. But she decided that she would only depart when she had enough money to live in comfort. She longed to be rich and sometimes when she thought of her husband and their miserable rooms her resentment was a physical pain.

Hank didn't know that she was salting a quarter of her salary away every week in a secret bank account. Neither did he know that she was augmenting her income by sleeping with Nathan Weitz, for which service she was well paid.

Weitz's location on Seventh Avenue, within walking distance of Times Square and Macy's, meant that when Nathan didn't require her company she could spend her lunch-hours window-shopping with her friend Bibi Jackson, who was the company's book-keeper.

One day, she and Bibi were walking up Fifth Avenue in bright sunshine when they stopped to peer into a bookshop.

The display featured copies of a new publication called *I am Cybèle*, smart in its black and white dust-jacket with the author's name in red. Beside it was a blown-up portrait of Lady Meredith and an announcement that she would be signing copies in the shop the following week.

As they looked at the photograph Bibi said, 'Know what, Al, you're the spittin' image of her. If you had grey hair and blue eyes, and you were a bit thinner . . . it's the shape of the eyes, really. Sort of going up at the corners, like the Chinese.'

'Go on! She's beautiful. And she's older than me.'

'You wouldn't be so bad if you took a bit of care, and had the money to dress up.' She took a hand mirror from her purse. 'You look at yourself next to her.'

Alice held the mirror up and swivelled her eyes from the portrait of Cybèle Meredith to her reflection. There was a similarity.

'You really think I could look like that?' she said.

'Sure! Why don't you try? Have your hair cut, get a make-up at Elizabeth Arden. Hank won't be able to resist you.'

She had said the wrong thing. Alice stiffened. 'No, thanks. That's what I'm trying to avoid. I've got it down to once a month now, and that's bad enough. I nearly throw up every time he gets into bed, he smells so bad.'

'Why don't you leave him?'

'I will one day, when I've saved enough money to get right away.'

'Where'd you go?'

'A long way. Europe, maybe. London. Paris. Vienna . . .' She said the words longingly, drawing out the syllables.

'I bet you will, too,' Bibi said. Lacking confidence herself, she often resented Alice's self-assurance and, especially, her good fortune in having, not one, but two men on the go.

They walked on, two dumpy women almost identically

dressed in neat navy-blue suits and white blouses. Nobody gave them a second glance, nor guessed that one of them, in her imagination, was living the life of a famous and beautiful author who could afford to buy anything she wanted, who was asked for autographs, who drank champagne and ate caviare – neither of which Alice had ever tasted – and slept with movie stars and politicians.

In bed that night with Hank, she found herself thinking about Cybèle Meredith's book. If she read it, maybe she could find out what that sort of life was really like. The next morning she bought a copy.

It took her three days to read it and when she had finished, her heart was pounding. A whole new life was opening up in front of her.

7

Arnold Gold found it difficult to be pleasant to his London landlady, because he was convinced the old hag was trying to get him between her sheets.

It was ten o'clock in the morning and any minute now, there would be a knock on his door and he'd hear her jolly voice: 'Here you are, Mr Gold, I've brought my *Sun* for you . . . lovely picture on page three today, dear! I know how you enjoy them!'

Sometimes he wouldn't answer and after a few minutes she'd go away, disappointed because she hadn't had a glimpse of him. Or that's what he assumed, because he couldn't believe that fat Mrs Kelly with her hair dyed autumn-leaf red was simply trying to be kind to a cross-grained, lonely man by handing over her newspaper when she had finished with it. In Arnie's world, there had been so few genuine humanitarians that he scarcely knew they existed. He had long since decided that nobody did something for nothing and had therefore concluded that Mrs Kelly must be trying to buy his body with her daily newspaper.

He heard the heavy footsteps, then the knock. 'Morning, Mr Gold! Here's the paper. How're you feeling today?'

He opened the door and glared at her. 'How would I be feeling in this filthy climate? And the bloody heating's not working.'

'We don't turn the heating on in summer, dear. But if you're cold, I could find a little electric fire . . .'

'Never mind. I'm going out, anyway.'

'That's a good idea. It's a lovely day. A nice walk to the park . . . Here's your paper, then.' She patted his arm and stumped off down the stairs.

As if anyone would want to bed you, Arnie thought scornfully, and it never occurred to him that few women would be interested in bedding *him:* a wizened old man in his seventies, whose shabby clothes hung on a skinny frame. Some years before, he had started to dye his hair and moustache after he read that the American president used Grecian 2000, and he had continued the habit. He was unaware that the slicked-back black hair and dark pencil-line on his upper lip fooled nobody. Looking in the mirror as he shaved, he still saw reflected the dashing young acrobat who had captured the heart of Etta Androwski, the Operatic Equestrienne. In his memory, the years had miraculously slimmed and glamorized Etta, and in many a Paddington pub he would bore chance acquaintances with tales of their torrid romance and exotic life in the circus before the war.

With the newspaper under his arm, he wandered out into Praed Street, and there was nothing exotic to be seen *there.* More than enough bloody foreigners, though. Paki shop-keepers ready to rip a man off; Eytie caffs that couldn't produce a decent cup of tea; Aussie tourists with loud, nasal voices; Arabic writing on the newsagents' boards.

He turned left and walked towards Hyde Park, increasingly bitter as he itemized his complaints against a world that had never paid him the living he believed it owed. A government too mean to give a native-born Englishman a decent pension for his old age. Bloody Etta, dying like that. The kid . . . what he'd sacrificed for her, and then what she'd done to him . . . if he could only have got his hands on the little bitch! Finally, old Billy Dando's son, young Billy, making him – Arnie Gold of the Flying Androwskis – wash up dirty dishes in his cheap café. And now, no job. No money. One frigging room in an old woman's boarding house in Paddington.

Life, Arnie decided for the umpteenth time, wasn't bloody fair.

He settled on a bench under a tree in the park and opened his paper to the page three girl. Not bad. Tits almost as big as Etta's. He looked his fill, then turned the pages listlessly, glancing at the headlines. Nothing much. Petrol prices up. Another mugging on the Underground. Chancellor says no tax cuts. Takeover threat to Harrod's. Dentist in sex scandal. Same old stuff.

A photograph on an inner page caught his eye. It was a portrait of a woman whose face rang a bell. No bimbo, this. Quite old, but not bad. Some movie star of a few years back?

Then he read the boxed caption and looked more carefully at the picture. As recognition dawned, his pulses began to race. The woman's name was said to be Cybèle Meredith. Like bloody hell it was. He was looking at Sybil Androwski. The step-daughter he hated. Even after nearly fifty years, he couldn't mistake her. Jesus! Sybil!

He took off his glasses, wiped the misted lenses, and read the caption again. *Lady* Meredith, they called her. She'd written a bloody book about her own life and won a prize. Thirty thousand quid. She lived in France, near the town of La Bergerie. That rang a bell, too.

Staring into space, he forced his mind back over the years. They'd played La Bergerie a couple of times. He remembered a one-horse place, sparse audiences, little laughter, even at Etta's squalling and his own clowning.

As he read the story for the third time, his thoughts quietened and he began to plan. First, buy her book. He'd be in it. She couldn't have left him out. They said here that it was a 'ruthlessly honest' book. Maybe he could sue her for defamation. She wouldn't have said anything good about him, that's for sure.

Or was there something better he could do? Like throw himself on her mercy for old times' sake? He had a little bit of money tucked away. Enough to go to France. She owed him something for the years he'd been put away, by God she did. Thirty thousand quid. There must be some way he could get his hands on a share of it. First, he'd read the book.

8

Charles McDonald strolled towards the mill-house, conscious, as always, of how much he loved Le Bas-Fond, and how much he would miss it if Cybèle forced him to leave.

At eight o'clock on a June morning, the surrounding fields were still dew-spattered. In the distance, sunlight glinted on the fast-flowing waters of the Dordogne. Closer, he could hear the rush of the stream and see it winding through the fields, separating around a tree-covered islet at the point where it swelled the main river. Above him loomed the big grey mill which had been his home for six years.

He perched on the stone wall that bordered the terrace below the house, and looked down into the stream as it scurried over the rocks. It was overhung with trees, and ferns reached into the water.

A path ran down a steep slope to the stream, crossed it on a hump-backed stone bridge and meandered on through fields to the banks of the Dordogne. It was his favourite walk.

The mill had not been active for years, and some previous owner had dammed the stream so the mill-pond could be used as a swimming-hole. The water was murky from its muddy bottom, but that never seemed to put off the young people. There were striped sun umbrellas over tables on the terrace and chairs scattered about. Swim-suits were draped on the wall.

Once the terrace had been part of the mill, housing the great wheel that had turned the grind-stone. The stone and the machinery had long since gone and the roof and walls had been taken down, opening the space to the sun. Only the wheel remained as a decorative feature, with its rectangular wooden scoops, or buckets, that had once been turned by the rushing mill-race. It was protected by a brick parapet a metre high and had been roped to prevent it from moving. It came to life only when it occasionally set up an eerie creaking on a windy night as it strained against the old ropes. Its bottom buckets reached down into what had been the race and was now a deep hole filled with stagnant water. The stream had been diverted to bypass it.

An open door led from the terrace into the house. It was Saturday, so nobody rose early, and the day's work-load was minimal.

Charles was enjoying his temporary solitude and the feeling that this tiny part of France belonged to him . . . until he reminded himself that in reality it no longer did. It belonged to Cybèle Meredith, and only her generosity had made it possible for him to stay.

He sighed as he remembered Cybèle, stubbed out his cigar and went inside.

There was no-one in the big hall, with its comfortable clutter of boots, straw sun-hats, espadrilles and baskets of logs. He had long ago given up making rules about tidiness, or insisting that belongings should be restricted to their owners' rooms. In winter, a logfire burned in a stone fireplace set into one wall. In summer, with the double doors on to the terrace open, people often gathered there to chat and drink wine in the candle-lit dusk, though the vast, warm kitchen was at all times of the year the centre of the house.

When Cybèle had bought the property and decided to convert a smaller house near the river for her own use she had said, 'I'm not interested in farming, Charles. I like the way you've been running the place, even if it hasn't made

49

you any money. You don't have to change anything, and the mill remains yours, to house your volunteers and organize as you like.'

She had offered him a token salary as manager, plus his accommodation and the freedom to use any produce the farm could provide. He had been grateful simply to be given the chance to stay at Le Bas-Fond and had taken her at her word that the mill-house remained his territory.

She rarely invaded it, but when she did, he had noticed that her mouth would turn down as her blue eyes swept over the disorder. Her own house was as perfectly maintained as money and two daily maids, brought in from the village when she was in residence, could make it.

He had originally bought Le Bas-Fond as an escape from a life in England which had become intolerable.

At fifty, his world had fallen apart with his wife's death and he had sold his house and fled to France. The mill had been in a state of dereliction, and for months he had worked from dawn until halfway through the night, making it habitable. By the time it was as he wanted it, he had regained his emotional equilibrium, but he had very little money left.

The property consisted of thirty hectares, including fields and a vineyard. It had to be made to pay for itself, but he had no experience of farming and insufficient money to hire local labour.

When the son of a former friend, hitch-hiking towards the South of France, turned up one day and offered to help to clear the vineyard if he could stay for a couple of nights, Charles saw a way which might provide assistance and the companionship which he was beginning to crave, as well as giving young people a chance to escape the stress of city life.

He put an advertisement in *The Times* asking for volunteers who would like a working holiday. In return for a few hours' labour each day, they would be lodged in a comfortable converted mill in a beautiful area of France, with plenty of free time and unlimited supplies of food and wine.

50

Within days, he had received a dozen replies, and accepted six.

He never had to advertise again. Male and female volunteers, who ranged from eighteen – his lower limit – upwards, passed on information about Le Bas-Fond to their friends, and he began to receive applications from all over Britain, America, Canada and Australia. They came from students, young men and women with jobs who were seeking a different kind of vacation, some who were jobless but desperate to work, even for nothing.

To each, he wrote a letter which set out, not the pleasures of Le Bas-Fond, but aspects which might not appeal: the accommodation was not luxurious, bedrooms would probably have to be shared, there was only one bathroom and no telephone. Domestic chores and cooking would be shared by himself and the volunteers; no shirking of the less pleasant jobs would be tolerated. Anyone who was unwilling to muck in, or did not get on with his fellows, would be requested to leave. The property was set in deep country, far from the bright lights.

This weeded out a percentage of enquirers, and those whom Charles then invited to join him tended to be appreciative, good company and hard workers. He required them to agree to come for a minimum of two weeks; some stayed for months, others returned again and again. He was often surprised at the quality of conversation and argument that raged around the big kitchen table and he watched with amusement as relationships developed. At least one had led to marriage.

But despite the free labour, he continued to lose money.

Because he knew little about wine-growing, he had at first been forced to hire experienced help to direct the volunteers in the vineyard. It was rewarding to send his grapes to the local co-operative and receive back the rough but palatable wine, but there was little profit in its production. His vinestocks needed renewing, but he had no capital to replace them. He reared lambs and calves, but their sale hardly covered his household expenses. He turned over two fields to vegetables and fruit, kept most of it for the table and sold the rest in the

51

nearest market for a pittance. The tractor that had come with the property was old and constantly broke down. If there was not a mechanically-minded volunteer in residence, it cost precious francs to repair. He had brought his aged Mercedes from Scotland but it was past its best, and parts were expensive.

After four years, his bank balance was so low he knew it would not be long before he would have to sell up.

Le Bas-Fond's nearest small town, a few kilometres away, was La Bergerie, so-called after the sheep-pens which had once stood on its outskirts.

During the sixties and seventies, it had seen a steady influx of foreign residents, who had come to the Dordogne after discovering that property could be bought there for a quarter what it would cost on the Côte d'Azur.

Retired British, Dutch and Scandinavian bankers, businessmen and service officers took up permanent residence with their wives. Smaller houses and cottages were snapped up by an international covey of artists and writers and potters.

Unusually for this part of France, the new residents did not include any Germans, and Charles discovered the reason when, not long after his arrival, he stopped to read a plaque on a brick wall outside the village. Incised in stone were the words: 'At this place, in 1943, twenty women and children, innocent inhabitants of La Bergerie, were massacred by the Nazi occupiers. In Memoriam.' There followed a list of names, some of which he recognized from signs on the bars and shops.

He was gradually to realize the deep and bitter hostility to the wartime enemy which survived among the relatives and descendants of the dead. Any stray German tourist was rapidly made aware that he was unwelcome: barmen, waiters and shop-keepers refused to serve him, asserting stolidly that in a half-full restaurant there were no tables available, that a crowded bar was about to close, that whatever goods he asked for in the shop were out of stock. It was an unwritten rule that no-one would sell property to a German.

The hostility was largely kept alive by the owner of the

village's one hotel, a sixty-year-old former Resistance fighter named Victor Sézille, whose mother and young sister had been killed during the massacre. He was a big man with a powerful body and a square, sullen face which usually sprouted a dark stubble of beard. His family had lived in La Bergerie for generations and he regarded himself as an arbiter in local affairs. A normally silent man, he could erupt into violence if angered. Many of the locals, Charles discovered, were afraid of him and went along with his dictates in order to keep the peace.

His wife was a pallid nonentity who scarcely spoke in his presence. Their one son, Paul, was a swaggering, eighteen-year-old lout who dominated his own age-group, leading a gang of teenage bikers who roared off to Bergerac every Saturday and spent the evening in drunken carousing.

Every year, on the anniversary of the massacre, Sézille led a procession through the village. Relatives of those who had been killed would place flowers in front of the memorial and he would make an impassioned speech, reiterating his implacable hatred of the murderers and exhorting his audience neither to forget nor to forgive.

Former allies or not, Charles sometimes wondered how the villagers really felt about the well-heeled foreigners who had come to live among them. Some months ago there had been cases of vandalism against foreign cars – coins scraped along the paint, aerials twisted and wing mirrors broken – and several thefts from foreign-owned houses while their owners were away. It was assumed that Paul Sézille and his cronies were probably responsible. Representations were made to the local police, who shrugged and said that, without direct evidence, there was nothing they could do.

This had resulted in the setting up of an unofficial neighbourhood watch scheme.

At a meeting, held under the guise of a cocktail-party, it had been agreed that whenever any foreign resident was away, his neighbours would take it in turns to visit his house, at varying hours, two or three times each day or night. Since word of the scheme had got round, there had been no further break-ins, but Charles believed that it had widened the social division between locals and foreigners, as it was clear that only locals had been suspected.

However, nothing was said and the general atmosphere remained friendly enough, at least partly because the incomers' money had brought increased prosperity to the town.

Charles's appearance at Le Bas-Fond had attracted a stream of callers from the expatriate community, and when invitations to drinks, barbecues, suppers and lunches began to arrive, he assumed that he had been accepted.

A few of the older inhabitants at first voiced doubts about his unconventional life-style with a houseful of young people, muttering irritably about 'hippy communes', but when they found that the volunteers were well-behaved and did not try to take over the town's bars, the doubts faded.

One man who had become his friend was a retired RAF Squadron Leader, Henry Franklin, who had been responsible for inaugurating the watch scheme. He lived with his wife, Emily, in a former barn which they had converted into a comfortable home. They had created around it a Surrey cottage garden: herbaceous borders filled with roses, lupins, pansies, forget-me-nots, nasturtiums and marigolds, neatly surrounding green lawns.

A bluff, cheerful man, Henry strode the country lanes with his ancient spaniel and shouted greetings in English to everyone he passed. He made no concessions to living in a foreign country, spoke not a word of French, grumbled because the local shops did not stock Marmite, and had all the right-wing prejudices of Colonel Blimp. Despite this, he was generous and good-natured and most of the locals regarded his eccentricities with tolerant amusement.

Charles had been poring miserably over his account books when Henry phoned one summer morning.

'I need a favour, dear boy,' he said. 'Emily's invited this formidable woman to supper tonight. She's staying with the Dunnetts for a week. Scares the pants off me . . .'

'Get to the point, Henry.'

'I know it's short notice, but will you join us and even up the numbers? Emily hates having an extra female.'

'I'd face the most formidable woman in the world for Emily's cooking. Who is she?'

'Cybèle Meredith. Something to do with clothes, I'm told. Brought up in France, but lives in London. Beautiful, successful, rich, but she's too bloody intelligent. Nothing she can't talk about.'

Charles laughed. 'What's formidable about that?'

'Makes a man feel a damn fool.'

That evening Charles dressed in his one surviving dark suit and put on a tie for the first time in weeks.

Cybèle was wearing pale grey silk trousers which exactly matched the colour of her hair. Her fine white cotton shirt had a stand-up collar, long, full sleeves and was cinched in at the waist by a wide belt. There were silver studs in her ears and silver chains around her neck. By contrast with her polished elegance, Emily Franklin and Deirdre Dunnett might have stocked their wardrobes from a charity shop.

As they shook hands, Charles was aware of narrowed eyes assessing him and understood what Henry had meant. This *was* a formidable woman.

Apparently her reaction to him was favourable, because she set out to charm him, and succeeded. He found her amusing and good company and, unlike Henry, refused to be overawed by her intelligence.

During supper, she told him that she was thinking of buying a property in the area.

Only half-seriously, he said, 'You'd better look at mine. I'm thinking of selling.'

Unexpectedly, she took him up on it and the next day she arrived at the mill.

As he showed her around, she asked probing questions and he told her about his ambition to run a virtually self-sufficient farming community where he could live simply, away from the city rat-race, and where young people in need of escape, as he had been, could come and go freely.

'It's in no sense a commune,' he said firmly. 'I'm the owner

55

and boss, though I try not to make it too obvious. I used to worry about taking advantage of the kids, asking them to work without being paid, but most of them seem to regard it as a privilege. They love being outside in the clean air, and enjoy the tough physical work. They say they've never slept so well. Those who have cars and a yearning for civilization can go into La Bergerie or even Bergerac or Bordeaux for an evening. And they organize their own entertainment . . .' He stopped. 'Sorry! I must be boring you.'

'Far from it. Now tell me about yourself, Charles. What brought you here in the first place?'

Suddenly, he was no longer forthcoming. 'I was fed up with my life in England and decided to make a break. That's all.'

She looked at him curiously, but did not pursue the matter. 'Why do you want to sell?'

He told her about his financial problems, and ended, 'I only want to break even, but the problem is that to achieve that, the place needs an injection of capital which I haven't got. As things are, I won't be able to carry on for longer than a few months.'

They were walking towards the stream, on the banks of which stood a double cottage which had once housed farm-workers. Since he had plenty of accommodation in the mill, and no spare cash, he had been forced to let it fall into disrepair.

Cybèle stopped. 'That is beautiful!'

He looked at it with her eyes, for the first time seeing it not as a ruin but a graceful, rectangular building with bougainvillea growing up the walls and a terrace sheltered by a vine-covered trellis. Its old, reddish-grey brick glowed in the sunlight. From its windows there were views across the fields on one side, and over the stream, towards the Dordogne, on the other.

Talking almost to herself, she said, 'Rebuild the terrace, gut the inside. Create space. Bedrooms upstairs, each with its own bath. It could be a jewel! Make a garden . . .' She turned to him and, with scarcely a pause for thought, added, 'I'll buy the property, at your price. This house will be mine. You'll

56

keep the mill and run it as you always have, as my manager. As far as you're concerned, nothing need change.'

It was clear that she did not expect any argument and, bemused by her decisiveness, beguiled by her assertion that nothing would change, he eagerly grasped the life-line she had thrown.

Two months later the legal formalities were completed and Cybèle had engaged an architect to transform the cottage into a villa.

Charles, with renewed financial security, invested in new farm equipment, built a glass-house to raise vegetables, and increased the numbers of cattle and sheep. Because there were always volunteers who liked to work with animals, he bought a donkey, some goats and geese and hens.

Within a year, with all expenses covered, his increased production enabled him to hand Cybèle a small profit.

He acted as her overseer while the cottage was being rebuilt and was amazed by the amount of money she was prepared to spend to achieve what she wanted, when she wanted it. Because she paid her builders more than the going rate, the work was finished inside six months.

She moved in almost at once to write the autobiography for which, she told him, she had already been given a substantial advance.

Every now and then she either invited him to join her for a drink, or he asked her to the mill for supper. The drinks, at which only the two of them were present, were pleasant enough, but the suppers were something of a strain. No matter how gracious she was to the young volunteers, her glossy presence intimidated them and, as one of them told Charles resentfully, 'She makes us all feel so bloody shabby, and she looks at the house as though she thinks it needs a good scrub.'

He admitted to himself that it was a relief each time she departed for London for a few days. Despite her determination that they should each preserve their privacy, her personality was too strong to allow her to be ignored, and her very presence on the property was a disturbance to the even tenor of his life. But because his gratitude to her was sincere and, on the whole, he liked her, he would not allow himself to become resentful.

When she had finished her book, she returned to England, and for a while she only visited the cottage for a week or two at a time. It was during the most recent visits that he had begun to notice a subtle change in her attitude towards him. Their evening conversations, as they sat under the trellis on her terrace, became more personal, less light-hearted. She started to probe into his life, asking questions which he had to field tactfully, because there were areas in his recent past which he had no intention of sharing with anyone.

She told him about herself and confessed that she was bored with her current way of life. She had achieved almost everything she wanted. With her book finished, she was ready to embark on something new. To his dismay, it emerged that this would be centred on Le Bas-Fond, where she proposed eventually to take up permanent residence.

One night, just before she was due to return to London, she said, 'I do believe, Charles, that you and I, as partners, could build this place up into a profitable enterprise. How many hectares of vines do we have?'

'Two.'

'We could treble that, couldn't we? Set up our own winery, eventually sell our own label.' Her face was young and eager in the flickering light of the candles under their pink glass shades. She leant forward and gripped his hand. 'The competition from other countries is fierce now, and the best Bordeaux and Burgundy are being sold in London like stocks and shares. Pension funds invest in them the same way they invest in paintings. They're almost out of the ordinary person's reach. But wines from the Côte de Castillon are good, cheaper, and virtually unknown in England. That's the market we could exploit.'

Charles listened with increasing unease. 'Cybèle, you're talking about making a Bordeaux Supérieur. We're not equipped for that. We've only produced simple table wines. We'd have to spend a fortune to bring up the quality of the soil and grub out all the vinestocks. We'd have to plant Merlot and Cabernet Sauvignon and it would be three or four years before we got our first harvest. People think they can just come into France and decide to be wine producers without giving it any thought or planning, but it can't be done in a hurry.'

She frowned. 'I've thought a great deal about this. I'm not worried about the time it would take, nor the cost. I need an interest and it's something I'd like to do. Now the book's published, I can give it my full attention.' She paused. 'Of course, it would mean minor changes. We'll need expert advice and trained workers; your volunteers couldn't handle it alone. But think of the fun we'll have, as partners. I've never worked with a partner before, Charles, nor wanted one.' She added softly, 'But I believe I'm tired of being alone.'

He finished his martini and stood up. 'If you're serious, I'm going to have to think about this, Cybèle. I don't believe I'm the person to deal with such an ambitious project.'

'But I am, my dear. I've never failed yet when I've undertaken something, and I don't intend to now. I'm going to make you rich.'

'I really don't . . .'

She moved closer to him and for an appalled moment, he thought she was offering an embrace, and stepped backwards. Apart from the fact that she was many years his senior, he felt no physical attraction to her.

She smiled mockingly, and he had an uneasy feeling that she had read his mind. 'Think about it. I realize this can't be an immediate decision. I'll be in London for a couple of months, then I'm going to the States for three weeks. We'll talk about it when I get back.'

He moved through the hall towards the kitchen, where the volunteers had gathered for breakfast. There was cheerful conversation and the smell of bacon frying.

Maybe, he thought, this would be the last lot of volunteers. If he stayed at Le Bas-Fond, they would be replaced by experienced permanent farm-workers. There would be no more evenings of animated discussion and argument around the kitchen table. He would no longer be the willing recipient of their confidences, nor the guru to whom they came with their troubles. The peaceful days of outdoor work punctuated by siestas to read or listen to music, swim in the mill-pond or simply stretch out in a field enjoying the view, would be gone. He knew instinctively that Cybèle would not tolerate such free and easy working arrangements. She would want every moment of the day organized.

During her absence he had set the problem of his future aside, but the time was approaching when he would have to make up his mind. To leave Le Bas-Fond would be heart-breaking but even worse would be having to fend off a strong-minded woman whose idea of a partnership might reach beyond business.

A pile of post was waiting beside his place at the table. After a general good-morning, he poured himself a cup of coffee and looked through it. There was a letter from Cybèle.

Watched by the volunteers, he opened it.

After a moment, he looked up and said, without expression, 'As you've no doubt seen, this is from Cybèle Meredith. She'll be back in about three weeeks.' He paused. 'No cries of joy? She's also invited a French journalist down to work with us. Apparently he wants to do an article about her life-style here. She says he's to be treated like any other volunteer.'

Neither was this greeted with any enthusiasm. Claire, a Yorkshire girl who had been at the mill for several months, said resentfully, 'Why should we have to put up with him, following us around with his little notebook? I hate bloody newspapermen, always twisting what people say.'

'I don't expect we'll see much of him. Cybèle is the one he's interested in.'

She wasn't appeased. 'The place isn't the same when she's here, either.'

He stood up. 'No . . . well, let's get the show on the road. Anyone want to come into the market with me? Maybe she won't stay for long.' But there was no optimism in his voice.

PART TWO

1

Lady Meredith looked unreal, Alice thought, a character from *Dallas* or *Dynasty*: impossibly sleek and groomed, her creamy skin faintly flushed (artificially) on the cheek-bones, the colour of her clear blue eyes enhanced by blue-shadowed lids, not a silver hair out of place.

She was sitting behind a desk piled with copies of her book, looking up with a special smile as each was presented for her signature, writing neatly: With best wishes, Cybèle Meredith.

Alice had been standing in a queue for ten minutes, clutching the book, watching her with a mixture of excitement and resentment. No woman had a right to be so composed, so invulnerable. She hugged to herself the thought, *I could change that.* I could crack that smile in pieces.

Three places from the table, she drifted into fantasy, hearing her own voice saying softly: 'Hi, Mom, I'm your daughter, Alice. Twin 2.' Seeing the beautiful face crumple in disbelief. Then, as she produced the grubby pink card, the dawning recognition, acceptance, delight.

'You'd like me to put your name? Of course. Alice Lynam. To Alice Lynam, with best wishes . . . Thank you so much!'

And she was walking away, aware that the eyes that had flicked up at her had been blank, the smile automatic. Next time they met, her mother wouldn't remember this fleeting contact. It didn't matter. Alice would change that soon enough.

That night, she surprised Hank by presenting him with a handful of dollars.

'What's this?' he said suspiciously.

'You haven't been out for ages. Go on down to Casey's. Have a few drinks. Do you good.'

Such manna rarely came his way and he wasn't about to

query the reason for it. Ten minutes later, he was lumbering along the uneven pavement towards the bar.

Alice hurried downstairs to her neighbour, Ella-May Doonan, who had been looking after some dress-boxes for her. They contained the travel-trousseau she had been secretly collecting for the past week: a tight, sequinned evening sweater in shocking pink, with a matching satin skirt, for the parties to which she would certainly be invited as Cybèle Meredith's long-lost daughter; a purple jump-suit with a silver collar for less formal occasions; a loudly checked black-and-white jersey suit, not too unlike the one Lady Meredith had been wearing today, she thought, and a frilly blouse to go with it; high-heeled black strappy sandals; three pairs of fancy black panty-hose.

Unable to resist showing off, she displayed them for Ella-May's admiration, presented her with a thank you box of chocolates and warned her once again not to mention her purchases to Hank.

Ella-May was delighted to be part of the scheme. 'You got a right to spend yo' money any way you like, honey,' she said. 'I been lyin' to my Johnny how much my clothes cost for twenty years. No chance I'll tell Hank. But what's he gonna say when he sees you wearing them?'

'We're going on a holiday. I want to look good for him, as a surprise,' Alice said shyly.

Upstairs again, she tried on her new clothes, then packed them away in the back of her wardrobe.

She sat down, lit a cigarette, and began to plan. She had read in the paper that Cybèle Meredith was returning to her home near the town of La Bergerie in the Dordogne after she had completed her tour of the United States. That would be the place to reveal herself, in her mother's own home, no other people around, where she could show the evidence of her birth.

Since Bibi had pointed out her resemblance to Cybèle and she had read the book, she had made up her mind that they were mother and daughter. As a child, she had often wondered about her parents, but in her wildest dreams she had not anticipated such luck. A mother who was rich, titled, famous . . . the future for Alice Lynam was looking good. She spared a passing thought for her twin. Good thing she'd never surfaced. Alice had no wish to share the loot.

The one snag was Hank. She went cold at the thought of him finding out she was planning to leave him. He could ruin her plans. Something, she thought grimly, would have to be done about Hank.

At midnight, he came home. After some difficulty finding the key-hole, he managed to let himself in.

As he dragged himself up the steep, narrow stairs, he was singing softly to himself, 'I'm a Yankee Doodle Dandy, Yankee Doodle do or die . . .' Liking the sound of his voice, he increased the volume as he repeated the phrase, dizzily stumbling from stair to stair, with frequent pauses.

Behind closed doors, the other residents listened and endured. They knew from experience that Hank, drunk, should be left alone.

'That poor little Alice,' Ella-May whispered to Johnny, 'I sure enough don't know why she stay with that man – and wanting to give him nice surprises, and all!'

He reached the top step and stood, swaying, his head thrown back as he roared out the words, '. . . born on the fourth of July!'

Then he was tumbling backwards down the stairs and the last thing he felt was an agonizing crack as his head hit the floor and his neck broke under the full weight of his body,.

At his last dreadful cry, doors were flung open. People emerged from their rooms and stood, their eyes searching the darkness. Ella-May was the first to see the great heap of flesh and bones collapsed at the bottom of the stairs and, as Johnny turned on the light, her wail rose to the roof. For several seconds it was the only sound that broke the silent horror.

The door on the top floor opened, and Alice came out, a flowery dressing-gown over her night-dress. She took a couple of steps on to the landing, looked down and recognized the body. A hand covered her mouth, but she did not make a sound. Then she ran down the stairs and threw herself on the floor beside Hank. As she crouched over him, the watchers saw her lips tenderly touch the side of his head.

Three weeks later, she gave notice to Nathan Weitz, saying she was going away for a while to escape from her sad memories.

Bibi Jackson accompanied her to the airport to say goodbye.

'Didn't I say you'd do it, Al?' she said, as they drank a last cup of coffee together. 'You're looking great. The hair-cut . . . it's just like that woman, you know, the one who wrote that book. And the dress! Wow! You could go *anywhere*. I just bet you're gonna pick up some Frenchman who talks like Maurice Chevalier and owns a château in Paris. You'll end up a countess, at least.'

To her irritation, Alice didn't share what was meant to be a joke. Instead she smoothed her hands complacently over her tightly brassiered breasts, which ballooned under the shiny polyester bodice of a scarlet shirt-waister. Silver rings she had picked up in Macy's dangled from her ears. With no need to worry any more in case Hank should question her about the source of her wealth, she had gone on a spending spree and was as confident as Bibi that she now had the right clothes for any social situation.

'I wouldn't be surprised if you're right,' she said thoughtfully. 'Everything's going my way now.'

Bibi had so far managed to hide her envy, but she couldn't resist saying, 'And it all started with Hank's fall, right? You been lucky, Al.'

'That's a terrible thing to say! Oh, God, poor Hank. I never meant those mean things I used to say about him. I miss him every moment of the day.' She sniffed, and scrabbled in her bag for a tissue.

That, Bibi thought as she watched her, is bull-shit if ever I heard it. You never had such a good time as since he died. She swallowed her annoyance and said, 'You'll write, won't you?'

'Of course. I'll tell you *everything*. You're my best . . . my only friend, come to think of it. And you know what, Bibi, if I hook that French count, you'll be the first person we'll invite to the château!'

2

Klaus Fischer's gloomy villa overlooked West Berlin's Kleiner Wannsee, its ground stretching down to the waterfront. There was a clear space in front, otherwise it was surrounded by thickly planted bushes and trees which shadowed it for most of the day. From his upper windows, he could see the little steamers making their regular circuits of the beautiful string of lakes that were the Berliners' favourite weekend resort. In summer, the water was bright with yachts, and the bays swarmed with bathers. He sometimes envied their happiness but he was never tempted to join them, recognizing that he had almost lost the ability to enjoy unproductive pleasure.

On the far shore, the remains of the Wall that had once divided Berlin followed the coastline, punctuated by watch-towers, and as he had stared at it he had often wondered what the hell he had fought for.

Unlike many former soldiers, he thought of the war not as a comma, but a full-stop in his life. It was as though, one day in 1939, the carefree young Adolf Klaus Fischer had died, and a different man had moved into his skin.

He had been a junior officer in a Panzer division stationed outside a small town near Karlsruhe, not far from the French border. With a few hours' leave one fine autumn day, he was strolling down the village's main street, handsome in his uniform and peaked cap, when he saw the girl from the circus.

She was sitting outside a café. She had fair, shoulder-length hair and extraordinary blue eyes that slanted up at the outer corners. Thin, with pale, fine skin, her looks had a waïflike charm that was totally unlike the Germanic ideal. He thought she was beautiful.

As he stared, a group of drunken soldiers from the camp surrounded her table. He saw one of them lean over and drag her towards him, his hands pawing her while the others laughed.

Rage such as he had never experienced flooded over him. He reached the group and dragged the man away. Just in time, he remembered that he was an officer and controlled his overwhelming urge to beat him to the ground. The other two had already recognized his rank and managed to sway to attention. A moment later, the three of them were hurrying away, relieved to have been dismissed with only a tongue-lashing.

He had bowed to the girl, who whispered her thanks. Then he said, 'Fräulein, may I buy you another coffee and try to persuade you that not all soldiers have the manners of pigs?'

She had looked him up and down, then smiled and nodded.

The following day, they met again, and every day after that, whenever he could leave his unit for a few hours.

At the end of a week, he rented a hotel room, and there they made love. Naive and untutored in sexual matters, he assumed that no other man had penetrated her, simply because she was young.

After that, they used the hotel room every day. She had asked him not to come to the circus. 'There are too many people around. We couldn't be alone,' she explained.

Throughout their relationship, he did most of the talking, sometimes in his halting French, sometimes in German, which she spoke fluently. He had never talked so openly to a woman before, and shared with her his fears, his dreams, his hopes. He told her about his childhood in Hamburg as the only son of a lawyer; how he had been planning to study economics after leaving school; how he had gone into the army instead and would take his degree when the fighting was over. He asserted his unshakable loyalty to the Fatherland, but whispered his doubts about Nazism and the Austrian who had led the country into war.

She rarely talked about herself. He knew that she had grown up in the Cirque Dando, which had set up its tent in a field a few kilometres from his camp. The fact that war had been declared and the German army was poised to march into France appeared to have had little impact in its enclosed world.

He knew that her mother had died only a few days before their first meeting and that she was the circus's unofficial wardrobe mistress. Otherwise she told him very little until the day she arrived at the café to meet him with her left cheek swollen and bruised, her eyelid half closed.

Head high, she made no attempt to hide the disfigurement, pretending not to notice the curious glances of passers-by.

'My step-father did it,' she said briefly. He had not known she had a step-father.

'For God's sake, why?'

'I discovered he had stolen some money my mother left me. When I asked him about it, he was angry and he hit me. I must get away. That's what the money was for. I've been waiting for an opportunity to leave.' She looked suddenly desolate. 'Only I have nowhere to go.'

'Yes, you have,' he said. 'You'll go to Hamburg and stay with my parents until I come home.'

'I can't afford the fare.'

'Tomorrow I'll bring money. More than enough. I'll put you on the train. But will you be safe tonight?'

She nodded. 'He won't attack me again.'

'How can you be sure?'

'The ring-master and his wife have promised to look after me.'

Because he was on duty at the camp in the evening, he had to be satisfied with that. The next day he gave her all the money he had and they arranged that they would meet in their café the following afternoon and he would take her to the railway station.

He waited for her as he had done every day for the past three weeks. Only this time she didn't come. After an hour, he went to look for her and discovered that the circus had packed up secretly during the night and fled into France.

69

At first he refused to believe it. Frantically, he searched the little town. He went to the hotel where they had made love in a small dark room, but she had left no message.

And she had taken his money.

His fellow-officers talked among themselves about the change in him. Overnight their cheerful companion became a morose, tormented loner who spent his free hours drinking himself into oblivion. He prayed that she would write, but she never did.

He was scarcely aware of time passing as the weeks extended into months. The war's tempo quickened and his division began the drive westwards. Holland was crushed, Belgium and France capitulated. He found some relief from his misery in aggression, and fought without regard for his own life.

He never forgot Sybil Androwski. Through the terrifying months on the Eastern front, then in the field hospital where the injury to his foot was treated, then in shattered post-war Berlin, she often seemed to be closer to him than the people he was with. Sometimes, lying on the edge of sleep in his hospital bed, he would actually *feel* her body beside him and come to consciousness with his arms outstretched, to find that there was no-one to embrace.

Because he had not been a member of the Nazi Party, and spoke adequate English and French, he worked with the Occupying Forces for several months after his discharge, processing refugees from the Eastern Zone. Hard work was the one thing which took his mind off her.

Day after day, he enquired for the Cirque Dando among Frenchmen he met, but no-one had heard of it. When it was possible to travel, he covered Western Europe, pursuing any touring circus of which he had news. Some of the artistes had heard of the Dandos but no-one knew Sybil Androwski and several assured him that the troupe had long since been disbanded. Finally, he had to give up.

When his job with the refugees ended, and he joined the ranks of Berliners who were slowly starting to rebuild their lives, he found a job with the publishing firm of Ellmann

Verlag. Through his single-minded dedication to work, he rose over the years to become, first, its senior editor, then head of the company.

Somewhere along the way, he married a dull, worthy woman named Carlotta. Humbly devoted to him, she died in 1980 without knowing that throughout their marriage the shade of another woman had shared her marital bed. They had no children and this, for him, was a major disappointment.

They bought their house in Wannsee during the seventies. After Carlotta's death he stayed on there. It was too large for a single man, filled with heavy, dark furnishings, neither welcoming nor comfortable, but his home was not important to him. His life began and ended with work and he frequently preferred to stay overnight in the apartment which was kept for his use at the top of the publishing house. His personal life was barren and loveless.

Inevitably, over the years, his memories of Sybil had blurred, though there were still times when they surfaced so vividly it might have been only days since they parted.

Reading her book had shaken him. It wasn't simply the revelation that Cybèle Meredith was Sybil Androwski, nor the humiliation of her contemptuous version of their affair. It was because she made it clear that her twins had been born about nine months after she had left him. They *could* have been his. Or were they the children of the step-father, who had apparently been sleeping with her at the same time?

When he had recovered from the first shock, his need to find out had become an obsession. Waiting for her reply to his letter was a painful period.

'I'm worried about Herr Fischer,' his secretary Kati told her friends. 'So pale, so quiet, and he sits in his office doing nothing. It isn't like him. I have to remind him to sign his letters, he won't read manuscripts, he refuses invitations . . .'

Then Sybil's letter arrived, inviting him to meet her at her villa in France. 'There is an adequate hotel in the nearby town of La Bergerie, and I will reserve a room for you,' she wrote.

'We can spend as much time together as you need, and I'm sure we can wrap up our discussion in a couple of days.'

The Sunday before he was due to go to France, he sat in his study in the Wannsee house, looking once again at the English edition of her book.

Compulsively, he re-read the section that had turned his life upside-down, although he already knew it almost by heart.

3

Extract from *I am Cybèle*

I was sixteen when Etta had her first stroke. It happened after midnight, in that dark silence when death always seems to be closest.

Arnie's hysterical shouts woke me. I lit the lantern and saw Etta lying on their bed, her mouth open, breathing in deep, rasping gasps. The left side of her face had sagged and she was unable to move her left arm. Her eyes were terrified and saliva bubbled from her mouth.

I borrowed young Billy Dando's bicycle to ride into the nearest town for a doctor. The streets were deserted, and I had to knock up the owner of a bar for directions. The doctor was not pleased to be called out, but when he arrived at our caravan, he instantly made arrangements to remove Etta to hospital.

Her stroke was not as serious as it might have been. He told us that the paralysis would probably wear off and she should eventually regain her speech.

'When will she be able to work?' Arnie said.

'What sort of work does she do?'

'She's Etta the Operatic Equestrienne. Rides a horse and sings.'

The doctor's eyebrows shot up. 'She's as likely to be able to fly to Mars. She's going to need nursing for weeks.' He looked towards me. 'Lucky her daughter's on hand.'

So when she was allowed to return to the caravan, I became Etta's nurse. I washed and dressed and fed her, I cleaned her up. Arnie, of course, did nothing.

It was the low point in my life, especially since, just before it happened, I had been secretly planning to leave the circus as soon as an opportunity arose.

I had already decided that my future was in the world of fashion. For the past couple of years I had been designing and making costumes for several of the artistes, who liked the robes I made for Etta. I was flattered by their admiration, so at first it didn't occur to me that I had found a way of earning money. When I finally told Olga Zakarova, one of the Russian gymnasts, that I would appreciate a token payment, I learned that Arnie had been there before me, setting a price on my work and keeping the proceeds himself. I made a scene, accusing him of theft, but he said the money was rightfully his for having maintained me for so many years. My mother was too cowed by him to protest.

I knew that she had some cash hidden under her costumes, which were folded in an old trunk, so I decided I would have to steal enough of it to get to Paris. I intended to look for work with one of the great couturiers of whom I had read: Worth, Chanel, Poirier, Lelong.

But then she had the stroke, and I was trapped.

Although Billy Dando took little interest in the behaviour of his troupe outside the ring, his wife insisted that Arnie should move out of our caravan while Etta was in hospital. She was worried about me because, like most of the other women, she was well aware of his sexual proclivities. Unfortunately, her protectiveness didn't go far enough.

I kept the caravan door locked, but Arnie had a key. A few nights after Etta had been taken away, he tiptoed in and flung himself on me, clamping a hand over my mouth to prevent me from calling out. I struggled, but he was strong and wiry.

When he entered me, there was pain, and the next morning the sheets were blood-stained.

Nevertheless, I found a curious satisfaction in the episode. Throughout my life I have sought new experiences. More importantly, I realized that Etta's embarrassed warnings about men and the horrors they could inflict on a girl no longer applied to me. I now knew what it was all about. It didn't make me like Arnie Gold any better, though. When I threatened to report him to Lucille Dando, he simply laughed. 'You do, love, and you and your mother will be out in the gutter. You wouldn't want to see poor old Etta, in her condition, without a home, would you? I been waiting to get my hands on you for a good while, and as long as you're nice to me, I'll look after you. If you're not, I'll dump the pair of you. Etta's no good to me or the circus now.'

He came to me at least once a week after that. Even when Etta returned, he would creep into my bed on the other side of the curtain that divided our living quarters.

Eventually she did partially regain the use of her limbs and was able to struggle from her bed to a chair. She could splutter a few reasonably comprehensible words, but it was clear that she would never return to normal.

Her act was sorely missed in the Cirque Dando, as it was one of the comic highlights. Arnie was angry, because without her, he was just another clown and his income was halved.

His demands on me became a bore. I found him physically repulsive, with his hairy, bony body and beer-scented breath. But as long as Etta was alive, I had to put up with him. He constantly repeated his threat to throw us out if I rejected him. I couldn't complain to the Dandos. We were already a burden on the circus and if he were to lose his job, we would have to leave, too. The other performers probably guessed what was going on, but since I never complained, they minded their own business.

The worst aspect of the affair was that he became jealous of other men and started picking fights with friends I'd had for years, accusing them of 'bothering' me.

The only thing that kept me from total despair was my

sewing. I worked hard on an old treadle machine in the caravan, creating costumes for acrobats and wire-dancers, jugglers and animal trainers, and off-duty dresses for the women. I learned how clever design could flatter the body and how to combine colours and fabrics.

Eventually, I even managed to keep some money back from Arnie, because my customers would occasionally give me a little extra for myself after they had paid him. I hid it with Etta's hoard in the wardrobe trunk.

The situation remained like that for more than a year, until Etta had, within a week, two more strokes, the second of which killed her. We had crossed into Germany three months before, and had been touring towns near the border, so we buried her in a tiny cemetery near Karlsruhe. I was surprised how much I missed her.

The circus was so cushioned in its own world that the war, which had been declared on 3 September, hardly impinged on us. We had been moving on every couple of weeks, setting up our tent whenever we could find a suitable site. Audiences were good, because local people, more sensitive to the situation than we were, seemed to need entertainment that would take their minds off an uncertain future.

Not long after Etta's funeral, I was having a cup of coffee on the terrace outside a local café when some drunken louts from the nearby army camp began to harass me. I was perfectly capable of getting rid of them myself, but a young officer raced up, seeing himself as a knight in armour coming to the rescue of the damsel in distress. He ordered them off, then asked if he could buy me another coffee.

He wasn't unattractive, so I said yes. His brown hair was brush-cut, he sat straight-backed and clicked his heels whenever we met. He was painfully polite and later on he bowed stiffly from the waist each time we separated after we had made love, which made me laugh.

I knew from the start that he was attracted to me. Oh, God, how he talked! And always about himself. It was as though he wanted to lay his dull life out as an offering before me.

Because it made a change from Arnie, I went to bed with

him. I don't think he'd had many women before, if any, and the whole experience seemed to overwhelm him. He took it for granted that we were now betrothed and informed me that we would marry as soon as the war was over.

As far as I was concerned, he was an interesting enough experience, but I had no intention of marrying him.

In fact, during the three weeks of our liaison, I was preparing to leave the circus. Now Etta was dead, I was free, and I had the money that we had hidden in the wardrobe trunk. Or rather, I thought I did.

One afternoon, I decided to check on the amount. Arnie was working in the ring on a new act with the other clowns, so I opened the trunk. The money had gone. He was the only person who could have taken it.

When he came to the caravan, I demanded it back. It had been my mother's, now it was mine. He had no right to it. We embarked on a raging quarrel and finally I shouted that he repelled me, that I found his love-making disgusting as well as boring and that I was leaving, with or without the money.

This time, he didn't laugh. He swore at me, then hit me on the head and face so that within minutes great red and purple marks came up and my eye started to blacken.

I managed to get away and went straight to the Dandos.

I cried as I reported what he had done, then told them the whole story of how he had raped me, forced himself on me regularly ever since and stolen Etta's money.

Billy was a bumbling old fool who always wanted to avoid trouble, but his wife Lucille was a tough Frenchwoman, hardened by her life on the road. She insisted that Arnie should be fired immediately, and I think Billy was pleased to have an excuse to get rid of him. He hadn't any real talent as a clown and was out of practice as an aerialist. After Etta's stroke the Dandos had kept him on out of compassion for her and me.

To escape the coming brawl when they tackled him, I fled into the village and met the German. He became emotional when he saw my face, and wanted to rush to the circus and kill my step-father. I managed to talk him out of that and

76

summoned up more tears as I told him how my money had been stolen.

By the time I got back to the caravan, Arnie had gone, and Lucille had got my money back. I've always been sorry I missed his departure. The female artistes had descended upon him and the Bulgarian strong-woman held him while others flung his clothes into a suitcase. Then they frog-marched him to the railway station and shoved him on to the first train out of town, shouting threats about what they'd do if he ever came near me again. A number of local people roared with laughter at the sight of this terrified man cringing from the mob of angry women.

The next day, I met the German as usual, and he gave me a wallet full of money. I was to use it to go to his parents' home in Hamburg. The war, he said, wasn't going to last long and we'd be married as soon as he returned.

By now, the Dandos had woken up to the fact that there was a war on. Many of the performers were French and were not enthusiastic about being caught in Germany. They decided to return to France, and hope to keep ahead of the conflict as they made for Paris, where they believed they would be safer. We left quietly that night.

I never saw the German again, but I was to meet Arnie under very different circumstances.

We had no trouble crossing the border because even then the circus had a special freedom.

In France, the Dandos regained their confidence. Instead of hurrying to Paris they decided to make a wide sweep south to Lyon and St Etienne, then turn north-west towards Tours, Le Mans and Rouen, where we had always drawn good audiences. We still suffered from a sublime and misguided confidence that we were immune from involvement in other people's wars.

It was April 1940, when we reached Evreux, not far from Paris, and by then something had occurred that put paid to my plans to look for work in a fashion house: I had discovered that I was pregnant.

I'd never been very careful about calculating my dates and must have missed three periods before I realized what had happened.

I'd heard women discuss their pregnancies and I knew there were ways you could get rid of an unwanted child. Desperately, I drank glasses of neat gin and fell into drunken sleep in my caravan. I galloped horses around and around the ring, bouncing in the saddle as Etta had, to the astonishment of performers who knew how much I disliked riding. I took baths so hot I emerged with my skin flaming. I even forced myself to climb a ladder, then tumble off it. All I did was sprain my wrist.

When, finally, I confessed what had happened to Olga Zakarova, and we worked out the approximate date when I must have conceived, she told me it was too late for an abortion.

'You are a stupid girl!' she exploded. 'Why didn't you come to me before?'

'I thought I could manage by myself.'

'*Idiote!* And that awful Gold is, of course, the father!'

In fact, I didn't know. Nor did I much care. It was either Arnie or the German – and I didn't wish to bear the child of either of them.

'You must have the baby in Paris, and let it instantly be adopted,' Olga said. 'Billy's changed his mind. He wants to go south. At last he's afraid of the war, so we're moving to Algeria. Maybe you can join us afterwards.'

But I was no longer thinking of Paris as a mecca. Being there during a war, alone and pregnant, was not at all what I had envisaged and I had already thought of an alternative.

'I'll go to England,' I said. 'I have relations there. I'll go to my uncle.'

Olga looked dubious. 'How will you cross the Channel? Already the British are being driven back in Belgium and Normandy.'

'I'll find a way.'

She shrugged. 'Go soon. You are starting to show. You are carrying a large child.'

In fact, I was carrying twins, though I didn't realize it until they were born.

When I waved the Cirque Dando goodbye outside Evreux it was the loneliest moment of my life. I stood by the roadside and watched the painted wagons and caravans which had been my home since I was born, disappearing south. When they had gone, I turned north. My only luggage was an ancient carpet-bag which had belonged to my father. I had discarded everything that would not fit into it.

The May weather was cool, so I was able to hide my condition under a loden cloak one of the Austrian eques-triennes had given me. Underneath it, my money was stuffed into a little leather bag slung around my shoulder. When I reached the coast, I planned to use some of it to hire a boat to take me to England. The rest would, I hoped, see me through until the child had been born and disposed of for adoption, and I could find work.

I'd made enquiries about the progress of the war from local people, and knew that to the north the British were moving towards Dunkirk and Ostend. German troops were advancing towards the sea in the south, to cut them off.

There was a constant sound of distant gunfire, and two or three men I spoke to declared that France and Belgium would fall any day and the British army would be defeated.

Calais or Dunkirk seemed to be my best bets to pick up a boat and I told myself confidently that if I could join up with the retreating British, they would help me. I spoke English without any accent and had decided that I would call myself by my mother's maiden name. As Sybil Jones, an English girl who had been caught in Europe by the war, I had a right to demand their assistance. It wasn't possible, I thought, that an army of 400,000 men could be wiped out.

After half an hour by the roadside I managed to pick up a lift in a farm-truck that was carrying a load of cabbages to Amiens. There were two men in the van, so I had to squeeze into the back, among the boxes. I told them I was on my way to join relations in Dunkirk.

It was not until much later that I discovered our route directly crossed that of the German drive to the sea. Had we been a few days later, we would have been in the line of fire from the Allied rearguard.

As it was, the roads were jammed by civilian refugees. The further we went, the more people there were, fleeing north, south and west, on foot or in any kind of vehicle they could commandeer: farm-carts, bicycles, cars ranging from ancient, rattling antiques to Rolls Royces. From my perch on the cabbages, I saw women pushing prams, with older children clinging to their skirts, men with hand-carts piled with belongings. I wondered whether they knew where they were going or whether, like lemmings, they were simply motivated by an instinct to move.

Throughout the day, Stuka dive-bombers roared above us on their way to attack the British and French forces.

My own worry was not the threat of attack, but whether the old truck's rattling progress over the rough roads might cause a miscarriage. I wouldn't have minded losing the child – or, as it turned out, children – but I did not want to be ill and immobilized in the middle of a battle.

The farmers dropped me in Amiens, where the gunfire was much closer, and I decided to spend some of my precious francs on a room for the night. After being turned away from one hotel after another, because all the accommodation had already been taken up by refugees, I found quarters in a pension near the cathedral. It was a small, dirty place and the sheets had not been washed since the previous occupant had slept in them. I was exhausted and feeling rather ill, so I didn't worry too much.

If I could get a lift the following day, I thought I might make it to Calais by nightfall.

Unfortunately, when I emerged the next morning, everyone else seemed to have the same idea. There were cars on the road, but even the rare driver who was not already carrying a full load was unwilling to stop in case he should be swamped by would-be passengers. Many already had people balancing on their running-boards.

I joined the procession moving on foot towards the town's outskirts and the Route Nationale which led to Abbeville. The children I was carrying grew heavier with every step, and the weight threw me off balance so I rolled from side to side like a sailor in a rough sea.

I had left the town when I saw, of all things, a circus. It had been camped beside the road and was getting ready to leave. There was an air of frantic activity. The tent had been pulled down and everyone was in motion, packing trailers and caravans. I heard a lion roaring, and an elephant trumpeting, and it was like coming home as I smelled the circus smell of sawdust and animal dung.

A tall, thin man with shiny black hair and a waxed moustache was standing near a truck. Everyone else was in rough working clothes, but he was wearing riding breeches, boots and a tweed jacket. Since he was issuing orders I guessed that he was the ring-master and, probably, the owner, so I went up to him.

He was talking to a man in dungarees and took no notice of me for a moment.

When he did, his greeting was hardly welcoming: 'So what do you want, mademoiselle?' Then he looked at me more closely and said, 'Excuse me. Madame.'

I was as brusque as he: 'If you're going north, I'd like to join you.'

'Certainly not!' He turned away.

'M'sieu . . . I belong to Le Cirque Dando. My name is Sybil Androwski. I need to get to the coast.'

'Doesn't everybody?' But his eyes narrowed. 'You were with old Billy Dando?'

'My father was Lajos Androwski and my mother was Etta . . .' Even at that moment I couldn't bring myself to give her ridiculous title. 'She was an equestrienne who sang.'

'Etta the Operatic Equestrienne! I remember her. One of the best comic acts I've ever seen. Why have you left the Dandos?'

'They've gone south. I want to get to relations in England before . . .'

He understood. 'We're making for Dunkirk, though God knows whether we'll get there or what we'll do then. Maybe He'll show us how to walk to England on the water. There might be a room for you in our truck. Go and see my wife.' He pointed to a dark, florid woman who was helping to pile neat coils of rope in a van.

Compared with my seat among the cabbages, the truck was luxury, although I was squeezed between the ring-master, Jan Saloman, and his wife Céline.

We worked our way north but because of the amount of traffic we were still short of Calais at dusk.

For most of the day, we were under fire. As well as the refugees there were hundreds of dazed British and French soldiers wandering along the roads. Many of them had been separated from their regiments during the retreat and appeared to be unsure where they were heading.

The roadsides were littered with prams, bicycles and carts which people had abandoned as they fled for shelter from the bombing.

In one field, I saw rows of army vehicles and equipment which the British troops had been forced to leave behind. Saloman told me that they drained them of oil and water, then left them with their motors running, knowing they would seize up and be useless to the enemy. For the same reason they had set alight piles of discarded supplies of clothing and blankets. As we crawled past, one of the circus men raced across and dragged out half a dozen grey army blankets which had not yet been burned. Saloman gave me one.

The animals suffered from the noise and crowds. The lions kept up a continuous roaring. The horses reared and shivered and those that were being transported in boxes beat a tattoo against the sides with their hooves. The elephant trainer, an Indian, kept up a continuous, soothing murmur as he walked beside his beasts.

Some guardian angel must have been looking after us, because we remained untouched by the bombs or the fighters which dived low to machine-gun the fleeing crowds.

During the afternoon, in an effort to move more quickly,

we turned off the crowded main road and came on to a lesser one which Saloman said ran more or less parallel. It was certainly empty of traffic, but was so narrow that the circus's big lorries and trailers had to slow down to a snail's pace and it didn't seem to me that we had gained anything.

As darkness fell, the air-activity lessened and finally ceased. Saloman decided to find somewhere to camp overnight so the animals could be fed and watered. He was more concerned with them than with the humans, who had been snatching snacks on the move.

Céline Saloman had shared their tomatoes and salami with me and during the morning we had bought some fresh bread as we passed a village *boulangerie.* Its owner had been baking steadily for two days, his wife told us, and as soon as a batch of bread came from the oven it was bought up by refugees. 'For us, this war is not so bad,' she said.

It was dark, with intermittent moonlight, when we emerged from some wooded country and saw, to our right, a stretch of unfenced grass a few hundred metres wide. Saloman decided to stay there and we pulled off the road.

Beyond it was a large building, surrounded by a high stone wall with an arched wooden doorway.

I was stiff from sitting in the truck all day and volunteered to take a bucket and ask whoever lived there for fresh water.

As I walked over the grass I noticed that some people were building little fires in the open to cook their meals. It occurred to me that the flames could attract the enemy's attention, but we were not yet wise in the ways of war, so I didn't think much about it. After all, the air-raids had stopped.

The door had a grille set into it at eye-height. I peered through, but could see nothing in the darkness. As I glanced up, I noticed a cross above it, and realized that the place was either a nunnery or a monastery. I tugged an iron bell-pull. Nobody came, and after a few minutes I turned the handle, which was a ring of twisted iron. The door opened into a courtyard. There was rubble and broken glass everywhere and part of the building was a ruin, its small Gothic windows without glass, its roof gaping, great holes in its blackened walls.

Then I heard many voices chanting. I climbed over some fallen stones and found an opening that led to an inner courtyard.

Half a dozen flickering oil-lamps lit a strange scene. In the centre knelt a circle of cloaked figures, around a dozen white-clad bodies which were stretched out on the ground. The kneelers were swaying as they intoned a prayer.

I went closer and saw that the prone shapes were the bodies of young girls. The mourners were nuns.

Someone touched my arm. It was another nun. She put a finger to her lips and drew me away, through a door, into the building.

A lamp in a niche showed me that she was young and her face was tear-stained.

'Who are you?' she said. 'Why have you come here?'

I told her my name and that we were camping outside the wall. 'What happened?'

'The Germans bombed us this afternoon. There was a direct hit on the wing where our novices live. They were all killed.'

I could think of nothing to say. As we stood, staring at each other, the nuns' voices were drowned by the sound of an aircraft. Almost simultaneously, there was a series of explosions and the ground shook. People started to scream.

Nuns appeared from the courtyard, their eyes wide and terrified. I heard one whisper, 'Mother of God, not again!'

The screams were coming from the direction of the circus. I ran across the courtyard and reached the door, followed by a black flutter of nuns.

Where I had left a peaceful, tidy camp, bodies were lying everywhere. Instead of the few little fires that must have attracted the bombers, trailers and lorries were in flames. I started towards where I had left the Salomans, but their truck had sustained a direct hit and was a mass of twisted metal. As far as I could see, all that was left of Céline and Jan were some blood-stained rags which had been scattered by the blast.

Nearby one of the baby elephants was lying on its side,

dead. Beside it, its mother, with a great wound in her side, was trumpeting in agony.

A white horse plunged past, eerily fluorescent in the moonlight. It was dragging the body of a man who had become entangled in its trailing bridle.

Then I saw the lion, standing a few yards away. His eyes were fixed on me and a throaty roar rumbled in his chest. Beyond was his cage, its iron-barred door hanging open. On a trailer next to it there was a second cage, where two lionesses were pacing up and down.

I had been brought up to be unafraid of our circus-trained animals, but this lion and I were strangers. The urge to turn and run was almost irresistible, but I knew that any big cat would attack a moving target, and my only chance was to remain immobile.

I stood, holding my breath. There was movement all around us, and sounds, but the lion wasn't distracted. It was as though we were isolated in our own silence. After what seemed like several minutes, but was probably a few seconds, there was a noise nearer at hand and the lion's head swung around. Then it plunged forward. As I screamed and stumbled back, it fell dead almost at my feet.

A man carrying a rifle knelt beside it. Blood was running from cuts on his face and his shirt was in tatters. There were tears in his eyes as he put his hand gently on its mane, then he said, 'Maybe he's better off than we are,' and walked towards his lionesses. He raised his rifle and shot them both.

Lit by the fires, the nuns were bending over the dead and wounded. The few circus people left alive were wandering around, dazed, looking for their friends. There were explosions as flames reached the petrol-tanks. Shattered vehicles littered the grass.

My cloak and my carpet-bag, which contained everything I owned, were now part of the wreckage of the Salomans' truck. I picked up one of the army blankets, which was lying on the ground, draped it around my shoulders, and left. Fortunately, I had been carrying my wallet.

Wanting to get as far away from the carnage as possible, I

walked for nearly two hours. Somewhere I must have taken a wrong turning in the darkness, because I found myself in deep countryside, on a narrow, unmade road. My feet were so heavy I felt as though I was wading through soft sand.

When I was about to collapse from exhaustion I saw the outlines of a group of farm buildings ahead. The moon had been obliterated by clouds and there was no way of telling whether a farmhouse adjoined them. I felt my way along a wooden wall and found a door which creaked open when I pushed it. There was a smell of hay, but there didn't seem to be any animals, so I went forward, step by step. I could hear rustlings, which I assumed were rats, but I was too tired to care. A stack of hay would be as welcome as any bed.

Then the sounds took on a different quality. I felt myself gripped from behind, jerked against a man's hard body, and a hand was clamped over my mouth.

Instinctively, I fought, twisting and kicking, trying to close my teeth on the hand, but he was tall and strong and his grip didn't loosen, even when we fell together on to a pile of hay. As I momentarily stopped struggling and sagged back, one of his hands slipped down and pressed against my breasts.

I heard a gasp, then a voice said softly, in halting, heavily accented French, 'Si vous criez, je vous tue! Comprenez?'

I managed to nod, and his hand released my mouth. 'Qui êtes-vous?' he whispered.

'You hurt me!' I said furiously, feeling blood trickling from my lip where he had pressed it against my teeth.

'English? My God! What are you doing here? And keep your voice down!'

'I'm looking for somewhere to sleep. What are *you* doing here?'

'Trying not to be captured. There are Germans all around us. Didn't you know?'

I stood up and tried to brush off some of the hay that was clinging to my clothes. 'You're a soldier?'

He introduced himself as Lieutenant Dominic Stone. After an attack in the morning he had become separated from his division and had no idea where he was. An hour before, he had almost walked into a German detachment. Like me, he had sought shelter for the night.

A wave of dizziness overtook me. I staggered, and fell against him. His arm went around me and I heard another gasp as he felt my swollen waistline.

He helped me to sit into a deep, comfortable pile of hay.

'I'm Cybèle Androwski . . . Sybil, I mean.' Unconsciously, I had given my name the French pronunciation to which I had become accustomed at the circus.

He repeated it, 'Cybèle.' Although it was hardly the time to think about such trivialities, I realized for the first time how much I preferred Cybèle to Sybil, and in that moment decided to adopt it as my name in future. It was mistakenly spelled the English way only once after that, in the hospital where my babies were delivered.

He settled down beside me and said, 'We have a lot of time to fill in. Tell me about yourself, Cybèle.'

Because we were alone in the middle of a war, and might be dead by this time tomorrow, I told this stranger, whom I hadn't even seen clearly, everything that had happened to me, including the fact that I was unmarried, pregnant and that I was going to relations in Brighton. Towards the end, I have no recollection at which point, I must have simply stopped talking and fallen asleep.

When I became conscious again it was full daylight. Dominic Stone was lying asleep beside me and I was able to study him. He looked very young and vulnerable, with smooth skin and tumbled light brown hair. There was a golden fuzz on his chin and long eyelashes swept his cheeks. I moved, and he was instantly awake. His eyes were a clear, light blue.

For a moment, we looked at each other in silence, then he said, 'Good morning, Mademoiselle Androwski.'

'Good morning, Lieutenant Stone.'

He stood up and stretched. 'I'm going to check out this place, then we'll get moving.'

Although he must have known I'd be a drag on him, I don't think that it occurred to him to leave me.

'What about the Germans?'

'With any luck, they'll have moved on. We'll go north and hope to link up with our lot.'

'You can't go anywhere safely in that uniform,' I said.

'I'm hoping there's a farmhouse nearby. Maybe we can find a friendly Frenchman who'll lend me some civilian clothes.'

We were in a big wooden barn and sunshine was slanting down through the roof, where several tiles were missing. He went to the door, opened it and peered out. Then, with an intake of breath, he pulled it to and put his finger to his lips. 'Jerries!' he breathed. 'Burrow into the hay and keep still.'

We had barely covered ourselves when the door was opened. Dust was tickling my nose and I was afraid I was going to sneeze.

A voice snapped, in German: 'There's nothing here. Stand them up against the wall.'

There were more sounds: several men talking, followed by shots, groans, and silence. Then the same voice said, 'That's it. Let's go!'

We stayed where we were. Half an hour must have passed, then we heard shuffling footsteps outside.

Dominic rose from the hay, looking like a scarecrow with straw sticking to his hair and uniform. Cautiously, he opened the door, looked around, then went out. I followed, to find myself in a cobbled yard. Opposite the barn, a woman was crouched over two men who were lying at the foot of a stone wall. They were both dead, their heads resting in pools of blood. One was wearing a British uniform, the other a farmer's overalls.

We went over to her and Dominic touched her shoulder. She looked up at us, too dulled by shock and sorrow to be frightened. She gestured towards the farmer. 'My husband.'

We followed her to the farmhouse and had barely reached it when neighbours started to arrive. One or two were openly hostile and advised the widow to have nothing to do with us, but she took no notice. She gave us some clothes and a breakfast of coffee, bread and ham. When we had finished, she directed us towards a minor road that led north and would take us into Dunkirk. She had heard that the town was still in Allied hands.

As we were leaving, she said to me, 'In your condition, you're walking?' I nodded.

Still dry-eyed, in control of herself, she said, 'Come!' and led us to a barn where there was an old bull-nosed Peugeot. 'Take it. I won't need it any more. I can't drive.' She shrugged away thanks, saying, 'Helping two English to escape is little enough to pay them back for what they did.'

The car was in a terrible condition, its engine wheezing, its springs broken, its tyres almost bald. Its maximum speed was less than thirty miles an hour. But it was faster than walking, and gave us some protection.

Even on the small roads, we twice came upon columns of German troops, swinging along with the confidence of men who knew they were winning the war. They had seen so many French refugees that they hardly glanced at us, though one or two laughed at the car and shouted insults.

Once again, aircraft were roaring overhead and we heard bombing, shelling and rifle fire.

At mid-day, there was an explosion which had nothing to do with the fighting. The car lurched across the road, out of control, and came to rest with its bonnet halfway through a thick hedge. One of the tyres had blown out. There was no spare.

'So now we walk,' Dominic said grimly.

'How far do you think we are from the coast?'

'Twenty or thirty kilometres. With luck, we might reach Dunkirk tomorrow.'

'And you'll be able to find your battalion?'

'God knows where it is. Or if there are any of them left. They must have scattered all over the country. Cybèle, have you thought what you're going to do when we get there?'

'Hire a boat and sail to England.'

He raised an eyebrow. 'Has it occurred to you that the entire British army is probably trying to do the same thing, and that there might not be any boats?'

'I'll get there somehow.'

He smiled down at me. 'I'm sure you will.'

It was curious that although I'd known him for less than twenty-four hours, I felt totally at ease with him. As we'd driven, and now as we walked, we talked, each interested in the other, sharing reminiscences, experiences, hopes. There was a sympathy between us such as I'd never known with a man before.

Carrying my weight, I tired quickly and we slowed to a plod. He put his arm around me to help me along and the physical contact created an excitement which I knew instinctively that he shared.

We had eaten nothing since breakfast. Before darkness fell, we reached a Normandy farmhouse, and decided to risk going in to beg some bread and, perhaps, a bed for the night. The Normans, we told each other, were on our side.

There was a pole extending from a window on the farm's upper floor, with a white flag attached to it. Its significance escaped us, so we knocked at the door.

A woman came. She was short and dark, with a flat nose and a small, mean mouth.

'Madame, could you sell us some food?' I said. 'We are English and we're on our way to Dunkirk.'

'No!' She gestured at the flag. 'You have lost the war. Go away!' She started to close the door, but Dominic put his foot in the gap. He drew out his army pistol, which he had stuck into his belt. Followed by a stream of abuse, we went into her kitchen and took enough bread, cheese, pâté, ham and tomatoes to keep us going for a couple of days. Then we left.

That night we lay under some bushes with my blanket over us. Before we went to sleep, Dominic said, 'Cybèle, when we get back to England I don't know what's going to happen. I guess I'll be sent overseas, but we'll meet again. I'll come and find you in Brighton.'

'Perhaps I won't be there,' I said. 'I might not like being with my uncle.'

'Then you must find me. My mother and father live in Church Row, Hampstead.' He paused. 'Even if I'm away, if you're ever in need of friends, don't hesitate to go to them. They'll help you.'

'I could hardly ask strangers . . .'

'You only have to mention me and they won't be strangers any more. I'll write and tell them about you as soon as I get back. We're not going to lose touch.'

'I wouldn't want to see them before the baby's born,' I said.

'No. But afterwards . . . What will you do about the child?'

'I'm going to have it adopted.'

We reached Dunkirk the next day.

The great pall of black smoke that covered it was visible for miles, and hundreds of Allied troops were pouring into the town, crossing roads and ploughed fields, wading through ditches, climbing barbed-wire fences. Some had requisitioned bicycles. We saw one man riding a cart-horse and another was carrying a black puppy. The wounded were being helped along by their comrades.

Dominic stopped several of them and asked about his unit, but the chaos was such that no-one knew the whereabouts of his own group, let alone anyone else's.

Dunkirk was a shambles. Buildings had been razed by bombs, streets were littered with rubble and fallen electric wires. Scarcely a window remained unbroken and wrecked cars were abandoned on every corner.

Ever willing to seize an opportunity to make a fast buck, a few café-owners were doing a thriving trade among the troops, and in some areas there was a curious atmosphere of gaiety, despite the constant air-attacks. It was a strange and chilling scene because no-one appeared to be in charge, and we knew how close the Germans were. I began to believe that, indeed, the British army was about to be wiped out.

We walked along the shore, and reached a stretch of beach where some order had been restored. A seemingly endless line of soldiers snaked along the water's edge. There were a few ships standing several hundred yards offshore and little boats were ferrying out a couple of dozen men at a time. It was a pathetic effort when one saw the thousands who were patiently waiting.

91

We approached an officer who seemed to be organizing the evacuation. Dominic introduced me as an English girl who, for obvious reasons, needed immediate transport. He simply shook his head and pointed to the waiting men. Already the boats were being dangerously overloaded. Anyhow, he said, a woman would probably be safe enough with the Germans.

We went back into the town. I was so tired that I scarcely cared what happened to me. The officer was probably right. I could speak French and German. I'd survive. I tried to persuade Dominic to leave me and join the queue on the beach, but he refused.

As we walked along the inner harbour, we saw half a dozen French *poilus* boarding a fishing boat.

We hurried across. One of the crew said they were going to take the men to a port along the coast which had not yet fallen to the enemy. We offered them money to return and take us across the Channel. They refused, but as we turned away, one of them called, 'Try Jean-Paul in the Café du Port. Maybe he'll help you.'

The café was in a noisome side-street which had so far escaped the bombs. It was a gloomy little place which had not even attracted the British, and the only customer was an elderly Frenchman who was slumped over a table, an empty brandy glass in front of him. When we asked for Jean-Paul, the barman pointed towards him.

He looked up sullenly and when I explained what we wanted, he shook his head. 'Cross La Manche at a time like this? Not me.'

'But you have a motor-boat? We'll pay.'

He looked at his empty glass, then back at us. 'How much?'

I glanced at Dominic and he whispered, 'Try twenty pounds.'

When I named the equivalent in francs, he said, 'Double it, and I'll think about it.'

'I haven't got that much,' Dominic said.

'I have. Shall I tell him yes?'

We had given in too easily. Jean-Paul's eyes narrowed. 'And the same again for my time and trouble.'

Living among circus men had taught me a vocabulary of abuse which I imagine was equalled by few young women at that time. I let fly with a stream of invective that widened his bleary eyes. 'And not one centime more!' I ended. 'Keep your bloody boat. It'll be requisitioned anyway, and you'll get nothing!'

That touched a chord in his avaricious heart. We had almost reached the door when he shouted, 'Hey! I'll take you. Only you pay me first.'

'When we're on board,' I said.

He didn't like that, but greed won, and he stumped out ahead of us.

It was a long walk over cobbles and rubble, through narrow alleys and over sand, until we reached a tumbledown boat-house on a lonely inlet. The door had a formidable padlock on it, but a child could have pushed through the rotten boarding of the walls. I wondered how long it would be before desperate troops had sought out all the vessels their owners hoped to keep hidden.

Dominic helped Jean-Paul to push a small, dirty motor-boat down the slipway. There was an inch of water in the bottom. It hardly looked as though it could cross the harbour safely, let alone the English Channel. Fortunately, there was no wind, the water was calm and the assault from the sky seemed to have diminished.

It took Jean-Paul a dozen abortive tries before the engine caught and we were on our way.

He only growled when Dominic handed him the money we'd agreed on, and had not otherwise spoken a word. He didn't appear to have a compass and I wondered how he was going to find his way across the thirty-odd miles to England.

Clouds had covered the sun and, in late afternoon, it was growing cold. Muffled in my blanket, I was better off than Dominic in his cotton work-jacket, but although he was shivering, he never complained. We sat together, holding hands, as the shore retreated and we reached the open sea. In the distance, we could at first see several ships, presumably awaiting their complement of troops, but soon even they were out of sight and we were alone.

I glanced constantly at my watch as we chugged along and the minutes moved slowly. The water in the bottom of the boat rose and, still without a word, Jean-Paul tossed Dominic a tin mug. He baled, but it didn't make much difference. We seemed to settle lower and lower into the water. At one point, he said, 'Can you swim?' and looked relieved when I nodded. But how long could I stay afloat, with the extra weight I carried?

The boat's engine missed occasionally and once cut out altogether and had to be re-started.

We had been travelling for an hour and a half when the clouds began to break up and the setting sun appeared just above the horizon. It threw reddish-gold streaks over the water and silvered the white tops of the choppy little waves.

Dominic smiled at me. 'It's a good omen.'

Those were the last words he ever spoke. Above us there was suddenly the noise with which we were all too familiar: the scream of a diving aircraft. The sun must have lit up our boat and a stray German plane had spotted us.

Dominic flung himself over me and we tumbled into the bottom. I heard the rattle of machine-gun fire, then a terrible cry. The boat lurched to one side, and righted itself. I was unable to move under Dominic's weight.

'Let me up!' I gasped, but he didn't move. 'Jean-Paul, help me!' There was no response.

The aircraft's engine faded and there was silence.

Eventually I managed to push Dominic away and sit up. He was lying on his stomach with water slopping around him and his back was covered in blood. I lifted his head. His eyes were open, but there was no life in them. Jean-Paul had disappeared. I guessed that he had been shot and fallen overboard.

The boat, without anyone to steer it, was zigzagging wildly. A kind of automatic pilot seemed to take over my movements. I climbed over Dominic's body and grabbed the wheel. With no idea how far the boat might have turned off-course, there was nothing to do but keep it straight and hope that eventually

I might reach some land. I no longer cared whether it was England or France.

And then the engine stopped, and there was no way I could start it. Darkness had fallen, a wind had sprung up and every now and then a wave threatened to swamp the boat.

I went back to Dominic and put my arms around him, lifting his head into my lap. For an hour, I clung to him, telling myself that this was only a nightmare; he had simply gone to sleep and would soon wake up. I talked to him, and now and then I bent and kissed him. At one point, I took his wallet and papers from his pocket and tucked them down the neck of my dress.

It was after eight o'clock when I saw the dark shape of another boat. It carried no lights, and it was steering directly for me. I began to call. My screams grew increasingly shrill as I realized that I was going to be run down. It swept on and its bow missed the motor-boat by a few inches. I lost my balance and sprawled over Dominic, still screaming. It was as though I was being tossed in a blanket and my boat scraped against the bigger one. Then it tipped over, waves swamped it and I was in the water.

As I struggled to free myself from the blanket tangled around my shoulders, there were shouts from above and a torch-beam was focused on the sea a few yards away. It swept slowly around until it caught me. I waved. Voices called out, in English, and a rope was dropped. I grasped it and was drawn towards what turned out to be a fishing trawler from Ramsgate, which was part of the rescue fleet. Men reached down and dragged me on board. Someone wrapped me in a great-coat.

I don't know how long it was before we reached England. The deck was crowded with soldiers who had been brought from Dunkirk. Some were wounded and huddled silently against the bulkheads, others were so exhausted they had not even wakened when the boat stopped to pick me up. I told them as little about myself as necessary, and could not bear even to mention Dominic.

In Ramsgate, women had organized supplies of cocoa and sandwiches for the returning troops. They were astonished to see me brought ashore – even more so when they realized my condition. But my escape story was no more bizarre than others they had heard and I didn't have to answer too many questions. One woman took me to her home and put me to bed.

The next morning, because my wallet had been lost in the water, she lent me enough money to go to my uncle in Brighton.

Before leaving, I asked for note-paper and wrote a brief letter to Dominic's parents, enclosing his papers. I told them what had happened and how he had died helping me to escape from France. Because I didn't want to see them yet, nor have them look for me, I simply signed the letter 'Cybèle'.

4

There were times when Julia Leander missed her husband so badly that she wondered how she could endure the rest of her life without him. Thirty years to go, if she was unlucky. Thirty years of living alone, belonging to nobody. Gitta, the adoptive mother she adored, had died two years before. Suzy was a loving daughter and they were as close friends as any mother and child could be. But she had left the nest when she was eighteen and was often abroad, working. Now she was in France, it might be weeks before she returned and Julia found herself suffering a severe bout of loneliness and depression.

It wasn't even as though Alex had been a good husband. Charming, certainly, lovable, good-looking, with the dark auburn hair and brown eyes Suzy had inherited. But he had one fatal flaw: he was a gambler.

At first she had regarded his compulsion to bet even on a couple of ants crossing a path as an amusing aberration. After their marriage, she was to discover that it was an addiction which nothing would cure. He would bet on horses, greyhounds, cards, fruit-machines, but most of his money went on the roulette tables, where he was consistently unlucky. Monte Carlo was his natural habitat, and during the early years, if he'd had a brief run of success, he would whisk Julia off there. On two occasions she'd had to cable Gitta for the air-fare home.

He had been born to a prosperous farming family and when he and Julia had been married for two months, he inherited nine hundred valuable acres in Hampshire, plus a sprawling flint house with twelve rooms. Five years later, he was eighty thousand pounds in the red and had sold off most of the property. After three more years, he sold the house, and they moved into a small flat in Pimlico. Suzy was moved from her private school to a London comprehensive.

At one point, Julia went to a meeting of an organization called Gamblers Anonymous and suffered the humiliation of begging strangers for help. An earnest young man came to the flat and told Alex how he, too, had once gambled away a fortune. 'I was just as miserable as you, old chap,' he said solemnly. 'Since I reformed, I'm a new man.'

Alex laughed at him. 'But I'm not miserable,' he said. 'I'm having a great time.'

When their total assets shrank to fifty pounds, he took a job, the first he had ever had, as secretary of a genealogical society. For six months, until the auditors moved in, he financed his gambling from cheques sent by Americans anxious to trace their family roots. Only his charm and his apparently genuine repentance saved him from prosecution.

At that point, Julia finally realized that it was up to her to keep the family afloat.

She had attended art school for a couple of years before her marriage, and had a talent for illustration. She took her portfolio to a publisher and won a contract to illustrate a children's book. Then she wrote and illustrated a book of her own. It was a success, and she was launched into what was to become a successful and lucrative career.

She relieved Alex of all financial responsibility and made him a generous allowance. Never having suffered from false pride, he was delighted.

Suzy was thirteen when he was mugged as he was walking home from a West End club in the early hours of the morning – walking because he had gambled away his last penny. Two youths jumped him in a dark alley near Victoria Station. When they were eventually arrested, the police told Julia that they had been after money for drugs. Angry when they discovered that Alex had nothing, they had beaten and stabbed him, and left him to die in the gutter.

Although he had caused her a great deal of unhappiness, her love for him had not wavered. Later she told Suzy, 'There were so many good things that after he died the bad ones didn't seem to matter. We laughed together and we enjoyed the same books and plays and there was nothing I couldn't talk to him about. As far as I know, he was never unfaithful.' Always a realist, she added, 'He was too busy gambling to take on other women.'

She was determined that Suzy should not suffer more than necessary from his death, so she hid her loneliness and concentrated on preserving a stable home-life. Gitta was probably the only person who realized the extent of her suffering.

Eventually, she got over it, and only rarely fell into one of the secret depressions that had dominated her life during the first years of solitude.

In her studio now, she wished she'd said to hell with work and gone away with Suzy. On the other hand, her daughter had seemed to need to be by herself for a while.

The telephone rang.

'Julie darling?' Damien Bennett, Suzy's agent, was recognizable instantly because of his irritating habit of shortening or lengthening the given name of anyone he liked. 'I've been trying to raise Suze. Could she be with you?'

'She left for France this morning. I thought she told you.'

'She did, but I hoped I might catch her. A job's come up in Paris. It might have changed her mind about this ridiculous holiday. She doesn't *need* a holiday, Julie! What's got into her?'

'I think she does, you know. She's broken up with Clive and she's generally fed up with modelling.'

'I can't imagine why. Who's she gone with?'

'No-one, as far as I know.'

'I don't believe it! That's what she said, but she's never done such a thing before and I had weeks of work lined up. There's something funny about this trip, Julie.'

'Rubbish!' But she felt a sudden frisson.

She put the telephone down and walked back to her drawing-board. What *had* caused Suzy's sudden decision? Hoping for a clue, she summoned up the memory of their conversation the day after she had come back from Morocco. They had talked about Clive, and Cybèle Meredith and, for the first time in years, about Julia's family – or lack of it – and her mislaid twin. Why had Suzy brought that up out of the blue? She already knew all there was to know . . . this, Julia thought, is ridiculous! She simply wanted a holiday, and when she rings to say where she is, I'll join her. There's nothing to worry about.

She was reminded suddenly of Gitta. When Suzy was a difficult adolescent, sullen, unpredictable and suffering from a severe attack of teenage rebellion, Julia had exploded: 'When will this end, for God's sake? When can one stop worrying about one's kids?'

Gitta had said simply, 'Never!'

'You still worry about me?'

'Always. Worry, worry, worry. When you were married to that man and he made you so unhappy . . .'

'Not always.'

'. . . And when he died and left you alone. So selfish! And when you must work so hard to keep the child. And now I worry because *you* are worried.'

She smiled at the memory and her depression lifted.

It was six o'clock. She washed her brushes and stuck them in a jar, then went downstairs and poured herself a gin and tonic, ashamed of her brief wallow in self-pity.

There was a photograph of her adoptive mother above the drinks trolley. Gitta was still missed by everyone who had known her. The picture had been taken when she was in her twenties, and very pretty. Later, she had put on weight, her face had coarsened, her skin become florid and the thickness of her lips and nose more pronounced. But her gaiety and compassion had never altered. If it hadn't been for her, Julia's childhood would have been very different.

She was ten when Gitta had told her that she was not her natural daughter, but had been adopted when she was six months old.

'It was during the war, and I read this story in a newspaper about little twin girls who had been deserted by their mamma,' she said. 'Such a tragedy! Such a thing for a woman to do!' Affected by emotion, Gitta's Austrian accent always became more pronounced. 'I made Godfrey come with me to the children's home. It took me two weeks to persuade him, and when we got there, one of the twins had gone to another family. But they let us have you, and eventually we adopted you. I have been very lucky. Other women have to take what God sends them. I was able to *choose* you.'

So Julia had been carried off to a mansion in Sussex, the adopted daughter of Sir Godfrey Harrap and his Viennese wife, who had married when Godfrey was Counsellor at the British Embassy in Austria before the war.

When Gitta died, she had inherited a considerable amount of money and had used some of it to buy her present house. The rest, invested, meant that with the proceeds of her books she would have no financial worries for the rest of her life. She had Suzy, many friends and she enjoyed her work. She was, she often told herself, a fortunate woman.

It was only during the bouts of loneliness that she would think about her lost sister, and fantasize about one day meeting her. Would they recognize each other? Would they instantly feel the bond that was supposed to exist between twins? Would such a meeting mean that she need never be lonely again?

Unfortunately, no matter how hard she tried to produce in her mind the idealized picture of this mirror-image of herself, her inexplicable suspicion persisted that the real woman would turn out to be very different.

5

Christian Morel's first impression of life in Le Bas-Fond was that it was both noisy and untidy.

He drove down from Paris a few days before Cybèle Meredith was due to return from the United States and arrived at the mill after dark on a balmy June evening. From a rutted, unmade road that wound through a vineyard, he saw a large stone house. Light streamed from its open front door, and most of the downstairs windows were illuminated. Voices and music came from inside. There was a terrace curving around to the left, on to which a set of double doors opened, and below it the house-lights were reflected in a stream. To one side, he could see the dramatic shadow of a great mill-wheel.

He parked his car outside the door and as he walked up the two wide, shallow steps, he heard what sounded like a party: many people talking at once, the chink of glass and china. There was a smell of onion-flavoured cooking. He had driven all day, without stopping for lunch, and was hungry.

Discarded coats, hats and boots were scattered about a large hall. He found a bell and pressed it, but there was no reaction. After a moment he walked in and turned towards the source of the noise, an open door on the right.

It led into an enormous kitchen. There was an oak table in the centre, around which several people were sitting. On it there were carafes of wine, baguettes in long baskets, earthenware dishes of butter and a great round of Brie. At a catering-sized stove a pink-faced girl enveloped in a butcher's apron was ladling onion soup into dishes from a brown *soupière*. She dropped a round of toasted baguette in each, then sprinkled grated cheese on it and slipped it under a grill. A bearded young man carried the plates to the table.

Everyone seemed to be talking at once, including the cook

and the waiter. The decibels were raised by a Sibelius symphony coming from a music-centre set on the stripped pine dresser that stretched along one wall. On the shelves above were rows of jewel-coloured jars of jams and pickles, each neatly covered by a mob-cap made of red-and-white checked gingham. There were peaches and pears bottled in *eau de vie*, baskets of green and red tomatoes and a wooden wine-rack filled with bottles.

Bunches of dried herbs and grasses hung from beams blackened by generations of wood-smoke from a stone fire-place at the far end of the room. Now it contained a basket stuffed with graceful pampas plumes.

Christian stood, unnoticed, outside the doorway, and studied the group. They were a mixed bunch. Half a dozen appeared to be in their twenties or early thirties; two men and a woman were older. Most were dressed informally, in jeans or shorts and t-shirts. There was only one girl apart from the cook. Sitting at the table, she had a small, triangular face and pouting lips. She was newly sunburned, with a peeling nose and white sun-glass circles around her eyes.

He looked at the older men with more attention, wondering which of them was Charles McDonald.

A couple of minutes passed, then the cook saw him. Her sudden stillness attracted attention. The chatter faded, heads swivelled, and eleven pairs of eyes focused on him.

He stepped forward and said in English: 'Now I know the effect Medusa had! I apologize for startling you, but the door was open and no-one heard the bell.'

A broad-shouldered man who appeared to be in his fifties stood up. He had a lined, lived-in face and thick brown hair, touched with grey at the temples. Christian's instant reaction was that he had the look of a man you'd like to be sitting next to when the pilot of your aircraft announced that one of the engines was on fire and he was going to make an emergency landing: a look of strength and composure. Hand outstretched, he said, 'It hasn't worked for months. You must be Christian Morel. Charles McDonald. I wasn't expecting you until tomorrow.'

102

As they shook hands Christian said, 'There wasn't too much traffic so I decided not to spend a night on the road. It is inconvenient for you, my arrival? Perhaps I should go to an hotel tonight?'

'Good Lord, no! We have elastic walls and, anyhow, there's plenty of room. Two of our volunteers left yesterday. You've had a long drive. Hungry?'

'Extremely.'

One of the younger men had already pushed a chair into a space at the table and as he sat down the cook set a bowl of onion soup and a glass of red wine in front of him. 'Hi,' she said. 'I'm Claire, and if you don't approve of my cooking, you'd better go to that hotel, because you'll be stuck with it here.' She was a cheerful, stocky girl with mousy hair cropped to a couple of inches all over her head.

He took a mouthful of the soup and was able to say honestly that it was delicious.

As he ate, McDonald introduced the rest of the party.

'You won't remember all the names, but you'll sort them out in time,' he said. 'Claire's our cook when she isn't dealing with the animals. The black beard is Arthur. He's practically a permanent resident. Been here for nearly a year.'

'He likes to think the place would fall apart without his genius for organization,' Claire murmured.

Arthur had been handing the plates. His mouth tightened as he glanced at Christian. 'If somebody didn't organize this lot there'd be right chaos.' He had a strong North Country accent.

'The second beard is Rob. Comes from Toronto. He's a doctor in his other life. Been spending a couple of months here every year since he graduated. He's pretty useful with sore backs and aching muscles.'

'Which you will certainly suffer if you've never worked in a vineyard before,' Rob said. 'Have you?'

Christian shook his head. 'I'm looking forward to it. It'll make a nice change from hunching in front of a word-processor.'

There was a chorus of derisive laughter, and Claire said,

'We'll see if you're so cheerful after your first eight hours' hoeing.'

McDonald went on. 'The lady with the sunburn is Olivia, our latest recruit. She doesn't say much, but thinks a lot. At least, we assume she does.'

Olivia was staring at Christian with embarrassing interest out of eyes made owl-like by the white circles around them. 'You're a journalist, aren't you? Are you going to write about us all?' Her voice was high-pitched and breathy.

'I'm mainly here to interview Lady Meredith.'

'Have fun!' Arthur said caustically. 'She's your real Medusa. One look from her can turn the strongest man to stone.'

McDonald said, 'The last two of the younger generation are James and Tim. They're actors.'

'Who happen to be resting at the moment. As usual.' Tim reached over the table to shake hands. He was small, neatly made, with a mobile, cherubic face. James, who appeared to be the youngest of the group, was slender, with dark, brooding good looks.

Christian nodded and smiled. He suddenly realized how tired he was and already names and faces were blurring. He mopped his soup-plate with a piece of bread and wondered how long it might be before he could decently excuse himself and go to bed.

'That's the kindergarten,' McDonald said. 'Now for the senior school. On your right, the best cook in the district despite being English, Emily Franklin, and her husband, Henry, ex-Squadron Leader, Royal Air Force. They're two of the original foreign inhabitants of La Bergerie, which is our nearest town.'

Franklin had a luxuriant moustache and iron-grey hair and was more formally dressed than the rest, jacketless, but wearing a white shirt and a red paisley tie. His wife could only be English, in her sleeveless cotton sun-dress with a white cardigan slung over her shoulders.

'How d'you do?' Franklin boomed. 'Pleasure to meet you, old boy. Bloody good English you speak. How come?'

'I've worked in Fleet Street. Now I divide my time between London and Paris.'

'Always wanted to be good at languages. I've been here nearly ten years and the best French I can manage is *je t'adore* and *merci millefois*. Before and after the event! Hah!'

'For Heaven's sake, Henry!' his wife said wearily. 'You'd better get out of the habit of making those awful jokes before Cybèle arrives. Welcome to le Bas-Fond, M. Morel. I'm sure you'll enjoy your stay with Charles.'

Christian cut himself a triangle of Brie and accepted another glass of wine. He noticed that as soon as a carafe was emptied, McDonald replaced it with a full one. A civilized man, he decided.

'Right, then,' Henry Franklin said briskly. 'Let's go back to what we were talking about before you arrived, young Morel. Call you Chris, do they?'

'In England, always. I'm afraid I interrupted you . . .'

'Not at all. Who knows, you might be able to contribute a few ideas. What d'you know about the Hundred Years' War?'

Christian blinked. 'Well . . . I know we won.'

Franklin laughed. 'So you did, and that's what this conference is about. Ever heard of the Castillon Festival? No? Maybe you'd better catch him up on it, Charles.'

As Claire poured coffee, Charles explained: 'Castillon's about ten kilometres away. It's where the last battle of the Hundred Years' War was fought in 1453, when the French finally chucked the English out of France. Historians reckon that the result of that war was the antagonism between France and England which lasted until we became allies in the First World War.'

'Sometimes wonder if they really like us even now,' Franklin said. 'But whether or not, every year the locals celebrate the battle in Castillon with a festival. They recreate the war, soldiers in full armour, sword fights, horsemen with lances, others carrying heraldic banners. It's set on a hillside below the château, which is floodlit. Everyone in medieval dress, tunics with heraldic emblems on 'em: lions, unicorns, crowns, clover leaves and so on, in all the colours of the rainbow. There are fireworks and dancing and it's pretty spectacular. Only trouble is, I for one am a bit bloody tired of celebrating a British defeat!'

Revived by the food and wine, Christian said, 'So you would like to change the course of history?'

'Can't do that. But I had an idea that seems to have gone down pretty well. Trouble is, Castillon normally has a population of around three thousand, but the festival's become so popular that an average of eight thousand tourists pour in and it's lost all its local feel.

'I've done some research and it doesn't seem impossible that a bit of the battle might have spilled over into La Bergerie. I suggested that we might hold a festival of our own. Get a few visitors, good for the local shop-keepers and hotel, and it'd be a bit of fun. Keep it small and manageable, though. No film-stars or politicians from Paris muscling in for the publicity like they do in Castillon. The local people love the idea. They've already formed committees and there are to be stalls and a funfair, music and dancing . . .'

'And will you also recreate the battle?'

'Old Charles here had a better idea. As a climax to the second day, a *real* contest between the French and the English, with no foregone conclusion.' He waved a lordly hand. 'Your turn again, Charles.'

Charles sighed. 'I'm not sure I'd have started this if I'd realized what it'd entail, but once Henry has the bit between his teeth there's no stopping him. I thought an obstacle relay race might be organized between the French and the expatriate residents. There are enough of us living here to field a team . . .'

Franklin's moustache was quivering with enthusiasm. 'We'll do it in medieval costume. That'd involve the women. They love dressing up. We're going to mark out a course which will start here at Le Bas-Fond and wind through the fields into La Bergerie, through the town and back again. Several kilometres, with each relay member covering a section. A prize for the winning team. Victor Sézille already thinks he's won it.'

'He would,' said Arthur. 'I bet he'll try to take over the whole thing.'

'Victor Sézille runs the Hôtel des Fleurs,' Charles explained to Christian. 'He's the town's king-pin – or likes to think he is.'

'He's absolutely convinced the Froggies – excuse me, Chris, that's said with affection – will win,' Franklin said. 'He's going to head the organizing committee and he's already chosen a team of the heftiest young buggers in the village, including his awful son.'

Claire leant forward. 'The competitors could each carry one of those medieval banner things to pass on instead of a baton. If anyone dropped it, he'd have to go back to the beginning. It'd make it more difficult going over the obstacles.'

'Good idea! I'll make a note. We don't want the young blokes to have all the fun, so Sézille and I agreed that each team would include three old gents like us, the over-fifties. The ladies will love seeing us make fools of ourselves clambering over walls and falling into streams.'

Christian's brief surge of vitality had begun to fade. He became aware that McDonald was speaking to him.

'Chris, this won't be of much interest to you. Would you like Olivia to steer you to your room?'

He nodded gratefully, stood up and wished the party good night.

Olivia led him upstairs, into a bedroom with a bare, wooden floor. It was furnished like a school dormitory, with two iron-framed beds, two wardrobes and two chests of drawers. But the beds had good sprung mattresses and clean sheets and the room was scented by bunches of dried lavender stuck in jam-jars.

'I hope you'll be comfortable,' she said. 'You've got the room to yourself. Tim and James share and so do Arthur and Rob.'

'So I am not inconveniencing anyone?'

'Oh, no. We're a bit short of volunteers at the moment.' She giggled. 'Two Italian girls came last week. They spent one day working in the vineyard and then they left, covered

107

in midge-bites.' She slanted a glance up at him. 'I was sharing my room with them, so now I'm by myself, too. I'm just down the hall. Second door on the right. If there's anything you need . . .'

There was an undisguised invitation in her eyes, but he ignored it. His welcome to this house had been warm, but his reason for being here was far from friendly. He had no intention of allowing himself to be distracted from his mission: to destroy Cybèle Meredith as she had destroyed his mother.

6

There were flowers and fruit in Cybèle's hotel suite, a box of chocolates tied up in red satin ribbon on the table, a selection of expensive shampoos, bath lotions and creams in the pink bathroom, a thick pink towelling robe hanging behind the door. She cast a swift, approving glance around. It was the suite she always had when she came to Paris and even though she was only staying for one night, nothing had been neglected.

A bell-boy who looked about twelve years old carried in her matching set of Louis Vuitton luggage. She gave him a generous tip and as he was about to leave, took off the card that was pinned to the ribbon on the chocolates, and handed him the box.

'Take these.'

'Madame?'

'They're for you.'

His veneer of adult self-possession fell away as his small face lit up. 'Truly, madame?'

She smiled. 'A present.'

There was satisfaction in his childlike gratitude, bought so easily with chocolates she didn't dare to keep. If she did, she would eat them, and at her age, extra pounds were added too easily.

She glanced at the card. 'To welcome you once again, dear Cybèle. Max.' He should have known better.

The telephone rang. 'Darling! Lovely to hear your voice. How *are* you after that terrible flight?'

'I'm well, and the flight was comfortable, thank you. The chocolates are delicious . . . so thoughtful, Max.'

'You're an amazing woman. I would be simply *dead*. How long are we going to have the pleasure of your company?'

'Only until tomorrow. Then I fly down to Bordeaux.'

'You will, of course, dine with me tonight.' Max Harrison had been a director of her French company, Cybèle et Cie, for nearly twenty years.

Although he had a spiteful tongue, which she suspected was frequently directed against herself, he also had an unrivalled knowledge of the Paris fashion world. It was said that he had been the *petit ami* of at least four of the great couturiers, male and female. As a writer she'd often had cause to thank him – and pay him well – for advance knowledge of new trends, shapes and colours when they were scarcely more than scribbles on a drawing-board.

She said, 'Thank you. And I'll drop in to the shop this afternoon. It will be a social call, but nevertheless, you don't need to tell them I'm coming.'

One of the ways in which the exclusive dress-shops that bore her name were kept up to the mark was that she never gave advance notice of her arrival. Her staff knew that any shortcomings revealed would result in, at best, a humiliating dressing-down, at worst, dismissal.

On this occasion, her visit turned up nothing about which she could complain. She spent a satisfactory couple of hours supplementing her own wardrobe before returning to the hotel to dress for dinner.

Max was waiting for her at the Tour d'Argent.

It was always a pleasure to be escorted by him, she thought, as he kissed her hand. His manners were impeccable and together they were a spectacular couple, their good looks hardly diminished by age. At fifty, Max's dark hair had silvered at the temples, which complemented his permanent, sun-lamp tan. A few inches taller than she, he was immaculately dressed in a silver-grey suit which she knew he had deliberately chosen because it would set off any colour-scheme she chose, in this case a shocking-pink silk sheath with her favourite pearls.

As they walked to their table she was aware of heads swivelling towards them. She smiled and raised her face towards his, tightening the loose skin under her chin.

Several people greeted them and two men rose to embrace her. One was the chairman of a New York department store, the other a Swiss fabric manufacturer. Both were extravagant in their expressions of delight at seeing her again and gratifying in their compliments on her beauty.

As she and Max dined, he retailed the latest Paris gossip but she found herself less amused than usual. It seemed that these days the men and women making news were a younger generation, few of whom she knew.

Anticipating the onset of boredom, she interrupted him ruthlessly. 'I've been out of touch, Max,' she said. 'I find it difficult to be interested in people I haven't even met.'

He apologized charmingly. 'I've been indulging in trivial chat when what I really want to talk about is you. Did I congratulate you on the success of your book? Of course you know they're reprinting the French edition.'

'I heard. It's going well in America, too. In the last three weeks I seem to have signed my name in a million copies.'

'You've had wonderful publicity. The Harrington prize was a triumph.'

'I enjoyed that,' she acknowledged. 'I'm planning to use the money to go into the wine business.'

'Good God! Why?'

'A new interest. I have land at Le Bas-Fond which has never been properly developed. I'm going to extend the vineyard, in partnership with Charles McDonald.'

'Are you, indeed? The handsome hippie. That should be quite a partnership.' Max had never met Charles, but there was a touch of jealousy in his use of the nickname that didn't displease her.

'He's far from that,' she said calmly. 'Intelligent. Interesting. Something of a mystery man.'

'How so?'

'He always changes the subject when I mention his past. It's as though his life started when he bought Le Bas-Fond.'

'Could be something nasty in his wood-shed. Better find out before you commit yourself to a partnership.'

'I intend to.' She refused another cup of coffee and said, 'I feel like a stroll. It's been a long time since I've walked in Paris on a spring evening.'

'Of course. We'll stroll for as long as you like, then pick up a taxi.'

'I wouldn't dream of asking you to come. I know walking isn't your favourite pastime. I'll be perfectly all right.'

'Absolutely not! It isn't safe.'

'Max, I know Paris like the back of my hand. It's the safest city in Europe.'

'Not any more, my dear.'

She shrugged. 'If you insist. For fifteen minutes, then.'

They walked in silence, and as she looked at the grey stone buildings with their shutters and balconies, the tree-lined *quais*, the bridges, the floodlit spires of Notre Dame, memories invaded her mind. She had been to Paris hundreds of times since the war, and lived in the present. Why was the past so vivid now?

She paused, looked down on to the *quai* below and saw a ragged *clochard* huddling against the wall. Suddenly, it was as though she could hear again the cracked voice of another tramp, even more ragged, calling her name: 'Sybil! Sybil Androwski . . .'

As they moved on, her arm linked in Max's, she began to tell him about that night.

After a few moments, she glanced up and saw him staring ahead, his face blank. She stopped and said, 'You seem to be

111

listening to distant voices, Max. Have I already told you all this?'

He smothered a yawn, and murmured, 'No matter, my dear. As always, it's fascinating.'

As always?

She said, 'I'm tired of walking. A taxi, I think. And thank you for a delightful evening.'

Her cold voice left him in no doubt that she had recognized his flash of malice and he cursed himself. Why the hell had he said 'as always'? Because she *had* told him the bloody story before, that's why. He had also read it in her book. But his future depended on Cybèle's goodwill, and he had many times seen her ruthless disposal of people who had irritated or offended her.

He was at his most charming while they waited for a taxi. She refused his escort back to the hotel. He embraced her affectionately, with protestations of his undying love, but she did not respond. Neither did she wave as the taxi pulled away, and he was frightened.

But Cybèle's mind was on herself for the moment, not on him. Was she turning into an anecdote-bore, constantly forcing her reminiscences on anyone who would listen? The eighth deadly sin was to inflict boredom. To avoid that possibility, she thought grimly, the memories that had been brought to the surface as she was writing her book must be reinterred.

Nevertheless, justifiably bored or not, Max had been insolent. A slow anger began to burn as she recalled his flagrant inattention, the yawn, the insult of those words 'as usual'.

He had been useful to her over the years, but the warmth between them had always been superficial. For their own reasons, each was wary of the other and she suspected that he would not be above inflicting a quick stab in her back if it would enable him to take over Cybèle et Cie.

She paid off her taxi outside the hotel and took the lift to her suite. Flattering pink lights had been switched on, the bed had been turned down, her ivory satin night-gown unfolded on the pink blanket – she had long ago instructed the management that she did not care for duvets.

She undressed, removed the contact lenses no-one apart from her optician knew she wore, and began the long preparation for bed. No matter how tired she was, she never neglected the ritual, which began with fifteen minutes of exercise. Then she removed her make-up with cleansing milk, washed with a rough, granular cream, and splashed her skin with astringent. She massaged lotions around her eyes and on her throat, patted night-cream over her face and burnished her hair with a brush whose bristles she had covered with a strip of fine silk.

A stranger's naked features looked back at her from the mirror, a woman still beautiful, but many years older than the ageless Cybèle the world knew. She put her elbows on the dressing-table and with her finger-tips drew up the skin at the points of her jaw, below her ears. A face-lift? She had previously resisted the temptation because she loathed hospitals and distrusted doctors. But maybe the time was approaching . . .

In the morning she would cover the fine lines with make-up, shaping and colouring eyes and mouth, emphasizing cheek-bones and jaw-line. She would not emerge from her room until the restoration was complete and the years had been removed.

Her appearance would be particularly important tomorrow, because Charles McDonald was meeting her at the Bordeaux airport. She intended to marry Charles. Not because she was in love with him – she had not loved any man since Dominic Stone – but because she was tired of being alone.

It was only recently that she had begun to look into her future and see loneliness. She had no family and no close friends. Her address book was filled with the names of people whom she considered no more than acquaintances.

She needed someone now with whom she could share the rest of her life. Charles was attractive, kindly, thoroughly presentable.

As she stared at her reflected image, she shivered suddenly.

He was many years her junior. She'd kept age at bay so far, but how long could she continue to do so?

She did not doubt her ability to win him. In the past, when she had set out to charm a man, usually in order to achieve some professional advancement, she had never failed. There was no reason why Charles should be different from other men.

But first she must get rid of those young volunteers at Le Bas-Fond. She had never approved of them, believing that they used the place as a base for free holidays, working only when they felt like it, taking advantage of Charles's easy-going supervision.

They also made her uncomfortable. In her world, she rarely found herself in the company of young people who did not regard her with awe and admiration. Many of the volunteers had university degrees in subjects as diverse as archaeology and computer sciences and tended to treat her with unconscious condescension, assuming that much of their talk was incomprehensible to her. She did not care to be made to feel ill at ease by children.

The girls were frequently attractive and articulate and seemed to regard Charles as one of themselves, treating him with an affection which she also found irritating. He belonged (almost) to *her* generation, not theirs, and it would not bode well for the future partnership she had in mind if he spent too much time with them. There would be a temptation for him to make comparisons.

She stood up and was aware of the ache in her hip. An X-ray had revealed the beginnings of arthritis. Another reason to capture him as soon as possible, before she could no longer conceal the disability.

Before she went to bed, she took from her suitcase the leather-framed photograph of Dominic Stone without which she never travelled, and set it on her side table. His mother had given it to her and she had packed it away only during her marriages.

The hand-tinted face, frozen at the age of twenty-one, with its clear blue eyes, white teeth and even features, the fine, floppy hair hidden under his officer's peaked cap, looked back at her with its unchanging smile.

She had known him for so short a time, but his memory had dominated her life for nearly fifty years. One reason she had married her first husband was his resemblance to Dominic.

Her thoughts drifted back to her arrival in England after his death . . .

7

Extract from *I am Cybèle*

It was a damp and windy day when I reached Brighton. I walked along the seaside resort's promenade. There was barbed wire on the shingle beach and the piers were deserted and forlorn. Few people were around and there was little to indicate that across the Channel thousands of soldiers were patiently awaiting either rescue or (more likely, I thought) death.

Before I left the Dandos, I'd had no personal animosity towards Germans, going along with the prevailing sentiment because it suited me. Now, having seen the young novices' white-clad bodies and witnessed the destruction of the Salomans' circus, the assassinations in the farmyard and, worst of all, Dominic's death, I found myself suffering a depth of hatred which surprised me.

I reached the address to which I had been given directions at the railway station. It was a tall, thin house with a basement and a wrought-iron balcony on the first floor, one of a terrace of similar houses in a crescent overlooking the sea.

The front door, whose paint was cracked and peeling, was opened by a grubby child of indeterminate sex who stared at me, sucking its thumb. Before I could say anything, it shouted, 'Mum, it's a lady!'

A woman wearing an apron over her cotton frock, her feet encased in fluffy pink slippers, shuffled along the narrow passsage. 'Yes?'

I said hesitantly, 'Aunt Enid?' She stared at me. 'I'm Etta's daughter. I've just come from France.'

There was a moment of silence as her eyes swept over me, pausing at my distended stomach. 'Well . . . we certainly weren't expecting you—Sybil, isn't it? Would you like to come in?'

She led the way into a dim, over-furnished parlour where she stood irresolutely. Finally she said, 'Would you like a cup of tea? Did you want to see Teddy? He won't be back from the shop until six.'

I accepted the tea and we drank it almost in silence, watched by the child and two older boys whom I assumed were its brothers. Their mother didn't bother to identify them.

'Come from France, have you?' she said after a while. 'War's pretty bad there, isn't it? They say our boys've taken a beating.'

'Yes.'

'Teddy's too old to go. But he's in the Home Guard.'

It didn't seem to occur to her to wonder how I had managed to reach England. 'Your husband with you?' was her next question.

'I haven't got a husband.'

Her eyes narrowed. 'But you're . . . aren't you?'

'Yes. I'm pregnant.'

'Get out of here, you boys!' she snapped. 'Go and play upstairs.' When they had gone, she said, 'What d'you want with us then?'

'I'd like to stay for a while. Until the baby's born and I can look for work.'

'That's impossible! For a start, we've got three kids and there isn't any room.'

'And to go on with?'

'What?'

'You said for a start. What other reason is there that I can't stay? Is it because I'm pregnant and I haven't got a husband?

116

You can tell your friends he was killed in France if you like. I don't mind.'

She glared at me. 'You were a right little madam when your mother brought you here before, Sybil Whatever-your-foreign-name is. You haven't changed. I don't want you living here in my house.'

'I think it's probably Uncle Teddy's house,' I said. 'I'll just wait for him, if you don't mind.'

She hurried out and I heard her telephoning. Soon afterwards, when I was alone in the sitting-room, Teddy Jones arrived, a heavily built, red-faced man with a soft, weak mouth, his few remaining hairs combed from a side parting across the top of his bald head.

'Well, well, it's little Sybil,' he said uneasily. 'This *is* a surprise. How's your mother?'

'She died a few months ago.'

'You should've written! Poor old Etta . . . I had no idea.' His eyes became moist.

'She often talked about you towards the end, Uncle Teddy,' I lied. 'She told me that if I was in trouble, I could always go to you.'

'She did? Old Etta . . . well, she was right, Sybil. And from what Enid said, you *are* in a bit of trouble. Right?'

I gave him a carefully edited description of my escape from France, emphasizing the dangers I'd faced and the horrors of the war. I didn't mention Dominic, knowing that if I did, I would break down.

At the end, he leant forward and patted my hand. 'You're a brave girl, Sybil. A real Jones,' he said emotionally.

'Thank you, Uncle. I'd be grateful if I could stay with you for a while. But I must tell you, I'm destitute. I have no clothes except what I'm wearing, and I lost all my money when I was washed overboard in the Channel.'

His face changed. 'I didn't expect . . . I mean, we're not all that well off, you know.' Then he rallied. 'But I suppose . . . I suppose we can put you up until – until . . .'

The English, I thought, appear to regard pregnancy as an unmentionable. 'Until the baby is born. I'm going to have it

117

adopted. Then I won't bother you any longer. I intend to find a job in London.'

'Good idea.' He hesitated. 'Who . . . ?'

Again I lied. 'Is the father? A young man my mother approved of. If it hadn't been for the war, we'd have been married by now.'

'And where is he?'

'A bomb,' I murmured. 'There was nothing, absolutely nothing left of him.'

So, to Enid's fury, I moved in, my domain a small room which I shared with the youngest Jones, who snuffled and squeaked and talked in his sleep.

After a couple of weeks, I learned that Uncle Teddy's assistant had decided to join the Land Army, so I begged him to let me work in the shop, for a token wage. Unable to resist a bargain, he agreed.

I learned a lot about my uncle during the next few weeks, including the fact that he was a sly, lecherous old man whose fat hands constantly had to be slapped away. He was also a cheat, instructing me to give his customers short weight whenever I thought I could get away with it.

The only good thing that happened during that time was learning that nearly all the British troops I had left in Dunkirk had been rescued.

As the months passed, my body swelled like a blown-up balloon and eventually I heard Enid telling Teddy that a friend of hers had said it was 'absolutely disgusting' to be served groceries by a girl in my condition. She made no attempt to keep her voice down. 'We're losing customers, Teddy, and it's that girl's fault,' she said. 'Another thing, I don't want her in the house any longer. It looks as though she's going to have the baby any minute, and if you don't get rid of her now, we're going to be landed with her *and* it.'

When he protested weakly, her voice became strident. 'I tell you, I'm not standing for it. She's not like us. She's *foreign*, and I don't want her around my children any longer!'

That night, after I had hauled my heavy body up the stairs, I counted the money I'd saved. I knew my time was drawing near. I had seen only one doctor in France, before leaving the circus. He had given me the probable birth-date, and told me that I was a healthy girl and should have no trouble. But the time had come when I must seek further medical help.

In order to get away from the Joneses, all of whom I now thoroughly disliked, I decided to go to London. I knew it was being bombed but anything would be better than remaining with my uncle and his wife.

I had no luggage. Teddy had prevailed on Enid to give me an ancient skirt, out of which I had cut part of the front to accommodate my bulge, and a couple of the horrible floral smocks she wore to do the housework. To travel up to London, I wore one of them with the skirt, and the tweed overcoat I had been given in Ramsgate. My hair was dull, my face was pale and thin, my stomach was enormous. I hated myself and I swore that after the baby had been born, I would never allow myself to look like this again.

I said goodbye to the Joneses, and Teddy was so relieved to see me go that, out of sight of Enid, he presented me with a five-pound note, a lot of money in those days.

When I left the Brighton train on Victoria Station, I saw another pregnant girl sitting on a bench on the concourse. I went up to her and asked if she knew of a hospital with a maternity ward. She gave me the name of one in South London. As I thanked her, she looked at me and said, 'Better get there quickly, love!'

When I was waiting for the train that would take me to the hospital, the first griping pain squeezed my stomach. I boarded the train and fell into a seat opposite a middle-aged woman wearing an Auxiliary Territorial Service uniform.

She saw me gasp and clench my teeth at a second wave of pain, and leant forward. 'Is that what I think it is, dear?' she said.

Unable to speak, I nodded.

'Where are you going?'

'To – hospital.'

I never knew her name, but I'll always be grateful to her. She helped me off the train at the next station and called an ambulance. My babies were born at four o'clock the next morning, twenty minutes apart.

When the first one emerged, the midwife said, 'It's not quite over yet, Mrs Jones. There's another one to come.'

'*What?*'

She actually laughed! 'Didn't you know you were having twins? Aren't you lucky then! Two for the price of one.'

When I had been wheeled back into a ward, a young nurse brought them in to me. All I saw were two little heads, each covered with a down of black hair, and waving arms. A pink card was tied on each right wrist with a piece of ribbon.

'You'll have to give us their names, dear,' the nurse said. 'Can't go on calling them Twin 1 and Twin 2 all their lives, can we?'

'Take them away,' I said.

I refused to feed them myself. The nurses argued, but one said that I was suffering from a post-natal reaction and I'd soon get over it.

Instead, the next evening, during an air-raid, I left the hospital, reasoning that despite the alleged English preference for dogs over children, someone would look after them a great deal better than I could.

I had already decided that as soon as I was free, I would go to Dominic's parents. They were the only contact I had and at least they would be able to advise me how to go about finding work.

When a tall, grey-haired man opened the door of their house in Church Row, I was almost exhausted and could only gasp, 'I am Cybèle.' That was enough; they remembered my letter. A woman, who turned out to be Dominic's mother, drew me inside.

They said later that they were horrified at my appearance. 'So thin and worn, my dear,' Mary Stone said. 'And those appalling clothes! A shabby overcoat over a hospital night-dress.' She laughed. 'We had no idea how beautiful you'd turn out to be.'

When they took me into a lighted sitting-room, I saw David Stone clearly. Apart from the grey hair, he was Dominic come back to life. For the first time since I had been rescued from the boat, I began to cry, and it was not until Mary had taken me upstairs and put me to bed that I recovered. The weeping must have been a kind of catharsis, because I have never cried for anyone since.

Nothing could have been more different from my welcome in Brighton. The Stones couldn't do enough for me. They wanted to know why I hadn't contacted them earlier. I had no intention of admitting my pregnancy, so I simply said that my experiences escaping from France had made me ill and I had been in hospital.

That was my entry into a kind of life I had never experienced. There were maids in the house and my meals were brought to me in bed. I had soft sheets and a tiled bathroom to myself, with fluffy towels. Mary gave me a lacy night-dress and a matching satin dressing-gown. I swore to myself that one day I would achieve this kind of life-style for myself.

Although the Stones were longing to hear the full story of my time with Dominic, they didn't pressure me, and insisted that I must stay in bed until I was stronger.

On the second day after my arrival I joined them downstairs for dinner. Although food rationing had been in force since January, we ate marinated mushrooms, chicken with a rich, creamy sauce flavoured with tarragon and brandy, and a lemon sorbet.

Afterwards, with a glass of Courvoisier in my hand, I told them how I had met Dominic and everything that had happened after that – editing out any mention of the real reason I had come to England. I described how he had saved my life in the boat by flinging himself on top of me, and how his body had slipped overboard into the water. Mary said later that it was clear from the way I talked that we had fallen in love.

The next day, they insisted that I must stay with them permanently, or at least as long as I wished.

During the following weeks, the war hardly seemed to touch me. The more I learned about the Stones, the more I liked them. They were well-to-do and generous, and as soon as I was mobile, Mary took me to Harrod's and bought me a complete wardrobe.

I learned that David owned a small company which published several magazines, including an old-established publication for women. Before they married, Mary had edited it, and she still wrote about the London fashion scene.

David's current occupation was less clear. He departed for the West End every morning and often did not return until late at night. He was frequently called away at weekends. It seemed to me that magazine publishing should hardly require such long hours.

As time passed, I became restless, and increasingly uncomfortable about living off the Stones' bounty. I spoke to Mary, but she laughed off my qualms, telling me it was their pleasure to have me in the house.

One day I found her going through a trunk in which she had stored clothes she no longer wore. 'I'm getting rid of them, darling,' she said. 'Take anything you like.'

I chose two or three dresses which she had discarded because their cut or trimming was old-fashioned. I borrowed her sewing-machine, adapted them to bring them up to date and altered them to fit me.

'I didn't realize you could sew,' she said.

'It's about the only thing I can do. I designed my mother's clothes, and my own. I used to remake them when we couldn't afford to buy new materials.'

She looked thoughtful. 'The government is talking about bringing in clothes rationing,' she said. 'When they do, we're all going to have to mend and make do. I've been thinking about writing a piece on that very subject. Why don't you do it instead? Take your dresses as examples to show what can be done with garments that might otherwise be discarded.'

That was my introduction to fashion-writing. She was pleased with the article I produced and I sketched my ideas as I used to sketch them for the circus artistes. The magazine paid me five pounds for it, and I wrote three more.

My new career came to an abrupt end early in October. The war had entered a different phase with the start of the London blitz the previous month. Bombs were raining down on the capital every night, the streets were piled with rubble and women and children were being evacuated to the country. From Hampstead Heath we could see the glow of fires that were engulfing areas of the city.

In Europe, France had capitulated to the Germans and a puppet government had been set up in Vichy. There was fighting in North Africa.

Seeing almost everyone in uniform and knowing I had no part in the excitement contributed to my restlessness and I mentioned to Mary that I was considering joining one of the women's services.

We had seen little of David for weeks. When he did come home, he looked exhausted and slept most of the time.

One evening, unusually, he was with us for supper. As we had coffee in the drawing-room, he said abruptly, 'How good is your French, Cybèle?'

'As good as my English. Maybe better.'

'You've often told us how much you hate the Nazis for what they did to your friends and to Dominic. Mary tells me you want to join the WAAFs or the ATS. How would you feel about something a little more – unusual?'

'Such as?'

Although only Mary was in the room, he lowered his voice. 'Such as going back to France.'

'How could I? The Germans . . .'

'We could get you there.'

'Who's we? What would I have to do?'

And then I learned what kept him away from home during the long hours. He was working with an organization devoted to co-ordinating resistance to the Germans in Europe: the Special Operations Executive. It had been set up by Churchill in July for the purpose of subversion and sabotage in all the occupied countries, and was now recruiting operatives.

'But why me?' I asked.

'Because you're about as unlikely a person for this work

123

as I can think of! And because you are brave and resourceful and speak perfect French.' He leant forward. 'You don't have to give me an answer now. Think about it. We'd want you in Paris, where the risk of being caught would be high. If you agree, you'll have to undergo several months of training, including parachute-jumping and how to operate a short-wave radio. We would then drop you into France and you'd be virtually on your own. It would be lonely, dangerous work, Cybèle.'

'But exciting,' I said.

'That I can guarantee.'

I didn't give him an answer until the next day, but I already knew that I was going to do it. To tell the truth, I was getting bored with my cushy life in Hampstead. I needed a challenge and this was it. It never occurred to me that I might be killed. Isn't everyone immortal at eighteen?

Six months later, I was parachuted into Northern France.

The last thing David Stone said before I left was, 'Make sure you come back safely, Cybèle. We need you.' When we embraced, I closed my eyes and pretended that Dominic was kissing me.

8

Arnie Gold sat on Victoria Station awaiting the train that would carry him on the first leg of his journey across the Channel and down through France to a reunion with his step-daughter.

Nobody noticing the bent figure, whose unnaturally dark hair and moustache contrasted sadly with his cadaverous, lined old face, could have guessed the anger that had dominated his thoughts since he read what Sybil had said about him in her book.

He hadn't expected her to be kind, but her undisguised

distaste for him – for *him*, Arnold Gold, who had kept her in comfort for years, who had even loved her for a while! – was a terrible revelation.

Even now the memory of how he had been run out of town by the circus women made him squirm. He could still see their grinning faces, hear the ridicule as he was frog-marched to the station. He could even feel the pain in his arm where the Bulgarian strong-woman had bent it up behind his back. Sybil had no right to tell that story, make him a laughing-stock!

And it was outrageous the way she'd twisted the truth. He'd never had to put his hand over her mouth in bed that first time. There was no need. It was almost as though she'd been waiting for him, eager as a cat on heat. She'd been good, too, and wanted him to teach her all the tricks. As for Etta's hidden money, he hadn't stolen it, it had been owed to him for all he'd spent on her.

No doubt about it, Sybil's kids were his. All in the genes, wasn't it? His own grandmother on his father's side had been a twin.

She'd taken everything from him, even his own children! His anger had settled into a determination that somehow he was going to make her pay.

He had consulted one of his drinking pals, a solicitor's clerk named Ron, about the possibility of bringing an action for libel.

Ron had considered the matter over his third pint of Guinness, then said weightily, 'Can't give you a proper opinion without reading the book, Arnie, but from the way you describe it, I'd venture to say, yes. Yes, you might have a case. Serious thing, accusing a man of rape and theft.'

That was all Arnie wanted to know.

The next morning, he told Mrs Kelly that he was going away.

'Really? Where to, dear?'

'France. See a relation of mine. We got some – business.'

'I didn't know you had any relations, Mr Gold. Especially in France.'

'Everyone's got relations. Anyhow, I'll be giving up the room.'

'How long will you be away? Would you like me to keep it for you?'

He thought for a moment. If his plan worked, he wouldn't be back in Paddington. Paris or Cannes, more like. 'No. Let it go. I don't know how long I'll be.'

Now, sitting on the station bench, his battered gladstone bag beside him, his mind returned to Sybil. She hadn't even had the decency to change his name. There it was, Arnold Gold, for everyone to see. She must have thought that it was safe to use it, because she clearly believed that he had died during the war. And no thanks to her that he hadn't, with what he went through after she'd shopped him to the Germans.

9

Extract from *I am Cybèle*

Coming as I had from a Britain suffering devastating air-raids, a London smothered under sand-bags and rubble, Paris was a revelation. France having capitulated, it had so far retained much of its gaiety and charm. The women were as well-dressed as they had always been, and for those who could pay, there were few food shortages. The main difference from the Paris I had visited two or three times before the war was the German soldiers who crowded the pavements, confident as though they owned the place. Which, of course, they did.

I arrived with a new identity. I was Sylvie Andros, with papers proving I had been born in Angoulême, in the Charente, the daughter of Louis and Lucie Andros.

After my parachute landing near Chateaudun, south of Chartres, I was picked up by an elderly man who introduced himself simply as Michel. We travelled together by train to

Paris, and he took me to a house on the Left Bank, where I met Marie Masson. An efficient wireless-operator who could transmit Morse code at twenty-four words a minute, she was a brave and dedicated agent a little older than I.

Her Jewish fiancé had been arrested and sent to a concentration camp a few months earlier. Recently, she had received word that he had been executed. This had left her with a bitter hatred of the Nazis. I was to share her quarters in an attic apartment and sometimes at night I would hear her crying for her lost Jacob.

She was round-faced, with a mop of dark, frizzy hair, and her figure reminded me of Etta's: large and bouncy, the torso top-heavy over thin legs. But she had none of Etta's gaiety.

We got on reasonably well, although we had little in common. She had no interest in clothes or other frivolities, and her earnestness often irritated me. She believed that the only excuse an intelligent person had for remaining in Paris under the Occupation was to work for the Resistance, and she had no time for any Frenchman or woman who fraternized with the enemy.

'Chevalier, Darrieux, Cocteau, Guitry . . . I would stand them all up against a wall and shoot them,' she said.

In advance planning sessions before I left England, it had been decided that I should try to find a job in a fashion-house. It was my idea, because I saw no reason why I shouldn't combine my secret work with something that would be useful in the future.

Marie, who worked as a secretary in an advocate's office, had already made enquiries about available jobs, allegedly for a friend who was moving to Paris from the provinces. She had arranged an interview for me with a couturier who had premises just off the Faubourg St Honoré.

Emile was a stringy, middle-aged man whose narrow face wore a permanent expression of *hauteur*. He gave the impression – which might have been genuine – that he had nothing but contempt for the women who paid outrageous sums to be dressed by him.

After our brief interview, he said irritably, 'You'll do, I

suppose, but you're too chic, mademoiselle. Tell Madame Claude I said to find you something restrained and black to wear. You can start by picking up pins from the fitting-room floors – but remember to keep in the background. My customers do not like to be outshone by the help.'

He was egocentric, greedy and arrogant, but he was a brilliantly innovative designer. Shrewdly anticipating that senior members of the occupying forces would import their wives or mistresses to keep them company, he had adapted his styles to appeal to the fleshier German women as well as to the French, and had built up a profitable clientèle among them.

'Those women come in for fittings, and they will talk,' Marie told me. 'You will pick up useful information. When necessary, you will also act as a courier, carrying messages to our colleagues.'

My job was not exciting, but I enjoyed it. For hours on end I served in the fitting-rooms, holding scissors and tape-measures and picking up pins with a magnet. I watched the beautiful fabrics being draped, then shaped in the cutting-room. I delivered pieces to out-workers for embroidering.

And I listened.

The German customers often came in with friends and they gossiped endlessly. It never occurred to them that the black-garbed, silent girl who kept in the background spoke German almost as well as they did. I passed on to Marie any information which might have the remotest connection with the enemy's activities, and she transmitted it to London.

I achieved my first important coup on a Friday a few weeks after my arrival.

The mistress of an SS officer attached to the German Security Police's Counter Espionage Service was being fitted. She was a fluffy-haired blonde named Gertrud who was busily spending her lover's money replenishing her wardrobe, boasting to everyone that he would deny her nothing.

According to Emile, she had the brain of a retarded rabbit, and on this occasion, she was with an equally dim-witted friend.

They were talking maliciously about some Parisians they had met, in whose sophisticated company they had clearly been ill at ease.

I heard Gertrud giggle, and say, 'Alfried's going to take these Frenchmen down a peg this weekend. He knows all the people in Paris who work against us – I can't imagine why they should, I mean, they're better off now than they've ever been – and he's going to arrest them . . .'

During my lunch-hour, I slipped out to a public telephone, called Marie and told her what I had overheard. She swung into action, ordering me to report sick to Madame Claude and return to the apartment.

Because it was too risky to use the telephone, I spent the afternoon cycling around Paris, warning as many members of the underground as I could find.

On Saturday morning, just before dawn, the Gestapo raided a dozen houses and apartments at widely scattered points throughout the city, and arrested several of our people. But because of the warnings, at least half of those who might have been taken had been able to get away.

When I am asked about my time in Paris, I can honestly say that I was rarely afraid. It never occurred to me that I might be arrested like others, and executed or sent to a concentration camp, mainly because I didn't take the business of being a spy seriously. It was simply a game I was playing, in memory of Dominic Stone.

The second phase of my life in wartime Paris began when Emile called on me to replace a house-model who had left suddenly.

For the couture house, it was an important time, when potential customers came in to see individual garments, with a view to ordering.

This was a particularly luxurious collection – in fact, the last of its kind for some years. Shortages were beginning to be felt, leading to a time when, as it was later reported, 'elegant sobriety' would replace fantasy.

Among the more exotic garments I modelled, I remember

a red pyjama suit called 'Promise', a short sequinned black dress trimmed with swansdown and a turquoise satin evening-dress called 'Heartsease', whose bodice was thickly embroidered with pearls. There were furs, too: a coat made from Somalian panther skins, another from the fur of bear cubs.

Hats rose high above the head that year and Emile's extravagances included one fashioned from draped newspaper, another decorated with pressed flowers. Some shoes were made of wood, others had magnesium soles and glass heels.

Because silk stockings were in short supply, smart women wore the new 'silkless stocking', a dye rubbed on to the legs which was the forerunner of today's self-tanning creams, though then the colour only lasted until the next bath.

I was put into the hands of the hairdresser Antonio. He was currently taking his inspiration from the ancient Greeks and tortured my hair into a hundred curls which clung to my scalp as though sculptured in stone.

As a house-model, I spent my days either in frantic motion, flinging garments on and off, then gliding and turning in front of the customers, or sitting in the dressing-room, suffering acute boredom as I waited in my underwear for the next call.

One day I was modelling furs for a well-known actress, a member of the Comédie Française, who lived in luxurious sin with a wealthy SS colonel named Gerhard Hofer.

He always accompanied her to Emile's, and on this occasion they had another companion, a tall, good-looking young man in civilian clothes with fair hair and no curve to the back of his head.

I was aware that he was watching me with particular interest. Once he laughed and said to Hofer, in German, 'That one's for me!'

Later the same day, a note was delivered, inviting me to dine with him that night.

His name was Werner Speidel, and he was an economist attached to the administrative staff of the Military Governor.

I borrowed a dress from Emile, and we dined at Chez Pierre, a restaurant favoured by the Germans, on foie gras, followed by Chateaubriand steaks. We drank champagne and burgundy.

Afterward, he took me back to ....
Champs Elysées, where we made l............

The next morning I went straight to t..............
and did not see Marie until early evening.............
for my second date with him.

When I told her what had happened, she w............
first. He's a Nazi! How could you bear him to touc.......... .c.
Etc. Gradually, though, she realized that we had bee..... ...ered
an opportunity to gather information from a source hitherto
closed to us. The powerful Military Government, with its
headquarters in the Majestic Hotel, off the Avenue Kléber,
virtually controlled Occupied France, from the economy to
the police. Who knew what Werner might give away in
pillow-talk?

From what I had seen of him, I doubted that he would be
as indiscreet as fluffy little Gertrud's lover, but I found the
prospect of playing Mata Hari exciting, and I had enjoyed my
taste of a life that was gradually being closed off from ordinary
Parisians.

Transport was becoming difficult, and bicycle taxis were
replacing petrol-driven cabs. In cinemas, the lights were kept
on during newsreels, to prevent demonstrations by pro-Allied
audiences. Soon potatoes would be sent from Germany to feed
people who could not afford to buy food on the black market,
and soup kitchens would be set up.

On the other hand, the Bourse had reopened, there was
horse-racing at Auteuil, brothels flourished, caviare could be
bought in the luxury shops, theatres and concert-halls were
crowded, and the city's leading auction-house, the Salle Druot,
took a record forty-seven million francs at a sale of fine art.

For those with money, who did not object to fraternizing
with the enemy, life was still sweet.

I saw no reason why I shouldn't share the goodies, as long
as I didn't forget why I had come to Paris.

The morality of the situation did not bother me. Werner
was an enthusiastic, if unexciting lover, and since he did not
attract me, I was able to detach myself from the whole
performance, while pretending enough passion to keep him

...ompany, I played the part of a frivolous girl
... interested only in clothes, sex and the good life.

He wasn't a wholly bad man, but he had been brought up in the Hitler Youth Movement, the son of committed Nazis. He worshipped the Führer and had been programmed to believe in the Master Race, to hate Jews and support their total extermination.

Like many of the Occupiers who were far from home, he hadn't had a woman to talk to for months, and in me he found a wide-eyed, appreciative listener as he boasted about the achievements and future plans of the Military Government. London was pleased with my reports.

Marie had started to worry about the length of time she had spent in the same apartment with her transmitter. She had seen in our vicinity a car which she believed carried a wireless-detecting machine and was already cutting her transmissions to a minimum so there would not be time for their location to be traced. Nevertheless, she decided it was time to move, and found new accommodation near the Gare du Nord. I said I would take over the apartment, and wasn't displeased at the prospect of having it to myself.

In future, I was to communicate with her by telephoning a coded message, giving a meeting-place, where I would pass on my information.

Werner and I had been lovers for several weeks when, after work one evening, I was walking home alone along the Seine.

I stopped for a moment and leant on the parapet, looking down on to the quai. A ragged *clochard* was peeing against the wall at the bottom of some steps. He glanced up.

As I walked on, I heard a cry: 'Sybil! Sybil Androwski!'

Before I could gather myself together, he had dashed up the steps and was standing in front of me. It was my step-father, Arnie Gold.

He was a horrible sight, in dingy, frayed trousers and a filthy shirt, with a piece of sacking around his shoulders. He wore no socks and there were gaping holes in his shoes. Unshaven, he stank of a combination of urine and old sweat.

He reached out his hands as I backed away, and his voice

was a high-pitched whine. 'For God's sake . . . no, for Etta's sake . . . you gotta help me, Sybil!'

'Talk French, you idiot!' I hissed. 'What are you doing in Paris?'

The words spilled out. 'I been here for months. God, I've had an awful time! You don't know what it's been like. I've lost my papers. If the Gestapo found out I was English . . . I been eating out of garbage-tins, picking up cigarette-ends. I'm starving, Sybil.'

Desperate to get away, I opened my hand-bag and handed him a few francs. 'That's all I've got. I have to go now.'

His attitude changed. From a fawning beggar, he became vicious, and grabbed my arm. There was still surprising strength in the muscles trained by years on the trapeze. He thrust his face into mine. It was twisted and ugly. 'Hang on, Miss! You're not getting away so easily. Bloody prosperous and healthy you look. I bet you're one of them Nazi whores, living on the fat of the land. So let's go to your place and find some more money, and then we'll have a nice talk and a bottle of wine or two.'

Knowing I was in a dangerous position, I pretended to give in. 'I live off the Boul' Mich',' I said. 'I've got some money there.'

He didn't loosen his grip as I led him in the opposite direction from the apartment.

'So what you been doing, Syb? Still with old Dando? Hey, if he's in Paris, maybe I could join up again. I mean, after all this time . . .' His voice trailed off, and I guessed that he was remembering his ignominious departure from the circus.

'The Dandos are in North Africa,' I said. 'Why don't you follow them there? I'll give you the fare.'

He ignored me. Instead, his fingers pinched my arm. 'Everything that happened to me was your fault, you little bitch!'

I wasn't ready to quarrel with him, so I was conciliatory, and asked him what had happened after he left the circus.

'Couldn't find a job. Ran out of money. Thought I'd do

better in Paris. I was bloody wrong. Gestapo everywhere, and me with no papers.'

'And you a Jew,' I murmured.

'Don't even whisper it! You know what they're doing to Jews? Bloody trainloads of 'em are being sent off God knows where, packed in cattle-trucks.' He shuddered. 'I heard what's been happening in the camps: forced labour, starvation, gas-chambers . . .'

We reached the bustling, crowded Boulevard St Michel, lined with shops and restaurants, and moved towards a terrace where a group of German officers were sitting around a table. Arnie glanced at them uneasily and tightened his grip.

We were almost opposite them when I began to struggle and scream for help. They looked around, saw a smartly dressed girl apparently being attacked by a tramp, and leaped up.

Arnie swore, then let me go and fled, zigzagging through the crowds with his sack flapping.

I sobbed, 'He was trying to rob me!'

He was already out of sight. Seeing that there was no point in pursuing him, they dried my tears and insisted that I should sit down with them and have a brandy. Then I thanked them, assured them that I was unhurt, and went on my way.

The incident had shaken me, and I realized that I must make sure it didn't happen again.

I was convinced that he wouldn't rest until he had discovered where I lived. If he were to see me with Werner, and suspect that I was leading a double life, our whole network of agents would be in danger. At best, he would probably try to blackmail me.

When Werner came to see me that evening, I told him about the *clochard* who had accosted me.

'It's happened several times. He frightens me,' I said. 'He wants money, and there's something strange about him. I'd swear he isn't French. Tonight when I told him to go away, he said, "You wouldn't be mean to old Arnold, now, would you?" ' I widened my eyes innocently. 'Arnold? Isn't that an English name, Werner?'

'How did you get rid of him?' Werner said.

'Some officers came to my rescue and he ran away.'

'Do you know where he went?'

'I saw him first on the *quai* near the Pont Neuf. I expect he went back there.'

The next day, Werner informed me that the tramp would not bother me again.

A few months later, he was transferred back to Berlin.

10

A few yards beyond the turn-off that led to Le Bas-Fond, a big blue Volvo carrying a GB plate was skewed across the narrow road. A girl was leaning into the boot, hauling out a red and white hazard triangle.

As he stood on the brake and blasted his horn, Charles McDonald still had a moment to admire the shape of long slim legs and firm buttocks.

'For God's sake, what does that idiot think she's doing?' Cybèle snapped.

He pulled on to the verge. 'I'd better go and see.'

The girl turned. Her face was half hidden by sun-glasses and her hair was covered by a scarlet scarf tied under her left ear. She was wearing gold gypsy ear-rings, black jeans and a red cotton shirt, unbuttoned and knotted in the front so a couple of inches of tanned flesh showed above the jeans. She looked chic and sexy and, despite the simplicity of her clothes, expensive.

''Afternoon. Need some help?' he said.

She raised her hands despairingly. 'The bloody thing won't go.'

'What happened?'

'God knows! It stopped. Just like that. I came round the

corner and suddenly there was no power, no nothing. I think it's had a heart-attack and died on me.'

'Petrol?'

'A full tank.'

'Would you like me to try and start it?'

'I've tried. But go ahead.'

He sat behind the wheel and turned the ignition key. Nothing happened. As she said, it was as though the car had died. He got out and regarded it dubiously.

'Do you know anything about these cars?' she said.

'Damn all. It wouldn't even help if I were to look under the bonnet. As far as I'm concerned, all engines look alike, dead or alive. Weren't you able to steer it off the road?'

'Even the power steering went. It was so heavy I could hardly turn the wheel. I'm making for a place called Le Bas-Fond. I'll have to walk there and use the phone to call a garage. D'you know how far it is?'

He smiled. 'I should. I live there.'

She pushed her glasses up on to her head, revealing thickly lashed brown eyes. She was an extraordinarily pretty girl, her creamy skin unblemished even without any make-up, her generous mouth untouched by lipstick. When she smiled, it was as though a light had been turned on, and he was momentarily dazzled.

'Are you Charles McDonald?'

He nodded.

'I'm Suzanne Leander . . . Suzy. I was on my way to ask if you'll let me work as a volunteer on your farm for a while. I tried to get your phone number before I left London, but directory enquiries couldn't trace it . . .'

'We don't have a telephone.'

'. . . so I decided to come on the off-chance.'

'Why?'

'Why? Oh . . . I needed to get away for a while. I wanted a change. Something different from the work I'd been doing.'

'What had you been doing?'

'I was working for – working for a photographer.'

'Ah. Too much time in the dark-room? Not enough fresh air?'

'Something like that.'

His eyebrows lifted and she saw that he had noted the evasion, which had been instinctive. Modelling, with its connotations of mindlessness and vanity, would hardly be a recommendation to a man requiring assistance on a farm.

She said, 'If you'll help me to get my car out of your way I'll find a public phone and call a garage, then come and see you.'

'OK. Hop in. You steer and I'll push.'

But without power the steering was too stiff for her and although Charles managed to move the heavy car a few inches, all they achieved was to straighten it so there was even less room to pass than before.

'Oh, shit! Now what do we do?' she said.

A cyclist turned off the main road and slowed as he came towards them. There was a pannier behind his saddle, filled with groceries.

Charles called, 'Chris! Come and lend a hand!'

He was a large young man wearing Levis, blue trainers and a denim shirt open to the waist. A fine gold chain glinted around his neck. His brown hair was thick, wavy, ruffled by the wind. He picked up his bicycle as though it was a feather and propped it against the hedge, then looked from Suzy to the car. White teeth gleamed as he smiled. 'Yours? This is quite an achievement, mademoiselle. Only a lady driver could have managed so successful a blockade on a perfectly straight stretch of road.'

'Very funny,' she said. 'Are you going to help us to shift it or not?'

Charles intervened. 'Christian Morel, Suzanne Leander. She was on her way to see us when her car packed in. You know anything about Volvos, Chris?'

'Everything. I owned this model once.' He patted the bonnet. 'What happened? You have petrol?'

'Of course I have petrol! It stopped. That's all. Without

137

warning. If you know everything, I'm sure you'll be able to tell me why.'

'Probably a fuse,' he said calmly. 'I would guess, the one that controls the petrol pump. Number seven. It is always number seven. Do you have any spares?'

'I don't know. I've never seen any fuses. Where are they?'

He opened the front passenger door. 'How long have you had the car, mademoiselle?'

'Nearly a year.'

'You obviously haven't bothered to read the handbook.' He reached below the glove compartment and pulled off a rectangular panel to reveal a line of fuses. At the bottom of the panel was a holder which contained several spares. 'The previous owner was a sensible man,' he said. She didn't miss his emphasis on the sex of common-sense.

He replaced one of the 16 amp fuses, then the panel cover, and made a theatrical gesture. 'All yours, mademoiselle. It's fixed.'

Hoping against hope that this chauvinist clown would be wrong, she slid into the driving-seat. Her temper was not improved when she caught him exchanging an amused look with Charles McDonald.

The engine purred as soon as she turned on the ignition.

He leant against her window. 'Would you like me to turn her? There's not much room.'

'No, thank you.'

She swung the wheel and reversed straight into a shallow depression by the side of the road. When she changed gear, the wheels spun in soft earth. Without comment, grinning at each other, the two men pushed the car back on to the hard surface. For a moment, she contemplated the pleasure of running them down, then she made a pistol-shape of her right hand, pointed the first two fingers at them and said, 'If either of you mentions women drivers . . .'

A cool voice interrupted. 'Charles, how long is it likely to be before we can continue?'

Cybèle was standing by the Mercedes. She surveyed them,

and nodded to Christian Morel. 'I'm delighted to see you, M. Morel. When did you arrive?'

'Several days ago, madame. Welcome back.'

'We'll arrange to talk when I'm settled.' Her eyes flicked away from him. Meeting her frosty blue gaze, Suzy recognized a flash of hostility and wondered whether Cybèle had identified her as the ''gauche teenager'' of eight years ago. She thought, she looks as though she's X-raying me to see if my underwear is clean.

Charles said, 'Cybèle, this is Suzanne, who has appeared out of the blue and wants to work with us for a while. Lady Meredith.'

Suzy held out her hand, which Cybèle barely touched.

'Another of your would-be volunteers, Charles?' she murmured. 'What a pity we don't have room for her.'

'Oh, I think we might . . .'

'You wrote to say you had a full complement. And we mustn't forget that we're going to discuss some changes.' She put her hand on his arm. 'Do let's get on. I'm sure M. Morel will get this car out of our way so Miss . . . er . . . can leave.'

'One moment,' Charles said quietly. 'As it happens, we do have room for another volunteer. A few days ago two Italian girls took one look at our rather primitive conditions and fled. If you'll agree to stay for at least two weeks, Suzy, I'd be happy to have you.'

'Thank you. I'd like that.'

'I'll see you at the mill, then. Chris will guide you.'

Cybèle's face was expressionless as they returned to the Mercedes.

'Let's get out of their way,' Christian said. 'Do you want to turn her? I'm sure you're perfectly capable.'

'No. I've made enough of a fool of myself today. You do it.'

Somewhat to her disappointment, he executed a perfect tight turn to put the car on the right-hand verge so Charles could pass.

'How about giving me a lift to the mill?' he said. 'I could load the bike into the boot.'

'All right. You might as well drive, since you know the way.'

Warmth had kindled briefly, but as they drove towards the mill, his face was sombre and he replied in monosyllables to her attempts to make conversation. She studied him covertly. He was arrogant and self-satisfied, but not bad-looking in his way, tall, muscular, with blunt features and a firm jaw. Now a vertical line was creasing his forehead between dark eyebrows and his mouth was compressed into a straight line. When he laughed he had appeared to be in his late twenties. Frowning, he looked older, and formidably grim. She wondered what had caused the change.

Le Bas-Fond was in sight when she said, 'Lady Meredith owns this place, doesn't she? How well do you know her?'

She saw his hands tighten on the wheel. 'I've met her once.'

'Is that why you volunteered to work here?'

'No. I'm a journalist. I've been commissioned to do a piece about her life at Le Bas-Fond.'

'I thought Charles McDonald implied that you were a volunteer.'

'I'm helping out as well.'

'At least Lady Meredith seemed to be pleased to see you. She didn't exactly welcome me.'

He glanced at her. 'I can tell you the reason for that. You're too attractive.'

She smiled, ready to acknowledge a compliment, then saw that his face had not changed. He was simply making an observation. 'Don't be ridiculous!' she said.

'I'm told she doesn't care to have good-looking women around the place because she doesn't want Charles McDonald's attention distracted from herself.'

Suzy looked at him curiously. 'You don't seem to like her much.'

'I don't have to. All I have to do is produce my story. An objective report, no?' He turned the car into a big wooden barn which already contained a red MG. 'Now I will take you inside. Your luggage?'

She hauled an overnight bag from the back seat. 'That's all I have.'

'You travel light.' He took it from her and they walked out on to the rough, gravelled drive that led to the front door. She pulled the scarf from her head and her copper hair fell loose and gleaming to her shoulders.

She was pleased to recognize a flash of interest in his eyes. 'You're full of surprises, mademoiselle . . .'

'For heaven's sake, stop being so formal. My name's Suzy. What d'you mean, full of surprises?'

'You don't look like a girl who can travel with her wardrobe in one small bag. I was anticipating a set of matched luggage full of designer clothes.'

'Sorry to disappoint you. I leave that to Lady Meredith. Did you see the Vuitton bags in the back of Mr McDonald's car?'

'I did. You also look as though you would be more at home in a Porsche than an elderly Volvo.'

'I want to live out my full span and I can't be bothered with status symbols. If I have a crash in the Volvo, I'll be the one who walks away.'

'I hope we never meet at speed on a narrow road. Mine's the little red status symbol in the shed.'

'I didn't mean . . .' she began, then said crossly, 'How is it that you manage to wrong-foot me all the time?'

He led her into the kitchen. It was empty, but there was a smell of something savoury cooking in the oven.

He went to the door and shouted, 'Claire!'

A small, sun-burned girl appeared. 'Claire's gone out to have a talk with the donkey,' she said. 'Is the *daube* burning?'

'Not as far as I know. Olivia, this is a new volunteer. Suzanne, who says she's to be called Suzy.'

Olivia's expression reminded him of Cybèle's when she had caught sight of Suzy in the lane: a long, unsmiling look, registering without pleasure the other girl's appearance, followed by an unenthusiastic 'Hello. How long are you here for?'

'As long as Mr McDonald will have me.'

141

'I suppose you'll be sharing my room then. D'you want to come and see it? You'll have to make up your own bed.'

'I'd like to. I'm sorry if this is going to put you out.'

As Suzy preceded her up the stairs Olivia pressed close to Christian, batted her white eyelids and whispered, 'See you later, Chris.'

He carried in the groceries he had been commissioned to buy in La Bergerie, thinking that Olivia was beginning to become a nuisance.

On his first day she had taken it upon herself to show him around the farm and vineyard, clutching at him for support whenever they reached a rough patch of ground. In the evening, she had seated herself next to him at the dining-table, pressed her leg against his and gazed with rapt attention whenever he spoke.

Later that night, she had knocked on his bedroom door. 'Chris, there's a gi-normous spider just above my bed! Please could you come and kill it for me?'

The spider was about half an inch in diameter. He had dispatched it with a rolled-up newspaper. Saying good night, she reached up and kissed his lips. He had detached himself hurriedly and returned to his bed.

At breakfast the following morning she made much of their midnight meeting, kittenishly describing her fear of spiders and his bravery. He caught Charles's sardonic eye on him and resented the conclusion which Olivia had clearly meant to be drawn.

His first favourable impression of Charles McDonald had been confirmed. He was the pivot around which the diverse personalities of the volunteers swung: easy-going but decisive when necessary, friendly, humorous and sympathetic. There seemed to be no age barrier between him and the younger people.

When Chris and Claire were collecting eggs from the hen-run one morning, she had remarked, 'He really *understands*, you know? You feel you can say anything to him and he won't be shocked.'

'What's his background?' he asked idly.

She hesitated. 'He never talks about himself. I know he was married once, so he's probably divorced. My guess is that he was some sort of businessman who was made redundant and used his golden handshake to buy Le Bas-Fond. He adores the place and the good atmosphere's entirely due to him. He's a marvellous listener and he never offers advice unless you ask for it, just lets you get things off your chest.' Peering up at him earnestly, she looked like a hedgehog with her sharp nose, round eyes and spiky hair.

'Do many people have such things to get off?'

'Oh, Lord, yes! Lots of us come here to escape from something or other. I originally came because I'd just broken up with my boy-friend and I was feeling suicidal, a real mess. Charles found me crying one day, and made me talk about it. It was the first time I had and it was like getting rid of a bloody great weight.

'And take Arthur. His problem was that he couldn't decide where he belonged in the scheme of things. His parents are working-class but he got a scholarship to read politics at Cambridge. After he graduated, he discovered that he had nothing in common with his family any longer. He was ashamed of his roots, and ashamed of being ashamed, if you see what I mean. When he arrived, he tried to hide his insecurity by being aggressive and opinionated. The rest of us thought he was a pain in the neck, but Charles used to take him for long walks and let him off-load his hang-ups. He's much less stroppy now.'

With a writer's curiosity about what made people tick, Chris said, 'How about the others? Olivia? The actors?'

She shrugged. 'Don't know much about Olivia. She hasn't been here long – and she likes boys better than girls, so we don't talk much. James and Tim are gay, of course. James's parents simply won't admit there could be a homosexual in the family, and they've made his life hell. He and Tim came here because they had to get away for a while. They soon discovered that neither Charles nor the rest of us give a damn what they are as long as they behave like reasonable human beings.' She looked at him sternly. 'We all love them. How do you feel about gays?'

'The same as you, I guess. They lead their lives and I lead mine. I have no prejudices. And Rob?'

'He went into medicine because his father was a doctor. What he really wanted was to make furniture. He's been coming here for years, whenever he can take a vacation, and Charles has given him one of the barns as a work-shop. He made the big table in the kitchen and a couple of beds, and he can mend anything.' She paused. 'On the whole, we're a fairly well-adjusted lot now, and it's mostly due to Charles.' Her voice sharpened. 'We're worried that Lady Meredith is after him for husband number three. God, it'd be a disaster! Not only because she'd ruin Le Bas-Fond. She'd *smother* him.'

During his few days at the mill, enjoying life in the open air and his healthy exhaustion after the physical work, Chris had pushed his own reason for being at Le Bas-Fond into the back of his mind. Cybèle's arrival today had brought it to the surface.

With the last of the supplies stowed away in the kitchen cupboards, he went on to the terrace and looked down into the mill-pond. There had been no recent rain to stir up the mud and the water was clear and still. In it, he saw again the image of his mother, as she had been for as long as he could remember: a wreck who existed in an alcoholic haze. Sober, she found her life intolerable, the pain of her twisted back unbearable. He had never forgotten how she had once said, 'Because of that woman, there isn't a moment when I can forget my body.'

Once she might have been good-looking, but she had become a withered bag of bones who rarely washed or combed her thin grey hair. In the end, she had lived out her last tormented nights, hoarding sleeping-tablets, then swallowed them with half a bottle of cognac.

He had found her body when he paid his regular morning visit to the room he rented for her in a small Left Bank hotel. She had made a final, pathetic effort to clean herself up, put

144

on her one good dress, then composed herself on her bed. The empty brandy bottle lay on the floor.

The note she had left on the side-table ended: 'If you ever meet the woman Cybèle, who called herself Sylvie Andros, I want you to tell her what she did to me. I hope you can find some way to make her suffer as I have.'

His life as a free-lance magazine-writer was full and busy, but in his early grief he had made sporadic attempts to trace Cybèle-Sylvie, without success. Eventually, he had accepted that it was hopeless, but although he had given up the hunt, he had never stopped hoping that some time, somewhere, he would meet her.

Then he had seen the book *Je m'appelle Cybèle* in a Paris bookshop. Intrigued by the title, he bought it, and discovered that Cybèle Meredith, née Sybil Androwski, was also Sylvie Andros, the woman who had shattered his mother's life.

His anger had mounted as he read her specious tribute to the bravery of her Resistance colleague, Marie Masson.

There were extracts from English reviews of the book on the back of the dust-jacket, including one which described it as 'ruthlessly honest'.

Ruthless, yes, he thought. But not honest.

That evening, Charles had invited Cybèle to supper at the mill.

She swept in at eight o'clock and the volunteers, grouped around the table with glasses of wine in front of them, automatically sat up straighter. She was wearing a deceptively simple dress which Suzy recognized as a current-season Yves St Laurent, in off-white silk, its sleeves and high collar piped in black. Her high-heeled pumps were covered in the same silk.

She was gracious to everyone, recognizing Arthur and Rob from previous visits, nodding to Christian and Suzy, shaking hands with the two actors and Olivia.

As Charles, the one person in the room who appeared wholly at ease in her presence, poured the Perrier she had requested, the volunteers returned to their own conversations.

Only Christian and Suzy were silent as they watched her.

From above their heads, music thundered. Cybèle glanced up. 'My dears, one can hardly hear oneself think! What on earth is it?'

Charles said, 'It's one of Claire's tapes. U2, I believe. The Joshua Tree album.' He looked around complacently as the volunteers applauded.

'Well done!' Rob said. 'We're introducing Charles to the pop scene, Lady Meredith. He needs to broaden his musical interests.'

'But you can't *like* that stuff, Charles,' she said.

'Not all of it. But I'm willing to be instructed by my youngers and betters, for a while, at least.'

'I can think of no good reason to listen to that noise.'

Arthur opened his mouth to challenge her, but the music stopped and there were footsteps on the stairs. Claire arrived, her face scrubbed and shining, on a breathless flow of words. 'So sorry, everyone. Hullo, Lady Meredith. Has anyone checked the *daube*?'

'I did,' Suzy said. 'It looks great.'

'You're the new one. Hullo, I'm Claire. Sorry I wasn't here when you arrived, but our donkey was lonely, so I took him for a walk, and then I had to have a bath.' She frowned. 'Don't I know you? You look sort of familiar.'

'Maybe we met in London some time.'

'I never go to London.' Her face suddenly convulsed. 'Hang on . . .' She ran out, pounded upstairs. Everyone waited, their eyes fixed on Suzy, who sighed, guessing what was coming.

Claire came back, waving an old, dog-eared copy of *Harpers and Queen*. She slapped it down on the table and pointed to the cover. 'I knew it! You're Suzy Leander.' They craned forward to look at the sleek, bejewelled girl in the photograph, her copper hair swept up, bare shoulders rising from a ruff of gold satin. 'And there's more . . .' She flicked through the pages. 'There! that's really why I recognized you. Norman Parkinson called you the Face of the Year.'

'It was some time ago,' Suzy said defensively – and wondered why she always felt the need to excuse herself.

146

'Six pages of you. Wow!' She handed the book to Charles. 'Look!'

Each volunteer reacted in his own way. The men moved their eyes from the pictured girl to the living one with various degrees of interest. Charles looked surprised, Christian amused. Claire said, 'What fun to have you here!' Olivia, after one glance, remained ostentatiously unimpressed.

After a moment, Cybèle said, 'I recognize you, too. I believe you've done some modelling for my magazine.'

'A little.'

'Who is your agent?'

'Damien Bennett.'

'I remember now.' Her voice was sweet and deadly. 'My dear, you must speak to him severely! He has an inflated idea of your value. My editors have had to look elsewhere for models whose fees are more realistic.'

'I set my own fees, Lady Meredith,' Suzy said serenely. 'If I'd realized that *Cybèle* was having financial problems I'd have been delighted to help you out by reducing them.'

'Oh, we can always find the money to pay for real quality,' Cybèle murmured.

Suzy began to laugh, turning the bitchy repartee into a joke. 'You win, Lady Meredith! Game, set and match.'

Charles chuckled.

'Seconds out for the next round,' muttered Arthur.

' "There's plenty of time to win this game, and thrash the Spaniards, too," ' James added.

Triumphantly, Suzy capped the quotation, bowing towards Cybèle: ' "The game is done, I've – no, *she's* won, she's won!" '

'Mon Dieu! The lady is educated!' Christian said.

Cybèle's face had stiffened during the quick-fire exchange. She forced a smile, but her eyes shifted uncertainly around the table and Suzy suddenly saw an elderly woman unable to cope with the mockery of a younger generation. She thought remorsefully, she knows we're laughing at her.

But within seconds Cybèle had recovered her poise and the brief awkward moment passed.

147

Claire began to serve the supper, which was more elaborate than usual in honour of the guest: hors d'oeuvres of raw vegetables from the garden, with freshly made mayonnaise, thin slices of sausage and olives, followed by the *daube* of beef, bacon, onion and garlic which had been simmered for hours in red wine, with tiny new potatoes and a green salad. The meal ended with a variety of cheeses.

As the wine flowed, so did the conversation and only Cybèle made little effort to join in, mainly talking in a low voice to Charles and picking at her food.

As Suzy passed her plate for a second helping of *daube*, she heard her say, 'I have a problem. Those two girls you found me last year tell me they can't work for me any longer. They've taken jobs in Bergerac.'

'I'll look for someone else, but it isn't easy these days. Most of the willing women have been snapped up by the permanent residents.'

'I'm sure you'll do your best. With arrangements for your festival looming, I must have help in the house.'

Suzy leant forward. 'Excuse me. I couldn't help over-hearing. Charles, I don't know what work you have in mind for me, but I'd be happy to help Lady Meredith out.'

They looked at her in astonishment.

'You?' Cybèle said. 'Impossible!'

'Why?' This was what she wanted: a chance to get close to the woman she believed was her grandmother and find out whether or not it would be wise to bring her together with Julia. So far, apart from the brief moment when Cybèle's defences had crumbled, she had found nothing much in her to like. But the more she studied her, the more convinced she was that her guess was right. Every now and then she saw her mother in Cybèle's eyes, in the shape of her face, in the graceful hand-gestures as she talked, although Julia's were more impulsive, less controlled.

'Are you serious?' Charles said. 'I mean, for God's sake, what would Norman Parkinson say to the Face of the Year becoming a house-maid?'

'I told you, one of the reasons I'm here is to get away from my job. I need a change.' She turned to Cybèle, a question in her eyes.

Cybèle nodded slowly. Already this girl and Charles seemed to be on the best of terms, and she was far too alluring, with her tawny beauty, graceful young body and quick wit. This would be a way of removing her from his orbit for at least part of each day. In a week or so, she could be found to be lazy, inefficient and deceitful, and her dismissal from Le Bas-Fond arranged.

'Let's give it a trial,' she said briskly. 'But I warn you, I'll treat you exactly as I would any local girl. You can come every morning from nine until twelve. That will suit you, Charles?' It was more a statement than a question.

'I suppose so. If you're really sure that's what you want, Suzy?'

'I'm sure.'

That night she lay in her narrow bed, listening to Olivia's uneven breathing, knowing that she was awake, too.

Olivia didn't like her, and she suspected that the reason was Christian Morel. Over the years, she had become resigned to such antagonism from women, but she had never grown used to it. Naturally friendly and without envy herself, she couldn't adjust to the fact that her looks and her job were identified in some female minds with a predator, out to devour their men.

If she has her eye on that over-sized, conceited Frenchman, she's safe enough, she thought. Even if he were interested – which he clearly isn't – I wouldn't want him under any circumstances.

Her mind drifted back to Cybèle Meredith. If no man was a hero to his valet, no woman could be a heroine to her house-maid. Her ladyship would hardly be able to maintain her image of invulnerable perfection from nine o'clock every morning. When the real woman emerged from behind the mask, Suzy intended to be there to meet her.

*

149

For his own very different reasons, Christian's thoughts were also focused on Cybèle.

Tonight, he had observed her first, brief show of weakness, when she had suddenly looked lost and out-of-place among the younger people. It had been an unexpected glimpse beyond the diamond-hard facade.

He knew that Suzy Leander had noticed it too. Her laughter had faded, and a few minutes later she had obviously tried to make up for the jokes at Cybèle's expense by offering to work for her. He frowned. She had been almost too eager to help out. Why on earth would she want to be a servant to a difficult woman?

Then light dawned: she made her living in the world in which Cybèle was a powerful figure. Ergo: any favour Suzy did her could immeasurably enhance her own career. So there had been nothing coincidental in her arrival at Le Bas-Fond at this time. It must have been part of a scheme to get close to Cybèle.

He had brought Cybèle's book with him and now he picked it up. Irritated because he had actually found himself feeling sorry for her discomfort earlier in the evening, he turned to the pages which he knew would refuel his anger . . .

11

Extract from *I am Cybèle*

I had been at Emile's for nearly a year when, bored with acting as a clothes-horse, I persuaded him to let me become a *vendeuse*, assisting Madame Claude in the showroom. This gave me greater opportunities to collect useful information from the customers.

During that year Marie moved half a dozen times, to set up her transmitter in different parts of Paris. We met when necessary, each time in a different place: outside the Opéra, in railway stations, the Montparnasse Cemetery, the Luxembourg Gardens. We never stopped to talk, but as we passed, we bumped into each other, apparently accidentally. Pausing to apologize politely, I would slip my written message to her. We had agreed that this was a safer method than the alternative of using letter-drops as some of the agents did.

My life was becoming increasingly dangerous. It was discovered later that the Gestapo had known far more about us than we suspected. They had traced many of our addresses and safe houses and frequently found it more valuable to follow the movements of an agent rather than arrest him immediately. Others were taken in, some were turned, some tortured until they gave names.

The technique for tracing transmitters had also improved and as the months passed I noticed that Marie was becoming thinner, her face drawn with anxiety, and she had developed a nervous tic under her left eye.

One winter evening we had arranged to meet near the Eiffel Tower at seven o'clock. I walked up and down for an hour, but she didn't arrive.

From a public telephone, I called another Resistance contact, a man I knew as Raoul, who lived in a small hotel in the Rue de la Huchette. He told me to go home while he made enquiries.

At ten o'clock, my telephone rang.

He wasted no words. 'Marie has been arrested. They'll make her talk. You must get out at once.'

At that moment, I heard sounds outside the apartment. I looked out of the window and saw a dozen SS men emerge from three cars.

I said, 'She's talked!' and put down the receiver.

They were pounding on the street door. I knew it would take our ancient concierge a few minutes to stumble out of her room and let them in. The building had no lift and they would then have to climb five steep flights of stairs to my rooms.

There was a back entrance to the house, but I had to assume

151

it would be guarded. I ran to a fire-escape that rose to a skylight opening on to the steeply sloping roof. I climbed up over the wet, slippery tiles, reached the ridge, then slid down the other side, terrified that I might lose my grip and fall into the street. I was halted by an iron guttering. There was a six-foot gap, above an alley, to the next building, and no way I could get across.

I looked down into a black void and saw a concrete ledge protruding above the window of my bathroom. I let myself down so that, facing the wall, my feet were on the ledge and I was able to cling to the guttering with my hands. Unless the Gestapo made the same climb over the roof, I was not visible from any window or from the street.

It was freezing, and snow began to fall. I was wearing heavy trousers and a thick sweater, but they were inadequate protection against the cold. I stood, plastered against the stonework, praying that the ledge would not give way.

Then I heard voices and knew that they had reached my apartment.

A few minutes later, the skylight was opened, but it was now snowing heavily and all I saw were powerful torch-beams above the ridge before, apparently satisfied that no-one could have escaped that way, they retreated.

After what seemed an age, I heard the cars being driven away.

I waited for as long as I could, until I was afraid that my icy limbs would no longer support me. Shivering uncontrollably, I had difficulty climbing back on to the roof. My fingers had frozen on the iron guttering and skin ripped off as I pulled them away.

I crept down the fire-escape. The building was dark and silent.

The apartment door was open. I waited, listening to the silence, then went in. There was no-one there, but the place was a wreck. Furniture had been overturned, upholstery ripped, drawers emptied, my clothes thrown in heaps on the floor. In my panic, I had forgotten to take my – or rather, Sylvie Andros's – identity papers, and they had been removed, together with a bundle of francs I had hidden inside a cushion, for emergencies.

From the window, I saw that one car was still outside. The Gestapo was awaiting my return.

In the dark, I bandaged my bleeding fingers and changed into dry clothes, piling on several sweaters.

I hoped that they would not now be bothering to guard the back exit, assuming that I was out and knew nothing about the raid. I went down the back stairs and reached the alley safely.

It was as though the city had died as I hurried towards the narrow Rue de la Huchette. There were no people, no lights, no sounds, and my footprints were quickly filled in by the falling snow.

Raoul had already made arrangements to conduct me to a safe house on the outskirts of the city while a set of false papers was obtained. The following day I was on my way to Spain.

I never saw – nor wanted to see – Marie Masson again.

During their first interview, Christian had asked Cybèle, 'What do you think happened to Marie?'

She shrugged indifferently. 'I have no idea. My contact with the Resistance ended after I was passed down the escape route into Spain. From there I came back to England.'

But he knew what had happened to Marie. The version of events recorded in Cybèle's book was pure fiction. She had herself been the traitor, had caused Marie's arrest, torture, descent into an agonizing old age, and suicide.

He had grown up with Marie's story, to which she returned compulsively so often that he knew it by heart. After he had read *I am Cybèle* he had written it down and the sheets of typed notes were now folded into the back of the book. He glanced at them and it was as though he could hear again his mother's voice, harsh with hatred.

'Sylvie Andros was a whore, Christian! From the moment she came to Paris, I knew it. She picked up her first lover a few weeks after she arrived, and moved from one man to the next. All of then Nazis. The people who had murdered my Jacob. She provided some useful information, but what I could never forgive was that she *enjoyed* what she did to get it. She used to tell me about their love-making and the wonderful meals she'd had while most people starved. She always wore beautiful clothes, for which the men paid.

'It was a relief to get away from her when I moved out of the apartment we'd been sharing.

'I had to pretend to like her, but to tell you the truth, I suspected her from the start. I often wondered what her background was. Of course, her name wasn't Sylvie Andros. One day she said to me, "Here in Paris I'm Sylvie, but that's not me. In real life, I am Cybèle."

'People thought she was charming, but I soon found out that she was hard and selfish. She took everything she could get from the men, then laughed at them and said how easy it was to fool them. Ah, she thought she was so smart!

'When I was arrested, I discovered that what she called the "pillow-talk", from which she had got much of her information, had worked both ways.

'Her lover then was an SS officer named Fritz Bauch and he interrogated me when they took me to the Gestapo building, which had once been the Sûreté Nationale.

'They tortured me, but I didn't speak, not even when Bauch told me it was Sylvie who had informed on me. That was the worst moment. He said that she had told him everything, so there was no point in keeping quiet. He showed me a list of names and wanted me to confirm that they were Resistance agents, but I said nothing.'

From Paris Marie was sent to a prison in the industrial town of Pforzheim, near Karlsruhe, which housed mainly political prisoners. After a month, she was transferred to Dachau. There she was starved, raped, tortured and finally suffered the spinal injury which gave her excruciating pain until the end of her life.

When the war ended, she spent months in hospital, emerging a semi-cripple.

She returned to Marseilles, where she had been born, and

made a meagre living manufacturing face-creams and cheap cosmetics in a back-street factory.

In the mid-fifties, having been constantly in and out of hospital for work on her spine, she met a doctor named François Morel, a gentle man some years older than herself. Suffering guilt because he had spent the war years in safety in America, where he had been a student, he mistook compassion for love, and married her.

The rest of her story Christian knew from bitter personal experience.

Even as a child, he had been aware that his parents' marriage was not a normal one.

Marie had started to drink before he was born, partly to dull her pain and partly to blur the memory of her imprisonment. As the years passed, the memories became more insistent and she talked constantly about Sylvie Andros.

She spent more and more time in bed, drunk. Her husband dealt with his patients, and then returned home to clean their apartment, minister to her, prepare meals and try, even in his exhaustion, to be an adequate father.

Finally, he could stand it no longer. Christian was twelve when he was called into his father's surgery and told that he was leaving. He had met a woman who loved him and they were going to set up house together.

'I will never neglect your mother, nor divorce her,' he said quietly. 'I have arranged for a woman to come in daily, and money has been put aside for her. Will you come with me, Christian?'

Because he loved his mother, in spite of everything, he said, 'No, I'll stay with her.'

He took over his father's role, fetching and carrying for her, racing home from school to prepare meals, enduring her alcoholic ramblings for hour after hour.

But as he grew older, and she increasingly lost her grip on reality, he realized that if he was to have any kind of a future, he, too, had to get away.

When he was seventeen he went to his father, in desperation, for advice.

Contented with the woman with whom he still lived, but had never been able to marry, François agreed to take up at least part of the burden. He employed a nurse to look after Marie full-time, and he visited her every day. Caring about nothing but her past and the pain she suffered, she hardly seemed to notice that Christian had gone.

He escaped to Paris, where he went to the Sorbonne, then moved into journalism and began to make a name as a magazine feature-writer. When his father died, he transferred Marie from Marseilles to the hotel near his apartment where, after a year, she ended her life.

And now he had found Sylvie Andros, and had gathered nearly all the material he required for a feature which would tell the truth about her career as a 'Resistance heroine'.

PART THREE

1

La Bergerie's six-man Festival Committe was meeting in a back room of the Hôtel des Fleurs, with Henry Franklin and Victor Sézille as joint chairmen.

The discussion had concentrated on the course over which the two relay teams would compete. Each team was to consist of ten members, of whom three would be of advanced years, the rest younger. The expatriates had chosen blue as their colour, the French red.

It had not been as easy as Henry expected to find ten expatriates who could compete on equal terms with the French, who could be drawn from a much larger pool. In fact, so short was the supply that a Dutch potter and a Scandinavian property developer had, after some opposition from the French committee members, been elected honorary Englishmen for the occasion.

Henry would lead the Blue team, with Charles McDonald and Frank Dunnett, the former banker from London, who had been voted the fittest of the available seniors. Of the remaining seven, four were the volunteers at Le Bas-Fond, plus a young Scots painter named John Grant, the Dutch potter, Hans Winkel and the Swede, Lars Svenson.

The three French seniors were Victor Sézille, a butcher named Maurice Simon, and Louis Prévert, a lawyer. The younger men were a mixed bag of locals, including Sézille's son, Paul.

Rivalries were already fierce. Henry was determined that this, unlike the Battle of Castillon, would result in a British victory. Sézille was equally determined that it would not.

There were naturally more supporters for the Red team, but the foreign residents were noisy fans of the Blue. Many people

159

were now wearing strips of coloured cloth pinned to their clothes, indicating their allegiance.

The previous day, the Franklins' fourteen-year-old grand-son, Anthony, who was spending the summer in La Bergerie, had returned from an outing with a bruised nose, the result of a fracas with a farmer's son who had objected to his description of the French team as 'bloody Frogs'.

A women's committee had been formed to provide the costumes and the barbecue which would follow the relay. Books were being consulted for pictures of authentic fifteenth-century costumes, and members of the teams could be seen through windows standing self-consciously as they were measured and fitted in bright satins by their mothers, wives or girl-friends.

At the mill, Claire and Olivia had borrowed a sewing-machine from a neighbour and were making costumes for the Blues, helped by Suzy when she was free of her duties with Lady Meredith.

There had been advance publicity in local newspapers and indications were that at least some of the visitors to the Castillon Festival would move on to La Bergerie a few days later.

With the weekly committee meeting drawing to a close, Charles said: 'I've been saving a bit of good news. As you know, the relay will start and finish at Le Bas-Fond. Lady Meredith has advised me that she'll present a case of champagne to every member of the winning team and half a case of Bordeaux to each loser.'

There were murmurs of appreciation and Sézille growled, 'I hope you like Bordeaux, messieurs.'

Charles smiled, but said nothing. He and Sézille were friendly enough on the surface but he found the man's insistence on maintaining old enmities both depressing and offensive.

They rose to leave, and reached the front of the hotel as a taxi drew up. A man paid off the driver and limped towards the entrance. Sézille stood in his path. 'Monsieur?'

His French was fluent, but heavily accented. 'I believe

Lady Meredith has reserved a room for me.'

Franklin and Dunnett went on their way. Charles was about to turn towards his car when he saw that the French committee members had formed a wall in front of the hotel's entrance, with Sézille's hulking figure in the middle. The new arrival, an elderly, stooped man whose left foot was twisted out at an angle to his leg, was standing in front of them.

He heard Sézille say, 'Where have you come from?'

'From Berlin. My name is Fischer.'

'There are no rooms.'

'But Lady Meredith . . .'

'There are no rooms.'

Fischer's face was bewildered. 'This is ridiculous! I have been told to come to this hotel. Lady Meredith wrote that my room was reserved some weeks ago.'

'She didn't tell me you're German.'

'What does that matter? I assure you, I am perfectly able to afford your prices.'

'Money has nothing to do with it. No German finds a room in my hotel.'

Fischer's confusion gave way to shocked understanding as he looked at the Frenchmen's implacable faces.

He said quietly, 'Perhaps you will tell me where I should look for accommodation?'

'Not in La Bergerie.'

Charles moved forward. 'Sézille . . .'

'Keep out of this, monsieur. It's none of your business.' Sézille's face was flushed and his protuberant eyes were wide with hatred.

Controlling his temper with difficulty, Charles turned to the German and said in English, 'Perhaps I can help you. Lady Meredith told me she was expecting someone to arrive today. May I give you a lift to her house?'

In English as fluent as his French, Fischer said hastily, 'No! I mean . . . I'm not ready . . .' He stopped. 'I'm a little tired after my journey. I cannot burden Lady Meredith with this problem. But if you could suggest an hotel . . . ?' Charles saw that his face was set in lines of pain.

161

'My car's across the road.' He picked up Fischer's suitcase and guided him away from the hotel, aware of hostile French stares.

The German subsided gratefully into the passenger seat. 'That was not a nice experience. After so many years . . .' He sighed. 'I suppose that in my life-time what we did will never be forgotten.'

'Victor Sézille lost his wife and daughter during the war,' Charles put out his hand. 'I'm Charles McDonald.'

'You're very kind, Mr McDonald. I'll be even further in your debt if you could help me to find somewhere to stay. I'm afraid I'm feeling rather unwell.'

'I'd be delighted to offer you a bed at my home, Le Bas-Fond, if you don't mind simple accommodation.'

'Surely Le Bas-Fond is where Lady Meredith lives?'

'It's her property. I share a converted mill with some young people who help me in the vineyard and farm.'

'She doesn't stay with you?'

'No. Her villa is about half a kilometre away from the mill.'

'In that case, I accept your invitation with thanks.' He leant back against the seat and stretched out his lame leg. Catching Charle's glance, he said, 'We have our souvenirs of the war, too. This happened on the Eastern Front. Being cramped in aircraft and cars does me no good.'

When they reached the mill, he mounted the stairs with difficulty. His face was gaunt and there were dark circles around his eyes. Charles took him into his own room.

'I am not normally so disabled,' he said apologetically. 'My leg will improve after a rest.'

'We have no telephone, but I'll send someone down to tell Cybèle Meredith you've arrived.'

'Thank you, but I would prefer to leave that until tomorrow. If I might just stay here quietly . . . ?' He looked around the room. 'I'm afraid I am displacing someone. Is it you?'

Charles took some clothes from his wardrobe. 'No problem. There's a spare attic room. I often sleep there when the house is full. Bathroom along the corridor. I'll get one of the girls to put fresh sheets on the bed.'

Fischer subsided into a chair. 'I am most grateful.'

'A German? *Here?* Charles, what have you done?' Claire said. 'The village will send us to Coventry!'

They were gathered on the terrace. It had been a warm day and several of the volunteers had swum in the mill-pond. Suzy, in a scarlet bikini, was topping up her tan in the late afternoon sun, watched appreciatively by the men, jealously by Olivia. As usual, there was wine on the table and Claire, declaring that it was too hot to cook, had provided plates of hummus, pâté, cold ham, salami, finely sliced red peppers, radishes, olives, tomatoes sprinkled with basil, crisp lettuce in a dressing made with walnut oil. There were fresh baguettes and dishes of sweet butter, home-made mayonnaise and a yoghurt dip laced with garlic.

Charles had taken a tray up to Fischer, and found him lying on the bed, his leg propped up on a pillow. He apologized again for being a nuisance and they chatted for a few moments.

'I am Lady Meredith's German language publisher,' he explained. 'I've come here to discuss sections of her book. You know her well, Mr McDonald?'

'Reasonably. She's owned this place for a couple of years. I suppose you'd call me her farm manager.'

'You find her . . .' he sought for words . . . 'interesting?'

'She's highly intelligent. Haven't you met her?'

He shook his head. 'I think she must be an unusually forceful woman. Not so?'

Charles looked at him curiously. There was an intensity in his questions that indicated more than a casual interest. 'She's certainly strong-minded. But I'm sure you'll find her charming.'

'She is well-liked?'

'Well . . . yes, of course.'

'And lives here alone? She has no family?'

Unwilling to gossip about Cybèle, Charles nodded, and went to the door. 'I'll leave you to rest now. I hope you'll be comfortable, Herr Fischer. Do join us on the terrace later if you feel like it.'

'Thank you, but I think not. I will sleep, and prepare to visit Lady Meredith tomorrow.'

A little later, Claire reported that he had left his tray outside his door and the light was out.

'But you must be mad, Charles,' she repeated. 'You know how Sézille and the rest of them feel.'

'Bugger Sézille,' he said. 'He's a mannerless lout. I'm damned if I'm going to pander to his obsessions. Fischer's an old man. He had paid off his taxi and he was clearly in pain.'

'Funny he didn't go straight to Lady Meredith.'

'I can understand it. He probably realized he needs to be on the ball for any conference with her.'

'You don't think having him here might make Sézille call off the relay?' Arthur said.

'I'm sure it won't. He'll probably be gone in a day or two. Anyhow, the arrangements are too far advanced. I saw some of the advertisements today. Fifty francs for a place on the route and entry to the barbecue afterwards. Proceeds to children's charities. Everyone invited to wear costume if they like. We've worked out the route today, a total of about ten kilometres, beginning and ending on the banks of the stream over there.' He gestured towards a field beyond the mill-pond. 'The youngsters will run just over a kilometre each and we senior citizens rather less, thank God. Sézille's worked out some formidable obstacles, ranging from swinging across the stream on a rope to shinning up a ladder, climbing over the roof of the hotel, then dropping ten feet on to a mattress on the other side.'

Rob groaned. 'He'll get us killed.'

'You can thank Henry that there'll be a mattress. Sézille wanted you to jump on to the concrete.'

Upstairs, Klaus Fischer heard the laughter from the terrace, but had no wish to join the group. All his concentration was on his imminent confrontation with Cybèle Androwski.

He had often lain awake at night, planning his campaign, and had decided not to reveal his identity immediately. His excuse that there were parts of her book which needed revision for the German edition would give him the opportunity to question her, to find out how much she really knew about the twins' whereabouts and the identity of their father.

There was little danger that she would recognize him. He had checked his appearance in a mirror against a photograph taken in 1939. The smooth-faced young officer with hair cropped to little more than bristles and innocent brown eyes bore no resemblance to the mirrored image of an elderly man with a gaunt, lined face, sunken eyes peering through horn-rimmed spectacles, and thick white hair. Hunched shoulders and the injury that caused his body to lean sideways as he walked made him appear to be shorter than she would remember.

He shifted in the bed to ease his aching leg. His greeting in La Bergerie today had shaken him, not only because of the underlying threat of violence in the Frenchmen's undisguised hostility, but because the unavailability of a hotel-room could upset his plans. He was reluctant to impose on a stranger's hospitality indefinitely, and it might take several days to find out what he needed to know. Tomorrow he would have to look elsewhere.

2

When Cybèle emerged from her bedroom the morning after Fischer's arrival, Suzy was already at work, singing as she washed the marble tiles of the sitting-room floor. Her face lightened with the dazzling smile that would, Cybèle thought sourly, make any man her slave.

''Morning, Lady Meredith. Sleep well?'

'Yes, thank you. Please don't forget to dust the decanters. And pay attention to the windows. I noticed streaks on the panes yesterday.'

'I'm sorry, I'll be more careful. It's such a lovely day, I've set your breakfast table on the terrace. Sit down and I'll bring your coffee.'

Cybèle moved to the french windows. She had intended to have breakfast on the terrace, but it was irritating that the girl had anticipated her.

For nearly a week, she had been searching for faults to find with Suzy Leander, which would give her an excuse to complain to Charles, and insist that her stay at Le Bas-Fond should be terminated. But there had been no faults. She worked well, never wasting time. The village girls who preceded her had moved lethargically and spent much of their time gossiping. She didn't stop even for mid-morning coffee and showed no resentment at the manifestly unfair complaints Cybèle manufactured from time to time.

Although Cybèle had found, to her own surprise, that she could not dislike the girl, her determination to remove her from Charles McDonald's orbit remained. So far, she was satisfied that their relationship had not progressed beyond casual friendship. She intended to make sure it stayed that way.

There had been no apparent change in his attitude, but their relationship had not progressed since her return. His defiance of her clear indication that he should not give Suzy house-room still rankled, although she had hidden her annoyance. Since then, she had twice invited him to join her for drinks. On the first occasion, he had made the excuse that he had to attend a meeting of the Festival committee. On the second, he had brought Christian Morel with him and had left after one drink, saying that he knew Chris was anxious to conduct a preliminary interview with her.

Morel, too, was an irritation. She had assumed that a couple of hours' talk would be sufficient for his requirements. Instead, he had begun probing into details which, he suggested, she might have left out of her memoirs. He had been particularly interested in her wartime work with Marie Masson and had seemed to doubt her protestations that she knew nothing more about Marie's arrest than she had recorded. He showed no signs of being ready to return to Paris. During their second

166

interview the previous day she had said, 'Surely you know enough about me by now? You can use whatever you need from my book. You must be getting bored with life away from the city.'

'Far from it,' he said. 'I've asked Charles if I can stay on for a while. I'm not going to miss the Festival.'

'Don't you want to write your article?'

'The deadline's not for another month. Anyhow, I'll probably write it here and fax it to Paris.'

Sitting under the vine-covered trellis on her terrace, she found herself increasingly exasperated. Things were not going as she had planned and would not, it appeared, until their wretched Festival was over.

In the meantime, on the if-you-can't-beat-'em-join-'em principle, she had offered to help the girls with the costumes they were making, and was spending a couple of hours each afternoon in their sewing-room. She was enjoying the work, and the memories it revived of Etta and the circus. Having been asked by the committee to start the relay and present the prizes, she was designing a spectacular medieval dress for herself.

She was pouring a second cup of coffee when she heard a soft American voice behind her.

'Pardon me, are you Lady Meredith?'

A woman with reddish-brown hair cut into a kind of bush was standing on the grass, clutching a suitcase. As usual, Cybèle noticed her clothes first: a cheap jacket and skirt in black and white checks, worn over an unsuitable, frilly blouse. Her stilt heels kept sinking into the ground so she had to lift one foot after another to keep her balance, like a high-stepping pony. Her face was pink and moist and rivulets of sweat were streaking her heavy make-up. She was smiling nervously.

'Where did you come from?' Cybèle said sharply. 'The front door is on the other side of the house.'

'I hitched a lift from the station to the bottom of that lane, and the man said I could take a short cut over the fields, only it was much further than I expected.'

'You have obviously come to the wrong place. Who are you looking for?'

'For you, Lady Meredith.'

'Why?'

'Well, I wanted . . . I've travelled all the way from the States to see you, because . . .' She took a deep breath. 'Because I'm your daughter, Alice. That's why.'

After a speechless moment, Cybèle stood up and said, 'I must ask you to leave at once.'

She put her suitcase down and her voice was pleading. 'Please! I've come all this way. I read your book and I knew right away. I can prove it, too.'

'You and at least half a dozen others,' Cybèle said grimly. 'You aren't the first, Miss . . . Mrs . . . Whatever your name is. If you won't leave, I must telephone the police.'

'Wait a minute! Just one . . . Listen! I'm Alice Lynam, but my name used to be Jones. That was the name you used when you went to the hospital. You said so in the book, only you never said what sex your twins were. Well, I know. We were both girls, and we were born July 1940. The hospital was called St Christopher's. And there's something else . . .' She scrabbled in her plastic hand-bag and drew out a small square of pink card. 'Look at that! "Jones. Twin 2, 6lb. 4 oz. Born 4.20 a.m. Female."'

Cybèle stared at the card and saw the waving arms of her babies, each wrist encircled by a tape securing its label. 'I don't believe it,' she whispered.

'It's true. My Mom – I mean the one who adopted me – gave me the card when I was a little girl. You recognize it, don't you?'

'You forged it . . .'

'How would I have known what to put on it? How would I have known the name of the hospital? You never said in your book.'

'No . . . no, I didn't.'

There was, for a moment, triumph on Alice's face, quickly replaced by a gentle smile. Mentioning the hospital's name had been a risk. If Cybèle had denied knowledge of it, all her plans would have been wrecked. But she hadn't, and Alice's last doubts about their relationship vanished.

As she studied her, Cybèle saw for the first time a resemblance to herself in the brown eyes that slanted up at the outer corners. The women was overweight but there were high cheek-bones under the soft flesh and her nose was well-shaped and slightly tip-tilted. My eyes, my nose, she thought. It could be true. And then: But I've never *wanted* a daughter! And what does *she* want?

As though reading her thoughts, Alice said, 'Please don't think I'm going to inflict myself on you. I just wanted to meet you, to see my mother and know that I have, well, someone.' She lowered her eyes. 'My husband died a few weeks ago. I'm all alone now.'

'I'm sorry . . .'

She picked up her suitcase. 'I quite understand that you don't want anything to do with me. I'd hoped – but it doesn't matter.' She smiled bravely.

'What are you going to do now?'

'Oh, have a little holiday, I expect. I've never been to France before. Then I'll go back home.' She turned away and brushed a hand over her eyes.

Suddenly, Cybèle realized that she wanted to know more about this woman who claimed to be her daughter.

She said abruptly. 'Sit down and have some coffee. At least we can talk for a while.'

Alice sat. She looked around at the green and manicured lawn, the flowering shrubs and pots of scarlet geraniums. Through the french windows she could see a big, marble-floored sitting-room, furnished with deep cane chairs and cushions covered in cool green and white chintz. There were vases of flowers, and paintings on the walls. A portrait of Lady Meredith hung opposite the doors which led to the terrace. Decanters and glasses stood on a brass-topped trolley. She sighed happily.

Suzy was upstairs, making Cybèle's bed. She folded the fine, coffee-coloured satin night-gown (no sixty per cent

169

polyester in this one) and put it under the pillows, with their frilled cases, the initials C.M. embroidered in a corner of each.

She dusted the two leather picture-frames on the dressing-table. Each contained a photograph: one of a young soldier, the other of a distinguished-looking man with grey hair. When Cybèle had first shown her around the villa she had said briefly, pointing to the older man: 'My first husband.' She had made no attempt to explain the other.

Although she was not the easiest person to work for, Suzy was more amused than irritated by what she called to herself 'Madam's nit-picking'.

Once or twice, she had picked up hints that there might be a lonely, vulnerable woman under the protective carapace, a woman who, if it hadn't been for her fear of competition, might have responded to overtures of friendship. When she had volunteered to help with the costumes for the Festival, she had been unusually hesitant, had looked pleased when her offer was accepted.

The previous afternoon, Claire and Olivia had been discussing men and Claire had said, 'The worst thing about ending a relationship is going home at night to an empty flat, knowing the telephone isn't going to ring.'

Suzy had seen Cybèle nod, though she said nothing.

She's had to be tough to achieve what she has, she thought. Julia and I have had it easy compared with her. Neither of us was raped at the age of sixteen. We've always had people who loved us and who we loved. We missed the war, and neither of us has ever been forced to fight for our position in the world.

She heard a call, and looked out of the window.

'Suzy, we need more coffee, please,' Cybèle said.

'I'll come and fetch the pot.'

She reached the door that led onto the terrace, and saw the woman who sat facing Cybèle.

'My God, what are you doing here?' she gasped. But even as she spoke, she realized she had made a mistake. 'I'm sorry! I thought you were . . .'

She caught her breath as her eyes fixed on the pink card lying on the table. She stepped forward, then looked at the woman again. Not Julia. But the resemblance was uncanny. She was heavier, and the hair was wrong: dyed reddish-brown and standing up in a travesty of Cybèle's silver halo instead of Julia's sleek, dark cap. But the features were almost identical.

'Coffee, Suzy!' Cybèle said. 'This is a – a friend of mine from America.' She glanced at her watch. 'And then you can go. I'll see you tomorrow.'

Unable to take her eyes off the other woman, Suzy said, 'I haven't finished upstairs.'

'Never mind. You've done enough for today.'

'Well, if you're sure . . .' She shook her head as though to clear it and stepped back into the sitting-room.

Pausing, she heard Cybèle say, 'Now, tell me about yourself.'

Charles was standing with the German visitor on the terrace when she reached the mill.

Still bemused, she was about to pass them without recognition when he spoke. 'Suzy! You look as though you've been hit by a blunt instrument.'

'What? Oh, sorry. Charles, who's the American woman who's come to see Lady Meredith?'

'I've no idea. She didn't tell me she was expecting anyone apart from Herr Fischer.' He turned to Fischer. 'I don't think you've met the most decorative of our volunteers, Suzy Leander.'

She smiled mechanically as they shook hands. 'This woman seemed to turn up out of the blue. One moment she wasn't there, the next she was. Are you sure Cybèle didn't mention her?'

'Quite sure. But there's no reason why she should have.'

'She said she was a friend from America.'

'And this lady is staying with Lady Meredith?' Fischer said. 'They're sitting on the terrace, having coffee.'

Charles said, 'Why are you so concerned? Cybèle has just

171

come back from America, presumably it's someone she met there. Was something wrong?'

She blinked rapidly and looked at the two men as though seeing them for the first time. 'No, of course not. I was just wondering whether you knew if she'd be at the villa for long. I could get a room ready for her.'

'You live with Lady Meredith, Miss Leander?' Fischer asked.

'No, I just work for her.'

'Indeed?' His eyes took in her impeccable grooming, the shining hair and graceful carriage.

Charles laughed. 'She might not look like a house-maid, but she's volunteered to help Lady Meredith out until we can find someone else.'

'I see. Perhaps, if there is a guest, this is not a good time for me to visit Lady Meredith?'

'Why don't we go down and find out?' Charles said. 'I can assure you, if she finds it inconvenient, she'll say so.'

3

'Tell me about yourself . . .'

Alice sat back, looking at the mother who had abandoned her when she was twenty-four hours old, and who was now going to pay . . . and pay . . . and pay for what she'd done.

This place was even better than she had dreamed. Not a château, maybe, but near enough. And there'd be men around somewhere, to liven things up. Oh, boy, what she'd have to write to Bibi would turn her green!

She had rehearsed several times the story she would tell Cybèle about her past life, leaning heavily on the pathos, especially poor Hank's death. She always thought of him as 'poor Hank' now, forcing tears into her eyes when she mentioned his name.

She took a deep breath. 'Well . . . I was sent from the hospital to a children's home. Then I was adopted by some people named Lawson, who lived in Lambeth. I don't know much about them, to tell you the truth, because they were killed by a V2 rocket when I was three years old. Seems as though I attracted bombs, doesn't it?

'The house was wrecked, but I was dug out of the ruins, right as rain.

'Mrs Lawson's younger sister, Mavis, had just got married to an American named Stan Bukowsky who was in England with the US Air Force. I don't think she wanted me to live with them but Stan said it was her duty and she went along with it because she didn't want to rock the marriage. I mean, he was good-looking and seemed to have lots of money, a real catch. And she'd always wanted to go to America.

'But just after that he was shot down and killed over Germany, and she and I were left alone.

'She didn't have parents, or anything, so after the war she thought that the best thing she could do was to go to the States and find his people, who lived in Massachusetts. She wrote to them just before we left, saying she was bringing me over, pretending that I was their grand-daughter. She thought they'd be keen to look after us if I was his. He'd told her that they were rich and had an estate on Cape Cod, only when we got there, she found that it was all lies. His father was a plumber and his mother worked in a bar. They didn't have any money and they didn't want us. They said we could only stay with them for a few nights, then we'd have to find somewhere else.' She paused, and said sadly, 'I didn't have a very nice childhood, but it was worse for Mom – that's what Mavis made me call her – a girl in her twenties, stuck there in a strange country with a baby, and not even enough money to get back to England.'

'What did she do?'

'I gotta be honest with you, Lady Meredith, she – she went on the streets. It was all she *could* do. It was awful for me. I grew up hearing it all going on in the next room, every night a different man.'

173

Suddenly, Cybèle was back in the caravan, listening to Arnie and Etta behind the curtain, covering her head with blankets to shut out the sounds.

'What happened to you?'

'I was only fifteen when Mom died, and one of the teachers at my school – I'd gone to eight different schools around Massachusetts by then – was sorry for me, and took me in. I learned to do speed-writing and type and as soon as I could, I got a job. I worked in Boston, then I moved to New York, and that's where I met Hank.'

'Hank?'

'Hank Lynam. My husband. Oh, Lady Meredith, we did love each other! Poor Hank . . .' The tears appeared on cue. 'And then he died unexpectedly. For a while, I thought I was going to die, too. God, the loneliness, you can't imagine! I had no-one in the world . . . until, when you were in the States last month, I read your book, and I realized . . .' Her lower lip trembled. 'You won't have recognized me, of course, but one day I went to the bookshop and you signed the copy I'd bought. You were so beautiful, and so nice, that I thought, why don't I just go and visit with her, and tell her who I am. I needed to get away for a while, and I'd saved a bit of money, so – I came.'

She leant forward. 'It's enough to have seen you, Lady Meredith. I'll go now.' She stood up and said wistfully, 'This place is beautiful, you must be very happy here. I'm so glad for you.'

She picked up her suitcase, teetering on her ridiculous heels.

Cybèle was aware of two emotions with which she was unfamiliar: compassion and guilt. Though she felt no surge of maternal affection, she no longer doubted the woman's identity. Her appearance and her evidence were too convincing. Her clothes were shoddy and she was obviously not well off, but she was not unattractive. Might it not be a rewarding exercise to take her in for a while and show her how to dress and behave, a kindness which would assuage this uncomfortable guilt?

Her thoughts were interrupted by movement inside the

174

villa, and Charles appeared at the sitting-room door.

'Sorry to arrive unexpectedly,' he said. 'But I've brought
. . .'

Not seeing the second man who was still in the shadows
of the room, she said, 'Charles, the most extraordinary thing
has happened! This is Alice Lynam. She believes she's my
daughter!' She paused to increase the impact of her next
words. 'And I think perhaps I do, too!'

Open-mouthed, Charles looked from one woman to the
other: the younger dumpy, cheaply dressed, eyes modestly
lowered; the older, elegant in white linen trousers and a loose
turquoise shirt, her face alight with an interest and animation
he had rarely seen. Superficially, they were totally different
and yet, as his eyes moved from one face to the other, he
detected a resemblance in the features and the shape of the
eyes, though Cybèle's were blue and Alice Lynam's brown.

He stepped forward, his hand outstretched. 'This is a
surprise! I'm delighted to meet you, Miss . . . Mrs . . . ?'

'It's Mrs, but call me Alice, please,' she said shyly. 'I'd
better go, Lady Meredith. I mean, you won't want to be
bothered, with your friends here.'

'No, you must stay!' Cybèle said decisively. 'I've made up
my mind. I remember the cards that were tied to the twins'
wrists, and you're right, I've never told anyone the name of
the hospital where you were born. You're my daughter, and
we should get to know each other. Charles, my dear, will you
send Suzy down to prepare a room for Alice?'

'I will, of course, but you have another visitor. Herr Fischer
has arrived from Berlin.'

For Fischer, the anticipation of seeing Cybèle had been
strain enough, but now, it seemed, this other woman was one
of the children he had been determined to find, and he had
been unprepared for the shock. The scene had blurred and for
a moment he had feared that he was going to faint.

'Oh, Lord!' She swung round as he stepped hesitantly on
to the terrace. 'Herr Fischer, do forgive me, but I imagine you
heard what we've been saying, so you won't be surprised that
I'd forgotten you were arriving.' Her voice was warm and

175

contrite and Charles saw the elderly man blink as she focused her charm on him.

He limped forward, in command of himself again, and bowed over her hand. Then, for the first time in fifty years, he looked into the blue eyes he remembered so well. The face was thinner, the high cheekbones more prominent, and all traces of the youthful innocence he had loved in Cybèle Androwski had disappeared. Under her wide-brimmed straw sun-hat, fine lines were visible around her eyes and mouth, and her hair was silver. But she was still a beautiful woman, with the figure of a young girl. There was no trace of recognition as she smiled at him.

He turned towards Alice Lynam and bowed over her hand. The likeness to Cybèle was there. But was there anything of himself?

In his concentration, he forgot to release her hand. She giggled, and squeezed his. Shocked, he realized that she was flirting with him, and stepped back. Although they had not even spoken to each other, he was aware of an instinctive distaste.

Cybèle was talking to him: 'I know you want to discuss the book, but if you aren't in a hurry to get back to Berlin, may we leave it for today? I'm sure they'll make you comfortable at the hotel, and perhaps you might like to see Le Bas-Fond. Charles would be delighted to show you around.'

Charles smiled inwardly, wondering if she was even aware of the arrogance of her assumption.

'I'm afraid I'm not at the hotel.' Fischer's voice was hoarse, and he cleared his throat. 'It seems that the owner does not care for Germans. Mr McDonald kindly came to my rescue, and I spent last night in the mill.'

'We were delighted to have you, and do stay as long as you like.' Charles glanced at Cybèle and said, with a trace of irony, 'If you'd care to be shown around, Lady Meredith's wish is, of course, my command.'

That evening, Fischer joined Charles and the volunteers at

supper on the terrace. The air was soft and warm, with a slight breeze and despite his preoccupation with what had happened earlier, he realized that he was enjoying himself. His working life in Berlin allowed for no such informal contacts, and he felt suddenly younger as he listened to the chatter and laughter. Suzy, sitting on his right, unobtrusively made sure that he had everything he needed.

Inevitably, the talk kept returning to Alice Lynam's extra-ordinary appearance.

'Charles, do you believe her?' Claire said. 'You don't think she could be a fake, after Lady Meredith's money?'

'Apparently she's proved her identity to Cybèle's satisfaction.'

'What does she call her? Mom?' Arthur said.

Charles laughed. 'While we were having coffee Cybèle told her that under no circumstances would she answer to "Mother" or any variation, that she had a perfectly good Christian name, and Alice was welcome to use it.'

Suzy, who had been unusually quiet, stood up and said, 'Charles, if you'll excuse me, I'm going to walk down to the phone. I have a call to make.'

'Mother? Hi, it's me.'

'Suzy! Where are you?'

'I'm at a place called Le Bas-Fond, in the Dordogne. You OK?'

'I'm fine, and I'm having a quiet gin and tonic. I've just finished the book.'

'Good, because tomorrow I want you on a flight to Bordeaux, where I'm going to pick you up in the car and bring you here.'

Julia's voice was hesitant. 'So quickly? I'm not sure I can. I mean, I have things to do . . .'

'Nonsense! You used to be able to take off with Alex at an hour's notice. I'm giving you twenty-four!'

'Is something wrong? You're not ill?'

'No, but there's a special reason why I want you to come down. Can't tell you what it is over the phone.'

'I've never heard of Le Bas-Fond. Is it a village?'

'It's a farm, and it's run by a nice man called Charles McDonald, and there are eight of us volunteers who help him, trimming vines and looking after animals. I want you to come and see the place.'

'Trimming vines? Looking after animals? That doesn't sound like you. Would I have to stay there, too?'

Julia loved hotels and hated staying even in the homes of her best friends, pointing out, 'In hotels I don't feel I have to make my bed, eat breakfast with other people or help with the washing up. That's my idea of a holiday.'

Suzy said, 'I'll book you into the hotel in La Bergerie . . . that's the nearest town. Mother, do come!'

Her voice was as urgent as she could make it, and Julia responded. 'Of course I will. But I'll drive down. If I take tonight's ferry from Portsmouth to Cherbourg, I should be with you the day after tomorrow.'

'Will you find your way? We're rather in the wilds.'

'Don't worry, I'm a pretty good map-reader. What's the name of the hotel?'

'L'Hôtel des Fleurs. It faces the square. You can't miss it.'

It was dark as she walked back to Le Bas-Fond, wondering whether she had done the right thing. But Julia had a right to be given the chance to meet her mother, and, particularly, the twin sister who had so often been in her thoughts.

In the lane where she had come to grief on her way to Le Bas-Fond, she was musing on possible scenarios for the meeting when she heard footsteps behind her.

She quickened her pace, then paused and glanced back. She saw a man's shadowy, hurrying figure and heard the rasp of his breathing, loud in the night's silence.

Living in crowded London had made her wary of muggers, but here in the lonely French countryside the threat was even more frightening, and without a moment's thought she exploded into panic-stricken flight.

As she ran, she thought of the Drummond family, shot as they were camping in Provence, and a young English couple brutally murdered more recently in Brittany. She remembered the last time she had been shopping in La Bergerie, and the louts who had whistled and shouted obscene suggestions at her from outside the hotel. Had one of them decided to try his luck at closer quarters?

She was still several hundred metres from the mill when her left foot landed on a loose stone. Her ankle twisted and she fell. She did not see a second man who was running towards her.

Dazed, she struggled to rise, then she screamed as arms went around her.

'For God's sake, I'm trying to help you! Are you hurt?' It was Christian Morel's voice.

'I'm all right . . . I think.'

He lifted her up. She put her foot to the ground, and pain shot up her leg. She leant against him. It was like being supported by a barn door.

'You should do your jogging in daylight, mademoiselle. This lane is not good luck for you.'

'Were you following me?' she demanded.

'Of course I wasn't. Why would I? I came out for a quiet walk. Nothing to do with you.'

'You've come from the mill?'

'Where else?'

'A man's been following me since I turned off the main road.'

'Did you see him?'

'Only a shadow.'

He lifted her as easily as if she were a child, sat her on a flat rock by the hedge, and disappeared into the darkness.

He was back in five minutes. 'No sign of anyone. Perhaps your shadow was a tree moving in the wind.'

'Trees don't sound like footsteps.'

'The rustle of a bird in the branches, perhaps?'

Through gritted teeth she said, 'There was a man. I did not imagine it.'

He shrugged. 'If you say so. But now he has gone. Can you walk?'

179

They turned towards the mill. Seeing her limping, he put his arm around her. She jerked away. 'I can manage by myself.'

The arm tightened. 'Don't be silly. You'll fall again. I assure you, I am not making advances to you.' Then, with an unerring instinct for the words most calculated to rub her up the wrong way, he added severely, 'It was not a sensible thing to do, coming out by yourself at night.'

'Oh, don't be so pompous! I had to make a phone call. It didn't occur to me there'd be any danger. It's peaceful here.'

'On the surface. But you should be more careful. There are some unpleasant undercurrents in La Bergerie. Has Charles told you what happened to Fischer?'

Diverted from her irritation, she said, 'Yes, and I can't understand how people can still be paranoid about things that happened nearly half a century ago.'

'That is perhaps because you are not French.' There was an undercurrent of bitterness.

'But Mr Fischer's such a nice man . . .'

'As far as Sézille's concerned, he's simply a German. And he's of an age to have fought against us.'

'Do *you* feel like Sézille about Germans?'

'No. My paranoia takes another direction.'

'Which is?'

'It's personal.' His tone cut off further enquiries and they fell silent.

After a few moments, he said abruptly, 'Are you convinced that Alice Lynam is really Lady Meredith's daughter?'

'Yes, I am.'

Her firmness surprised him. 'No doubts? In spite of the way she turned up out of the blue?'

'No doubts. Why are you so interested?' Light dawned. 'Oh, Lord! I'd forgotten why you're here. Are you going to write about her?'

He hesitated, then said, 'I think, not yet. I'm a feature-writer, not a reporter. I would like to know a little more about Madame Lynam. If she is a fake, that is one story. If she is what she claims, it is another. Either way, it's good stuff and, with luck, I can keep it to myself. I doubt that Cybèle will be looking for immediate publicity.'

'Maybe she won't want you to reveal it at all.'

He shrugged. 'Nothing she can do to stop me. It's her bad luck I'm on the spot.'

And maybe Julia's, she thought. She's never liked personal publicity. Damn Christian Morel . . . one more complication in an already difficult situation.

'What do you really think of Cybèle?' she asked curiously.

'I have no opinion. I told you before, I am an observer only. And you? What do you think?'

'I met her once, years ago, and I disliked her. Now . . . she doesn't *look* elderly, but she could be my grandmother . . .' She smiled inwardly. '. . . And she's still in there fighting. She hasn't resigned herself to becoming a has-been. OK, she's tough and dictatorial, but she's been successful in several fields, she's one of the most elegant women I've ever seen, and she's indomitable. I admire that.'

'That's quite a speech. I have to tell you I do *not* admire her Ladyship.'

She said mockingly, 'Could that be because she challenges your macho image? Are you a little afraid of a woman who's got where she is by using tactics as tough as any man's?'

'My dear girl, her tactics were entirely female. If you've read her book, you should know that she got where she is on her back.'

'That's a rotten thing to say! If she was a man who'd screwed around and become successful, you wouldn't equate the two.'

'Because men don't use sex as a substitute for ability.'

'How do you think Cybèle's managed to stay at the top? So she used every weapon she could to get there, but she's stayed because she's intelligent, shrewd and hard-working.'

'And cunning and ruthless in exploiting her sexual attraction.'

'You know, you're not objective about her at all,' she said. 'And I have a curious feeling that you know more about her than you pretend. What is it?'

181

'Nothing! I am tired of talking about Cybèle Meredith. May we find another subject?'

'Such as?'

He surprised her. 'You, for instance.'

'I'm very uninteresting,' she said lightly.

'Perhaps. But I will make up my own mind when I know more about you.'

'Sorry. I have no intention of being interviewed for your wretched magazine.'

'I assure you . . .'

But they had reached the terrace. She shook herself free of his arm and he stood aside, smiling sardonically as she faced a barrage of questions about her damaged ankle.

When she had explained what had happened, Charles said, 'Do you think it was one of young Sézille's gang?'

'He wasn't close enough to recognize.' She shrugged and shot an unfriendly glance at Christian. 'Maybe I over-reacted. *He* thinks I imagined the whole thing. There *was* a man, but maybe it was only someone harmless, out for an evening stroll.'

'I hope so.' But Charles still looked worried, and repeated Christian's words. 'I think you girls should be more careful about going out at night by yourselves. There's a growing atmosphere in the village . . . a sort of aggression I haven't known before, especially among the teenagers. I'm beginning to wish we'd never thought of this bloody festival. They're taking the race too seriously.'

Fischer said uneasily, 'Charles, I think perhaps my presence is a provocation. Tomorrow I must find a hotel elsewhere.'

'You'll do nothing of the kind,' Charles said vigorously. 'I'm not giving in to Sézille's ridiculous obsession. He must learn that he can't dictate how we run our lives.' There was a chorus of agreement from the young people.

'Thank you. If you are sure it will not create trouble, I would like very much to stay for a little while. Apart from my need to talk with Lady Meredith, I have not had such a happy few days for many years.'

4

Arnie Gold was shaking when he emerged from his hiding-place under the hedge. Bloody woman, running like that. And a man-mountain coming after him. What'd they think, anyway – that he was going to rape her? All he'd wanted was to ask the way to Sybil's. He'd been walking for hours when he'd seen her ahead of him, hadn't even been able to summon up the energy to shout. But he wasn't going to wait and explain anything to the big chap. Sliding under the hedge to stay out of his way had been instinctive – there had been many occasions in Arnie's life when he'd had to take such evasive action.

He plodded back towards the main road. His sunken stomach was rumbling its need for food. Getting down here from London had cost more than he expected and he only had nineteen francs left. A bit under two quid. Not enough for a bed and he'd been counting on Sybil to feed him. He looked at the fluorescent hands of his watch. Eleven-twenty. Too late to go to Sybil's, even if he could find the place. He'd need all his wits about him when he confronted her. Right now, all he wanted was to sleep. Well, he'd slept under the stars before, though not for a few years.

There was a heavy dew and with his rheumatics it was too damp to lie in the open, but there had been benches in La Bergerie's square. One of them would do for a bed, then tomorrow he would start off again for Le Bas-Fond.

It took him nearly an hour to reach the town, by which time he was scarcely able to walk.

La Bergerie was graveyard-silent and not a light showed as Arnie limped into the square.

It was a big unpaved space with a plane tree in the middle. On one side, plastic chairs were piled on tables and closed umbrellas drooped above them. In the starlight, he could make out the words Hôtel des Fleurs above an awning. He'd been in there earlier and asked its unpleasant landlord how to get to Sybil's.

He found a bench under the tree, placed his shabby gladstone bag on it to serve as a pillow, and stretched out. His old bones had no cushions of fat and as he twisted and wriggled, trying to find some comfort, he thought bitterly of the woman who was the cause of his suffering.

She was to blame for everything bad that had happened to him, from that awful day when the circus women had man-handled him on to a train, to the night in Paris which had heralded the worst years of his life.

After fleeing from the Germans in the Boul' Mich' he had huddled against the wall on one of the *quais*, shaking from a mixture of cold and anger. The sacking around his shoulders was no protection against the night air, but even chillier was the memory of Sybil's treachery.

He had been awakened at midnight by a heavy boot nudging his rib, and driven to a brightly lit building which was full of large, well-fed, hard-eyed men, some in the black shirts of the SS, some in military uniforms, others in civilian clothes – and these frightened him most of all, because they were the Gestapo.

He was taken to a cell-like room and left alone, his terror increasing by the minute. Sybil was the only person in Paris who knew his name. She'd done this to him. He prayed to the God in whom he had never believed: just give me a chance to tell them who she is. I'll do her in, so help me!

But God didn't answer his prayers. After twenty-four hours during which he was given neither food nor water, a couple of military policemen took him outside and hustled him into a police van. They might have been deaf and dumb for all the notice they took of his pleas to be allowed to talk to someone in authority. An hour or so later he was disgorged into an internment camp which he subsequently discovered was north-east of Paris, where he was to remain until the war ended.

He was lonely, frightened and always hungry. The internees were given *ersatz* coffee and dry bread for breakfast and supper, with bowls of a kind of sour paste made from cabbage, swedes or mashed peas at mid-day. The guards amused themselves by beating up the prisoners and there was scarcely a day when his body was free of bruises.

His great terror was that his Jewish origins would be discovered. But since he had not been circumcised and had lost his papers, they did not identify him. He told them that he was Irish and his name was Arnold Murphy.

For ever afterwards when the memory of those years came back to him, he would sweat and become short of breath, for his life had been a compound of such discomfort and fear that he would willingly have exchanged it for a return to the *quais*.

When the war ended, he joined the other prisoners racing for freedom as their guards fled. After some months in a refugee camp, he had managed to convince the authorities that he was British and been sent to England.

Unfortunately, he was little better off there than he had been in Paris. His years abroad had made him lose touch with his family and he found that most of the relations he knew about were either dead or scattered to unknown addresses. A cousin took him in for a while but when Arnie, woman-starved for years, made advances to his wife, he was requested to go elsewhere.

One afternoon, broke and miserable, he had been sitting on a bench in Royal Avenue, just off the King's Road in Chelsea, when he saw a familiar face.

It was young Billy Dando, now in his early twenties, looking plump and prosperous.

If he wasn't overwhelmed with delight to see Arnie, he was not unkind, and offered to buy him a cup of tea and a bun.

It turned out that he had left the circus in Algeria and moved to London, where he had gone into the scrap-metal business. He had already made a great deal of money, some of which he had invested in a café in Fulham.

'Where's the circus now, then?' Arnie asked.

'Finished, mate. Dad died last year and Mum decided she'd

had enough. Sold the tents and the animals and the trailers and she's here, too. She's gone into the property market. There are houses all over the place selling for practically nothing, and you can claim war damages on most of 'em. She's just bought a five-storey Georgian terrace house in Pimlico for two and a half thou, and she'll get half of that back in reparations.'

Arnie remembered tough Lucille Dando without affection. She had led the women when they frog-marched him out of the circus. 'What does she want a five-storey house for?' he said.

Billy looked at him pityingly. 'Where you been, mate? There's a fortune to be made in property. Thousands of people left London during the blitz and now they're all trickling back. Need somewhere to live, don't they? Five-storeyed house equals five flats when she's converted it, and she'll sell the leases. She reckons to cover the cost of the entire house with one flat. How about you, Arnie? Seen anything of Sybil?'

'I stayed in Paris during the war. Lost my passport, couldn't get away. I had a terrible time, Billy. Terrible. And you know who caused it? That little bitch, Sybil. She set the Gestapo on to me. She never liked me, you know.'

'Christ, I'm sorry. Did you ever hear what happened to her?'

Even thinking about her angered Arnie. 'I hope she's bloody dead,' he said viciously.

'What are you doing now, then?'

'Looking for a job. You don't know if anything's going, do you?'

'I just might, at that. I need a washer-up in my café. Interested?'

'A washer-up?'

'I know it's not what you've been used to, but it might tide you over. Give you a chance to find something better.'

But Arnie never did find anything better. The years passed, and day after day he stood at a sink filled with greasy, khaki-coloured water and washed mountains of dirty dishes, and dried them, and stacked them on their racks. Eventually Billy turned the café into a restaurant and put up his prices. Because he was sorry for the old man, and against his mother's advice, he appointed Arnie caretaker of the premises and gave him a room in the basement, where he remained until he reached pensionable age, retired and moved to Mrs Kelly's lodging-house in Paddington.

Over the long years of apathy his bitterness against Sybil had lain dormant. Since he had read her book, it had flooded back with renewed strength.

5

As Cybèle sat in front of her dressing-room mirror, creaming her face, she was thinking, inevitably, about her newly discovered daughter.

They had talked together for hours, getting to know each other. Alice had shown herself touchingly grateful for having been allowed to stay in the villa and fulsome in her appreciation of Cybèle's generosity.

She appeared to be genuinely eager to be instructed in the ways of a more sophisticated life-style. When Cybèle mentioned that a loudly checked suit and frilly blouse were hardly suitable country wear, she had looked momentarily taken aback, then said, 'Of course, you're right. You have such marvellous taste. Only when Hank died, there was so little money left, and after paying my air-fare, I just had to make do.'

'We will go shopping together,' Cybèle said.

'But I can't afford . . .'

'I can.'

If she remained as humble and appreciative as she appeared, Cybèle thought, there was no reason why she should not be allowed to stay at Le Bas-Fond indefinitely. Making her over into a daughter who could be introduced to the world with pride would be an interesting challenge.

She was startled by a tap on her door.

'Yes?'

Alice called, 'May I come in? I just wondered whether you would like me to bring you a drink, some hot milk, perhaps, or a cup of tea?'

Cybèle loathed hot milk and never drank anything before she went to bed. Without opening the door, she said, 'Nothing, thank you. Good night.'

As the footsteps retreated, she decided that one thing Alice must learn was that her room was sacrosanct. It was her personal domain, where she relaxed in the knowledge that there was no-one to note the added years when she removed her make-up, nor the tired lines around her eyes, nor her arthritic limp. When she had closed its door, she was not to be disturbed and the only person other than herself who was ever permitted entry was her cleaner. No exception would be made for Alice.

Her need for some space which was entirely her own stemmed from her childhood, when only a curtain had divided the caravan and inadequately shielded her from prying eyes. Even during her marriages she had insisted on having one room set aside into which even her husband would enter only after knocking.

Her bedroom here in the villa was particularly personal, furnished without regard to cost. Her bed was covered by a magnificent Amish patchwork quilt she had bought in Pennsylvania. A turquoise sofa and two arm-chairs which picked up one of the quilt's dominant colours were set around a low table where, sometimes, she had her breakfast as sun poured in through the french windows that led on to her private balcony. Unlike the rest of the house, where the floors were marble or tile, the room was close-carpeted in pale grey Wilton. Through one doorway was a mirror-walled dressing-room with racks and cupboards for her clothes; through another, a turquoise and grey bathroom with thick, apricot-coloured towels which matched her robe.

The evening ritual completed, she moved from the dressing-room into the bedroom, and her eyes fell on the two photographs on her side-table: Dominic, with his unchanging smile, and her first husband, the only man in whose judgement she'd had total trust; who had loved her, but never really known her.

She picked up the leather frame. When they married, he had been nearly thirty years older than she was, but he was still attractive. He had been her lover and adviser for two decades and had set her on the path that had led to success.

Now, for the first time in years, she felt a need to talk to him, to find out whether she had done the right thing in acknowledging this daughter – his step-daughter – whose existence he had never suspected.

But if he were still alive, he would be nearly a hundred years old. Better that he had died when he did, before the handsome man in the photograph had finally deteriorated into senility. God, she might have had to nurse him as she had nursed Etta! That would have been intolerable. At least now she could remember him as he had been when she came back to London after escaping from France.

6

Extract from *I am Cybèle*

My second arrival in England was very different from my previous one. First, I wasn't pregnant. Secondly, I had somewhere to go, knowing that I would be welcomed.

A week after my escape from France into Spain, my flight to London and my de-briefing in what had formerly been a stately home in Sussex, I was once again ringing the bell of the house in Church Row, Hampstead. This time, Mary Stone opened the door. She kissed me with every appearance of delight.

David came home late that evening, when she and I were still sitting with our elbows on the dining-table, drinking coffee and brandies, catching up on news of the years we had been apart.

The look on his face made me wonder whether he had been prepared for my arrival, although I had telephoned Mary before leaving Sussex. I jumped up and threw my arms around him. He put his cheek on my hair, whispering, 'Oh, my God, Cybèle, I wondered if I'd ever see you again.'

For a few weeks, I relaxed, enjoying my release from the tensions of Paris. Although London was being battered by V-bombs and there was severe food and clothes rationing, the war seemed less immediate than it had in France, where I had been in daily contact with the enemy. Life with David and Mary was still remarkably comfortable.

Mary, who now worked for the Red Cross, was out most of the day. David took time off and we went for long walks, talking, talking, talking. He wanted to know everything about my life as an agent and the only thing I kept back was the extent of my personal involvements with the enemy.

One day as we were strolling on the Heath he said, 'What do you plan to do now, Cybèle?'

'I've no idea. Have you any suggestions?'

'How would you feel about coming into the publishing business? I think I could pull a few strings and get you cleared for work which might not be of national importance. You've done your bit, my dear.'

'What could I do in publishing?'

'There's a vacancy on one of our magazines for a fashion editor, and your experience in Paris would be invaluable. How would you feel about taking the job?'

'I'd love it!' I said. 'David, thank you!'

I reached up to kiss him on the cheek, but he pulled me roughly towards him. I heard him whisper, 'My darling!' and my grateful gesture became a long, passionate embrace: open mouths, tongues seeking each other, bodies straining together.

I was never in love with David, although I was fond of him. I married him eventually for two reasons. The first was because when I looked at him, I could see Dominic. Mary had once shown me some photographs of him as a young man and he was uncannily like his son. The second reason was that I knew his influence would be useful in my career.

It was an uneasy situation, carrying on an affair under Mary's nose, but whenever I suggested moving out of the house, David begged me not to, saying that he couldn't bear us to be separated.

At the same time, I was working as fashion editor of a drab little publication called *Living Woman*. I learned how to write an eye-catching lead paragraph, how to identify type-faces and lay out a page, how to shape austerity dresses with pins and bull-dog clips at the back so that in photographs they looked like high fashion. I wrote a series of features about Paris and my work with Emile which attracted hundreds of appreciative letters. I worked hard, often until late at night, and picked up all the information I could about magazine production.

Living Woman's editor was an elderly woman named Vera Siever who had been on the staff for thirty years, and had stepped into her present position as younger journalists went into war-work. She bitterly resented me and did everything she could to obstruct me. She cut my copy to ribbons, replaced the eye-catching photographs I chose with old-fashioned pictures of boring clothes, and continually called me into her office to complain about the frivolity of my articles. In some ways, she reminded me of Marie Masson.

I hadn't been there long before I realized that either she or I would have to go – and it wasn't going to be me.

At the back of the magazine, which came out weekly, we ran a couple of pages of London society news. Vera wrote the material herself and loved the opportunity it gave her to brush skirts with the upper crust. But she was lazy, and rarely bothered to read carefully the proofs of her paragraphs about weddings, engagements and births.

I was in the office alone one evening when an infuriated

man burst in, waving the latest copy of the magazine. He was the father of a young woman whose engagement had just been announced. Unfortunately, the type-setters had muddled three separate paragraphs, which Vera hadn't checked. As they appeared, his daughter was not only engaged to the wrong man, but she had just borne a son. He was threatening to sue the magazine; so was the man the girl was really engaged to and so was the 'father' of her alleged child.

Perhaps I could have covered for Vera, but she wasn't worth it. The next morning she was fired and I stepped into her shoes as editor. We published a fulsome apology to the injured parties and the suits were dropped.

My first recommendation in my new job was to change the magazine's name. *Living Woman*, I told David, sounded middle-aged. The war was in its final phase and I predicted that when peace came and young women were released from the services there would be a reaction against austerity, particularly in fashion. We needed to project a new image with a smarter, fresher title.

He thought for a moment, then he said, 'We'll call it by your name. Just *Cybèle*. It's young, sophisticated, unusual, but easy to remember.'

Cybèle it became, and has remained. Over the next couple of years, I transformed it from a pallid weekly into a luxurious, glossy monthly. Even as Executive Editor, I retained control of the fashion pages.

When I took over from Vera, I told David that I must insist on having a home of my own. After some argument, he agreed, and bought me the lease on a small apartment in Belsize Park.

He spent as much time with me there as he could, but we were finding the furtive hole-and-corner atmosphere of our affair an increasing strain. He kept saying that all he wanted in the world was to marry me, but at the same time he couldn't bear the thought of hurting Mary.

Eventually, she made the decisive move.

One evening, a few months after I had moved into the flat, she telephoned and asked me to supper.

192

Everything seemed as usual until the three of us returned to the drawing-room for coffee.

As she handed me my cup, she said, 'I'm leaving David, Cybèle. You can have him.'

David gasped, 'Mary . . . what are you saying?'

I had never heard her voice so hard. 'I've known from the time it started. Even before. I think you fell in love with her that first morning, when she was standing at the front door shivering like a sick kitten. I've put up with it, because I asssumed it wouldn't last. Since it has, I'm going.'

She left the house the next morning, and after a week, I moved in. A few months later, she was dead and we discovered she had known for nearly a year that she had incurable stomach cancer. Realizing that leaving him had been her way of protecting him from having to watch her slow death, David was distraught, and it was weeks before I could bring him back to normal.

We were married within a year.

I enjoyed being the mistress of David's house. When the war ended, we entertained a great deal and built up a wide circle of friends. Most of them were of my generation rather than his, but everyone liked him. He was urbane and charming, uninhibitedly affectionate towards me even in public, and we were apparently an ideal couple, despite the difference in our ages. I never let on that to me, he was more father than husband and that there were times when I longed for a partner nearer my own age. Often at night, I pretended that I was in bed with Dominic.

But then, as always, my career was all-important and I depended on David for support and advice. We modernized the magazine, and its circulation and advertising revenue increased steadily. I persuaded him to close down two of his less successful publications. This caused some resentment among the redundant staff, but the economies meant that more money was available for *Cybèle*.

As French couture recovered from wartime restrictions, I

began to make regular visits to Paris in search of contacts and information.

I became friendly with Christian Dior, who had spent the war years living on a farm, with wooden sabots on his feet, planting beans and peas which he sold in the market. When he burst on the fashion world in 1947 with his New Look of long, swirling, feminine skirts, *Cybèle* was one of the first magazines to feature his designs.

I met the woman who had always been my idol, La Grande Mademoiselle, Coco Chanel. She had been living in the Ritz with a German officer during the war and at that point had no intention of reopening her salon. Her Chanel Number Five perfume was still the first choice of fastidious women throughout the world, and its sales had soared at the end of the war, thanks to American servicemen who wanted presents for their wives and girl-friends back home. Even though she was in retirement, I often wrote about her for the magazine, quoting the aphorisms for which she was to become famous.

'Women cannot be friends,' she said once. 'You can love them or hate them, you cannot *like* them.'

And 'An ugly woman with a bright mind can turn herself with make-up into a *jolie-laide*. Clothes will do the rest.'

Finally bored with leisure, she produced her first post-war collection in February 1954. *Cybèle* devoted ten pages to pictures of it.

As the magazine became increasingly influential, I found myself leading a life which surpassed anything I had dreamed of during the nights when I had listened to Etta and Arnie Gold struggling and grunting in our caravan.

My year divided itself into three: one-third in London, one-third in America, one-third in Paris. Sometimes David came abroad with me, sometimes not. I was so busy working – and sometimes playing – that I hardly noticed whether he was there.

Because it was important to live up to the sophisticated image we had created for the magazine, I stayed at the best hotels wherever I was. In Paris, I took valuable contacts to lunch at Maxim's or the Relais-Plaza. In New York, I shopped at Bergdorf-Goodman for lingerie and accessories. I flew to Italy to buy my shoes and bags. I rarely had to pay for a dress in any major city. Fashion-houses were delighted to lend me anything I needed for grand occasions.

My writing became more acerbic, my criticisms of dull collections harsher. I had been told that more than one designer went bankrupt because of what I wrote about him. His fault, not mine. I always gave credit where it was earned.

As I moved around the world, I met Greek millionaires who invited me to spend vacations on their yachts in the Mediterranean; I went skiing in Gstaad as the guest of European royalty; I stayed with film-stars in their Bel Air mansions.

I saw less and less of David, but he was proud of my achievements and never reproached me for my long absences. After ten years of marriage, he was nearly sixty and had lost much of his appetite for social life. He preferred to stay quietly in our house in Hampstead – we had moved from the one he shared with Mary into a grander one overlooking the Heath – cared for by a married couple who acted as housekeeper/ cook and gardener.

It was inevitable that as we grew apart and he aged, our sex-life suffered. It was therefore equally inevitable that I turned to other men in New York or Paris. The affairs were, on the whole, short-lived and unimportant.

As my fortieth birthday approached, with the magazine swinging along successfully, my tranquil marriage and my elderly husband, I realized that I was bored. On the social front, I had discovered that millionaires are no more interesting than anyone else, apart from their money. I preferred the company of powerful, self-confident men of achievement, but it seemed that these days the men I met either kowtowed to me because of *my* power, or were overly aggressive, regarding me not as a woman, but a competitor.

In Paris and London, fashion designers were beginning to realize that it was difficult to survive on the production of haute couture alone. It was Chanel, I believe, who said ruefully: 'Couture is like a beautiful courtesan.

Everybody wants to sleep with her, nobody wants to pay for her upkeep.'

I found the challenge I needed in working out the solution to their problems. After weeks of thought, I believed that I had it.

First, I had to persuade them that while the salons would remain the outlet for their prestigious haute couture, it would not be demeaning if they were to design ready-to-wear collections to be sold at more reasonable prices in boutiques.

At the beginning, many of the designers I approached were not interested. Their leader was Cristobal Balenciaga, the son of a Spanish fisherman and a village seamstress, who announced grandly, 'I do not prostitute myself.'

But gradually, as their losses soared, a few others began to dabble their toes cautiously in the ready-to-wear pond, and found it warm.

One of the first was my former employer, Emile, with whom I had kept in touch after the war. He had always loved publicity, and when I promised him maximum coverage in *Cybèle* he agreed to design an exclusive ready-to-wear collection for me. Where he led, I knew others would follow.

Years later, I visited him in the mansion near Versailles to which he had retired. He then wore only brocade dressing-gowns of his own design and was the centre of a shifting population of beautiful young people who moved in and out of his life like butterflies. They included boys and girls because, he informed me, 'Gender is unimportant if I can take pleasure in looking at them. Looking, alas, is all I can manage now.'

I reminded him of the early days, and Balenciaga's implacable opposition to ready-to-wear. 'And what happened to him?' he said. 'The rest of us began to make our fortunes, but he refused to adapt to the sixties. When he retired in 1968, he said, "Why should I carry on? There is no-one left to dress." Such nonsense! Within a few years the poor darling was dead.'

Emile died in 1979. What he did not know then, which would have given him a great deal of malicious pleasure, was that in the mid-eighties Balenciaga's heirs finally succumbed and opened a ready-to-wear in Paris bearing the great name.

I looked for premises for my first shop in London. My aim was to provide a luxurious setting for women to buy elegant clothes which, although not exclusive, bore designer labels and would not financially cripple their middle-income husbands or lovers.

I discussed my scheme with David, who thought that it was a good one, but was shocked when I told him I intended to put my own money into it.

'The rule in business is that you never use your own money,' he said. 'I'd finance you, my dear, but at the moment, I simply don't have the capital. You must find another backer.'

That was the first intimation I had that all was not well with the publishing company. Concerned only with *Cybèle*, I hadn't taken much interest in the other magazines and had assumed that when one or other ceased publication, it was in order that more money could be poured into mine. I was to discover that there had been a steady loss on every magazine apart from *Cybèle* for several years, and only our profits were keeping the company going.

At that moment, however, I was too involved in my own plans to question him.

I met Sir George Meredith for the first time at a drinks party in Chelsea, though I already knew his name through newspaper reports, both in the gossip columns and in the financial pages.

He had become a multi-millionaire by buying moribund businesses, injecting money and expertise which put them back on their feet, then selling out at a profit. He had been knighted for his services to industry.

Unmarried, he was famous among London's glitterati for the skill with which he maintained in harmony two beautiful mistresses, one in Paris and one in New York. According to the columnists, each woman knew about the other and appeared to be content with the arrangement. George jetted between the two.

197

The party at which we met was crowded, noisy and dull, largely attended by stockbrokers, accountants and members of the legal profession. Most of the women appeared to have been dressed by chain stores. David and I were there because the host was the company's lawyer.

I was caught in a corner, surrounded by two lawyers and their wives when George arrived, alone.

There was a sudden hiatus in the buzz of conversation. I turned and saw him standing in the doorway: a massively built man with a square, bull-like head and a face whose crudely modelled features looked like a stone sculpture. Hard, grey-green eyes extended the monumental image. His springy grey hair was receding at the temples and a sensuous lower lip hinted at his sexual proclivities. He looked to be in his late forties. His size and physical vitality, combined with his compelling personality, made his presence impossible to ignore and diminished most men who stood near him. I was to find that they also had the effect of making women look – and feel – pleasantly fragile.

His voice was as powerful as his physique and even after I had turned back to my companions, I was able to follow his progress around the room as he boomed greetings and platitudes to the other guests. It was unfortunate for David that he and George converged on our group at the same time, from opposite directions. Next to him, David looked shrunken and old.

We were introduced. He kissed my hand and, turning his back on the rest of the group, murmured, 'I saw you from the door. You're the only reason I didn't leave immediately. Do you agree that this is an extraordinarily tedious gathering?'

I nodded.

'In that case, we'll depart, and dine together.'

He put his hand on my arm, but I gestured towards David. 'Sir George, this is my husband, David Stone.'

They shook hands. He looked David up and down, assessing the competition, then smiled and said, 'I know you by reputation, and your wife, of course. I have a friend in Paris who regards *Cybèle* as fashion's bible. You have cost me a great deal of money, one way and another, Mrs Stone.'

'Should I apologize?'

'Not at all. I enjoy spending it on beautiful women. May I have the pleasure of taking you both to dinner when we leave here?'

David shook his head. 'Thank you, but it's been a busy day. I'm planning an early night.'

He looked theatrically disappointed. 'You don't feel that you could manage even an hour or so at the Connaught?'

'I'm afraid not . . . but Cybèle? Perhaps you'd like to keep Sir George company, darling?'

'If she would . . . ?'

I accepted gracefully.

Our behaviour that first night was thoroughly circumspect, and I enjoyed myself. George had the gift of concentrating his entire attention on the person he was with. We talked easily and I found myself telling him about my plans for the shop, without mentioning my need for financial backing.

At eleven o'clock, we walked to Park Lane. His car was garaged under the building where he had a pent-house. He drove me back to Hampstead, saw me to the front door but, rather to my chagrin, made no attempt to kiss me good night. As he shook hands and turned to leave, he said casually, 'I'll be in touch, Cybèle. And by the way, your shop idea is interesting. If there's anything I can do to help you, don't hesitate to ask.'

Like a teenager, I waited for him to call, wondering whether it was him each time the telephone rang in my office or at home. I had found him physically attractive but, more important, I wanted to explore the extent of his interest in my shop.

When I had not heard from him after a month, I wrote him a note, asking if we could meet to discuss some business.

He phoned the next day, and we arranged to lunch at Claridge's. Afterwards, I went with him to his apartment high above Park Lane, and we became lovers.

I found out later that it amused him to show interest in a

199

woman, then neglect to follow up the first approach, rightly assuming that if she made the next move, his conquest was a foregone conclusion.

As a lover he was everything a woman could desire: virile, passionate, self-confident to the point of arrogance. I willingly became his third concubine and within a few days he had agreed to back me financially.

Less than a year later, I opened my first shop in Mayfair. Like the magazine, it bore my name and I stocked it with beautiful garments from Paris, together with bags, scarves, and perfume, all by big-name designers.

Our mirrors were pink-tinted, to flatter the customers, the decoration was subdued, with mushroom carpeting, pink walls and chairs covered in smoke-blue velvet. Against its restraint, the clothes and accessories stood out like jewels.

I now had two full-time jobs. As well as spending as much time as possible in the boutique, I still controlled the magazine and kept up my writing and travelling.

There was a dichotomy in my private life, too, as I tried not to neglect David, at the same time carrying on my affair with George. He was no more in love with me than I was with him, but we shared a strong physical attraction that increased as time passed. We never discussed his other mistresses and I was not jealous of them. My life, like his, was divided into neat compartments.

While I sometimes felt like the centre of a whirlwind, David had almost totally withdrawn from both business and social life, and shuffled around the house like an octogenarian. In hindsight, remembering Etta's last months, I believe he must have suffered at least one mild stroke, saying nothing about it to anyone. It had probably occurred when I was away, and at home I was so occupied with my own affairs that his deterioration hardly registered.

I have always loved Edith Piaf's song, *Je ne regrette rien*, because it expresses my own philosophy. But one of the few things in my life that I do regret was my callousness towards David during the last years. I didn't think of myself as callous at the time, but that's what my neglect amounted to.

The stroke that killed him occurred one night when I was with George. I arrived home in the early hours of the morning to find him lying dead in his bed.

In the days that followed, it was as though Dominic had died for the second time. David had been my last link with him and I mourned them both.

His will left me his entire estate and it was then I discovered that the publishing company was on the edge of bankruptcy. I sold everything I could, retaining only *Cybèle*, which was making a steady profit. Since I regarded it as my baby, I was delighted to be its sole owner as well as editor.

My first shop was a success from the day it opened, and I began to plan branches in Europe and overseas. It became my ambition to see my name on fascias in all the world's major cities.

George Meredith, I decided, was going to help me to achieve it.

7

A rough hand shook Arnie Gold's shoulder, and a voice shouted in his ear. For a frightening moment, he was translated back on to the *quai* near the Pont Neuf, about to be dragged off to Gestapo headquarters.

But this time the words he heard were in French: 'Come on! Up! Get moving!'

He was so stiff that he could hardly swing his legs to the ground. He sat up, rubbing his eyes. The empty square of the previous night had been transformed into a market. Stalls were being put up, trucks of flowers, vegetables and produce were arriving.

One of the market-traders was standing beside him. 'You're in the way, my friend. And you'd better not let the *flics* catch you. They don't like tramps in La Bergerie.'

Arnie blinked at him. 'I'm no bloody tramp!' he said hoarsely.

The man looked at his unshaven chin and rumpled clothes. 'So you say. Whoever you are, you're in the way.'

'I need some coffee.'

He gestured towards the hotel. 'In the bar.'

Arnie made his way across the square and leant on the bar. A fat youth regarded him with distaste, and when he ordered coffee and a croissant, said, 'Sure you can afford it?'

Revived by indignation, Arnie snapped: 'Don't you give me any cheek, *copain.* Coffee. Black.'

The youth's eyes narrowed. 'You aren't French. Where you from?'

'England. Not that it's any of your damn business.'

'OK. Thought you might be German. We don't like the Boche here.'

He was so hungry he wolfed down a stale croissant without complaint. It scarcely took the edge off his hunger, but his francs would not stretch to a second. He carried his coffee over to the door and stood, looking on to the square.

The market was already being invaded by shoppers. His eyes focused on a stall piled with fresh bread, then he saw two women near the bench where he had spent the night. One was small and plump, the other tall, slender, elegant in olive-green trousers and shirt. Her silver hair was half covered by a folded silk scarf and she wore a heavy gold bracelet on one wrist. He blinked and strained his rheumy eyes to see her more clearly as she moved towards the opposite side of the square.

By God, he thought, that's Sybil!

He hurried from the café and pushed through the crowds of shoppers, but he was too late. As he dodged around the stalls, the women got into a blue BMW and drove away.

As he shuffled back to pay for his meagre breakfast, he reflected on her appearance. She'd changed, all right. Very *grande dame* she looked. In fact, it was probably a good thing he hadn't managed to catch up with her. He glanced down at his trousers and jacket, crumpled into concertina folds after his night on the bench. He'd been wearing the same shirt for a few days, too, so he probably smelt a bit. Turning up at her house like this, he'd look like a bloody beggar. What he needed in the present circumstances was to be able to face her as an equal, demanding what she owed him for the way she'd ruined his reputation in her book. He smiled as he reminded himself of the magic word: libel.

But how the hell was he going to improve his appearance without any money? Couldn't even afford to have his pants ironed. And he was still bloody starving. Nothing like hunger for sapping a man's self-confidence. He'd learned that during the war. So food was the immediate problem, then he'd be able to think more clearly about what to do next.

In the old days, he'd have had no hesitation in nicking some fruit or bread from the market, but not being as spry as he used to be, that wasn't on.

Like a homing pigeon, he returned to his bench, now almost hidden by a dried-fruit stall, and sat down to consider his options.

He was looking hungrily at the stalls when he heard English voices. A grey-haired woman and a tall, military-looking man were buying dried fruit. The man wasn't even trying to speak French, making himself understood with gestures and slow, fortissimo English.

It could be that help was at hand. Arnie waited until they had completed their purchases, straightened his creased tweed jacket and stepped in front of them. They paused, seeing a gaunt, shabby old man with dark circles around his eyes and deeply dyed hair and moustache, an ingratiating smile on his face.

'Excuse me, sir,' he said, with as much heartiness as he could muster. 'Fellow-countryman. Heard you talking. Couldn't resist a word.'

'British, are you?' the man said. 'Tourist, eh? We live here. Hope you're having a good time.'

They were smiling kindly and he took courage. 'Actually, not a good time at the moment. Had a bit of bad luck. My wallet's been stolen.'

Their expressions changed to wariness, then the man sighed. 'I suppose I can spare a few francs . . .'

Arnie looked outraged. 'No, sir! Certainly not! I'm not begging. I need a bit of advice, that's all. I want to find a British consul, see what the government can do to help. I mean, what do we pay our taxes for, right?'

'The nearest consul is in Bordeaux,' the woman said.

His shoulders sagged, then he straightened them bravely. 'I'll find a way of getting there. Might manage to thumb a lift. Nice to have talked to you.' He staggered and reached for a lamp-post to support himself.

Behind him, he heard her say, 'Henry, he isn't well!'

He managed a smile. 'I'll be all right, madam. I just need a bit of a sit-down. Haven't eaten since yesterday. Couldn't bring myself to ask anyone for a hand-out.'

He turned away and heard her hiss: 'At least we could buy him some breakfast!'

He smiled to himself. Get the women sorry for you. It was a trick he'd tried a couple of times when he was on the road after he'd been thrown out of the circus. It had worked then, too.

There was a touch on his arm. 'I hope you'll give us the pleasure of joining us,' the man said. 'We're just off for a coffee.'

'I couldn't, really, sir . . .' He swayed and leant against the post again.

'Of course you could,' the woman said. 'And I'm sure we'll be able to find some way to help you.'

They led him to a café off the square, where they ordered coffees for themselves and a plate of ham and eggs and croissants with butter and jam for him. It was the best food he had ever tasted.

Tactfully, they didn't try to talk to him as he ate, which gave him time to think. If they lived in the district, it was odds-on that this pleasant couple would know Sybil. They might even have read her book. Wouldn't do for them to recognize his name. Not yet, anyway.

He put down his knife and fork with a sigh of contentment.

'Can't thank you enough,' he said. 'I'm most grateful to you both and I hope that when we're all back in the Old Country, you'll give me a chance to return the kindness.' He put out his hand and the man shook it. 'Name's – ah – Alfred Brown.'

'Henry and Emily Franklin. What are you doing in this part of the world, Mr Brown?'

'I'd been hoping to visit old wartime haunts, sir. Afraid my bad luck has put paid to that. I've been thinking, though. What I might do is try to pick up a few odd jobs, rather than depend on government charity. Perhaps you even know someone in the district who could do with a bit of help in the house or the garden, like? I've done some odd-jobbing in my time. I speak good French, by the way.'

'You were in France during the war?' Emily said.

'With the Resistance. Liaison with the French. That's why I wanted to come back, and I wouldn't mind staying for a while.' Carried away by the past he was inventing, he smiled reminiscently. 'We had quite an exciting time in those days.'

Henry beamed at him. 'I was in the RAF myself. Couple of old sweats, eh? Now, Mr Brown, I'll tell you what, and I know Emily will agree with me. I can see you're too proud to accept a hand-out, but I could certainly do with some help in the garden. We're not far away and there's a room above the garage you could have for a few days. Got its own shower and loo, and there's a gas-ring. Pay you the going rate. How about it?'

Arnie gave the impression of being grateful to the point of tears. Once again, he reached out and shook Henry's hand. 'I'd be delighted, sir! Anything I could do to help. I'm . . . I'm overwhelmed!'

'Right, then. We'll take you to the car, then finish our shopping and go home. We might even find you work with some of the other Brits in the district if you're not in a hurry to get away. There are quite a few of us.'

As they walked towards the car-park, Emily said, 'You didn't tell us how you happened to come here, Mr Brown. Were you actually in this area during the war?'

'I came down in forty-three to make contact with the local Resistance. I seem to remember a place called Le Bas-Fond. Do you know it?'

'We certainly do. Charles McDonald, who owns it, is a friend of ours.'

'He doesn't own it now, Henry!' Emily said. 'You always give the wrong impression. An Englishwoman, Lady Meredith, owns the property, Mr Brown. She bought it from Charles a few years ago. Did you know the place well?'

'Just in passing. Unusual name, it stuck with me.'

'We must take you there some day. Charles is our nearest neighbour.'

'I thought you said a Lady Meredith . . . ?'

'She has her own villa. Charles lives in the mill nearby and runs the vineyard and farm.'

'Tell you what,' Henry said. 'You must get together with Victor Sézille, too. He owns the hotel here in La Bergerie and he was in the Resistance. Maybe you even met.'

'I'm sure we didn't,' Arnie said firmly. 'I never actually came into La Bergerie. Kept out of towns as far as I could. Too dangerous.'

They reached the car-park and Henry unlocked a red Mini. 'You wait here,' he said. 'We'll be as quick as we can.'

When they had left, Arnie leant back and breathed deeply. He'd fallen on his feet all right. So what if he had to do a bit of gardening for the first time in his life? He was close to his goal. Clean himself up, make a bit of money out of the Franklins, then, he thought, Sybil, here I come!

8

Cybèle had gone up to the mill to see Charles McDonald. Eager to share the news of her good fortune, Alice was writing to her best friend, Bibi Jackson. As she sat on the terrace

in the evening sunshine, her pen moved busily, liberally
bespattering the pages with exclamation marks.

Dear Bibi,

Well, you'll never believe what's happened to me since
I left the Big Apple, as we used to call it! And it's all due
to you. If you hadn't seen that book by Cybèle Meredith
in the store-window, and said that you thought I looked like
her – do you remember? – I'd probably still be in the Bronx
instead of . . . only I'd better start at the beginning!

What I never let on to you at the time was that I went
back and bought a copy of the book. In it, Lady Meredith
mentions how she had twins during the war who she left
in a hospital when they were twenty-four hours old and she
hasn't seen them since. When I read that, I had the most
peculiar feeling that I might actually be one of them!

It seemed crazy at first, but the more I thought about it,
the more convinced I was. Remember how I told you I was
adopted as a baby, then taken to Boston? And how my
Mom had told me I was born in London during an air-raid
and that the hospital was bombed and my real mother had
walked out on me and my twin? It was just like what Lady
Meredith did! I've always kept a piece of card that was tied
to my wrist and said that I was Jones, Twin 2, born at 4.20
a.m. Well, that was the name she had called herself at the
hospital. I thought, that has to be more than coincidence!

Of course, I couldn't even think of doing anything about
it while poor Hank was alive, but when he died and I was
so unhappy, I thought, why not go to France, where I'd
found out Lady Meredith lives, and see her? Just to have
a talk about things, you know.

So that's what I've done and, do you know, I was right!
I *am* her daughter! She even remembered the identity card!
It's all been so exciting, I can't tell you! Here I am, living
in a gorgeous house and Cybèle (that's what she's told me
to call her) is the nicest, kindest woman in the world.

Today she took me into the nearest town, which is called
La Bergerie, to buy me some clothes because she says that

the things I brought with me aren't suitable for France. Well, I don't agree with her, but you don't look a gift horse in the mouth, do you? There wasn't much in La Bergerie – it's sort of a one-horse place with a few shops and bars and only one hotel – so we just had a look around the market then went on to a bigger place called Bergerac.

I can't tell you how much she spent on me! We bought dresses and shirts and trousers and skirts and shoes and sandals. I think some of them are a bit dull, to tell you the truth, because they haven't got any trimming at all and the colours are sort of drab, but my, were they ever expensive!

After the shopping, she insisted that I should go to the hairdresser because she didn't like my hair the way it was . . . remember how I had it cut like the photograph of her? Actually, I think, me being so much younger, she might have thought it made her look old by contrast, hers being white and all. Anyhow, mine's cut in a sort of bob now, just below my ears, and puffed out, with bangs. I think you'd like it – makes me look very *French*.

Here's the most exciting bit of all: I might never be coming back to New York, because I *think* Cybèle is going to ask me to live with her permanently! She has the villa here, and a big apartment in London, and she has more money than she knows what to do with. *And* she has nobody else to leave it to, so your Alice might be an heiress! Naturally this isn't something we've discussed, but I have a feeling that it could come off.

This place, Le Bas-Fond (which means the hollow, Cybèle says), is lovely, though rather out in the boondocks, with fields all round. Our villa has marble floors, and I have a beautiful room to myself, with my own bathroom. The furnishings are fantastic!

There's an old mill on the property which a friend of hers called Charles McDonald has converted into a house. It's a funny sort of place, and he has a load of boys and girls living with him (I wondered at first if there was anything *funny* going on). They work in the vineyard and on the farm, only they aren't treated as labourers. I mean, they all call him Charles and they eat together, that sort of thing. There's one girl, Suzy, who is quite pretty and she's Cybèle's maid. She comes in every morning to clean and give us breakfast. The first day I made my own bed, but then I realized that she was paid to do it, so I leave it for her now. Me with a maid! How about that?

In a couple of days, Charles is giving a dinner-party especially to welcome me. I'm going to wear my evening sweater with the sequins and the satin skirt.

I forgot to say that there's a man staying at the mill with Charles who rather fancies me! How's that for fast work? An Admirer already! He's German and he isn't young, but he's quite handsome, with thick white hair and a limp which is sort of romantic. He held my hand for ages when we met and I could tell at once that he was attracted. He's a publisher and he's here to talk about Cybèle's book, which they're translating into German.

Everyone's preparing for a festival that's being held in a few weeks. Should be fun. We're all going to wear old-fashioned costumes and there's going to be a relay race from Le Bas-Fond to La Bergerie and back. Cybèle and I will be sort of hostesses and she's giving the prizes. I'm looking forward to it because I'll have a chance to meet a few more people – especially men!

Well, that's all for now, Bibi. I'll write again pretty soon and tell you all about the party. Hope you are well, and give old Nathan Weitz a kiss from me. Who knows, you might do yourself some good there!

She was sealing the letter when Cybèle returned from the mill.

'I've been writing to my friend Bibi, in New York, to tell her how wonderful you've been to me, and how I love it here,' she said. 'Where can I post it?'

'Leave it on the table in the hall. Suzy takes my mail up to the mill every morning and the post-van collects it from there.'

Thinking smugly how envious Bibi was going to be when she read it, Alice addressed the envelope.

PART FOUR

1

Julia Leander arrived in La Bergerie early in the afternoon, had a light lunch and was in her room at the hotel when Suzy arrived.

After embracing her, Julia held her at arm's length. 'You *look* all right,' she said.

'Of course I am. I told you on the telephone.'

'I know. But you sounded peculiar. So urgent.'

'I wanted to see you.'

'That's nice. But why? Don't try to tell me that was all. I know you.'

'OK, there is something else. Let's have a coffee on the terrace and I'll tell you about it.'

She realized anew what an astonishing likeness there was between her mother and Alice Lynam, especially since Alice had changed her hair-style. Anyone seeing the two women together would know at once that they were twins. Not that there weren't differences: a coarseness about Alice's features that was missing in Julia's; an animation in Julia's expression that Alice's didn't have, despite her almost permanent smile. Their taste in clothes was different, too, though that was less noticeable now that Cybèle had taken Alice in hand. Today, Julia was looking years younger than her age, bare-legged, in a sleeveless, cream linen sheath with a Hermès scarf in red and yellow at the neckline, and scarlet espadrilles. She was lightly sun-tanned, wearing little make-up. Gold hoop ear-rings gave her a gypsy look. Even Cybèle couldn't fault her, Suzy decided.

As they walked through the lobby, Julia whispered, 'I don't much care for the man who owns this place. He asked me if I was a German, and I had the feeling that if I'd said yes, he would have thrown me out.'

'He probably would,' Suzy said. 'There's a dear old German staying at Le Bas-Fond because Sézille wouldn't have him here. Charles McDonald had to come to his rescue.'

'Is it because of the war?'

'There was a Nazi massacre of women and children. The locals have never forgotten, nor forgiven. They persecute any wretched German who strays into the area.'

They found a table in a shaded corner of the terrace, separated from the few other customers, and ordered coffee.

Suzy found herself reluctant to start her story. She felt as though she was standing on the end of a high diving-board. Once she launched herself, there would be no turning back.

'Come on, my love,' Julia said briskly. 'You look so solemn, I'm starting to worry again.'

The words rushed out: 'I've found your mother and your twin sister.' Julia's head jerked as though she had been struck, but she said nothing. 'Aren't you going to react?'

'I don't know how to. Is this a joke?'

'No. It's true.' She breathed deeply. 'It all started the night I got home from Morocco and turned on the TV . . .'

She recounted the facts as matter-of-factly as possible, and ended by producing from her pocket the identity card she had taken from Julia's desk. 'Alice Lynam's is identical, except that hers says "Twin 2, born 4.20 a.m.," ' she said. 'I think it was that which finally persuaded Cybèle that she was genuine.'

Julia sat in silence for several minutes, staring out into the bustling square, seeing nothing.

'It's almost too much to take in. Cybèle Meredith, of all people,' she murmured. Then, with a quickening of interest: 'What's Alice like?'

'To look at, she could be you, but she's . . . different. I keep expecting her to – to react like you and it's sort of bewildering when she doesn't.'

'I could have tried for ever to guess the reason you phoned and not anticipated this.' Julia's mobile face suddenly crumpled with apprehension. 'Suzy, I don't know how to handle it. If it isn't all a mistake – and I don't believe you'd have brought me down here if you had any doubts – suppose she – suppose *they* don't like me?'

'It isn't too late to back off. If you don't want to see them, we'll leave here tomorrow. We could drive down to the coast, have a holiday, then go home.'

'I couldn't bear that! Now I know, I must meet them. But I can't decide on the best way to go about it.' She brushed a hand over her forehead. 'What are you doing this afternoon?'

'I'm at your disposal. I'm cleaning house for Cybèle every morning and I've done today's stint. When I told Charles McDonald you were coming, he said I was to spend all the time I wanted with you.'

'You're Cybèle Meredith's *cleaner*?'

Suzy smiled at her astonishment. 'I volunteered. I wanted to get to know her.'

'And now that you do?'

'I dislike her a lot less than I thought I would. She's a difficult woman, but I have a feeling that she's lonely and that she's beginning to worry about getting old. She had to fight bloody hard to reach her present position and made tremendous sacrifices in personal relationships. Reading between the lines in her book, it seems that she has hundreds of acquaintances, but hardly any friends.'

'You don't make me warm to her.'

'Don't be put off. She can be very charming. And generous . . . she's bought Alice Lynam a whole new wardrobe. I keep wishing that she'd relax a bit, but she's not at ease with people my age. I've seen her with the crowd at the mill. Most of us are a couple of generations removed from her. We talk a different language sometimes, and she can't cope with it, so she protects herself by being prickly and standoffish.' She smiled. 'If anyone can break through her defences, you will.'

'Has Alice managed it?'

'Sort of. But I can't really believe they have much in common yet. That could change, of course. Alice's husband died recently, so I expect she's lonely, too.'

'So many isolated women . . .' Julia said sadly. 'Look, darling, would you mind if I had a few hours to myself to

215

think this over? I want to get used to the idea that I might be about to acquire a family – for better or worse. Can you fill your time? Perhaps you could come back around six and we'll go somewhere for a drink and supper. By that time, I should have decided what to do.'

'I can certainly fill the afternoon. I'll probably work on my tan for an hour or so. After that, we're still hoeing between the vines and Charles can do with every extra hand.' She paused. 'Mother, I want you to meet Charles. He knows Cybèle better than any of us. Why don't I bring him back with me and we can get his advice on the best way to approach her?'

'A stranger? I don't know . . .'

'Please! He's a man I would trust with my life, let alone a family problem.'

'If you really think . . . I suppose an outsider's view could be helpful. OK, ask him to join us. I trust your judgement.'

As she kissed Julia, Suzy said, 'I'll see you at six. And remember, if you change your mind, we can forget the whole thing.'

Julia watched her walk away, tall, long-legged in a brief denim skirt and a hot-pink cotton t-shirt that matched the scarf tying back her pony-tail. A group of men playing *boules* on the far side of the square paused as she passed, frozen in mid-movement. Two youths standing astride motor-bikes near her car whistled and shouted at her. Driving off, she made a derisive gesture at them with two fingers raised. It wasn't hard, Julia thought, to understand that a woman of Cybèle's studied elegance might find it difficult to relate to Suzy's generation.

As she turned to go into the hotel, she became aware that a man was watching her from the pavement a few yards away. Their eyes met briefly, then he hurried away towards a small car which was parked just off the square. She thought no more about him.

It was siesta time when Suzy returned to the mill, which appeared to be deserted.

She drove the Volvo into the barn and went up to the room

she shared with Olivia. Looking out of the window, she saw Charles and Klaus Fischer strolling towards the stream.

From past experience she guessed that Rob would be in the work-shop, where he was making another table for the terrace. The actors would be rehearsing scenes from Shakespeare somewhere and Arthur would be jogging grimly along the country lanes, preparing himself for the relay race. Olivia was probably with Chris, whom she trailed like an eager puppy, and Claire was almost certainly keeping the donkey company.

Suzy had discovered a little glade a few hundred yards from the mill where she usually went to sunbathe and read after lunch. She changed into her bikini and a towelling robe, and made her way to it through the fields. The air was warm and buzzing with insects, there was a scent of wild herbs and grass, butterflies flitted among the trees like scraps of white paper blown by the light breeze. She thought that this was a place where nothing should ever go wrong, where emotions should be gentle and violence was unthinkable.

She reached her glade, pushing through some bushes into a sunny circle of grass bordered on one side by the stream. Taking off her robe, she put it on the grass, removed her bikini top and lay down on her stomach, resting her forehead on folded arms.

Inevitably, her mind was on Julia's forthcoming meeting with Cybèle and Alice and once again she found herself questioning her wisdom in having set in train events which could upset the delicate balance of her mother's life. Would it have been better if she had left Julia undisturbed in the tranquillity she had achieved after the upheavals of her marriage to Alex?

On the other hand, now Gitta was dead, Suzy was the only family Julia had, and she was away a good deal. Getting to know Cybèle and Alice could add a new dimension to her life.

Against the insects' buzzing and the chirruping of a cricket in the bushes, her thoughts began to blur and after a few minutes she turned on to her back and drifted off to sleep.

She awoke with a start when a cool breeze blew over her.

Her eyes opened to a shadow which was blocking the sun. She sat up. Christian Morel was looking down at her.

She had never been self-conscious about her body and it didn't occur to her to cover herself. Her main emotion was irritation at his invasion of her territory.

'What do you want?' she said.

'I want to talk to you. Put something on, please.'

'Are you embarrassed? That's unusual for a Frenchman.' Her small, perfect breasts lifted as she reached for her bikini-top. She saw him swallow and look away.

'I see you're a puritan as well as a chauvinist,' she mocked.

'There's a difference between nakedness on a beach and in a field. But don't flatter yourself that you disturb me. All I'm interested in at the moment is talking.'

'About what?'

He squatted down on his heels. His face was hard, his grey eyes so intent that she felt he was trying to see into her mind. 'Just what are you up to?'

'What are you talking about?'

'I saw you with that woman in La Bergerie.'

'So?'

'I thought you said you were going to meet your mother.'

'That was my mother.'

His expression changed to bewilderment, then his mouth tightened. After a moment's silence, he said softly, 'So the leeches are coming to suck the blood, are they?'

'And what the hell does that mean?'

He rose in one fluid movement and stood over her. 'I've always thought there was something odd about your arrival out of the blue, and even more odd your eagerness to be the housemaid of Cybèle Meredith.'

A stress she didn't understand had thickened his French accent and it was her turn to be bewildered. 'I only . . .' she began, but he swept on.

'. . . Then I understood: it was because you wanted to put her under an obligation to you. Couldn't be bad for your career, the gratitude of Lady Meredith, eh?'

She laughed. 'Is that what you thought?' She rose to her

feet and put the robe around her shoulders. 'And just how does my mother fit into your little scenario?'

'You forget. I saw that woman. I don't necessarily believe that she's your mother, but she is without doubt the sister of Alice Lynam. The twin sister, I assume. At first I thought she *was* Alice. So I repeat, what are you up to?'

When Suzy was a child, her outbursts of temper had been explosive. According to her grandmother Gitta, who adored her, 'It is the red hair, and she is enchanting, like a leetle, angry squirrel!' Her parents had found her tantrums less amusing. In adulthood, she had made a conscious effort to control herself and these days her temper burst out only on rare occasions.

As she faced Chistian, she suspected that one of them was about to occur. 'You tell me what you think I'm up to.' Her voice was dangerously quiet.

'I think that the three of you are plotting to take Cybèle Meredith for everything you can. She's already spent thousands of francs on new clothes for Alice Lynam. Now, presumably, your "mother" is going to step in, claiming to be the other twin, to see what she can get her hands on. And you, I suppose, are going to be revealed as the loving grand-daughter.'

Eyes blazing, Suzy said viciously, 'Why are you so concerned? You dislike Cybèle. It shouldn't bother you what anyone does to her.'

She was right, he thought. Why should he care? His own object in coming to Le Bas-Fond was hardly less devious.

But he did care. Instead of the amoral, malevolent Cybèle his mother had pictured, he had found an ageing woman who had welcomed, with what seemed to him a pathetic lack of suspicion, a patently false 'daughter', because she had nobody else. He hadn't believed in Alice from the moment he met her. Now it was obvious that Suzy was in on whatever fraud they had planned.

As he looked at her beautiful angry face, he felt a pang of regret. Under other circumstances . . . He forced his thoughts back to the moment and said coldly, 'I propose to tell Charles

219

the whole story. Let him decide what to do about the three of you. I would guess that your days here are numbered.'

'You pompous, interfering idiot!' she exploded. 'Who the hell do you think you are to make judgements? Hasn't it ever occurred to you that you might be wrong?' She answered her own question. 'No, of course it hasn't! You think you're so bloody infallible, it makes me sick! Go ahead, share your little fantasy with Charles!'

She whirled around and ran through the bushes towards the mill.

Behind her, Chris called: 'If I'm wrong, tell me what you and your so-called mother *are* doing here?'

'Mind your own damn business!' she shouted.

As he walked through the fields with Fischer, Charles's mind, too, was on the arrival of Alice Lynam. In a woman as shrewd as Cybèle, her eagerness to accept Alice had been surprising, and he wondered what proof of relationship had been offered. Cybèle had simply said, 'I have no doubt that she is my daughter', without any further explanation.

But who the hell *was* Alice? She had arrived out of the blue from America, seemed to have very little money, and had already made herself thoroughly at home in the villa. When he had called in that morning to suggest a welcome party at the mill the following night, she had taken it upon herself to call Suzy down from upstairs, and issued brisk orders: 'Another pot of coffee for Mr McDonald, honey. And make sure it's hotter than the last one.' Suzy had winked at him as she murmured, 'Right away, madam.'

They reached the stream and paused on the bank, watching the shallow water bubble over rocks and sweep the fronds of a weeping-willow. A dragonfly hovered above the surface, its wings a fluorescent blue-green in the sunshine.

Fischer said, 'I can understand how you love this place, Charles. I believe I would never want to leave it if it were mine.'

'It belongs to Cybèle now. I'm lucky to have been able to stay on.'

'Why did you sell?'

'Couldn't make a go of it. Didn't have the capital to improve it.'

They strolled on in friendly silence. Charles had already come to the conclusion that Fischer was among the least troublesome guests he'd had. Undemanding and touchingly grateful for the fairly primitive accommodation he had been offered, he obviously enjoyed the young people's company. Unlike Cybèle, he appreciated their quick repartee, without having any compulsion to compete. He laughed at their jokes, was not offended by the frankness of their language and didn't attempt to patronize them. The result was that they had accepted him as one of themselves, addressed him by his christian name without asking permission and ministered to his comfort.

He had shown no eagerness to complete his business with Cybèle, and seemed happy to have turned his visit into a holiday.

Christian Morel, particularly, had taken to him and they'd had several talks, with the young man encouraging him to reminisce about his wartime experiences. Charles guessed that he was trying in some measure to make up for Fischer's unpleasant welcome in La Bergerie, and liked him for it.

Fischer interrupted his thoughts. 'Charles, what is your opinion of the young woman who claims to be Lady Meredith's daughter?'

'I was thinking about that a few minutes ago. Curious situation, isn't it? Perhaps she smiles a little too much, but she seems very pleasant, and anxious to fit in.'

'I suppose she is genuine?'

'Cybèle is convinced, and she's no fool.'

'Does she not intend to investigate her background?'

'Apparently not. And I don't feel I can suggest it. It's none of my business, after all. But I must say I hate the thought that she might be the target of a clever fraud. She's a wealthy woman, and I've always suspected that she's lonely, although she'd never let on.'

Fischer nodded. 'The fact that she would not admit to any

such weakness does not prevent one from wanting to protect her from being – what is that nice English phrase? Ripped off.'

Charles was momentarily surprised at his interest, then he said, 'Of course, you must feel you know her well through her book. We're so enjoying having you at the mill that I tend to forget you came here to work.'

'I forget it myself. I'm delighted that Lady Meredith is too concerned with her daughter to be bothered with the book at the moment.' His face became serious, 'It is none of my business, either, but I feel we should try to get to know Alice Lynam a little better.'

'I agree, and we'll have a chance tomorrow evening. They're both coming to the mill for dinner, to celebrate her arrival. It was Claire's idea. She isn't particularly keen on Cybèle, but the volunteers love any excuse for a party.'

When they got back to the mill, Suzy was perched on the terrace wall. After greeting them, she said, 'Charles, may I see you for a moment?'

'I will leave you,' Fischer said. 'I have one or two letters to write.' With old-fashioned formality, he bowed and limped off.

'I always expect him to click his heels,' she remarked. 'I like him, don't you?'

'Very much. What did you want to see me about? Has your mother arrived?'

'Yes. Charles, she'd love to meet you. Would you come into La Bergerie this evening and have dinner with us?'

'Why not bring her here?'

'There are things we want to talk to you about, sort of in private.'

He raised his eyebrows. 'Nothing's wrong, I hope?'

'Not at all. It's just . . . we need some advice. Will you come?'

'I'd be delighted. Only you'll dine with *me*.' He glanced at his watch. 'In the meantime, siesta's over. Are you going back into town now?'

'No. I said we'd meet mother at the hotel at about six

for drinks. What would you like me to do?'

'Will you take over the *pamprage*? Olivia's been doing it, but she complained of a bad back this morning.'

'Yes . . . what is *pamprage*?'

'Removing shoots which are growing from old wood on the vines, plus shoots that aren't bearing any flowers. Come on, I'll show you. We're working on the rows in the Old Plantation.'

She followed him around the mill-house to the vineyard, where the leafy vines were strung in neat rows. Wearing shorts, their sun-tanned skins shining with sweat in the afternoon heat, Arthur, James and Tim were already hoeing. They grinned as Suzy bent to the vines.

'Better tell Rob to get the horse-liniment out,' Arthur called. 'She's going to need her back rubbed tonight.'

'Any volunteers?' Charles said.

Three pairs of hands shot up but Suzy said primly, 'I think I'll leave it to the doctor, thank you.'

She had been working for fifteen minutes, and was already feeling the strain of constant bending as she cut the shoots, when Chris walked past her, on his way to start another row.

She sat back on her heels and looked at him. He kept his face averted and she wondered whether he had yet carried his accusation to Charles. The resentment which had been smouldering since their encounter by the stream revived at the sight of him. 'I hope you break your bloody back,' she muttered as he plunged his hoe into the sandy ground.

2

Charles was unusually quiet as they drove into La Bergerie to meet Julia, and Suzy guessed why.

They had almost reached the outskirts of the town when she said, 'Did Christian Morel talk to you this afternoon?'

Looking straight ahead, he nodded.

'He told you that he thought my mother and I were in cahoots with Alice Lynam in some plot to fleece Cybèle, didn't he?'

He nodded again.

'And you believed him?'

'Not – entirely.'

'How much *did* you believe?'

His tone was neutral. 'If there is any such plot, I'd be surprised if you were involved.'

Her next words surprised him: 'Oh, I'm involved in a plot, all right. You'll hear about it tonight. That's why you've been invited to dinner. What else did he say? About my mother, I mean.'

'Nothing. I didn't give him a chance. I told him that I was meeting her and I'd decide for myself.'

They reached the square. It was deserted apart from the inevitable *boules* players. The central plane tree was throwing a long shadow in the evening sunshine as Charles parked his old Mercedes near a lamp-post.

There were several people sitting at tables on the terrace outside the hotel. A woman stood up as they walked towards her. She was wearing a sleeveless apricot-coloured dress and had a fringed yellow silk shawl slung over one shoulder. On her feet were flat tan sandals with thongs wound around her ankles. From a distance, she looked little more than a girl.

All this Charles registered before his eyes lifted to her face.

Suzy heard his intake of breath and a whispered 'Jesus Christ!' Then he turned to her. 'That's your mother? *Alice?*'

'Yes, that's my mother. But it isn't Alice. It's Julia. Come and meet her.'

Moving as though on automatic pilot, he followed her on to the terrace.

'Charles McDonald, Julia Leander,' she said.

A smile lit Julia's face like the sun breaking through clouds. 'Suzy's told me about you, Mr McDonald. I'm so pleased to meet you.'

'Yes . . . I . . . how do you do, Mrs Leander?' He still

looked dazed and he was blinking rapidly. 'It's uncanny,' he muttered.

'My likeness to Alice Lynam? Suzy told me. She's convinced we're Lady Meredith's long-lost twins.'

'So am I, now. There can't be any doubt.' He shook his head as though to clear it. 'My God, I wonder how Cybèle is going to react to this? I presume you've come here to see her?'

'I didn't even know about her until a few hours ago,' Julia said. 'Do let's sit down. You've had a shock. I think you need a strong drink.'

'I do indeed!'

Victor Sézille came to take their orders. They sat in silence as they waited, Charles's eyes still glued to Julia. As he studied her, he began to see the differences from Alice. The features were similar, but Julia's were more delicate and her smile was wide and natural where Alice's sometimes looked as though it was painted on. Alice's hands had a habit of writhing nervously and her fingernails were bitten. Julia's hands lay still on the table, loosely clasped, the fingers tipped with long silver nails.

Surly as always, Sézille put the glasses down without bothering to clean the table of its damp rings, and slipped the bill under an ash-tray. Instead of leaving, he turned to Charles and said, in French, 'Is that German still at Le Bas-Fond?'

'Monsieur Fischer is still my guest, yes,' Charles said.

Sézille thrust his heavy head forward. 'You know how we feel about those people in La Bergerie. You're trying to cause trouble. Get rid of him before the festival, or you will be sorry.'

Charles kept his voice level with an effort, aware that Paul Sézille was standing behind his father, grinning. 'I won't be dictated to by you or anyone else,' he said. 'M. Fischer is an old man and the war's been over for more than forty years. Don't threaten me, Victor.'

Sézille walked away, his face thunderous.

'I told Suzy today that I don't like that man,' Julia said. 'I'd move, but I gather there isn't another hotel.'

225

The diversion had eased the tension between them. Charles raised his glass. 'Welcome to La Bergerie, Mrs Leander. I have a feeling you're in for an interesting time over the next few days!'

'I'm sure you're longing to know the whole story,' Julia said. 'I'll let Suzy tell you since she started it all.'

For the second time that day, Suzy recounted the events that had been set in motion the night she had watched Cybèle on television, then read her book.

'. . . and the advice we want from you, Charles,' she ended, 'is how to tell Cybèle. Will it be too much of a shock for her, acquiring two daughters – to say nothing of a grand-daughter – within a week? You know her a lot better than I do.'

'I don't want any dramatic confrontations,' Julia said nervously. 'I'd like her to be warned before we meet.'

He thought for a moment, then said, 'Cybèle's a tough lady. I'm sure she'll survive the shock. If you like, I'll break the news to her in the morning. You could come to the mill later, after she's had a chance to absorb it.'

'I'd be grateful – if you don't think I'd be taking the coward's way out?'

'Not at all. And I'll be happy to help.'

She smiled gratefully and he was surprised by the warmth he felt.

By the end of the evening, he had decided that she was the most attractive and honest woman he had met in years. Whatever might be the motive behind Alice's descent upon Cybèle, Julia wanted no more than to make contact with the mother and sister she had never known.

Following the brief scene with Sézille, they had decided not to dine at the hotel, but walked to a small restaurant a few streets away which Charles claimed served the best food in the district. Greeted as an old friend by the *patronne*, a large woman with black hair screwed back into a tight bun, he was informed that they were not to tell her what they wanted to eat, *she* would tell *them*.

They started with mussels stuffed with garlic and parsley butter, followed by *medaillons* of duckling with sour cherries, soufflé potatoes, and a salad. None of them could face dessert, so Madame set a cheese platter on the table, and left them to help themselves.

By then, Julia understood why Suzy had wanted her to meet Charles. He was sympathetic, intelligent, and had a store of inner strength that inspired trust. He talked little about himself, but questioned her with genuine interest about her books and her life in London.

It was nearly midnight and the restaurant was empty when they left. Arm in arm, Charles between the two women, they strolled back through the empty streets towards his car.

As he took the keys from his pocket, Suzy said, 'My God! Look!'

The windscreen was crazed and in the centre there was a round hole, where it had been hit by some heavy object. The wipers had been pulled off and the two wing-mirrors bent. Someone had ripped along the duco on both sides with a knife or a coin.

Speechless, Charles walked around the car.

'I'll bet it was that little shit Paul Sézille!' Suzy said. 'What are we going to do?'

'We're going to the *gendarmerie*. I'll haul one of the cops out of bed if I have to.'

But a sergeant named Jacques Millet, whom Charles already knew, was on duty. He listened to the complaint with a bored expression. 'Are you accusing Paul Sézille?' he said. 'You have proof that he did it?'

'Of course I haven't! I didn't see him. But his father told me tonight that if I didn't get rid of a German guest I have at the mill, there'd be trouble. Young Paul was listening.'

'That is hardly sufficient evidence. It could have been anyone. I must say, though, m'sieu, that inviting a German to the mill, when you know the feeling in the town, was provocative.'

'Jesus Christ! I will *not* be told whom I can invite into my own home! Are you going to do anything about the car?'

'I will make out a report,' Millet said. 'I expect your insurance will cover the damage.'

'That isn't the point!' Charles heard the shrillness in his own voice and gritted his teeth. 'Oh, hell . . . just do what you can.'

Seething, he marched outside to where Julia and Suzy were waiting. 'Jacques Millet is a friend of Sézille's, and I've remembered that there are a couple of Millets on the plaque listing the women and children who were massacred in 1944,' he said. 'He's not going to do a damn thing.'

'You can't drive that car,' Julia said. 'I'll give you a lift back to the mill.'

'I couldn't let you . . .'

'I've got a better idea,' Suzy said. 'May I borrow your car, Mother? I'll bring it in tomorrow and take you back to meet Cybèle after Charles has seen her.'

'Of course.' She held out her hand. 'Charles, I'm so sorry our evening had to end like this. And I want to thank you for – oh, for everything, your advice and your offer to be a mediator. I really wasn't looking forward to bursting in on her unannounced.'

He looked down at her and suddenly, the damage to his car was of no account. What did matter was that he would be seeing Julia Leander again tomorrow.

As they were driving home Suzy said, 'So what do you think?'

He had been concentrating on keeping Julia's image clear in his mind. 'Think? About what?'

'About what Chris Morel said. Are we plotting to do Cybèle down?'

'Good God, no! Nobody meeting your mother for a minute could think any such thing. Chris's imagination seems to have run riot. I'll set him right tomorrow.'

'No, don't. If everything goes well in the morning, may I ask Julia to join us at the dinner-party tomorrow night?'

'Of course you must. But why can't I tell Chris?'

'Because I want to see his face when we bring her in and he finds out what an ass he made of himself.'

3

The tranquillity that Charles had admired in Julia the previous night had been replaced by nervousness when Suzy arrived to collect her at eleven o'clock.

She was walking up and down outside the hotel. As soon as Suzy pulled up, she slid into the passenger seat. 'How did it go?'

'Amazingly well! I must say, Cybèle is one of the most unflappable women I've ever met.'

They circled the square, and Suzy saw that the damaged Mercedes was no longer parked by the lamp-post. Puzzled, she said, 'Where is it? Charles asked me to get the local garage to come and collect it . . .'

'They already have. I went to see them this morning. It should be ready for him in a few days. Go *on*, darling! What did she say?'

'Charles and I arrived at the villa while she and Alice were having breakfast. I suspect she was rather cross because I was late, but she didn't say anything because he was there. She asked him to join them and he said thank you, Suzy and I would like that – which made her raise her eyebrows – because we have some news for you. Then he told the whole story, word for word as I told him last night. He has a wonderful memory . . .'

'Do get on with it!' Julia said impatiently.

'She looked stunned when he'd finished, but she recovered almost at once. She wants to see you as soon as possible.'

'How about Alice?'

'The first thing she did was ask Charles if he was sure you – we, that is – were genuine. When he assured her that he was, she accepted it, but she didn't say much else. She seemed overwhelmed at the thought of meeting her twin sister.'

229

'I'm overwhelmed, too. But excited. At my advanced age, to find my family – especially to discover that my mother is Cybèle Meredith.'

'When she realized that she's my grandmother, too, she wasn't at all happy about employing me as a housemaid. I said I didn't mind in the least, but she announced frostily that it wasn't *convenable*!'

Julia laughed. 'She fired you?'

'I think she was in two minds whether to abandon her principles for the convenience of having a clean house, but Charles came to the rescue. He's heard that Sophie, one of the girls who used to work for her, doesn't like her job in Bordeaux and has come home. She's going to take over.'

'Charles seems to come to the rescue whenever required,' Julia remarked.

'I was right about him, wasn't I?'

'You were right – but you forgot to say how attractive he is, too.'

Charles had returned to the mill by the time they arrived at the villa.

Suzy led the way inside. Cybèle came forward, and paused in front of them. Wide blue eyes raked Julia from head to toe, then she looked towards a second woman, who had not moved from her place in a shadowy corner of the room.

'Unmistakable!' she said softly. 'The likeness is extra-ordinary.' She held out her hand. 'I'm still not sure how one greets a daughter one abandoned so long ago, but how do you do, my dear?'

Julia felt thin fingers grip her own. She smiled and, as Charles had the previous night, Cybèle felt herself bathed in warmth.

'I can hardly believe this has happened,' Julia said. 'I've often tried to picture what it would be like, meeting you.' She turned to the other woman. 'Alice? Have you wondered about me as much as I have about you over the years?'

Alice came forward, her arms outstretched. 'Of course I have!' she embraced Julia clumsily. Their cheeks touched, then she stepped back. 'We're twins, aren't we? Two halves of the same egg. Isn't this the most mar-r-rvellous thing, the three of us finding each other! Oh, we have so much to talk about!'

Involuntarily, Suzy thought, it's as though she's acting a part, speaking lines she has memorized.

But if her enthusiasm was over-effusive, Julia didn't notice. Tears came to her eyes as she looked at the mother and sister she had never thought she would find, and there was excitement in the knowledge that a new chapter in her life was opening.

4

Christian Morel was the only person at Le Bas-Fond who was unaffected by enthusiasm for the party Claire had organized to welcome Alice. Politely refusing to be involved in preparations, he spent the day working in the vineyard.

A long table had been taken on to the terrace, where it would be set with Charles's rarely used linen, silver cutlery and candles with red glass shades. Olivia, more hindrance than help in the kitchen as she pined for Chris's company, was set to arrange flowers while Claire and Suzy cooked.

'What's the matter with Chris?' Claire said as she decorated a *boeuf en croûte* with delicate pastry leaves. 'He's hardly spoken today.'

'Perhaps he's sickening for something,' Suzy said. 'Like an attack of galloping egotism.'

'You don't like him much, do you?'

'I neither like nor dislike him. He doesn't interest me.'

Claire drew veins in a leaf with the tip of a skewer. 'He's interested in you, though. I've seen him watching you. Olivia's noticed, too. She doesn't like it.'

'I can't help that.' Suzy was stirring almonds into melting

sugar to make praline for the top of an elaborate pudding Claire had devised. Her spoon moved more vigorously. 'He's a self-centred, conceited smart-ass!'

'Funny thing, I thought you said he didn't interest you enough to like or dislike.'

Suzy glared at her innocent face. 'OK, I *don't* like him. Let's not spoil a nice afternoon by talking about him. Shall I lay the table? How many will we be?'

'There's nine of us including Klaus, Cybèle and Alice, the Franklins. Oh, and Charles has invited a mystery guest. He wouldn't tell me who it is. Fourteen.'

The rest of the afternoon passed quickly as they worked. Christian was not mentioned again, but every now and then Suzy contemplated with pleasure the prospect of his discomfiture when the identity of the 'mystery guest' was revealed.

By eight o'clock everyone except the guests of honour had gathered on the terrace. The male volunteers had discarded their normal shorts and t-shirts in favour of shirts, ties and slacks. The girls were wearing the best they could produce from the meagre wardrobes they had brought with them.

There was a moment of silence when Suzy emerged, wearing a brief dress of black silk jersey which left one of her shoulders bare and clung to the curves of her body. Her feet, at the end of long, slim brown legs, were thrust into gold sandals.

A chorus of whistles broke the silence. Only Christian looked away with ostentatious indifference.

The sound of a car signalled Cybèle's arrival and Charles rose as she came from the front of the house. It was already dusk and nobody saw clearly the two women who followed her until they reached the brightly lit terrace. One was Alice. Suzy bent forward, kissed the second, and said, 'Everyone, this is my mother, Julia Leander, who is Mrs Lynam's sister – and Lady Meredith's other daughter.' As they gaped at her, she linked arms with Julia and moved around the group, introducing them individually.

By the time they reached Olivia and Christian there was a rising tide of amazed exclamations and questions. Cybèle, more relaxed than the volunteers had seen her, was clearly enjoying the drama.

'This is Christian Morel,' Suzy said. 'A clever journalist from Paris, who is convinced that you and I are frauds, Mother – leeches was the word he used – and Cybèle had better beware of us.'

Taken aback, Julia said, 'You must forgive my daughter, Christian, she has a habit of making unfortunate jokes.'

Suzy smiled maliciously. 'Of course it was a joke. Chris understands, I'm sure.'

For almost the first time in his life, he was speechless with anger and embarrassment.

Without giving him a chance to recover, she swept her mother off to meet Klaus Fischer, and as Charles opened the first bottle of champagne, the party, too, began to fizz.

Everyone wanted details of Julia's meeting with Cybèle, and Suzy's part in it. Christian, moodily drinking, wishing himself anywhere but here, heard it all, saw the two little hospital labels which were, Cybèle declared, incontrovertible proof of her daughters' identity, and discovered the enormity of his own mistake.

Apart from him, the two quietest members of the party were Klaus Fischer, whose eyes were fixed on Julia, and Alice, whose bright pink sequins sparkled in the lights, making her heavily powdered face look pale as a clown's. Cybèle had suggested that she should wear a simple blue dress they had bought the previous day, but she had decided to assert her independence, and put on the glittering top and tight satin skirt she had brought from New York. She had added a wide pink plastic bangle on each wrist and matching plastic ear-rings.

When she marched downstairs, Cybèle had looked her up and down, but said nothing. Only when Julia arrived, wearing wide-legged white trousers of heavy silk with a fine black cotton shirt, and no jewellery, had she begun to doubt the wisdom of her defiance. Cybèle had said, 'Ralph Lauren, I think? Perfect, my dear Julia.' Alice had gritted her teeth and neither of them guessed the smouldering resentment she felt as she kissed her twin.

Julia had no need for sequins to help her to sparkle and more than one man fell instantly in love with her. Arthur hovered around her like a wasp over a saucer of marmalade and Rob found himself wondering whether a sophisticated older woman could ever be interested in an impoverished Canadian doctor. Charles, temporarily squeezed out by the younger men, contented himself by watching her from the background.

She was interested in everyone, talked to them all and drew Alice into conversations whenever she sensed that she was being left out. She deferred, without any servility, to her mother, chatted with equal interest about publishing to Klaus and gardening with Emily Franklin.

'My dear, we have the most extraordinary old man with us at the moment,' Emily told her. 'We picked him up in La Bergerie, an Englishman named Alfred Brown, who'd had his wallet pinched. Henry said we'd give him a few days' work. He claimed to have done some gardening, but honestly, he doesn't know a weed from a wallflower! I have to tell him *everything*. He seems willing enough, though, and at least he can mow the lawn.'

'Beginning to wonder whether we'll ever be able to get rid of him,' Henry said. 'Keeps telling me how he'd like to stay here forever! I'm hoping I can find him work somewhere else.'

Overhearing, Cybèle said, 'If he can mow the lawn, I could give him some work, Henry. I suppose he could sweep the terrace, do other outdoor jobs like that?'

'I'm sure he could,' Henry said promptly. 'I can keep him going for a few more days. Like me to send him along to see you after that?'

'Yes. Thank you.'

Claire announced dinner and they moved to the long table. Charles seated Julia between himself and Klaus, while Cybèle queened it at the head of the table.

Many bottles of wine were opened and the meal was superb.

234

Even the volunteers lost their awe of Cybèle while she, in the position she liked best as a centre of admiring attention, was at her most charming, scarcely less beautiful than her granddaughter, in a deceptively simple white dress with a wide silver belt and silver jewellery.

Watching her, Suzy saw for the first time that it would be possible to love Cybèle.

Klaus Fischer, from his seat halfway down the table, was seeing once again the girl he had fallen in love with in Germany. As he looked from her to Alice, who was sitting opposite him, then at Julia, he was more anxious than ever to discover whether he or her other lover had fathered them.

It wasn't Alice as much as Julia who had reinforced his determination. Alice did not appeal to him. She was gentle, self-effacing, friendly towards everyone, but he had not enjoyed the sly assumption of familiarity with which she had greeted him, the prolonged pressure of her hand, her whispered disappointment when Charles seated her opposite, instead of beside him. Julia, on the other hand, was a woman he would be proud to acknowledge as his daughter.

As the meal ended, chairs were pushed back, coffees and brandies were poured and the young people cleared the table.

Cybèle moved from her place to sit next to Julia, opposite Alice.

Charles heard her say, 'Julia, my dear, tomorrow you will, of course, move into the villa with Alice and me.'

Julia shook her head and said gently, 'That's kind of you, Cybèle, but I think we all need some privacy while we adjust to each other. I will stay at the hotel, but I hope you'll let me spend as much time as possible with you during the day.'

Cybèle's frown was her normal reaction to argument, but then she nodded and, in an uncharacteristically affectionate gesture, put her hand over Julia's as it lay on the table.

Charles's eyes shifted to Alice and he was shaken by the flash of pure hatred that crossed her face as she looked at her twin sister. It was as though a mask suddenly lifted, revealing her true character in the narrowed, hostile eyes, flared nostrils and the mouth's convulsive spasm. It lasted for only a moment, then the mask fell again, but it had been long enough for him to recall the last time he had seen such an expression on a human face, many years ago, in Edinburgh. He glanced down at her hands, which were clasped in her lap. The thumbs were ceaselessly circling each other, betraying an inner tension that bore no relation to her features, once again calm and smiling.

For the rest of the evening, he responded automatically to conversation, and refilled his brandy-glass frequently, in a vain attempt to drown the nightmare that was struggling to the surface of his mind. He found himself unable to take his eyes off Alice, watching for the mask to slip again, but it never did. Her expression remained bland as she chatted to Julia with every appearance of enjoyment.

The party broke up just after midnight. Julia returned to La Bergerie and the Franklins went home, happy in the thought that they had found a way of terminating their odd-job man's employment without hurting his feelings.

As she prepared to leave with Alice, Cybèle said softly to Charles, 'Since I came back, we've hardly had a chance to talk. I find myself missing you!'

'You've had so much to occupy you. We'll get together soon, Cybèle.'

'Indeed, I hope so. We have a great deal to discuss.' She paused. 'The discovery of my daughters will not make any difference to my plans for us.'

The words sounded suspiciously like a threat.

Later, in the attic into which he had moved when he gave up his own room to Klaus, Charles sat on the edge of his bed, and he was frightened.

The picture of Alice's malignant face rose before him, and what was most disturbing was the target of her animosity. Suppose history were to repeat itself, this time with Julia as the victim? Oh, God, he thought, not again!

He rested his elbows on his knees and put his head in his hands.

How could he possibly tell Cybèle, on the evidence of a

single moment, that he suspected one of her new-found daughters might be mentally unstable?

He began to pace backwards and forwards and the walls seemed to close in on him. Quietly, he went downstairs. The mill was silent, apart from sounds of sleep from some of the bedrooms. He walked out on to the terrace. The night air was warm. The sky was clear and starry, trees rustled and the stream rippled over its stones. Normally, he would have breathed deeply, let the tranquillity wash over him and felt tense muscles relax, but tonight he found no peace.

As he walked to the wall he heard a soft voice: 'You cannot sleep either, Charles?'

Klaus Fischer was sitting in one of the chairs, still fully dressed, a glass in his hand. There was a bottle of whisky and a jug of water on the table in front of him. 'I have helped myself to a drink. You will join me?'

Charles poured himself a Scotch and sat down.

'An interesting evening,' Klaus said. 'But it appeared to me that you were not happy towards the end. I hope nothing went wrong?'

Charles suddenly felt an urge to talk. Bringing his apprehensions into the open might enable him to see them in a less menacing perspective, and he liked and trusted Klaus.

'I'm . . . worried,' he said. 'It's possible that my imagination is working overtime because of something that happened years ago.' He hesitated, 'Did you notice anything tonight that would make you suspect that Alice has taken a violent dislike to Julia Leander?'

'You are meaning the way Alice looked at her across the table. Yes, I noticed. And I thought that it was more than dislike. There was a . . .' He sought for a word: '. . . a malevolence that was frightening.'

'But dammit, there's no reason for it. They've only just met!'

'I also thought that perhaps I had imagined it, but if we both saw the same thing . . . You mentioned something that happened years ago?'

Charles sipped his drink. Then, looking sightlessly into the darkness, he talked for the first time since leaving Britain about the past which had nearly destroyed him. At first the words came quickly, then as he forced the memories to surface, more slowly and painfully. 'It was seven years ago. My wife and I were living in Edinburgh, where I practised as a psychiatrist. Laura was a social worker . . .'

Because they were childless, their work had increasingly invaded their private lives. In the evenings, watching TV or listening to music, Charles often agonized about how little help he could give to his patients, many of whom lived in a secret world of suffering which he seemed to be incapable of relieving. Each became his personal crusade. Laura, too, found it difficult not to become involved with her charges and would even, when their situations were particularly difficult, bring them into her home to stay for a while.

'There was this fifteen-year-old boy, Mark. He had a violent, drunken father who regularly beat him, and eventually died after a pub brawl. The mother was incapable of controlling Mark and he'd twice been in institutions for young offenders when he was assigned to Laura.

'She was desperately sorry for him, and brought him home. He told us he truly regretted his behaviour and intended to go straight.' He stopped.

'And did he?'

'Yes. He settled down and we liked him. At first he talked about finding somewhere else to live, but he seemed to be getting on so well that we didn't press it. Then, after he'd been with us for two months, Laura discovered she was pregnant. We'd been married for ten years and had almost given up hope of a child, so we were delighted, but we had to tell Mark that we'd need his room for the baby.'

He would never forget the spasm of hatred that had crossed Mark's face as he stared at them, so intense that it was like a knife-thrust. The look Alice had directed at Julia had been no less savage.

His voice sank to a whisper. 'The next morning, when I was downstairs in my consulting room, Mark murdered Laura. He stabbed her in the stomach a dozen times. I heard her screaming. When I got there, he was smiling. He said, "I got rid of it. Now I can stay in my room." '

'*Ach, Gott!*' Klaus breathed. 'She died?'

'Oh, yes. Mark was convicted and sent to a maximum security mental hospital. Three months later, I sold my house and everything we'd owned except the old Mercedes, and came to France.'

After a long silence, Klaus said quietly, 'There is no point now in my giving you sympathy for that dreadful event, but you have my admiration for the way you have come through it. I can understand your concern about Alice, but, Charles, there has been nothing to indicate that she has any tendency towards violence. Perhaps she is just a little jealous, reluctant to share her mother's affection with Julia. She will get over it.'

Charles sighed. 'Now I've talked about it, I'm sure you're right. I've over-reacted. I guess I'm influenced by my own guilt because I didn't recognize Mark as a psychopath.'

Klaus was shocked. 'You surely don't think Alice could be a – psychopath?'

He avoided the question. 'I just wish we knew a little more about her background.'

'She seems a gentle enough woman, too meek and eager to please, if anything; but we will observe her, yes? And you will keep an eye on Julia, I am sure.'

Charles couldn't see his features in the darkness, but heard a smile in his voice. Having shared it, some of his disquiet had faded. Too much to drink during the evening, the resurgence of guilt, the effect of his meeting with Julia, which he had not yet dared to analyse, had all combined to produce a heightened reaction to a momentary facial expression – perhaps no more than a muscular spasm.

'I will,' he said. 'Klaus, no-one knows what I did before I came here. I'd like to keep it that way. I'm afraid the kids would be a lot less willing to share their troubles if they knew I'd been a – a professional listener. And I particularly do not want to talk about Laura.'

'Of course. And I thank you for your trust.' He rose stiffly.

'Now I will go upstairs, and in the daylight tomorrow, we will see that there is really nothing to worry about.'

But as Charles lay in bed, vainly seeking sleep, phrases from the past came into his mind and there was no comfort in them.

Psychopaths begin as children who feel themselves rejected or cruelly treated. Cybèle had told him Alice's childhood had not been happy.

A psychopath is very good at flattering people in order to achieve his end. Alice had instantly recognized and responded to Cybèle's need for admiration and respect.

The psychopath can't love . . . He coldly takes what he wants, with violence if necessary, and grasps it without guilt. As Mark had tried to do.

Successful therapy for the character disorder known as psychopathy has proved all but impossible . . .

Finally, he remembered the chilling words of an American psychiatrist, Robert Lindner: *'There walk among us men and women who are in but not of our world . . . Often the sign by which they betray themselves is crime . . . of an explosive, impulsive, reckless type.'*

5

At the villa, Cybèle and Alice were in the living-room.

'That was some party!' Alice sighed. 'I never went to one like it. Oh, I'm gonna enjoy myself here, I just know it!' Unaccustomed amounts of champagne and brandy had combined to flush her face, and her voice had a strident note Cybèle had not heard before.

'Charles McDonald is an excellent host, and it was a great pleasure being able to welcome Julia,' she said. (And me, Alice thought. It was *my* party, remember?) 'A small whisky and then I'm going to bed. I don't imagine you'll want one.'

Her tone sobered Alice. 'No, thank you.' Then she said eagerly, 'Let me pour yours. Sit down and rest. You look tired.'

'I am not in the least tired.' She walked to the table, where decanters and glasses were set out.

With remorseless sympathy, Alice went on, 'I notice that you're limping a bit. Do you have a touch of rheumatism, or something?'

'Neither rheumatism nor anything else. And I must tell you, my dear, that I find discussions about my own or anybody else's health intensely boring.' She sank carefully into a chair below her portrait. She *was* tired, but had no intention of admitting it. She was also feeling distinctly out of sorts. The party, as far as she was concerned, had not been a total success. Charles had hardly spoken to her throughout the evening and Alice's attentions were starting to irritate her. I will *not* be treated like an old woman, she thought savagely.

Her mind drifted back over the day. She and Julia had been together for most of it, and Julia had described her life, showing no trace of self-pity or resentment for the way she had been abandoned. As Alice had sat beside them, taking little part in the conversation, Cybèle had felt a growing fondness for this other daughter. She was intelligent and well-educated, with a sense of humour and, despite her gentleness, a mind of her own. In fact, given a few years' training, was she not the kind of woman who might be capable of taking over the Cybèle empire? The thought was exciting. As a writer and illustrator, she must already know something about publishing. Unlike her twin, she had a strong sense of style, and her obvious ability to get on with all kinds of people would be an asset.

Alice's voice broke through her musing. 'I do love that portrait, Cybèle. It's the one your second husband had painted, isn't it? Gee, you must miss him a lot!'

'I don't miss him in the least, as you should realize if you read my book.'

There was a brief pause, then Alice said softly, 'I'm afraid

I just forgot, because I was thinking how lonely I am without my poor Hank.' She blinked tears into her eyes.

'Yes, well, I don't believe in looking back.' Cybèle rose. 'I'm going to sit outside for a while. I'm sure you want to go to bed.'

'I'll keep you company . . .'

'No need. I'll see you in the morning.' It was a clear dismissal.

When Alice had gone, she settled in a chair on the terrace. With time and solitude to consider her idea, it seemed increasingly feasible. She would retain control of her companies, but Julia would run them in London and Paris, under her guidance. She dismissed any notion that Julia might have her own ideas about the future. No-one would be foolish enough to pass up the opportunity for power and riches with which she was about to be presented.

Observing Suzy during the past days had led Cybèle to the conclusion that she was not, in fact, setting herself up as a rival for Charles's affections. Her manner with him remained casually friendly, as it was with the younger men – with the exception of Christian Morel, whom she clearly disliked. She, too, might repay grooming for future stardom within the company.

I am, she thought with wry humour, about to found a dynasty.

She lifted her eyes to the painting beyond the french windows. It was dominated by her own figure in the foreground. To one side, looking at her with an air of arrogant possession, was George Meredith, who had become her second husband. He had commissioned the portrait early in their relationship and, since she was still married to David Stone at the time, it had created something of a scandal. The artist had described the picture as a 'conversation-piece', and hadn't understood its implications. After George's death she had kept it on her wall only because it was a satisfyingly flattering portrayal of herself.

Now she whispered, 'George, you bastard, I've got your money and your title and now I have a family. A whole new life is opening up, and you have no part in it, because you're dead!'

Was it her imagination, or did the man in the painting seem to shrink and lose his arrogance? George had feared death. He had jogged and played strenuous games and lifted weights in order to stay fit, had given up smoking and drinking as age had crept up on him, had insisted on a high-protein, low-cholesterol diet. And had died of a massive heart-attack on the squash-court at the age of sixty. His appalled opponent had informed Cybèle that the expression on his face in death had been one of sheer terror.

She had managed a conventional appearance of mourning at his funeral, but her main emotion had been a lightness of heart she had been hard put to disguise. Only when she came to write her book had she felt free to express the pure pleasure she had felt in widowhood.

6

Extract from *I am Cybèle*

I decided to marry George Meredith because there were things I needed from him. The first was the certainty of his continued financial backing. The second was that I had a fancy to become Lady Meredith. It would be the ultimate social achievement of little Sybil Androwski, the seamstress of Le Cirque Dando.

George was not of my mind. He enjoyed his mistresses in Paris and New York and was reluctant to give up his freedom, although I was sure that my physical attraction for him outweighed theirs. Now that I was unencumbered by a husband, his demands became more urgent. When he was in London he could hardly bear a night to go by without making love, especailly as I was willing to satisfy even his more bizarre demands.

Sometimes he liked to come into my bedroom and find me wearing a virginal Mother Hubbard night-dress which, proud of his strong hands, he would rip from neck to hem before falling on me savagely in emulation of a rape. We ruined dozens of Harrods' finest cotton lawn night-dresses that way. He also liked me to fight him and scream for help so he could use his strength to subdue me. Mindful of neighbours, to whom he was indifferent, I made sure my shrieks were muted.

There were other times when he pretended I was a whore and made me dress in black lace underwear, my breasts bare, sheer black stockings on my legs.

I put up with his fancies because I hoped they were binding him more closely to me, and even pretended to enjoy the play-acting, but as far as marriage was concerned, he was slippery as an eel.

Outside the bedroom, he was generous and sophisticated company and it was a pleasure to be escorted by him. His size and his self-confidence ensured instant attention from waiters, shop-assistants and taxi-drivers.

His accent was faultlessly upper-crust and it was a long time before I discovered that he came from a working-class family and had been brought up in London's East End. One of his weaknesses was to pretend that his background was landed gentry, and as he was building up his fortune, he had adopted most of their pastimes. He shot grouse in Scotland in August and pheasant in Hampshire during the winter and rented a boat on the Spey for salmon and fished the Test for trout. He went to Ascot and Henley and Wimbledon and Covent Garden and Glyndebourne, had his shirts made in Jermyn Street, his suits in Savile Row. He kept a yacht on the Hamble, which he rarely used, and occasionally flew to Spain to stay at the Marbella Club. His Paris mistress was a countess and the one in New York was heiress to a department-store fortune.

Together with money-making and women, his third interest

was social climbing. Having virtually bought his knighthood, his final ambition was a life peerage.

My own career was flourishing. With the first Cybèle boutique a success, I persuaded him to finance a second in Edinburgh, a third in Dublin. All made a handsome profit.

Our first disagreement came when I decided to open a shop in Paris. 'France isn't Britain . . .' (*He* was telling *me*!) 'French women know about clothes. They don't want designer labels on second-rate goods.'

'We are not selling second-rate goods. Different, and slightly less expensive than in the salons. Catering for a different market. Women who can't afford ridiculous prices, but will pay for quality, plus a designer name.' I was patient, but he remained unconvinced.

'I'll think about it,' he said, and dismissed the subject.

I could have financed the shop on my own, but always kept David's advice in my mind. Let someone else take the risk. Anyhow, I wasn't in a hurry. With my work at the magazine, and the three boutiques I already had, my time was full. My international reputation had increased and I was constantly being asked to pronounce on fashion trends for publications in New York, Berlin, Paris and Rome. Careerwise, I had achieved almost everything I had dreamed of.

What it seemed that I could not achieve was marriage to George Meredith. As the months passed his sexual passion remained undiminished, but we still maintained our separate establishments, my house in Hampstead and his Park Lane apartment. We were generally accepted as a couple and one was rarely invited anywhere without the other. Nevertheless, I never felt wholly confident of my hold over him.

It was a fourteen-year-old schoolgirl who finally brought us together. Her name was Carmen and she came to clean George's flat one day when her mother, his daily help, was ill.

I had spent the night in the flat and George and I were together when she turned up. He was still in his dressing-gown.

She was small and round and pretty, with bold eyes, pouting

lips and well-developed breasts. Her hair was black and glossy and she wore dangling ear-rings.

She set to work willingly enough, covering her jeans and blouse with a freshly ironed overall, replacing her shoes with an old pair of red slippers.

I left for my office at the magazine after arranging to meet George at the flat at lunchtime and go on to a private view in a Mayfair art gallery.

I got back before mid-day, earlier than I had expected. As I let myself in, I heard sobbing from George's bedroom. Carmen was lying on his bed, naked, one plump arm hiding her face.

George came from the bathroom, holding a towel. He was wearing only his pyjama top and his face was pallid.

We stared at each other, then he said thickly, 'The little bitch asked for it! From the moment you left, she threw herself at me.'

From the bed, a high-pitched voice hiccupped: 'I never did! He – he raped me!' She sat up, her face swollen and red, eye-liner smudged on her cheeks.

'She told me she'd done it lots of times! Shit, she was a virgin!'

'What'll my Mum say? And my Dad?' She rolled off the bed, George tossed her the towel and she clutched it between her legs. 'It was horrible!'

'Get your clothes on,' I said. 'And you will not tell your mother or your father. This never happened, do you understand?'

But Carmen showed herself a child of her times, streetwise and cunning. 'Only it did, didn't it? He raped me and I'm not fifteen until next month. He could go to prison. I'm going to tell my Dad and he'll call the police.' She paused, then added, 'Unless you give me something . . .'

For once George seemed incapable of thinking clearly. He simply stood, blinking at her, pasty-faced and trembling.

'I told you, it didn't happen,' I said. 'I've been here all the time, so how could it?'

'You never! You've been out.'

'No. I was here. Do you really think the police would believe you rather than Sir George and me?'

All she could think of was to repeat, 'I'll tell my Dad.'

'If you like,' I said indifferently. 'Tell him to come and see Sir George. I think we can persuade him you're lying.'

'I want some money or I'll go to a doctor! He'll know. They can tell what's happened. It happened to my friend Sandra, and her Mum took her to the doctor . . .'

'If you were raped, it was some boy you've been with.'

'It never was!'

'Well, it certainly wasn't Sir George. Get dressed, and go home. Just forget the whole thing. If you make a fuss, *you're* the one who's likely to be sent to a – what do they call it? – a young offenders' institution.'

Her clothes were in a heap on the floor. As she made a grab for them, I steered George out of the room. He moved like a zombie.

'Christ, I feel sick,' he muttered. 'Her age . . . I had no idea. I thought . . . sixteen, at least. She . . . we were fooling around, and then – it was too late to stop. I tell you, she asked for it.'

I had no difficulty picturing the scene: the nubile little girl flaunting herself in front of this attractive, titled older man, thinking how she could boast about it later to her friends. She had led him on, let him fondle her, assuming she could say 'Stop!' as she did to boys her own age. And George, amused at first, then aroused by her youth, accepting her assertion that she had 'done it before', falling on her. He would have been excited, not inhibited, by her struggles.

'I'll give her money, it's the only thing that'll keep her quiet,' he said.

'Don't be bloody silly!' I snapped. 'You give her money and everyone will know there was a reason. Let her go and if she talks, we simply deny the whole thing and I'll say I was here all the time.'

'Oh, Christ, Cybèle . . .' He was almost in tears.

I patted his shoulder. 'It'll be all right, George. She won't

247

talk, and neither will I. No-one else need know that you raped a fourteen-year-old girl.'

We looked at each other. He needed my silence. If anything were to happen between us which would tempt me to break it, it could mean, at worst, a sordid prosecution, at best, social humiliation.

A month later, we were married at the Caxton Hall Registrar's Office and I began planning my boutique in Paris.

George recovered from his fright. Confident that as his wife I would not jeopardize my own position by giving him away, resenting the fact that I had trapped him into marriage, he dropped back into his old ways, flying regularly to Paris and New York to resume relations with his mistresses. I found myself annoyed by this as I never had been before we were married. I was not concerned that he slept with them, but that now they were invading *my* life, and my name was being linked with theirs in the sleazier gossip-columns.

He still came into my bed whenever he felt like it and each time his violent love-making was akin to rape. Although he hurt me, I never protested, knowing that indifference was my most effective weapon.

We managed to keep up an appearance of amity when we were in public, but any liking we'd once had for each other soured into mutual animosity. Life became a series of clashes in which each of us fought to maintain the upper hand. It seems odd when I look back that we never even discussed divorce, but this was possibly because our lives were so entangled, emotionally and financially, that separating them was more than we could contemplate.

As during my marriage to David, I had the occasional affair, only this time they were to assert my right to a freedom equal with George's rather than to satisfy any sexual urge. They made him very angry, because he couldn't bear the thought that people might suspect his love-making no longer satisfied me.

It wasn't easy living with a man I disliked so much but before it became unbearable, he died and I inherited his fortune.

The feeling I had was akin to that of a boxer who has won in the final round.

7

When Charles came downstairs the morning after the party, the volunteers had all gone about their business on the farm.

Fischer was sitting alone on the terrace. Charles poured himself a cup of coffee and joined him. 'Thanks for listening to me last night. You were probably right. I might have done poor Alice a grave injustice.'

'Probably, but I have a suggestion which could set your mind at rest. I hope you will not think this an interference . . .'

'Of course not. Go ahead.'

'I have a friend in New York, a professional researcher named Neil Simmonds. We met several years ago when he did some work for one of our authors. He has stayed with me in Berlin and I last saw him when I was in New York a few weeks ago. He's a young man, very bright, very discreet, who is employed by publishers and authors needing research which they have neither the time nor the inclination to undertake. It occurred to me that we might ask him informally to check on Alice's background. No-one need know, apart from ourselves, unless he discovers something . . . something . . .'

'Something Cybèle should know, for her own protection? It's a good idea, but where would he start? We don't even know where she lived.'

'I saw a letter from her waiting to be collected. It was addressed to a Miss Bibi Jackson, care of Nathan Weitz, Menswear, in New York. It would be a beginning, *ja*?'

8

Life for Arnie Gold had improved since he had taken up his post as odd-job man to Henry and Emily Franklin.

He was sitting in a comfortable chair in his room above the Franklins' garage, a glass of red wine beside him. On his table were the remains of a chicken casserole which Emily had provided for his lunch.

If it wasn't for his determination to make Sybil pay up, he decided, he could be happy here indefinitely. The work wasn't too arduous, and he only had to clutch his back and utter a muted groan when Emily was near for her to insist that he should take a rest. His room was comfortable and although it contained cooking facilities, she frequently brought him helpings from their own meals.

Unfortunately, the Squadron-Leader (as he called Henry with oleaginous respect) was showing signs of impatience. There wasn't a great deal for Arnie to do in the garden, apart from mowing, sweeping the terrace and raking the gravel drive. Emily had created an English cottage garden around the villa but after he had pulled up some of her half-grown plants, mistaking them for weeds, she had ordered him not to touch the flower-beds. Now he had been set to scrape down and repaint the window-frames. The Squadron-Leader had suggested that he might perhaps look for work elsewhere when he had finished.

That would be the time for him to pay his visit to Sybil.

From listening to his employers' conversations he had learned that she was a kind of queen-bee among the local expatriates. The previous evening, the Franklins had been to a party at which she had been present, and he had heard Emily remark how gracious she had been. Gracious! Little Sybil, whose squirming body underneath him he could sometimes still feel in erotic dreams!

He was considering how best to approach her when he heard Emily calling.

He carried his empty plate down the exterior staircase that led to the back of the garage, where she was waiting for him.

'Delicious, Mrs Franklin!' he said. 'You cook like a Frenchwoman, and I can't say better than that, can I?'

'Thank you, Alfred . . .' (He had to remind himself every day that the Franklins knew him as Alfred Brown, not Arnold Gold.) 'I wanted to see you because we've found someone else who could use your help when you finish here. Are you still planning to stay on in La Bergerie?'

'It's possible, madam,' he said cautiously, not wanting to close any doors just in case Syb should take a while to come across. 'With whom would it be?' In his new persona, he had adopted what he believed to be the manner and accent of a family retainer.

'You've heard us mention our friend Lady Meredith?'

His eyebrows shot up. 'I believe so.'

'With the festival coming up, she will have lots of odd jobs. You could finish your work here, then go to her. Charles McDonald says he can give you accommodation at his mill.'

'I'd be delighted, madam,' he said formally.

He had difficulty containing his elation. Couldn't be better. Only once he got to Sybil's, he wouldn't be doing any odd jobs. He'd be lying back in the lap of luxury.

Emily, who loved to gossip, said, 'An extraordinary thing has happened. Lady Meredith hasn't seen her two daughters since just after they were born, and they've both turned up at Le Bas-Fond, one from America and one from London. They'd never met, but they'd read an autobiography she wrote recently and realized she was their mother. They're staying with her now . . .' She saw that Arnie's mouth had fallen open. 'Is something wrong?'

He swallowed, but his voice was husky. 'Her – daughters?'

'Twins. Lady Meredith seems so happy that they've been reunited.'

251

'That's – nice. For her, I mean, if she hasn't . . . What a coincidence . . .' He was aware that he was babbling.

'Isn't it? And now, if your back's all right, Alfred, perhaps you'll carry on with the painting.'

'Certainly, madam.' He spoke mechanically and was relieved when she went back into the house.

What a bloody turn-up this was! Twin daughters. *His* daughters! This would take a bit of thinking about. What could be in it for old Arnie? There must be some way he could use it to his advantage. For instance, if Sybil cut up rough he could appeal to the girls' sympathies. Girls, hell! They'd be in their forties. Might even be wealthy and only too delighted to contribute to their Dad's well-being. In fact, he *could* be looking forward to a very, very comfortable future.

This, he thought, calls for a little celebration.

That evening, he knocked at the Franklins' front door and sketched a salute when Henry opened it. 'Evening, Squadron-Leader, just thought I'd let you know I'm going into La Bergerie for an hour or two. I wondered if you might see your way clear to a little advance?'

'Of course, Alfred. Nearly the end of the week, isn't it?' Henry did a quick calculation and handed over a bundle of francs. 'That should see you through.'

'Truly grateful, sir. Just a glass of wine or two, for old times' sake. If you felt like joining me . . . ?'

'Thanks, but not tonight. I understand from my wife that you'll be moving on to Lady Meredith's.'

'Very kind of you to mention me to her. I'm looking forward to meeting the lady.'

'I'm sure you'll get on like a house afire,' Henry said mendaciously. 'Good night, then, and enjoy your evening.'

La Bergerie had the deserted air peculiar to small French towns after dark. By eight-thirty even the *boules* players had left the square.

The only place showing signs of life was the Hôtel des Fleurs, where several youths with leather jackets slung over their shoulders were lounging around the front door. Arnie recognized the hotelier's unpleasant son among them and turned into a side-street, making his way towards the café at which the Franklins had bought him breakfast.

There was only one customer, a large young Frenchman who was leaning against the bar, a beer in front of him.

Arnie ordered a glass of red wine and took it to a table. This wasn't the most cheerful place for a celebration, but it was the only one he knew apart from the hotel.

The other customer was chatting with the barman about the forthcoming festival, which was all anyone seemed to talk about these days.

Arnie heard him say, 'It should be a good show. Everyone in town seems to be involved.'

'We're organizing a relay race, local people against the foreign residents.' The barman lowered his voice. 'I hear our boys have a few tricks up their sleeves.'

'Tricks?'

He winked. 'We won the Hundred Years' War, can't lose to the British this time, can we? I haven't seen you here before, m'sieu. New in the district?'

'Just a visitor.'

'Will you be staying for the festival?'

'Probably. So the locals are making sure they'll win?'

Realizing that he had been indiscreet, the barman said hastily, 'Only a rumour. Probably nothing in it. Another beer?'

'Thanks.'

Arnie felt a need for company. He took his empty glass to the bar for a refill. ''Evening,' he said. 'I heard you talking, m'sieu. May I join you seeing we're both on our own?'

Rather to his chagrin, being proud of his French, the young man said in English, 'Certainly. You're on vacation?'

'Staying with some friends.' He put out his hand, 'Name's Alfred Brown.'

'Christian Morel.'

'Nice part of the world this.'

'You know it well?'

'Passed through during the war. I was with the Resistance, actually.'

'So you are renewing old friendships?'

'In a manner of speaking.' He grinned. 'Hoping to renew one in particular. A lady.'

They bought each other a couple of drinks, then Morel rose.

'Think I'll stay on for one or two more,' Arnie said expansively. 'Haven't had a good raisey-glassy like this for a long time. Are you sure you won't . . . no? Well, nice to have met you. Might run into each other again some time.'

When Morel had gone, he sat down at a table. Inevitably, his thoughts turned back to his forthcoming meeting with Sybil and his two daughters.

With wine had come confidence. He saw himself marching into her house and the crumbling of her arrogance when she realized he meant business. He saw the delight of his daughters when he told them who he was. His entrance should be accompanied by music. Circus music, a fanfare, then one of old Sousa's great marches: *Washington Post, Gladiator, El Capitan*. He hummed under his breath: 'Pom, pom, tiddle-iddle, om-pom-pom-pom, OM-pom- pom . . .' and was taken back – Christ, so long ago! – to Le Cirque Dando.

He closed his eyes and saw again the Grand Parade. Billy in black breeches, scarlet coat and top-hat. Girls in sequins and feathers. The Amazing Androwskis, stars of the show, in their gold leotards with red trimmings. Himself, striding tall and straight, handsome with his black hair and pencil-line moustache, swarming up the ladder, then flying and somer-saulting free as a bird, using the air as his natural habitat. The applause: that was the best part, hearing the audience roar, being *loved*.

They were good times. He had been crazy about Etta then and couldn't believe his luck when, after Lajos's death, she said she'd marry him. He remembered the big, soft, cushiony body into which he would sink . . .

He looked down into his glass, was surprised to see a tear plop into the wine and feel wet tracks down his cheeks. Why the hell should he be crying? The good times were coming again, weren't they?

As Christian drove back to Le Bas-Fond he was thinking about what the barman had said: 'Our boys have a few tricks up their sleeves . . .' He must warn Charles McDonald that some chicanery was afoot.

He had switched from drinking beer to red wine with Arnie, and was feeling slightly drunk. Also depressed, because he was going to have to apologize to Suzy Leander for his accusations. He had avoided her all day, and even alone in the car the memory of the fantasy he had concocted after seeing her in La Bergerie with Julia made him feel hot with embarrassment. Their relationship had got off on the wrong foot the first day they met, and since then it had been downhill all the way. After she had fallen in the lane and he had picked her up, there had been a moment when things might have changed . . . Forget that! he told himself. Olivia had reported that she had a man in London. She wasn't a girl who would ever go short of an admirer, probably had to brush them away like midges on a summer evening. It wouldn't be any fun joining a swarm like that.

She was arrogant, irritating, imperious, too sure of herself, and didn't mean a damn thing to him, so why was he making such a big deal of saying sorry? Why did it matter what she thought?

Because she was one of the most attractive women he had ever met, that's why.

But she wasn't for him, and anyhow, he had other fish to fry. He had almost completed his interviews with Cybèle. It only remained to reveal that he knew the truth about her behaviour in Paris during the war, and see what she had to say.

Maybe he wouldn't even wait for the festival, but go back to Paris as soon as possible, write his story, free himself of his obligation to his mother and dismiss Suzy Leander from his mind.

He reached the turn-off to Le Bas-Fond and slowed as the surface became rougher.

After a few hundred yards, he saw Suzy's Volvo parked by the verge.

Then his headlights picked up a group of people. There was

255

a body lying on the ground and three men wearing helmets and goggles were surrounding a woman, their hands grabbing at her clothing. He heard her scream as she fought them, and realized it was Suzy.

He skidded to a halt, grabbed a tyre-lever from under his seat, leaped out of the MG and raced forward.

He shouted. The struggling group broke up. For a moment, the men held their ground, then they saw the weapon in his hand, and ran. He started in pursuit, but there was a roar of motor-cycles as they shot off into the night.

When he turned, Suzy was kneeling on the ground, her arm around Klaus Fischer's shoulders. Her hair was wild, her white shirt ripped open to the waist so it barely covered her breasts.

Gently, they lifted the old man to his feet. He stood shakily on his crippled leg, and suppressed a groan when he tried to put the other foot to the ground.

Christian carried him to the Volvo and edged him on to the back seat, where he lay with his eyes closed.

Suzy's body was trembling. He put his arms around her and she clung to him. He stroked her hair. 'It's all over. You're OK. Do you wish to tell me about it?'

She moved back, breathed deeply and said, 'We must get Klaus home. He needs a doctor. Those bastards kicked him.' She hesitated. 'I feel a bit shaky. Would you drive us?' He wondered what it cost her to ask for his help.

As they moved off, she said, 'They followed us from La Bergerie. They passed us on the main road, and were waiting here.'

'What were you doing in La Bergerie? You were at the mill when I left.'

'Julia's lent her car to Charles until his is repaired. She spent the day with Cybèle and Alice then came to the mill for supper. I was driving her back to the hotel and I suggested that Klaus might like to come with us. He hasn't been off the property since he arrived. It never occurred to me that there would be any danger. That damn town's usually deserted at night.'

'Did you recognize any of the men?'

256

'They were hanging around their motor-bikes near the hotel, but they were in the shadow of the big tree and I couldn't see their faces. I'd guess one of them was Sézille's son.'

'We must tell the police as soon as possible.'

'I don't think they'll be much help. Sézille seems to have them in his pocket. They didn't want to know when Charles reported the damage to his car. And the trouble is, I can't positively identify them.'

'What happened in the lane?'

'There was a motor-bike blocking the way. I had to pull up. They came out of the bushes, opened the passenger door and dragged Klaus out. They pushed him down and started kicking him . . .'

'Suzy tried to stop them.' The old man's voice was weak. 'She was very brave. I believe I fainted, because I was not even aware that you had arrived, Christian.'

The lights of Le Bas-Fond were ahead of them. Tightening his grip on the wheel, furious that he had let the attackers escape, Chris glanced at Suzy and said tightly, 'Did they hurt you?'

'They didn't have time, thanks to you . . .' She suddenly became aware of her semi-nudity, pulled the edges of her shirt together and managed a smile. 'As you told me, nakedness on a beach is different.'

'If you can make a joke, I think you must be feeling better.' He hesitated, then the words came in a rush: 'I was coming back to see you. I have to ask you to forgive me for what I said about you and your mother.'

After a pause which seemed to him to be ominously long, she said: 'I shouldn't have embarrassed you the way I did last night. Julia said she could understand what made you think we might be frauds, turning up at Le Bas-Fond the way we did, out of the blue.'

'So is it possible we might start our – relationship again? Perhaps to be friends?'

'I think we could give it a try.'

Rob, the doctor, announced that Fischer was shocked and

bruised and his knee was badly swollen, but no bones were broken. He must rest, preferably in bed, for several days.

In his room with Charles, Fischer said, 'I'm afraid my presence here causes nothing but trouble. Those young men were after me. I regret very much that Suzy was involved. It will be best if I leave as soon as my leg will support me.'

Charles was sitting beside his bed. 'If you feel you must, I can't argue. You've had a horrible experience. But we'll all be sorry to see you go.'

'Thank you. I hope a reply to my letter will arrive from Simmonds while I'm still here. By the way, some good has come out of this episode: Christian and Suzy have become friends.'

'I'm pleased to hear it . . . though I know one person who won't be.'

'The little round-eyed Olivia? Ah, she is not suitable for him. He is a clever young man with a streak of real toughness beneath the charm. He needs a girl who can stand up to him.'

Charles grinned. 'I foresee a pretty turbulent relationship, but it should never be boring – my God, what a pair of old gossips we are! We've practically got them married off, and they hardly know each other.'

'It is amusing to speculate, yes? There are many complicated relationships in Le Bas-Fond. It is like a bubbling pot. I think also of Alice Lynam and Lady Meredith, and the beautiful Julia – and you.'

'Why include me? I'm just the lid which tries to keep the pot from boiling over.'

'I notice things. Lady Meredith is lonely, and so are you, I suspect. This is an impertinence, but perhaps it is allowed since we are friends. Are you – interested?'

'In marriage to Cybèle? Good God, no! May I tell you something in confidence? I might be leaving here soon. You know she wants to start a winery, with me as her partner?'

'She has mentioned it. You do not like the idea?'

'I said I'd think about it, but I couldn't bear to watch the place being turned into an industry. Cybèle is a business-woman. She thrives on constant activity and she doesn't care

258

who suffers as long as she gets what she wants. I couldn't live like that. I only hope that she doesn't ride rough-shod over Ju – over her daughters.'

'I'm sure Julia has the strength to cope with her. She is a rather special person.'

'I think so, too.' He rose. 'I'll let you sleep now, and remember, if you change your mind about leaving before the festival, we would all be delighted.'

9

As predicted, La Bergerie's police showed little interest in Suzy's report of the attack, saying that since she could not identify any member of the gang, there was nothing they could do. Jacques Millet did not fail to point out that the continued presence of a German at Le Bas-Fond was highly provocative.

Julia spent most days with Cybèle and Alice and dined either with them or at the mill. Charles had banned Suzy from driving into the town at night and happily took on the task of chauffeuring Julia back to the hotel.

As they were strolling along the river-bank after supper one night, she told him, 'Cybèle asked me again to move in with her and Alice, but I've refused. I really need a bolt-hole. In large doses, Cybèle can be a little – over-powering. I'm not in danger in La Bergerie – it would be very foolish of a hotelier to allow one of his guests to be attacked. It's Suzy I'm worried about. Now she's got over the shock, she's so angry I'm afraid she might try to force a show-down with the Sézille boy.'

'I wouldn't worry about that. Since she and Chris Morel declared a cessation of hostilities, he's attached himself to her like sticking-plaster. He won't let her go off the property alone.'

'I like him, don't you? He's nicer than the last man she had an affair with – not that I think it's gone that far with Chris.'

She raised an eyebrow and added, 'But I'm watching for signs and portents.'

'What happened to the last man?'

'She gave him the push just before she left England. He was a humourless, self-satisfied snob. It was a relief to hear she'd come to her senses.'

'I've always enjoyed watching the progress of Le Bas-Fond's romances. You'd be surprised how many have started here.'

'I wouldn't be surprised at all. You seem to be able to bring all kinds of people together in harmony.'

There was a full moon and the air was soft and warm. Above them, the lights of the mill made it look like an ocean liner and ahead they could see Cybèle's villa outlined against the trees. The only sound was the splash of water over stones.

Charles slipped his arm through hers. She smiled up at him, thinking that it was a long time since she had met a man she liked so much.

'Talking of harmony, how are you getting on with Cybèle?' he asked.

'Very well. We talk endlessly. Today I asked her about our father, but it's as she said in her book: she doesn't know whether it was her step-father or her young German lover, since she was sleeping with them alternately. And she doesn't care. She's convinced that Arnie Gold died in a concentration camp and she has no idea what happened to the German. She doesn't even remember his full name, only that his Christian name was Adolf.' She added reflectively, 'I must say that of the two he'd be my choice.'

'Does it bother you, not knowing?'

'Not in the least. I loved my adoptive father and while I fully accept that Cybèle is my mother, I can't picture myself as the daughter of either of those men.'

'How does Alice feel?'

'She hasn't said anything about it.'

'Has she told you much about herself?'

'She doesn't talk a great deal, but it's fascinating, and rather sad, finding out how different her life and mine have been.'

'You've never sensed any – antagonism on her part?'

'No, of course not. But . . .' She stopped.

'But what?'

'She's never anything but friendly, and it's delightful to have a sister, but my upbringing was so happy and luxurious compared with hers that it must be difficult for her not to feel some resentment.'

'She's looking more like you every day,' Charles remarked. 'Yesterday she was wearing a pair of white trousers and a red shirt exactly like yours.'

'She bought them in Bergerac. I've always thought the obsessive twin thing, two people dressing and behaving alike, especially as adults, was a bit distasteful. But it isn't like that with Alice. I think she's genuinely trying to improve herself, and Cybèle hasn't been very tactful about the clothes she brought from America.'

He was aware again of the unease which had settled on him after he had intercepted Alice's hate-filled glance at Julia on the night of the party. Neither he nor Fischer had seen any further manifestation of a psychopathic personality, but now it occurred to him that there was something distinctly unhealthy about her eagerness to transform herself into a replica of her sister.

Odd things he had noticed, each insignificant in itself, coalesced in his mind. Alice had cut her hair into a fringe like Julia's and had taken to using the same kind of make-up: a coral lipstick and pale green eyeshadow, very different from the heavy layer of cosmetics she had worn at first. She was attempting – not always successfully – an English accent and he had noticed that she was even imitating some of Julia's mannerisms: the way she lifted her voice at the end of a statement so it almost became a question, the low gurgle of laughter when she was amused.

Was all this, as Julia had said, simply a recognition of her own shortcomings and a desire to learn from a woman she admired? Or could jealousy be at the root of it? Cybèle had made no secret of the fact that she had a greater rapport with Julia than Alice. She had several times showed impatience when Alice had revealed ignorance of a subject under discussion and had not hesitated to put her down.

Alice appeared to be meek, deferential, desperately anxious to please. Was it possible she believed that by making herself over in the image of Julia, she could keep Cybèle's affection to herself?

If she failed, what then?

The spectre of Mark's face, at once smiling and hate-filled, rose before him. Mark had murdered Laura's baby because he had been jealous of it.

A psychopath coldly takes what he wants, with violence if necessary . . . and feels no guilt.

Julia was still talking about her sister. 'Sometimes it's almost as though she's watching me, making mental notes. It's flattering, no-one has ever thought I was worth using as a model before. My daughter frequently tells me I look a mess.'

They were on the bank just below the villa, and paused, looking out over the water, hearing the louder rush of the stream as it joined the river a few hundred yards away.

Almost before he realized what he was doing, Charles had put his arm around her shoulders and drawn her towards him. 'She's wrong. You could never look a mess.' He bent and kissed her. For a moment, her body stiffened. Then she relaxed and her lips parted in eager response. He felt the soft hillocks of her breasts pressing against his shirt, was aware of a genital hardening and intensity of desire he had known all too seldom since Laura's death. His hand slid over her body, fumbling for the buttons of her shirt.

It was a mistake. Too soon. She jerked back and her eyes were wide and startled. She said, 'This is absurd, Charles! Two middle-aged people who hardly know each other behaving like teenagers!'

He took a deep breath to calm himself. 'Could it be that teenagers know the right way to enjoy themselves in the moonlight? And age has nothing to do with it! Have I embarrassed you?'

She turned back along the path, drawing her silk shawl

around her shoulders. Tentatively, he reached for her hand, half-expecting her to withdraw, but she didn't, and her fingers curled through his.

'You haven't embarrassed me in the least. I enjoyed kissing you,' she said frankly.

'May we do it again?'

'Not at the moment. I need time to get used to the idea that I might not be past it – whatever it is – after all.'

As they walked back to the mill, absorbed in their own thoughts, neither of them knew that, from a darkened window in the villa, there had been a sullen, envious witness to their embrace.

As they disappeared into the darkness, Alice switched on the light in her bedroom.

Not only was Julia Leander trying to squeeze her out of Cybèle's favour, she was going after all the available men. She encouraged the young volunteers to hang around her and she was even getting cosy with Klaus Fischer.

He was still bed-ridden at the mill and earlier in the day Alice had visited him. She had been looking forward to an intimate chat, because she knew he really liked her, but Julia was perched on the end of his bed. She'd pretended to be pleased to see Alice but she'd been annoyed, Alice could tell. She wanted *everything* for herself: all the men as well as Cybèle's attention – and, of course, her money.

Suddenly, she was calm again, smiling as she went to the pretty marquetry table in front of the window. She lit a cigarette – Cybèle didn't like her smoking anywhere else in the house – and took her writing materials from the drawer. It was time she caught Bibi Jackson up on the latest news of her good fortune.

Dear Bibi,

Here I am again. Haven't heard from you yet, which is no way to treat your best friend, but I thought I'd write anyway.

Things are still fabulous here. Almost every time we go

out Cybèle buys me some more clothes. I only have to say that I need something, and she shells out.

One peculiar thing has happened. A woman named Julia Leander has turned up, claiming to be my twin sister. I was sort of doubtful about her at first, I mean, whether she wasn't just some sort of con-artist, only it seems that we look so alike we have to be twins.

I'm kind of sorry for her, because it turns out that she had such a disadvantaged childhood compared with me. I never told you this, Bibi, but I was brought up in a great big house with a park all round it and I had my own pony and everything. Julia was poor and her Mom was, to say the least, a Loose Woman!

I think she's trying hard to be like me. You remember how I always had a talent for drawing? Well, she pretends she's an artist, too. It's sort of pathetic. You can see she envies me. Cybèle likes me best so I expect she feels a bit left out. She's got a daughter named Suzy who some people think is pretty, but I think she's common-looking, with reddish hair and slanty eyes. She has a good body, I'll give her that, and doesn't she know it! She flaunts herself in front of the men wearing a bikini that isn't much more than a couple of pieces of ribbon. She calls herself a model – and you know what *that* means!

Remember the German publisher I told you about, who had his eye on me? He's still keen and who knows what might happen? He's loaded!

Would you believe, I have another Admirer, too! He's the Englishman who runs Le Bas-Fond for Cybèle and he's *so* handsome . . . wow! Aren't I lucky? Which one would you advise me to take, Bibi?

Do hope *you* have managed to find yourself someone. Has old Nathan shown any interest?

We had a big welcome party at the mill the other night. I wore my pink and the sequins looked terrific in the lights on the terrace. It was all fabulous, men in tuxedos and all us girls in evening-dress. There were toasts to Cybèle and me and I sat between Klaus and Charles.

Remember that festival I told you about? Our costumes are nearly finished and mine's beautiful. I'm a sort of princess with a long dress which I wear over lots of stiff petticoats. Even though I shouldn't say it, I look pretty good!

Well, that's all for now. Hope this finds you in good shape, as it leaves me – though I don't suppose your life has changed much in old New York. Take care!

With love from your friend, Alice

10

At eight o'clock one evening the week before the festival, a car skidded to a halt at the front door of the mill.

The air was hot and sticky, and the volunteers were lying about on the terrace in various stages of collapse after a hard day's work.

Heads turned as a man hurried around the corner of the house.

'Where, please, is Charles?' he said.

On cue, Charles came from inside, carrying a fruit-laden jug of iced sangria. 'Hans! Nice to see you. Come and join us. A drink?'

Hans Winkel was the Dutch potter who had been invited to join the expatriates' team for the festival relay race. He was a short, shy young man who jogged several kilometres every day and was frequently seen doing press-ups outside the tiny cottage which was his combined home and studio. When he wasn't exercising or relieving stress by meditating, he produced pottery in earth colours and primitive shapes which was displayed on tables outside the cottage and sold well to passing tourists. Everyone liked him and he had thrown himself enthusiastically into preparations for the race, stepping up his training so he had less time than ever for his work. He and Claire had become friends – another incipient romance which everyone at the mill was watching with interest.

'Thank you, no drink. May I see you in private?'

'What's the problem?' Claire said.

His round, pink, normally cheerful face was worried. 'I must speak with Charles.'

They went inside. Ten minutes later, the party on the terrace heard his car drive away and Charles returned.

'What on earth's the matter with him?' Claire said.

'He can't take part in the relay. He has to go away for a few weeks.'

'But that's ridiculous! He didn't say anything to me and we were jogging together this morning. What's happened?'

Charles shrugged. 'Lord knows. All he said was that something had come up. He's leaving early tomorrow and won't be back until after the festival. I told him he was letting us down badly. He was upset, but he wouldn't change his mind.'

'Who can we get to take his place?' Arthur said. 'Fit young Brits are pretty thin on the ground around here. They're all kids or . . .'

Charles supplied the words he had hesitated to add: 'Elderly gents. So are fit young Scandinavians and Dutch. It took long enough to persuade Lars Svenson to take part . . .'

The telephone rang inside the house. Rob went to answer it.

He came back, shaking his head. 'Speak of the devil. That was Lars. He can't race, either.'

'Why not?'

'He says he has to go unexpectedly to Nice to look at a block of apartments he might buy. Sorry and all that, but he's leaving tonight.'

'Shit!' Charles said. Then, with certainty: 'Something's happened. This isn't just coincidence. Lars wasn't all that struck on taking part but he seemed to have been more enthusiastic lately. Hans, on the other hand, has been keen all along.'

Claire rose. 'I'm going to find out what's going on. May I use your car, Suzy?'

'Of course. Where are you going?'

'To see Hans.' She grinned and added in a deep voice: 'I got vays of making him talk!'

When she returned an hour later, they were still on the terrace and had been joined by Julia, who had walked up from the villa.

'So what's the problem?' Arthur said.

Claire helped herself to a glass of wine and sank into a chair. Her face was sombre. 'It's horrible. When Hans was at the market this morning, someone destroyed all his pottery. Six months' work, smashed into little pieces. It was on the tables outside his cottage . . .'

'Hang on!' Rob said. 'You mean he went away and left the pots outside? Unguarded?'

'He always does that. It doesn't appear to have occurred to him that anyone might steal them. He said, "One must trust people, no?" He puts prices on the pots and customers post the money through a slot in the door. Until today, he hadn't lost anything.'

'There had to be a first time,' James said.

'Right. But it wasn't stealing, it was vandalism. It was as though someone had taken a broom and swept everything off the tables on to the ground, then jumped on them. When I arrived, he was sweeping up the mess and he was almost in tears. It took quite a while to persuade him to tell me about it.'

'It's appalling, but why does he have to go away?' Charles said.

'They – whoever they are – left him a note saying that if he didn't withdraw from the race, they would come into the house and destroy the few pots he has left, and break up his wheel and his kiln. Charles, he's devastated – because he's letting you down as well as about what's happened, but he says that all he can do is go away until the festival's over. The pots are his only way of making a living and he can't risk losing anything more.'

The volunteers had never seen Charles look so angry. He turned to Chris. 'This must be what the barman meant when he told you those sods had some tricks up their sleeves to make sure they won the race. It's intolerable! I'm going to see Sézille. He's obviously behind it.'

Julia spoke for the first time. 'I wonder if he is,' she said slowly. 'I've talked to him a few times, Charles, and although he has this obsessive hatred of Germans and almost fanatical determination to win the race, I honestly don't believe he'd stoop to that kind of destruction. His son Paul, on the other hand . . .'

'Would stoop to anything,' Suzy said. 'I bet it was him and his gang.'

Tim Clarke, the second of the two actors, said: 'What made Lars pull out? He's a property-developer – no pots to smash there.'

'More threats,' Claire said. 'He phoned Hans this morning and told him that obscene graffiti had been sprayed over the walls of his house and a window had been broken. He'd had a note, too. It said that if he didn't withdraw from the race, this was only a beginning. The next damage would be more serious. Lars said that the race didn't mean a thing to him and he wasn't going to risk his house.'

'So what do we do?' Arthur asked. 'Pull out and cancel the race?'

'I'm tempted,' Charles said. 'We should never have got involved in this competition. Henry and I thought the relay would create a bit of friendly rivalry. Instead it's turning into a full-scale war. The atmosphere in the town gets steadily worse. The other day a small boy actually chucked a stone at my car – your car, Julia. Fortunately he missed – and yelled: *"À bas les sales Anglais!"* '

James said. 'The other night Tim and I went into the hotel for a drink and it was bloody uncomfortable. Paul was behind the bar and he virtually ignored us. Several of his friends came in after us, and were served first. We were like lepers.'

'We finally left without a drink and they all laughed as we went out,' Tim added. 'But I'll tell you what, Charles, I don't think we should withdraw from the race. It's just what they want: they'll be able to boast that the French beat the British without firing a shot.'

There was a roar of agreement.

'That's all very well,' Charles said, 'But we're two short in the team. No chance of persuading Hans to change his mind, I suppose, Claire?'

'No. I tried. He's already packed, and he leaves in the morning.' She looked momentarily happier. 'He's promised he'll be back the day after the festival, though.'

'That doesn't help us. Anyone got any ideas who we might approach?'

A hesitant voice came from the darkness where Chris was sitting next to Suzy. 'I suppose – I suppose you wouldn't permit me to become an honorary Briton for one day and let me join the team?'

'Good God! That never occurred to me,' Charles said. 'But I don't know . . . you wouldn't be too popular with the French. I doubt if they'd even wear it.'

'Why could you not say that I am half English and therefore eligible?'

'Are you?'

'No. But in view of what has been done by the French team, a small lie is justifiable, I think.'

'I'll have to talk to Henry and Sézille, but if you're serious, Chris, I'm sure we can come to an arrangement.'

'We're still one short,' Arthur said. 'You know the Franklins' grandson is staying with them. He's a smart kid, only fourteen, but big for his age and pretty fit. How about him?'

'Good idea. I'll ask Henry tomorrow. And then I propose to pay Victor Sézille a visit and tell him that if this persecution doesn't stop, we're pulling out. We'll withdraw the use of Cybèle's property and the prizes she has offered, and the whole festival will collapse.'

11

In Alice's bedroom, Cybèle and her daughters were trying on their festival costumes.

As they lined up, side by side in front of the mirror, Cybèle felt an unusual warmth at the sight of herself flanked by the younger women, pleased to see that she looked hardly older than they did. They were, she reflected, a good-looking trio now that Alice had been persuaded to tone down her wardrobe and her make-up.

She had designed the robes herself, basing them on fifteenth-century paintings, and they were as flamboyant as anything she had created years ago for the circus. None of the local women, cobbling fancy-dresses from cheap fabrics and their own wardrobes, would hold a candle to them.

Alice had suggested that she and Julia should wear identical garments, but this Julia had firmly rejected.

Instead, Cybèle had designed Alice a dress with a turquoise satin top and a skirt in blue and gold brocade. Several feet of trail swept the floor at the back. It was heavy, but Alice was so enchanted by her spectacular appearance that she didn't complain.

Julia's train was shorter, made of a rich furnishing fabric with a crewel-work pattern of roses in pink and green. Her dress was pink satin with green panniers over her hips.

Cybèle's gown was gold satin, the skirt flaring out from a tight bodice. Her train was gold brocade and gold ribbons bound her silver hair. The effect was sumptuous and even more eye-catching than her daughters', which had been her intention.

As they looked into the mirror, she pronounced, 'Not bad at all. We may be proud of ourselves, I think.'

'Proud of you, Cybèle,' Alice said quickly. 'We could never have thought up designs like these, could we, Julia?'

Julia was struggling out of her dress. 'They're beautiful, but thank God we only have to wear them for a few hours. Mine weighs a ton.'

'Oh, but isn't it worthwhile? I mean, the way we look . . . I'd love to have lived in those days, wouldn't you, Cybèle?'

'Certainly not! The people were disgusting. They only took a hot bath once a year. Julia, my dear, would you help me with this ribbon?'

Unwinding the ribbon from her hair, neither of them noticed Alice tighten her lips. Always Julia, she thought. She always asks Julia, never me.

When they had put the costumes on hangers, Cybèle looked around the room with distaste. Alice had managed to turn it into a reflection of herself. The pretty setting which had been created for guests was now scattered with her belongings. It smelled of dead cigarettes and the ash-tray was overflowing. Powder had been spilled on the dressing-table's glass top. A cotton bra and a greyish nylon petticoat lay on the button-back velvet chair, and the bed's white crocheted quilt was bumpy and creased. This daughter still had a great deal to be taught about civilized living.

'Would you mind putting the costumes away in the hall cupboard, Alice?' she said. 'Julia, I'd like to talk to you in my room for a few minutes.'

She was inviting Julia into her room? Alice had never been allowed through the door. And *she* was being dismissed like a servant.

Julia followed Cybèle into her immaculate sanctum, and was waved to a chair.

Cybèle let herself down on to the edge of the bed. As she sat, she felt a twinge of pain in her left hip and was unable to hide an awkward movement of her leg. She glanced at Julia to see if she had noticed, but her face was impassive. She thought, how long can I go on hiding it? If only this bloody festival was over so Charles and I could arrange our futures.

But first, there was Julia.

Wasting no words, she said, 'I have decided to appoint you executive director of my company.'

Julia gasped. 'You've *what*?'

Noticing that the door was slightly open, Cybèle rose and closed it. 'You heard me, my dear. I propose to spend most of my time down here from now on. Perhaps you know that Charles and I intend to go into the wine business. I need someone I can trust in charge of the shops and the magazine.' She smiled. 'And I like the idea of keeping them in the family.'

'Cybèle, it isn't . . .'

But Cybèle swept on: 'Obviously, you will work under my guidance for a while, but after watching you, and talking to you, I know you'll be able to handle the job. You have a flair for design, you clearly have a strong fashion sense and you get on with people. That's important. I have well-trained staffs, but there must be someone in overall control. I also want a buffer between myself and them. I'll continue to provide ideas, you will pass them on and see that they are carried out. You've told me that you enjoy travelling and you will be able to do a great deal from now on. We have shops in Rome, Berlin, Copenhagen and San Francisco as well as Paris and the UK.'

Julia tried again, 'Please, Cybèle . . .' but her mother held up an imperious hand.

'At first, you will be paid a salary – a very generous one; far more than you make from your little books – but eventually you will become my full partner, with an equal share of the profits.' She sat back and watched the expressions chase each other over Julia's face: bewilderment, a frown, disbelief. 'You're surprised? I don't wonder. It's the chance of a life-time.'

Julia said steadily, 'It's an extraordinarily generous offer. I'm overwhelmed . . .'

'It's for my own sake as much as yours. When will you be ready to start?'

'. . . But I'm afraid that it won't be possible for me to accept.'

'Nonsense! You're the perfect person for the job. You

needn't worry about your inexperience. Remember, I'll be behind you.'

'It isn't that. Cybèle, I hate to sound ungrateful, but I have my own career. I can't give it up.'

'I expect you'll be able to find time to turn out a book now and then, though I can't pretend it won't be a demanding job. I sometimes find myself working eighteen hours a day. But it's never less than stimulating.'

There was a touch of desperation in Julia's voice. 'Please do understand! I *love* what I do. It isn't something I could fit in with another job, and I'm not cut out to be a business-woman. I don't understand anything about finance or retailing or magazine production.'

'You will soon learn. Don't you realize this is your chance to make more money and become more powerful than you could ever have imagined? I control a very successful com-pany.'

'But I don't *want* to be rich and powerful! Since Alex died, I've made my own life and maybe I'm just too old or too stick-in-the-mud to change it. I inherited some money from Gitta and with what I make out of my books, I live comfortably and I have the freedom to do as I please. That's important to me. Cybèle, I'm touched and flattered that you think I'd be capable of succeeding you, but I have to refuse your offer.'

Cybèle's blue eyes had turned to ice. 'I can hardly believe what I'm hearing. Any sensible woman would jump at this opportunity.'

'Then please offer it to someone else. There's Alice. She's had experience in business in New York. With your help, she could handle it far better than I.'

'Alice? Impossible! She means well but she couldn't control a corner shop, let alone an international company. She has neither the flair, the background nor the personality.' She stood up. 'I'll give you time to think this over, Julia. I'm sure you'll realize you're making a mistake. We'll leave the subject until after the festival, then we'll talk again. You might discuss it with your daughter. There would be room for her in the company and by refusing, you'd be depriving her of an

273

exciting future. She could, after all, eventually inherit from you.'

Julia rose and said quietly, 'Cybèle, please don't let this spoil our relationship. I'd hate to lose you when we've only just found each other.'

'We'll talk about it later,' Cybèle repeated. 'I'm hoping that our relationship will become a great deal closer, but that will be up to you.'

When Julia went downstairs, Alice was standing in the living-room.

Julia kissed her cheek and said with forced cheerfulness, 'I'm dining at the mill tonight. See you tomorrow.'

Alice didn't respond. The words she had heard from outside Cybèle's door were beating like hammers in her head: 'I have decided to appoint you executive director of my company . . .'

For once, Suzy and Julia found themselves alone on the terrace in the late afternoon. The volunteers were scattered around the farm. Charles, whose car had finally been repaired, had gone into La Bergerie to confront Victor Sézille and meet the Festival Committee. Christian had accompanied him. Klaus Fischer was upstairs.

Julia was silent and abstracted.

'What's the matter?' Suzy said. 'You're not usually so quiet.'

'I've had a disturbing interview with Cybèle.'

'About what?'

'She wants me to join her company. As what she calls an "executive director".'

'You? But you're the last person . . .'

'That's what I tried to tell her, but she wouldn't believe it. She said I was to think it over and we'd talk again.'

'Mother, you'd loathe it! You're an artist, not a business-woman.'

'I know. But at the end she said something that's been worrying me . . .'

'Go on. What was it?'

The words came out in a rush. 'She implied that if I refused I'd be doing you out of a position in the company, and eventually inheriting it.'

'Oh, for God's sake! Look, I've come to admire and like Cybèle during the past few weeks, but I have no desire to work for her.' She added urgently, 'Darling, her whole life has been dedicated to achieving power and making money, and good luck to her. But all you and I have ever wanted is freedom and a modicum of comfort – which we've achieved. No way would I want a life-style like hers.'

The tension left Julia's body. 'I can't tell you what a relief it is to hear that. It's what I thought but I couldn't bear to do you out of a chance to improve your prospects, if that's what you want.'

'Well, I don't. Neither do I give a damn for inheriting the company. As far as I'm concerned, she can leave her fortune to found a home for indigent hamsters. I'll take care of my own future.'

Charles emerged from the house, carrying a bottle of white wine and a tray of glasses. 'You look peaceful. May I join you?'

'Only if you're going to share that wine,' Suzy said. 'Julia's had a stressful afternoon with Cybèle and I've been grubbing weeds out of the vegetable garden. I'd never realized what hard work hoeing is.'

He looked at Julia. 'Nothing wrong, I hope?'

'Not really. I'll tell you about it later.'

As he was pouring the wine, Christian appeared and sat down next to Suzy.

'Did you talk to Victor Sézille?' Julia asked.

Charles nodded. 'Chris came with me. We attacked him on two fronts.'

'How did he react?'

'At the beginning, he was inclined to scoff. But when we told him that Klaus was bed-ridden after a physical attack, that Suzy had been threatened with rape and Hans and Lars had been terrorized, he looked genuinely shocked. Either he's

275

a bloody good actor, which I don't believe, or he knew nothing about it.'

'Did you tell him we suspect his son was involved?'

'Yes. He said it was an intolerable accusation, but I had the feeling that his heart wasn't in it. I'm damn sure that he knew we were right. I told him we were going to call in the Bergerac police and he began to collapse – which is another indication that he believes Paul could be responsible. He adores that kid, though God knows why, he's a thoroughly nasty piece of work. Then Chris put his oar in . . .'

'I said I was planning to write a piece for a national magazine about racial prejudice in France and that it would feature his persecution of a crippled, seventy-year-old German publisher who had been invited to La Bergerie by the world-famous author Cybèle Meredith. I would point out that not only had he been refused room at the inn, but had been attacked by M. Sézille's son, whose prejudice appears to extend to other foreigners as well.'

'And what effect did that have?' Suzy asked.

Charles said, 'His mind works slowly, but it didn't take him long to realize the effect a story like that would have. He's deferred to in La Bergerie because he's a bully and a loud-mouth, but there are quite a few locals who don't agree with his prejudices and only go along with him for the sake of peace. The publicity would ruin him personally and possibly wreck his business.'

Chris added: 'To say nothing of scaring off tourists, thereby causing the town's bar-owners, restaurateurs and shop-keepers to lose money – to which they would not take kindly. Anyhow, he grovelled. He said he would withdraw Paul from the relay team. He begged me not to write the article and said that if we'd agree not to contact the police, he'd do everything he could to make sure that nothing of the kind ever happens again.'

'D'you think he can control Paul?' Suzy said.

Charles said, 'I'm sure he'll do the best he can, but Paul doesn't take kindly to any authority, even his father's. He's had two or three jobs since he left school and been fired from all of them. All he cares about is leading his biker friends into mischief. They drink too much and I suspect they're into drugs. On one or two occasions it's only been Victor's influence with the police here that has kept him out of gaol.'

'What happened at the committee meeting?' Suzy said.

'The French agreed to everything . . . led by Victor. There were no objections to Chris taking part, and Henry says his grandson will be delighted to make up the team, so we're back in business.' He turned to Chris, 'And you, my lad, had better get into some serious training. We're working out the obstacles for the race and some of the French team's ideas are pretty fearsome.'

'Like what?'

'Like shinning up a fifteen-foot brick wall on ropes. Like doing a Tarzan across the widest part of the stream – and anyone who falls in has to do it again. Like crawling under a hundred yards of tightly stretched netting. Like pushing a loaded van over a rough field. Like climbing a drainpipe, then crossing the roof of the hotel and jumping down into the road. And so on. Every competitor will have to negotiate at least two obstacles and there'll be a good deal of running to be done between them. The easier obstacles will, of course, be reserved for us senior citizens. The race will start and finish, after circling through La Bergerie, in the field just below us.'

'I must have lost my mind,' Christian muttered. 'I weigh nearly a hundred kilos. I hope your ropes will carry the strain.'

'You could always take some exercise and lose weight,' Suzy suggested.

He stood up and stretched, a lithe, sun-tanned man with wide shoulders, well-muscled limbs and a flat stomach. 'There is no time like the present. May I invite you, mademoiselle, to accompany me on a run?'

'No, thanks. I've been hoeing the pea-bed all day.'

'Then your spine needs stretching!' He pulled her out of the chair and when she held back, heaved her up in a fireman's lift and carried her, laughing and protesting, around the corner of the mill.

Julia said thoughtfully, 'I really do believe she has met her match in that young man.'

Charles shifted his chair nearer hers and reached for her hand. 'I might have envied them once,' he said.

Wearing shorts and trainers, Suzy had no difficulty keeping up with Christian as they jogged through the field that led down to the stream. They didn't pause until they had covered nearly a mile along its bank and reached the fence that marked the eastern boundary of Le Bas-Fond. It was a warm evening and both were covered with a sheen of sweat.

He sank on to the grass. 'Let us rest for a few minutes. My sedentary life has not prepared me for such exertion.' He pulled her down beside him.

'Rubbish! You aren't even breathing heavily.' She rolled on to her stomach, supporting her chin in her hands. For a few minutes they lay in silence, their bodies lightly touching, and discovered that the slightest movement seemed to pass an electric current between them.

Startled by the effect, not ready to surrender to it, Suzy moved away and said abruptly, 'Tell me about yourself, Chris. We've had so little chance to talk by ourselves. Who *are* you? Are your mother and father alive? Do you have brothers or sisters? Where were you brought up?'

He sat up so suddenly that she jerked back.

Are your mother and father alive? During the past few days the object of his visit to Le Bas-Fond had been pushed into the back of his mind. Now it surfaced again and he seemed to hear his mother's voice, whispering her hatred of the woman he knew as Cybèle Meredith.

He looked down at the copper-and-gold girl with whom he now recognized he was in grave danger of falling in love. She had only known her grandmother for a few weeks, but already he had seen signs of a growing family loyalty. If it were sufficiently strong, there might be no place in her life for the man who presented Cybèle to the world as a liar and a traitor.

Suzy was watching him, puzzled. The darkness on his face reminded her of the first time they met. He had been cheerful, smug in his macho triumph as he diagnosed the fault in her Volvo. Then, as he had driven to the mill, he had become grim and withdrawn, as he was now. There could be no connection between the two occasions, so what was wrong?

He met her eyes and his face cleared. Recklessly, he thought, the hell with the future. It can take care of itself. He moved closer to her. 'I was brought up in Marseilles. My father was a doctor and he and my mother are dead. I was their only child. End of story.'

'Can't you expand a little?'

'Not now. I have better things to do.'

He bent towards her and his lips found hers. The weight of his body came down on her. She had no chance to break free, but she didn't want to. In the past, she had never been able to give herself wholly to a man. One part of her brain had always remained coolly analytical: his lips were too wet; he was sweating; he needed a shave; he was too hairy, too fat.

As Chris's limbs wound around hers, she found herself swept by a physical desire that blotted out thought.

When their lips and tongues finally separated and they drew apart, gasping, his hands began to stray over her body. Too honest to make a pretence of maidenly reluctance, she slid her own hand down to his waist, fumbling at belt and zip. Within seconds, both were naked and he had entered her, hard and demanding.

They reached a climax at the same moment, he with an exultant shout, she with a joyous exhalation.

Fifteen minutes later, dressed, spent by mutual passion, they were sitting on the river-bank, hands linked, feet dabbling in the water.

After a few minutes, he said, 'Where do we go from here?'

'Must we go anywhere? I'm happy where we are.'

'I think you understand me. You know what is meant by a *coup de foudre*?'

'A clap of thunder?'

'It means also love at first sight.' His mouth twisted sardonically. 'With us it was not exactly that, but I do not

279

want it to be the other *coup de foudre*: the storm passes and we are again strangers.'

'That wouldn't be possible. But, Chris, we haven't known each other long. Don't let's rush things, say anything we might regret later.'

'Perhaps we don't have so much time.'

'What on earth does that mean?'

He stood up, pulled her to her feet and kissed her. 'It is possible that when you get to know me better, you will like me less.'

'Actually, you seem to improve on acquaintance.'

'You also. So now we run home and pretend to everyone that nothing has happened. It is a great nuisance that you are sharing a room with Olivia. I would like to be able to visit you at night.'

'You, on the other hand, do have a room to yourself. Perhaps some time, after Olivia has gone to sleep . . . ?'

'There will be a warm welcome awaiting you, mademoiselle. But talking of Olivia, there is something I wish to be made clear . . .'

'Let me guess. She told you I had a man in London. Is that it?' He nodded. 'Well, I did. But I broke with him before I left England. As far as I was concerned the affair had already been dead for months.'

'Why did you tell Olivia about him?'

'Because you'd warned me that Cybèle didn't want any rivals for Charles's favours. Imagine me setting up in competition with my grandmother! Anyhow, while I was waiting for Julia to arrive, I thought I'd have a better chance to get to know her if she could be convinced that I wasn't interested in Charles. We were all swapping girlish confidences one day while we were making the festival costumes and I pretended I was already involved. It did make a difference, too.'

His arm went around her as they turned towards the mill. Again the touch sent a shock through her body. What the hell has happened to me? she thought. Then: as if I didn't know!

12

Alice watched Cybèle covertly as they sat at supper under the arbour. She had been preoccupied ever since Julia's departure after their conference in her bedroom.

The table was set with a red-and-white-checked cloth and white Rosenthal china. As always, there were flowers and candles, even though, with only the two of them, Alice had suggested that they might as well eat in the kitchen.

'I find no pleasure in a meal surrounded by dirty dishes in a room that smells of washing-up water,' Cybèle had informed her. 'Even if there are only two of us, there's no excuse for lowering standards.'

You and your standards! Alice thought. Brought up in a caravan . . . I bet you ate off newspaper same as I did.

The evening was too hot for a heavy meal, so Sophie had left a *salade niçoise* in the refrigerator. There was a fresh baguette and a ripe, round farmhouse Brie rested on a wooden platter beside a red bowl piled with fresh fruit.

Alice ate heartily, but Cybèle picked at her food. She spoke for the first time when Alice cut herself a second triangle of Brie: 'You keep complaining about your weight. You certainly aren't going to lose any this way. You're pounds heavier than Julia.'

Meekly, Alice returned the Brie to the platter. Normally she would have had to make an effort to control her anger at the disparaging comparison with her sister. Now she smiled inwardly, hugging to herself the knowledge that she had a secret weapon which would certainly drive a wedge between Cybèle and Julia. It was to be the first step in her campaign to win for herself the goodies which had been offered to her sister.

She had not failed to observe that Cybèle treated Charles

281

McDonald as her own property, constantly demanding his attention, touching him possessively, addressing low-voiced remarks to him alone. In fact, generally behaving like a woman with marriage in mind. Just wait until Alice told her what was going on between him and Julia! But the revelation must be saved until it would have the maximum impact. She was confident that she would recognize the moment when it arrived.

As they were drinking their coffee, Cybèle said, 'Henry Franklin phoned to say that the odd job man who has been working for him is coming on to us tomorrow. I must warn Charles to make one of the attic rooms ready for him.' She added irritably, 'I really can't think why he doesn't have a telephone.'

'Can't you insist that he gets one?'

'I probably will, eventually. He claims that one reason he came here was to get away from the phone, but it's most inconvenient having to go up every time I have something to say. I'd much rather ring and get him down here, away from that houseful of people.'

I bet you would, Alice thought.

Cybèle drained her coffee-cup, dabbed her mouth with a napkin and stood up.

'I'm going for a walk. Would you clear the table? Sophie can wash up tomorrow morning.'

She made her way through the field that lay in the opposite direction from the mill, absorbed in thought.

Of her newly discovered daughters, she had no doubt which one she preferred. From Alice, she got attention and flattering envy, but Julia, who neither flattered nor envied her, had awakened in her an affection she had never felt for another woman, and she had been confident that the future she had planned for her would bind them more closely together. It had been a shock when Julia claimed that she preferred to continue turning out her piddling little books, but now her first anger had settled into determination that a way must be found to persuade her to change her mind.

George Meredith had worked on the principle that every

man had his price, and usually he had been proved right. Why should Julia be different from anyone else? It might take time, but she could be won over eventually. It was not possible for a woman to reject the financial rewards and prestige she and Suzy had been promised.

Alice's future also had to be decided. She was irritating at times, but malleable, and she had indicated that she would like to remain at the villa. There seemed no reason why she shouldn't be allowed to stay on as combined companion and house-keeper.

As she walked back towards the villa, her mind turned to the vineyard – and Charles. She was so deep in plans for both that she hardly registered the sound of a car moving down the lane towards the main road.

She reached the terrace and Alice appeared in front of her, small, dumpy in the white trousers and red shirt she had bought in imitation of her sister. 'There's someone to see you. He's just arrived . . .'

Cybèle followed her inside. An old man, thin as a stick-insect in a shabby sports-jacket and crushed trousers, was standing with his back to her, gazing up at her portrait.

He heard her footsteps on the marble floor and turned. Without recognition, she looked at the slicked-back black hair and thin moustache that were so ill-matched with his lined, sagging face and yellowish skin, the sunken eyes and veined, clawlike hands.

'Hello, Syb, been years, hasn't it?' he said softly, and she knew who he was.

She took a step backwards, groped for support, found Alice and clung to her.

'Arnie?' she whispered. 'Arnie Gold?'

13

Earlier in the day, the Squadron-Leader had made it clear that the time had come for Arnie to move on. 'Sorry about this, old chap, but my daughter's coming from London for the Festival, and we'll need your room.' To make sure there was no argument, he added, 'I've just telephoned Lady Meredith and she's expecting you in a day or two.'

Arnie's brief glimpse of Sybil in the market-place, chic, polished, expensive-looking, had undermined the confidence with which he had started his journey from England and he had not been unwilling to postpone their confrontation. Now it appeared that he no longer had any excuse for putting it off.

In the evening, the Franklins went out to dine with friends. He had laid in a bottle of wine, and settled down for a few drinks in his comfortable room over the garage.

He'd leave for Le Bas-Fond first thing in the morning. Nothing to be nervous about, was there? Damn it, he only wanted what he was entitled to, a share at last of the good life that Sybil had denied him. All those years he'd taken care of Etta and her . . .

By the time he had finished the bottle his courage had returned. There was no time like the bloody present. I'll go now, he resolved, give young Syb a surprise. And her – his – daughters, too. Fanfare of trumpets. Watch out, girls, here comes Arnie!

He lurched to his feet, pulled his gladstone bag from under his bed and pushed his few clothes into it. He drained his glass as he scribbled a note to the Franklins: 'Many thanks for past favours, sir and madam. Am moving in with Lady Meredith. Hope to see you again soon. Yours truly, Alfred Brown.' He grinned as he signed it. They were in for a surprise when he re-emerged as Arnold Gold, not the odd-job man, but Lady Meredith's step-father and former lover. Father of her children.

Carrying his bag, he walked unsteadily into La Bergerie. Another glass of courage before he found a taxi? Why not?

He went into the bar where he had met the young Frenchman. Tonight there were only a few local customers, who ignored him.

Solitude didn't spoil the flavour of the wine, though. Three drinks later, he swayed out into the night and found a taxi parked on the square.

'Le Bas-Fond, the residence of Lady Meredith,' he ordered grandly.

It was nine o'clock when he reached the villa. As he fumbled for change, his eyes roamed over its façade with bleary appreciation. Nice and bright, with its illuminated windows and the wide terrace, sheltered by a vine-covered trellis. A lawn, too, just like England, but without the bloody herbaceous borders Emily Franklin made such a fuss about.

He paid the taxi-driver, and it wasn't until the cab had moved off that he wondered uneasily whether he should have told him to wait. What if Cybèle wasn't home, or tossed him out on his ear? Not much danger of that, though, he reassured himself, he had too much on her. He put his bag down and pressed a button which was set into a shiny brass plate at the side of the front door.

After a moment, it was opened and a round face peered at him. The maid, he thought. She'd have a maid, for sure. Wouldn't demean herself by answering the door, would she?

'Hullo, love,' he said. 'Lady M. in?' He chuckled. Fancy him calling Sybil Lady M.!

'She'll be back in a few minutes. Oh! Are you the new gardener?'

'You might say that. In a manner of speaking. Going to let me come in?'

'She wasn't expecting you until tomorrow.'

'She'll be pleased to see me, love. I'll guarantee that.' The fresh air was going to his head and his voice was slurred.

'Surprised, too. I'm an old friend, see. Known her since way back when . . .'

He went past her, releasing a breath that filled the air with stale wine fumes, and stood at the top of two wide, shallow steps that led from the hall down into the living-room.

'Very nice!' he said. 'Very nice indeed! Done well for herself, Syb, hasn't she? And just look at that!' Steadying himself with a hand on the wall, he went down the steps towards Cybèle's portrait. 'That's her, innit? She's certainly come up in the world since I knew her . . .'

He heard footsteps and turned towards the french windows.

There she stood, little Sybil Androwski, who he'd slept with all those years ago, who now called herself Lady Meredith and who, if this house was any indication, was even richer than he had imagined.

His lips stretched into a smile. 'Hello, Syb, been years, hasn't it?'

She looked as though she was going to faint, and grabbed the maid.

'Arnie? Arnie Gold?' The words were hardly more than an exhalation of breath, then she said, 'I – I thought . . .' She stopped.

'Thought I was dead, didn't you? Nope. Here I am, love. No ghost. Give us a kiss and I'll prove it to you.'

He took a couple of steps forward and a wine-laden miasma enveloped her as she backed away.

His eyes shifted to the other woman, who he could now see was too informally dressed to be the maid.

'Here, you wouldn't be one of the twins, would you?' he said.

Simultaneously, Sybil said, 'No!' and the woman nodded.

'Well, well, well! Give us a look at you, then. You don't know who I am, do you? I'll tell you: I'm your old Dad!'

Alice took in his shabby clothes, cracked shoes, the rheumy eyes and uneven yellow teeth. 'You can't be!'

'I am, too. Aren't I, Syb?'

'No!' Cybèle's voice was choked. 'You aren't! Don't believe him, Alice.'

'Oh, yes, I am. It was either me or that German, and I reckon it was me because I had you for months and you were only with him for a couple of weeks, right?' He moved over and stood beside Alice. Clasping a bony hand around her arm, he turned her so they were facing Cybèle. 'Can't you see the resemblance? Where's the other one, then?'

Although her face was still pale and sick, Cybèle had regained her poise. 'Why have you come here, Arnie?'

'I thought you'd never ask. Tell you what, let's all sit down and have a little drink to celebrate. Then we'll talk.'

'You've already had enough to drink.'

'Same old bossy Sybil! I'll decide when I've had enough.'

'Get him a glass of wine, Alice,' Cybèle said.

Hardly taking her eyes off him, Alice went to the drinks cabinet.

He sat in an arm-chair and as she handed him a glass he reached up and patted her bottom. 'Thanks, love, hope you'll go on looking after your old Dad as well as this.'

Her eyes were like brown marbles as she joined Cybèle on the sofa.

He leant back, looking around with satisfaction. This would do him nicely, and Sybil wasn't so formidable after all. It was going to be easier than he had expected.

'Well?' she said

'You want to know why I'm here? To get my rights, Syb, that's why.'

'I've no idea what you're talking about. As far as I'm concerned, you have no rights.'

'Oh, yes, I have. You know what you did to me in that book of yours? You called me a liar and a thief. That's libel. I asked a lawyer about it. You held me up to ridicule but out of the kindness of my heart I thought I'd give you a chance to put things right before I sue you.' His eyes misted with anger. 'You messed up my life, too, Syb. After that time in Paris, you put me in prison for years, you nearly got me killed.' He drained his glass and held it out to Alice. 'Get me another one, and never mind asking *her* if you should. This is your father speaking.'

Alice made no attempt to hide the look of loathing on her face as she took the glass.

'How did you find me, Arnie?' Cybèle's voice gave no hint of her panic.

'Read your book, didn't I? You mentioned your place near La Bergerie. We came through here once with the Dandos, remember? No trouble finding out where you lived once I got to the town. Lady Meredith's pretty well known around the district.'

Suddenly enlightened, she said, 'Have you been working for Henry and Emily Franklin? Are *you* the odd-job man who was supposed to come to me?'

'Well . . . that's what they thought.' He bared his teeth. 'Never told them who I really was, said my name was Alfred Brown. I took the job while I spied out the land, so to speak. Then the Squadron-Leader told me Lady Meredith needed a bit of help and wanted to see me. Couldn't help laughing! Anyhow, Syb, here I am, and here I stay, until we come to an arrangement.'

'Just what are you expecting?'

'Now I've seen the place, I reckon I'll stick around for a while.' He glanced at Alice. 'And my little girl who'll be happy to look after me, right? I'm looking forward to meeting the other one, too.' He raised his glass again and Alice refilled it without being told. 'If you don't want a libel suit on your hands, with a lot of nasty publicity, you're going to have to pay.'

'Suppose I agree to give you some money. What would you do then?'

His voice was increasingly slurred. 'I wouldn't shu – sue you. Can't guarantee you'd never see me again, though. I mean, I fancy getting together with my kids and their Mum from time to time. Sharing your lives, like.' He belched.

Unable to contain herself, Alice gave a strangled yelp. Jesus, he was worse than Hank! 'I'm not your kid!' she snapped. 'You're disgusting!'

'That's not very nice, is it? None of your business, either. How we settle things is between Sybil and me. And it's going to cost her. Even if you read her book, you don't know the half of what happened to me during the war. She *owes* me! I'm gonna stick around and you're gonna help her to make it up to me.'

With the return of anger, he stood up, then subsided abruptly as a wave of dizziness made his head reel. 'Don't feel too well . . .' he mumbled.

The two women lunged forward, pulled him to his feet and rushed him towards the terrace. He threw up on the grass.

Helplessly, Cybèle turned to Alice. 'What are we to do?' she whispered. 'I'd give him money, anything! But how are we ever going to get rid of him? Alice, he could ruin my life!'

Alice was almost unable to believe her luck. Cybèle needed her. Here was her chance to show what she was made of. She would see this dreadful old man off and Cybèle would be so grateful, nothing would be too good for Alice in future. The hell with mealy-mouthed Julia, she thought triumphantly, I'm taking over.

'Don't worry,' she said. 'I'll fix him so he won't bother us any more.'

'You'll never persuade him to go away! Even with money . . .'

Alice patted her shoulder. 'Leave it to me, honey. I'll think of something. First thing is, I'll drive him back to La Bergerie. Get him out of our hair for tonight, at least.'

When Cybèle was writing her book, it had never occurred to her that Arnie might have survived the war. After his arrest, she had scarcely thought of him again and when she did, she had simply assumed that execution had automatically followed his arrest. She had felt no guilt. Apart from loathing him personally, his knowledge of her identity put the entire underground movement in jeopardy. If he were to sue her, she shuddered at the effect his manifest poverty and the old, whining voice accusing her of betrayal would have on a court. The humiliation of being revealed as the former mistress of this unwashed down-and-out would be equally intolerable. The newspapers would love the story. She was well aware that she had made enemies during her rise to power. The thought of the malicious delight of her Paris director, Max Harrison, for one, made her cringe, and there would be others who would crow at her downfall.

She was too upset to think clearly, and frantic words tumbled out as she clutched Alice's arm. 'Call his bluff! Tell him that if he's still here tomorrow, I'll have him arrested. Tell him anything!' She went into the house and took out all the money in her purse. 'Give him this. Buy him a train-ticket. Just get rid of him!'

Alice turned to Arnie, who had straightened up and was clinging to the trellis. 'I'm going to drive you to a hotel where you can stay until tomorrow. Then you leave,' she snapped.

'Don't wanna go to a hotel. I'm going to stay here,' he muttered.

'No, you aren't. On your feet!'

He was too drunk to struggle as they guided him towards Cybèle's BMW, which was parked in the drive.

'We'll put him in the back. I can't stand the smell of him,' Alice said.

'Shouldn't I come with you?'

'Leave it to me.' She patted Cybèle's shoulder. 'You go to bed. Take a sleeping-pill. Tomorrow everything will be all right.'

Cybèle watched the car pull away. Arnie was slumped along the back seat, his eyes closed.

She had no real hope that Alice could persuade him to leave La Bergerie empty-handed. Tomorrow, she would offer him an allowance on condition that he never came near her again.

As she went upstairs, she realized that she had just seen an Alice she had not known existed. There had been no sign of meekness as she took charge of the situation. Her face had been hard, her voice sharp, and there had been something vicious in the way she had twisted Arnie's arm behind his back as she pushed him into the car. The transformation had been so complete that Cybèle found herself disturbed by the memory, but she was too upset to analyse it at the moment.

As she lay in bed, she listened for the car, but Alice had still not returned when she drifted into sleep.

They had been driving for fifteen minutes when Alice pulled into the side of the road and switched off the headlights.

The night was pitch dark, the stars and moon hidden by threatening clouds. Drops of warm rain and rolling thunder were presaging a summer storm.

She opened the passenger door, reached in and shook Arnie's shoulders. He muttered and twitched, but his eyes remained closed. She drew back her hand and slapped him hard on the cheek. Then she grasped his thin hair and tugged it. He jerked upright, banging his head against the car window.

'Jesus, I'm dying!' he gasped. 'What's happening?'

'Get out,' Alice said. 'We've arrived.'

'Leave me alone! Arrived where? Oh, God, I have to pee . . .'

'Not in the car!' She took hold of his jacket and hauled him out on to the grass. He was a skinny, fleshless old man and he weighed very little. He stood, swaying and fumbling at his trousers.

'Down there! You can go down there,' she said, and gave him a push which sent him stumbling forward. He took a couple of steps and the ground fell away beneath his feet. Unable to stop, he hurtled on, then fell and rolled down a steep incline that ran into the black, fast-flowing waters of the Dordogne. With a choking, bubbling moan, his head sank below the surface.

A flash of sheet lightning lit up the scene and Alice saw what looked like a bundle of old clothes being swept out towards the deep channel in the middle of the river. The storm broke. Huge drops of rain began to fall. The water boiled as the wind lashed it into waves.

She drove back to the villa.

She parked the car in its usual place in the drive and went up to the front door. When she opened it her foot kicked Arnie's gladstone bag.

She took it inside and opened it. The first thing she saw, on top of his shabby clothes, was his passport. Nobody, apart from herself and Cybèle, knew that Alfred Brown was really

Arnold Gold. It must stay that way. She thought quickly. There was a weed-covered pool in the stream below the villa, with overhanging trees and bushes. Because there was little movement of the water, a layer of silt several feet deep had built up on its bottom.

Carrying the bag, she went outside again. The rain was lashing down; thunder and lightning were almost continuous. Within seconds her clothes were soaked and her hair was clinging to her scalp in wet strands. She reached the pool, which was just below where she had seen Julia and Charles embracing each other. She found some heavy stones and put them into the bag to weight it. Then she pushed it through the weeds and watched it disappear into the oily water.

The next morning, Cybèle emerged from her bedroom at ten o'clock, to find her breakfast set as usual on the table under the vine. Through the french windows she could see Alice buttering a croissant. In the kitchen, Sophie was humming to herself as she washed up the supper dishes.

All traces of the night's storm had gone and the air was fresh and clear. Everything outside looked as though it had been newly washed. The grass below the terrace was green, the geraniums were bright and the sun gave a golden glow to the villa's mellow brick.

She moved more slowly and heavily than usual and for once she had not bothered to dress, but was still wearing her night-dress and a pale pink satin dressing-gown.

As she reached Alice she said, 'What happened last night? Will he be back today?'

'He won't be back at all. May I pour your coffee, Cybèle?' Meek Alice had returned.

'Yes. What do you mean, he won't be back?'

'I told him that we weren't going to be blackmailed and that if he stayed, we'd hand him over the police. I gave him the money, and made him promise to go away.'

'But will he? Where did you leave him?'

'Near the square. He was feeling better when we got to La Bergerie. He was going to spend the night in the hotel.' Her eyes were wide and guileless. 'We don't have to worry about him again, Cybèle.'

Cybèle took a deep breath. 'I am very grateful to you, my dear, though this seems too good to be true. I'm amazed he gave in so easily.'

Alice shrugged. 'I can be very persuasive when I like. It was just a try-on, honey. He thought he could bluff you and when he found he couldn't, and might go to prison, I guess he decided to cut his losses.'

'I couldn't have endured him a moment longer. Alice, what would I have done without you?'

'I was so glad to help, after all you've done for me. Now let's forget it. No-one need ever know he was here. Even the Franklins only knew him as Alfred Brown.'

'That would be best, wouldn't it? What happened last night will be our secret.'

'Yours and mine. Oh, Cybèle, whenever you need help, remember that you'll always be able to call on me. I'd do anything for you.'

Cybèle looked at her gratefully. 'I believe you would, my dear.'

PART FIVE

1

With a few days to go until the festival, normal life in Le Bas-Fond and La Bergerie had been suspended.

Charles had given up attempting to achieve more than the essential work on the farm, and the volunteers were fully occupied laying out the course of the relay race, putting up barriers to keep the public back, erecting the obstacles.

'This bloody festival is dominating everything,' he grumbled to Julia as they were walking by the stream after supper. It was the first time in several days that they had been alone. Safely out of sight of the mill, he slipped an arm around her shoulders. 'The locals can't talk about anything else.'

'They're certainly taking it seriously.'

'Seriously! They're preparing to fight the last battle of the Hundred Years' War all over again. A mob of little boys yelled insults at Christian yesterday, saying he was a traitor to his own people.'

'At least there hasn't been any violence. Your talk with Victor Sézille had the right effect.'

'Maybe. I don't trust Paul Sézille, though. I have a feeling he and his biker friends are helping to stir up the antagonism.'

'You worry too much. I'm sure everything will be fine.'

'I hope you're right. Generally the arrangements are going well. A fair and street entertainers are coming and there'll be music and dancing in the streets on the first night. The high spot of the second day will be the relay and barbecue. Most of the women in the town want to have a hand in preparing food – by the way, we're calling the barbecue a *pique-nique* now. The locals weren't too happy about sitting around on the grass eating charred meat, English fashion. They've extended it into a major banquet and we've had to hire long tables and benches. Fortunately, Cybèle's offered to pick up

297

the tab so the kids' charities will get a hundred per cent of the take.'

Julia said, 'She's one of the most generous women I've ever met. She's spent a fortune on our festival costumes and refused to allow me to contribute a single franc.'

He nodded. 'She was furious when she discovered I'd ordered medium-priced champagne for the winning team's prize. She made me replace it with Dom Perignon.'

They walked on in companionable silence for a while, then he said, 'Has she adjusted to your refusal to work with her?'

'She hasn't mentioned it again. Maybe she's waiting until after the festival to renew the attack, but I'm hoping that she might have decided to offer the position to Alice instead of me. I've noticed over the past few days that they're becoming closer and Alice is getting much more self-confident, almost assertive at times.'

'How about *your* relationship with Alice?'

'I still can't decide how she feels about me, and it's sad, because I would so like us to be real friends. We get along well enough, but I can't help thinking that she'll be happier when I go back to London.'

'I hope you're not planning to do that yet?'

She said evasively, 'Like everyone else, I'm not planning anything beyond the festival at the moment.'

They reached the stream and paused at almost the same spot where they had first kissed. Since then, although their mutual attraction seemed to have deepened every day, he had not attempted to take the physical relationship any further. For this she was grateful, because it saved her from making a decision she was not yet ready to face. She knew so little about Charles. He never talked about his background and on the one occasion when she had attempted a casual question, he had lightly, but definitely, avoided answering. She hadn't been able to prevent herself from wondering whether he was really interested in any deeper relationship than a passing flirtation with a reasonably attractive woman who would shortly be returning to her own world. Since Alex's death she had indulged in a few brief, unimportant affairs, but she found herself oddly reluctant to add to their number with Charles.

Even as she decided, in that case, that she must not give him any further encouragement, he turned her towards him, tipped up her face with a finger under her chin, kissed her gently, then released her.

He took a deep breath and, afraid that he was going to say something which could bring matters to a head, she rushed into speech. 'I suppose Klaus and Chris will both be leaving after the festival. Have they said anything?'

Not for the first time, she had the feeling that he read her mind. There was amused resignation in his smile, then he slipped his arm through hers and answered, 'Nothing definite. Chris told me the other day that he had almost all the information he needs for his article. He's planning one more interview with Cybèle. After that, I suspect that his movements might depend on Suzy.'

Grateful for his understanding, she said lightly, 'They really are an item, aren't they? Suzy goes round in a daze most of the time. I've never seen any other man have this effect on her.' She laughed. 'I believe they think nobody has noticed.'

'I wonder if anyone has noticed us? I feel slightly dazed myself.' She was silent and he added hastily, 'About Klaus, I expect he'll have to get back to Berlin soon. He and Cybèle have finished their alterations for the German edition of her book.'

'He doesn't seem to be in any hurry to leave.'

'I've managed to persuade him to stay for the festival. He's still lame after his beating, and I have a feeling that his life in Berlin is pretty lonely. In spite of the unpleasantness he's had to face, he says he hasn't felt so alive in years as he does with our young people, and I must say I enjoy his company.'

He didn't add that another reason Klaus had agreed to stay on was to await a reply from Neil Simmonds in New York to his query about Alice.

'Me, too,' she said. 'We've had several long talks. He cross-questions me about my life in London, and my work, and childhood. He's a good listener.'

299

'He's probably fallen in love with you, like Rob and Arthur and – the rest of us.'

She ignored that and said thoughtfully, 'The festival's become a kind of watershed, hasn't it? I have a curious feeling that afterwards all kinds of things will change.'

For Klaus Fischer, several things had already changed. The weeks at Le Bas-Fond had cured him of his bitterness at Cybèle's duplicity; he had discovered in himself a forgotten capacity for enjoyment; he had found in Julia Leander the daughter of whom he had dreamed.

Watching her stroll towards the terrace, arm in arm with Charles, he thought that it hardly mattered to him any longer whether he or Arnold Gold had fathered her. It was enough that in a short time he had come to love her as a daughter and she had accepted him as a friend. They had agreed that she would visit him in Berlin, and she had insisted that next time he was in London, he must stay with her. The knowledge that they were not likely to drop out of touch produced a contentment with which he was unfamiliar.

There was further pleasure in watching the development of her relationship with Charles McDonald. If she *was* his daughter, there was no man he would rather see her with.

As for Cybèle, she was not the Cybèle Androwski he had held in his imagination for so long. Try as he might, he could recognize nothing of the circus waif in the sophisticated, elegant woman she had become. During their meetings, he had manufactured editorial suggestions for her book as an excuse to study her. He had discovered that her mind was razor-sharp, her intelligence formidable, her charm undeniable, but he had actually found himself shuddering at the thought that he might have married her all those years ago and been impaled by the thrust of the ambition which dominated her life.

With the lifting of his years-long obsession, it was as though he had emerged into sunshine from the fog which had enveloped him since the day she had decamped with the circus.

Only one thing remained to worry him: Alice. Try as he might, because she was Julia's twin and also might be his daughter, he could not like her. Her ingratiating manner jarred on him and her secret nods and flirtatious glances were increasingly embarrassing.

Not for the first time, he wondered how much his reactions were influenced by what Charles had told him, and how seriously Charles's interpretation of a momentary expression on Alice's face had been distorted by the tragic death of his wife.

'All alone, Klaus?' Julia sank into a chair beside him. 'Where is everyone?'

'They have all gone to bed. Even the girls have been hammering in posts along the relay course since dawn. They were already yawning by eight o'clock, at the same time insisting that they were not in the least tired.' The smile he had used so rarely until recently removed years from his face. 'You have had a pleasant day with your mother and sister, my dear?'

'Yes, very. Have you heard that Cybèle is inviting us all to a champagne and caviare party the night before the festival? She was shocked to find that La Bergerie's little shops don't run to best-quality caviare, so we're planning a shopping excursion into Bordeaux in a day or so.'

As they chatted, he felt that it was impossible that this woman's twin sister could be a psychopath. Charles had been mistaken, a trick of light had distorted Alice's face and soon Simmonds's letter would reassure them that there was nothing unsavoury in her past.

At eleven o'clock, he went upstairs, leaving Julia and Charles talking quietly. Half an hour later, he heard Julia's car leaving for La Bergerie.

A little later, lying in the bed which was barely wide enough for his own large body, let alone the sleeping girl who lay in his arms, Christian's thoughts were bleak.

This was the third time he and Suzy had made love, the second time in his bed. She had crept in just before midnight,

301

when the mill was silent and everyone presumably asleep. He had heard the creaking of passage floor-boards and held his breath. Then the door had opened.

'Were you expecting me?' she whispered.

'I was afraid you weren't going to come.'

'I had to wait until Julia went back to the hotel. I thought she and Charles were going to talk all night.'

She slid down beside him and their bodies became one. Afterwards, she fell asleep, but he stayed awake and found himself suffering a severe attack of depression. The success of his mission in Le Bas-Fond would result in Cybèle Meredith's humiliation in the eyes of the world. The prospect that it could also mean Suzy would be lost to him became daily less bearable.

He moved restlessly, then stilled, afraid of disturbing her. The image of his mother lying dead in her lonely hotel-room returned, her pallid, pain-wracked face, lank hair and withered body as clear as they had been the day he found her.

The moon was shining through the window. Suzy's hair was spread on the pillow, its warm colour leached out by the cold blue light. She was sleeping peacefully, thick lashes sweeping her cheeks, her breathing soft and regular. It was a humid night. They were both naked, and the exuberance of their love-making had caused the sheet to fall on the floor. His eyes travelled down the curve of her breasts and waist, the swell of hips and the long, slender legs and his despair became a sickness that choked his throat and made his head throb. Marie had asked too much. He couldn't do it. But then he heard the echo of her tired, flat voice: 'Sylvie Andros was a traitor . . . she informed on me to save herself . . . there is never a day when I'm not in pain . . .'

He realized that Suzy's eyes were open and she was staring at him.

She whispered, 'What's the matter? You look as though you've had a nightmare.'

'I sometimes think I'm living in one.' He regretted the words immediately.

She swung her feet on to the floor and perched on the edge

302

of the bed. The dark, almond eyes were intent on him. 'Want to tell me about it? I've wondered, you know. Every now and then you seem to move into another world, and I get the feeling it isn't a very nice one.'

After a long pause, he said, 'Not now. I'll tell you after the festival.'

'Why after the festival? Tell me now!'

'No. I want to make the most of the days we have left.'

After she had crept back into her room, hoping that Olivia had not discovered her absence, she lay awake, her imagination creating one disagreeable scenario after another: he was married and was going to tell her after the festival; he was suffering a terminal illness; he was some kind of criminal; he simply didn't love her.

2

On that same evening, Alice was sitting on the villa's terrace, gloomily staring into the darkness, wondering how much longer she could endure spending night after night in this dump. Now that she had become accustomed to the luxury of her new home, she was noticing its shortcomings. It wasn't even equipped with television, for God's sake! She might not understand what they were saying on the French programmes, but at least the voices would break the silence. Recently she had found herself looking back on the Bronx with something close to nostalgia. At least it had been *alive*. There had been people, cars in the streets, lights, the comforting noises of a big city. Here cars never passed the door, there was not a light to be seen and the country sounds of insects and small animals only emphasized the solitude.

The inhabitants of Le Bas-Fond, who had seemed so promising at first, had turned out to be a dead loss. She had looked forward to outings escorted by Charles McDonald or

Klaus Fischer but neither had risen to her hints that it would be nice to investigate the local night-life – if, indeed, any existed. Neither had it occurred to the volunteers to include her in their visits to Bordeaux or Bergerac. Her only excursions off the property had been with her mother and sister, and she was bored with hanging around with women. Even old Nathan Weitz, fat and foul-mouthed though he was, would have been better company.

Cybèle liked to spend the evenings reading, as she was now, in the sitting-room, or listening to high-brow music. At the mill, people talked about subjects Alice didn't understand, discussed books she hadn't read, plays she hadn't seen, painters she had never heard of. All in all, the most stimulating event of the past few weeks had been her disposal of Arnie Gold. And now, in her boredom, she decided that the time had come to let Cybèle know that she required a more positive reward than gratitude.

Purposefully, she went inside. Cybèle was sitting under a standard lamp, her hair an aureole of silver, wearing a long navy-blue skirt. Her loose white cotton shirt was bloused over a wide belt and there were gold chains around her neck. Alice found incomprehensible her habit of dressing up even when there was no man around to see her. Her own preference in the circumstances would have been a comfortable dressing-gown and slippers, and a few rollers in her hair so she'd look nice the following day.

Putting on her most deferential manner, she said, 'I wondered if we might have a little talk? If I'm not disturbing you, that is?'

Reluctantly, Cybèle put down her book. 'What is it, Alice?'

A gentle reminder first. 'You haven't heard anything from Mr Gold, have you? I just wondered, you know, if we can be certain he's really gone.'

'He must have. I'm still not sure how you managed it.'

'I guess I just found the right words.'

'You know how grateful I am.'

'Yes, thank you. Cybèle, after the festival, I'll have to think about getting back to New York.'

'Surely not? I've been hoping you would stay here indefinitely.'

'I have to earn my living, and I've been offered a job back at Nathan Weitz and Company. They're in the fashion business, like you.'

'Really? I had no idea . . .'

'No. Well, I've had a lot of experience, you know. Nathan says I know as much about running a company as he does. I'd much rather stay here, but it's such an opportunity . . .' Her voice trailed off, then strengthened. 'Of course, if something turned up, I mean, working with you, for instance . . .'

After a long moment, Cybèle said, 'I wasn't going to say anything until after the festival, but since you've brought the subject up, I do have something to offer you. It might not be exactly what you've been planning, but I think you'd find it rewarding.'

'You know I'd do anything for you!'

'I'd like you to stay on as my housekeeper and secretary.' Alice was sitting in the shadows beyond the lamp's penumbra and Cybèle did not notice the change in her expression. 'I'm going to be busy reorganizing Le Bas-Fond, so I'll need someone to deal with the household chores and my mail. I'm sure you could manage that beautifully. Two or three times a year we'd move to the flat in London for a few weeks, and you'd look after both places when I'm abroad.' She smiled. 'How does that appeal to you?'

Alice managed to keep her voice steady. 'That wasn't exactly what I had in mind. I was thinking more of becoming a kind of partner in your company.'

Cybèle said kindly, 'I'm afraid that wouldn't be possible. Mine's a specialized business. You simply don't have the experience.'

She couldn't stop herself: 'I know a hell of a lot more about business than Julia does!'

'Has Julia spoken to you?' Her voice was sharp. 'No, she wouldn't have done that. So you must have overheard us talking. Alice, I'm sorry if you're disappointed, but I can't offer you a place in the company. Apart from anything else, we're centred in Europe and as an American you wouldn't understand our way of doing things. I will be sad if you don't feel you can stay with me, but of course I'll understand. You know what's best for your own future. If you do decide to stay, you'll be well-paid, I assure you.' She stood up. 'And now, I'm off to bed. Good night, my dear. Switch off the lights, will you?'

Alice watched the slim, straight-backed figure disappear upstairs. Her fingers were writhing furiously in her lap. She had a great deal more to say.

She heard water running in Cybèle's bathroom, the lavatory flush and footsteps above her head.

She waited for another few minutes, then mounted the stairs and, without knocking, opened Cybèle's bedroom door.

Her mother was sitting in front of the dressing-room mirror, massaging cream into her face. She was wearing a tailored black satin dressing-gown and her hair was tied back with a scarf.

She swung around as the door opened, and surprise turned to anger. 'I do hope you are not going to make it necessary for me to lock my door, Alice.'

Deliberately, Alice kept her voice soft. 'I'm sorry, Cybèle, but we hadn't finished talking. What I was going to say when you walked out, was that after the way I got rid of Arnie Gold for you, I had hoped for something better than a housekeeper's job. I mean, what would have happened if he'd stayed? You said he'd ruin your life.'

'It's because I'm grateful that I've asked you to stay on as my personal assistant.'

'Your servant! While Julia gets the fun and all the cash!' She made no attempt to disguise her bitterness. 'It's not enough! I want what you've offered her. And I've got something else to tell you: you're not going to have her for long anyway, not with what she has going with Charles McDonald.'

Cybèle's hand, which had continued to smooth cream up under her chin, stilled. 'And just what does that mean?'

'Haven't you noticed? They have a real thing going.'

'A *thing*?'

'I saw them from my window the other night. They were down by the river, necking like a couple of kids.'

'Necking?' She drawled the word with distaste.

'It was sort of embarrassing to watch. Julia's been chasing him. You know, like when she asked him to drive her into La Bergerie at night instead of Suzy.'

'I wasn't aware of that.'

'Oh, yes. And she invited him to supper at the hotel last week, just the two of them. I can't think how you could have missed it, although poor Hank did use to say that I was more observant than most people.'

With an effort, Cybèle kept her face expressionless. 'Thank you for telling me. Go to bed now, Alice.'

'I thought you'd be interested. And it makes a difference, doesn't it? To us, I mean. Think about it, Cybèle, and think about Arnie Gold and how you told me to get rid of him. And after the festival, we'll have another talk.'

Slowly, Cybèle stood up, and the look in her ice-blue eyes made Alice realize that she might have under-estimated her mother's will.

'We have done all our talking. I have made you an offer, which I will not, for the moment, withdraw. *You* think about it, Alice. But dismiss from your mind any hope of taking the position I offered to Julia. Will you please leave my room?'

Alice was panting as she reached her bedroom. She tore off her clothes. Then she fell on to her bed and had to put a hand over her mouth to prevent herself from screaming with fury. Julia and Cybèle! She hated them both.

As she continued to carry out the nightly routine of cleansing and exercising Cybèle went back over the conversation.

'Think about Arnie Gold and how you told me to get rid of him.' That had been an undisguised threat. Presumably Alice intended, if she wasn't given what she wanted, to circulate the truth about 'Alfred Brown's' identity.

But hadn't she, Cybèle, in the first shock of Arnie's apparent rise from the dead, lost her sense of proportion? Would it

307

matter all that much if people did know about him? Surely she had sufficient social clout to rise above the sniggering of lightweights like Max Harrison?

She would call Alice's bluff and show her that she could not be blackmailed. The hell with the opinion of the rest of the world. It had never bothered her before.

She wiped the last of the face-cream away with a tissue. Now it was time to consider the problem of Charles McDonald's affair – if that's what it was – with Julia. What angered her most was that they'd carried it on under her very nose and she hadn't been aware of it.

It was, of course, no more than a holiday romance, but holiday romances had a habit of developing into something more serious when the participants were thrown together for longer periods. She did not wholly accept Alice's malicious assertion that Julia had instigated the affair. In hindsight, she realized that indeed she had noticed, but disregarded, Charles's attention to her daughter. She had been so damn smug because he hadn't seemed to be attracted to the beautiful Suzy that she had never looked for another rival.

Surprisingly, jealousy was the least of her emotions. Charles was attractive, but she had never been in love with him, had even thought that if they married, she would be happy for him to indulge in extra-marital sexual activities which might prevent him from invading her privacy too often. What upset her most was the effect his defection would have on her plans to secure a companion for her old age and a partner in her winery.

Her facial completed, she went to the open window and stood, taking deep, regular breaths, her shoulders back and head held high.

As she got into bed, her eyes fell on her book, lying on the side-table in front of her photographs of Dominic and David Stone.

She picked it up for the first time in weeks. Here were all her triumphs: the rising graph of her success after George's death; her increasing stature in the fashion world; the continuing growth of her magazine and her shops. Here were the men who had loved her, others who had set out to do her down, the board-room battles she had conducted with zest and confidence.

Now there was a threat that she would be thwarted in both her personal and professional lives by two people far less shrewd than most of her previous opponents, because, incredibly, they appeared to be indifferent to the dazzling prospects offered by partnership with herself.

Her idle page-turning brought her to a section not far from the end of the book, where she had recorded the last major conflict in which she had been involved, when there had been a threat to the future of the magazine on which the entire structure of her career was founded. It had been a long, dirty battle, but she had won it, as she intended to win this time, for she had no intention of giving Charles up without a fight.

3

Extract from *I am Cybèle*

By 1980 *Cybèle* was established as one of Britain's most successful magazines. It appeared monthly, and sold twice as many copies as any comparable publication. I owned it outright and on the mast-head my name appeared as Editor-in-Chief, although most of the donkey-work the title implied was done by my competent èditor. This was inevitable, because I had to spend much of my time travelling and running the Cybèle shops.

I'd had several offers from larger publishing companies to buy the magazine, and refused them all, but one organization, headed by a man who had briefly been my lover, was more persistent than the others.

Mark Scott hated me because I had ended our affair instead

of letting it continue until he became bored, as had been the pattern with his previous mistresses.

He was a small, hatchet-faced man who was determined to build a publishing empire rivalling those of Murdoch and Maxwell. For years he had been quietly buying up local newspapers and smaller magazines, but when I knew him he still hadn't quite achieved his ambition. He had made a great deal of money, but had poured most of it back into the expansion of his business interests and the pursuit of power, which was even more important to him than money. He wanted *Cybèle* for the gloss it would add to his image.

I suppose I was flattered by his admiration at first, since he was nearly ten years younger than I. But he was a womanizer and a boring conversationalist, devoid of humour. The affair rapidly became a bore and after a couple of months I told him bluntly that it was over, which was a severe blow to his vanity.

I realized just how severe when I began to hear rumours that he was planning to publish a new magazine which would be a direct rival to *Cybèle*. Not long after that, he made another offer for the magazine. As usual, I turned it down.

Enticing advertisements for the new publication began to appear in the trade and general press and I realized that it was to be a 'spoiler' – a magazine with which Mark planned to cut into *Cybèle*'s sales and advertising so drastically that I would be forced either to sell or close it down.

I wasn't too worried at first, because we had a devoted readership. We had constantly updated the book in line with changing social conditions, bought work from the world's top writers and photographers which interested men as well as women. While retaining an up-market image, we eschewed the snobbery of other glossies and never patronized our readers, aiming our appeal at all classes.

If I had any doubts about Mark's intentions, they were swept away by the title he chose. The Frenchified *Félice* was in direct imitation of *Cybèle*. When the magazine appeared on the book-stalls after weeks of hype, it closely followed ours in layout and content. The first issue was, inevitably, a sell-out thanks to public curiosity, and our sales that month dropped by several thousand.

Then the dirty tricks started in earnest. Mark bought away several of the brightest members of my staff and suborned literary agents into allowing *Félice* first look at the work of their most prestigious authors. He also had a direct line to magazine distributors and I found that *Cybèle* was being hidden on many shelves by well-displayed copies of *Félice*.

We won back some of our readers during the ensuing months, but Mark's blanket advertising campaign on TV and in the newspapers caused a slight but steady seepage towards *Félice*. I realized that something drastic had to be done to halt it.

I began to plan my campaign and, as I had done before in a financial crisis, I called on the advice of two dead men: David Stone and George Meredith.

Alone in my flat one night, I closed my eyes and summoned their spirits to a conference, seeing them on my mind's screen: David as he had been when we married, wise, subtle, knowledgeable; George, ruthless, tough, single-minded.

I imagined them advising me as they had in life and could almost hear George's harsh voice summing up the tactics I should use: 'Screw the bastard as hard as you can.'

From David, I heard: 'I don't approve of using your own money in business, love, but this time, spend, spend, spend if you have to, to save *Cybèle*. You could even sell a shop or two if necessary.'

George: 'Give him a dose of his own medicine by going after the distributing companies. Buy up their shares until you have a controlling interest, then refuse to distribute *Félice*.'

David: 'Tell the press how Scott is attacking you because you rejected him as a lover. The gossip columnists will love it. He'll be a laughing-stock and that's something he won't be able to stand.'

George: 'You already know that some of your defecting staff don't like working for him. Buy 'em back, upping their salaries. I doubt if he'll be able to match you. The word is that he's already over-spent.'

311

David: 'Your magazine has one important advantage over his: yourself. Your reputation in the fashion world is unmatched. Put yourself in the hands of a good PR and let your name be splashed all over the papers. Every time it's mentioned you'll win back a few more readers.'

By midnight, I had all I needed to know from my two husbands, and their images faded.

I went to work. My broker bought up blocks of shares in two distributing companies and *Félice* disappeared from many shelves. I had always been cooperative with journalists and now it paid off. Paragraphs began to appear about my battle with Mark Scott, sympathetic to me, ridiculing him. I heard that he was beside himself with anger.

A clever public relations woman organized television appearances for me, and ITV offered me a series of six half-hour shows on the history of fashion. I was interviewed and photographed by the Sunday colour supplements, and the story of our fight appeared in *Time* and *Newsweek*. The three best members of my staff returned to the nest. They had never been happy at *Félice*, mainly because Scott, knowing little about magazine production, had constantly interfered.

Three months after my campaign started, *Cybèle*'s readership reached a new high and *Félice*'s had diminished to a point where advertisers no longer wanted to buy space in its pages.

The ninth issue was the last.

Mark Scott lost millions and has never challenged me since.

4

The weather changed. From being still and warm during the day, with cooler evenings and light breezes, a hot wind raced up from the Mediterranean. Branches tossed, the vines strained against their ties, and dust-devils swirled.

It began to blow at nine o'clock in the morning. The volunteers had all departed for their various tasks along the relay course, and to set up tables and benches for the *pique-nique*. Charles and Klaus had driven to the villa to discuss final arrangements for the prize-giving with Cybèle.

Only Suzy was at the mill, taking her turn at clearing the breakfast table and cleaning the kitchen.

As the wind began to whistle through the old building, doors banged and the great mill-wheel set up a high-pitched whine, straining against the ropes which bound it. A roof-tile crashed on to the terrace and the light outdoor tables and chairs were lifted like tumble-weed. Sun umbrellas were whipped out of their stands and two of them lurched over the terrace wall into the stream.

Suzy hurried outside. The hot wind dried her skin and tossed her hair as she carried the furniture into the hall. She splashed into the stream and pulled out the umbrellas, fighting to stay on her feet as the gusts caught them.

When she had cleared the terrace, she ran through the house, closing the ground-floor doors, then upstairs to shut the bedroom windows and pick up clothes, books and letters that had been blown to the floor.

Finally, Christian's room was the only one she hadn't checked. She pushed open his door with difficulty against the pressure of the gale through the open window.

What had been neat piles of paper beside his typewriter were now a white carpet. A copy of *I am Cybèle* was lying open and face-down beside his bed.

She collected the paper and picked up the book. As she did so, three typewritten sheets fell out of it. She glanced at them curiously and her attention was caught by the words at the top of the first page: 'This is the true story of Sylvie Andros's betrayal of the woman she knew as Marie Masson . . .'

She sat on the edge of his bed. Sylvie Andros? Surely that was the name Cybèle had used in Paris during the war? And Marie Masson was the Resistance worker with whom she had lived.

Her eyes moved down the page. What she saw made her

return to the beginning and go through it more carefully. A few minutes later, she put the manuscript down, scarcely able to believe what she had read.

'What the hell do you think you're doing?'

Christian was standing in the open doorway.

'I thought you were out . . .'

'I came back to make sure there was no damage from the wind. Why are you in my room?'

'I came in to shut the window. Your papers had been blown all over the floor . . .'

'So you decided to do some reading.' Towering over her, his face was hard and angry. Knowing that he had reason to be annoyed, at the same time irritated because he made her feel like a guilty schoolgirl, she said defiantly, 'Yes, I've been reading, and OK, I shouldn't have, but since I did, I'd like an explanation.'

'Of what?'

'Of this story about Cybèle and Marie Masson.'

'It's none of your business.'

'Yes, it is. Cybèle's my grandmother. Are you planning to publish this?'

'Probably.'

Light suddenly dawned. 'That's why you came down here! You were hoping to rake up more dirt!'

His voice was harsh. 'I'm going to correct this myth about Cybèle Meredith, war heroine, which she's been at such pains to circulate.'

'But how do you know this other story is true?'

'Marie Masson was my mother.'

'Oh . . . Jesus!' She stood up and said: 'That's the – the nightmare?'

'That's it. When my mother couldn't stand her life any longer, she committed suicide. There's no way Cybèle can be made to suffer the way she did, but when I realized who she was, I decided that at least I could set the record straight.'

'I've suspected from the start that your aversion was more than just macho-man's dislike for a successful woman. But you can't do this, Chris!'

314

'I told you, Suzy, it's none of your business what I do.'

She swept on, 'Even if what your mother told you is true, it happened nearly fifty years ago. She's dead. And you're going to accuse Cybèle of being a traitor and a liar, humiliate her and sour what's left of her life? To say nothing of what it will do to Julia and Alice.'

'Nonsense. They hardly know Cybèle. None of this will affect them.'

Her anger burst forth. 'You bloody insensitive idiot! I don't care so much about Alice, but for the first time in her life, Julia's found a real family. How do you think she's going to feel when you spread this scurrilous story that might not even be true? And you lied to everyone. Cybèle and Charles and the rest of us accepted your story that you only wanted material about her life at Le Bas-Fond. You didn't have the guts to tell the truth!'

He put his hands on her shoulders and gripped them hard. 'I intended all along to tell her eventually that Marie was my mother and hear what she had to say. I'd have faced her with it before if it hadn't been for you.'

'Me?'

His face was tormented. 'Do you think I've enjoyed the situation? I was afraid you'd react like this when you found out, and I couldn't bear to spoil things between us. That's why I decided to wait until after the festival. I thought, the more we got to know each other, the more chance there was that you'd understand my feelings.'

'I will never understand! You weren't even born during the war. You can have no idea what made Cybèle behave as she did.' She corrected herself: 'As your mother *said* she did. How can anyone our age understand the sort of tension she was living under?' She moved past him. At the door, she turned. 'Is it any good asking you to change your mind?'

He said flatly, 'I'm going to talk to her as soon as the festival's over.'

'You'll at least let her enjoy that? How thoughtful.' When he didn't react to the sarcasm, she said, 'And then I hope we won't see each other again.'

Julia had promised to help the women of La Bergerie to make preparations for *le pique-nique,* but first she drove to Le Bas-Fond to have breakfast with her mother. A few puffs of wind were already heralding the gale when she arrived. Cybèle was sitting alone at the table on the terrace.

'Alice has taken the car into La Bergerie to pick up some supplies at the market,' she said. 'Sophie wants to make us a *cassoulet.* She's turning into a good little cook. I think I'll take her on full-time after the festival. Charles and I are going to need extra help.'

Julia was breaking a freshly baked croissant that Sophie had collected from the bakery. 'You and Charles?'

'When we're in partnership. You know about our plans for Le Bas-Fond.' She hesitated. 'And, of course, there are the more – personal ones.'

'I don't understand . . . ?'

'I'm glad we haven't given ourselves away!' She leant forward, and smiled. 'I think I can't resist telling you, my dear. You'll be the first to know, but I beg you to keep it to yourself, at least for a while. We're not going to make any announcement until after the festival.'

'What announcement is that?'

'You must have seen what close friends Charles and I have become. Can't you guess what it is?'

Again Julia said, 'You – and Charles?'

Cybèle nodded. 'When I met Charles, it was as though I was beginning a new life. I need him, Julia. I've been lonely for such a long time and with him I feel I've been given another chance to find companionship and happiness.' Her voice dropped to a whisper. 'My last chance.'

She felt a pang of guilt as she saw Julia's expression, the brown eyes bewildered, her face suddenly drained of colour.

She hardened her heart. Dammit, she *did* need Charles, and Julia was young enough to have other chances.

With an obvious effort, Julia said, 'I'm happy for you. And – thank you for telling me.' She stood up, leaving the crumbled croissant on her plate, her coffee-cup half full. 'I'm sorry . . . I must go, Cybèle. I'm expected in the town by nine.'

As they walked to her car Cybèle put a hand on her arm. 'You'll say nothing, will you? Not to Alice. Not even to Charles. I wouldn't want him to know I've anticipated the announcement.'

'Of course not.' Her cheek was cold when Cybèle kissed it and she drove away without looking back.

That night, the wind was replaced by a brief, torrential rain-storm. It swelled the Dordogne's little tributaries, which surged into the main flow of the river, creating white-caps and sending miniature breakers crashing against the banks.

Three kilometres below La Bergerie, Arnie Gold's battered body was dislodged from between the rocks in which it had come to rest. It was borne down-river for a few hundred yards, then a cross-current tossed it up on to a tiny *plage* popular with holiday-makers from a nearby camp-site, where it was found the following morning by two small boys.

5

The day after the gale the weather returned to its normal gentle warmth and the wind was no more than a breeze. Julia arrived at Le Bas-Fond in the morning, to accompany her mother and Alice into Bordeaux to buy supplies for Cybèle's festival-eve party.

She was feeling heavy-eyed and depressed. Since Alex's death, no man had affected her as strongly as Charles. The discovery that he was apparently committed to Cybèle had left her with a sense of loss that surprised and shocked her. There was anger, too, that she had even momentarily been in danger of mistaking his light-hearted advances for something more serious.

She parked at the front of the house. As she reached the door, Alice came from down the stairs and stopped abruptly. 'I didn't think you'd be coming with us.'

'Wasn't I expected? I thought we'd arranged . . . ?'

Cybèle appeared from the kitchen. 'Of course you were expected.' She handed them each a straw shopping basket and led the way to her car.

They had almost reached it when Julia realized that she and Alice were wearing almost identical outfits, the white trousers and red shirt which were her own favourites and which Alice had duplicated.

'I wish I'd known you were going to wear that,' she remarked. 'We're going to look like Tweedledum and Tweedledee.'

She hoped Alice might volunteer to change, but she shrugged and said, 'It doesn't matter. We can't keep Cybèle waiting.'

There was heavy traffic in Bordeaux. Cybèle manoeuvred her BMW expertly into a parking-place as another car pulled out, ignoring the furious protests of a Frenchman who had been slower off the mark. She was, Julia thought, the kind of woman who would always manage to find somewhere to park, a taxi in rush-hour, the last table in a crowded restaurant.

She had previously telephoned an order for black, grey and red caviare to a delicatessen. When they collected it, she paid a bill which left her daughters open-mouthed.

Awed, Alice said, 'It'll be like eating diamonds!'

'And this isn't even the best quality – just the best available to us. The greatest caviare looks like golden beads and it used to be reserved for the Tsars. God knows who eats it now – only members of the Politburo, I suspect. The red is from salmon, not sturgeon, but I've bought some because it looks pretty.'

'How do you serve it?'

'With thin slices of Melba toast and pumpernickel. And no one must hold back! Luxury foods are no fun unless you can have *enough*.'

Julia always enjoyed the moments when Cybèle's façade

318

cracked to reveal glimpses of a less sophisticated personality, unashamedly revelling in treats which the young Sybil Androwski had been denied.

Alice's thoughts were less generous. This was the life-style of which she had dreamed, to be able to eat caviare and drink champagne whenever she desired. And it was almost within her grasp. No way, she vowed, was she going to allow Julia or Cybèle to rob her of any part of the splendid future to which she felt she was entitled.

She had been shocked to see Julia arrive at the villa, even more so by Cybèle's amiability. Surely it wasn't possible that she had decided to ignore Julia's affair with Charles?

They went from the delicatessen to a bakery, then to a crowded food-store to collect trimmings for the caviare: lemons, spring onions, farm eggs, smoked salmon, cucumber, tiny tomatoes and sweet butter, perfect grapes, peaches, strawberries, cherries, apricots, apples and pears to fill the crystal bowl which would be the centre-piece of a buffet table.

Cybèle moved from one counter to another. She had a presence that was impossible to ignore, and male assistants deserted other customers to serve her. Trailing behind, Alice was a dim, anonymous figure.

After following for a few minutes, Julia saw that her presence wasn't required, and told Cybèle she would break away and do some shopping for herself and Suzy.

Knowing that the others would be some time, she didn't hurry. She disposed of the essentials first, then decided to cheer herself up with some enjoyable extravagance. She bought perfumes for Cybèle, Alice and Suzy. From a gift shop she added a pair of tiny, exquisite silver ear-rings for Cybèle, a silver bracelet for Alice, a Mexican turquoise necklace for Suzy, a silk scarf and two pairs of black lace tights for herself. Having spent an agreeable half hour and a great deal of money, she strolled back towards the car.

She was passing the shop in which she had left Cybèle when a woman and two men, one in police uniform, hurried from the entrance and surrounded her.

The woman, who was small and middle-aged, with sharp

features and hair cut in a twenties shingle, peered into her face and snapped, 'This is the one!'

Julia's French, hesitant at the best of times, deserted her. 'What on earth . . . ?'

The man in civilian clothes said, in English, 'You will come with us, please, madame.'

'I'll do nothing of the kind! What is all this? Who are you?'

A few people paused and watched with interest. The men moved to either side of her, took her arms and forced her to walk into the shop between them. The woman pulled her basket out of her hand and followed.

She wondered wildly whether she was being kidnapped, but there was nothing secret in their actions. Rather than indulge in an undignified struggle, she held her temper in check until they reached an office at the back of the shop.

The woman set her basket on a desk and began to take out her purchases, one by one.

Icily, Julia said, 'You will kindly give me an explanation for this extraordinary behaviour.'

The men, standing between her and the desk, were watching the woman examine the contents of the basket, and did not reply. As Julia spluttered protests, they looked at the perfumes, the jewellery, the toiletries and especially a pot of black caviare, which had been carefully wrapped at the delicatessen, in paper bearing its name.

'What the hell are you doing?' she raged. 'How dare you interfere with my belongings!' She turned on the policeman. 'Why don't you stop them? Who *are* these people?'

He looked at her stolidly and did not reply. The woman spoke to him in French so rapid that she could not follow it. He pointed towards the hand-bag that was slung over her shoulder.

'You will show the purse, madame,' the other man said.

'Certainly not!'

The policeman grasped her arm while the woman slipped the bag off her shoulder, opened it and tipped the contents on to the desk. Comb, cosmetics, wallet, passport, change purse, a letter from Suzy, her key-ring, all fell out and the woman stirred them like vegetables in a pot. She handed the passport to the policeman, who opened it, looked at Julia's photograph, then at her, and went through its pages. The letter was handed to the other man, who read it.

This can't be happening, she thought. I'm being treated like a criminal. What do I do about it? No point in calling a policeman . . . he's already here. The British consul?

After a moment, she realized that the atmosphere had changed. The men had stepped back from the desk. The policeman directed a brief, angry tirade at the woman, then left the office.

'Madame . . .' The other man cleared his throat. 'I am afraid there has been a terrible mistake. My assistant . . .' He glared at the woman, '. . . thought that you . . . that she saw you . . .'

'Saw me what?' Julia said dangerously.

'Saw you take something from one of the counters.'

'She thought I was *shop-lifting*?'

He nodded, wretchedly.

'I haven't been near your shop for the past half-hour!' The woman, who looked as though she was about to burst into tears, was clumsily trying to re-wrap the parcels. 'Never mind that. Just put everything back in my basket. What is it I was supposed to have stolen?'

'A pot of caviare.'

She stared at him unbelievingly. 'You thought I *stole* that caviare? Can't you see where it was bought? I didn't even know you sold it here!'

'Not that one. We also . . . a pot is missing . . . it has been an error, madame.' He was a thin, sallow-faced man in a black suit. A nervous tic was shivering the skin under his right eye. 'You must allow me to make amends. Anything in the shop . . . anything you require . . .'

'All I require from you is an apology!' She picked up her shoulder-bag and shovelled its contents back, feeling that they had been defiled.

'I do apologize, most sincerely. I wish you would . . . some token? No? I hope you will forgive . . .'

Grovelling, he seemed younger than when he had

triumphantly believed he had trapped a shop-lifter, and she almost felt sorry for him. She said grimly, 'I won't take this any further, but I suggest that in future you think more carefully before you accuse innocent passers-by of theft.'

She turned her back on them and heard him say ominously to the woman, 'Wait here!' He scurried after her and bowed her out of the shop, dry-washing his hands as he muttered renewed apologies.

Still feeling the humiliation of having been marched under guard through the crowds, she hurried towards the car. It had been an extraordinary episode and she began to regret not having asked for more details, but all she had wanted was to get away.

As she began to think more clearly, she felt a chill. Alice had been in the shop, dressed almost exactly as she was, carrying the same traditional French marketing basket. Was it possible that *Alice* had taken a pot of caviare from a shelf and forgotten to pay for it? Or had she deliberately concealed it? The questions tumbled over each other. Why would she do such a thing when Cybèle had bought kilos of the stuff?

A half-forgotten incident came back into her mind. One day, when they were shopping in a store in Bergerac, Alice had admired some ear-rings that were lying in a tray on a counter. Later, at the villa, she was wearing them. When Julia remarked on them she said casually, 'I went back and bought them.' Julia had thought nothing of it at the time, but now she recalled that she and Alice had left the shop together and driven straight home. She couldn't have gone back for the ear-rings, but it would have been easy enough for her to slip them into a pocket as they passed the counter.

Cybèle and Alice were waiting for her in the car. She apologized for keeping them, but found herself tongue-tied when Cybèle said irritably, 'What on earth have you been doing?'

Now that she had thought of it, it seemed so obvious that the woman in the shop had mistaken her for Alice. Sharp-witted Cybèle, certainly, would not miss the implication, so telling them what had happened was tantamount to accusing

Alice of theft. She muttered something about having more to do than she had anticipated, and settled in the back of the car.

Preoccupied and unhappy, she hardly spoke during the drive home and when they reached the villa, had to make an effort to behave naturally. Hating herself for her suspicions, she watched Alice as they carried their baskets and carrier-bags into the kitchen and put away their purchases. There was nothing unexpected among them, but she noticed that instead of putting her hand-bag down as they unpacked, Alice kept it slung over her shoulder, then carried it upstairs with her.

Sophie had left lunch for them, and as soon afterwards as she reasonably could, Julia excused herself, saying she would be back the following morning to help prepare for the evening's party.

Neither Cybèle nor Alice appeared to notice anything was amiss.

She drove up the private road that led to the mill, intending to go straight back to the hotel and think out her problem.

Why would Alice steal cheap ear-rings when she had plenty of money to pay for them, and a superfluous pot of caviare?

Could it be an aberration caused by her age? Julia herself had sailed through the menopause early and hardly noticed it, apart from the ineffable relief of being released from her monthly periods, but she knew that other women were not so lucky, and sometimes indulged in irrational behaviour.

Worse was the possibility that these were not isolated incidents, but that Alice was a kleptomaniac, victim of a morbid and uncontrollable impulse to steal. One of Julia's oldest friends was a woman of otherwise impeccable character whose habit of stealing from the local shops was well-known in her village. Because she was generous and popular, the shop-keepers, after one of her forays, simply contacted her long-suffering family, who either paid for or returned the goods. It was unlikely that Alice would be as fortunate if her failing were discovered in France.

The lane wound around the mill and as she passed the terrace, Charles rose from a chair and waved. She was tempted to drive past, but knew that she could not avoid him indefinitely. She pulled up and leant out of the car. He came towards her, a solid, broad-shouldered man, his face lit by a smile of welcome. She watched him coldly, shamed by the memory of her response to his embrace on the river-bank, hating the cheap thrill he must have felt at the conquest of daughter as well as mother.

A few days ago she wouldn't have hesitated to tell him what had happened in Bordeaux, and ask for his advice, but now she wanted only to keep him at arm's length. The problem of what to do about Alice must remain hers alone. In any case, she didn't *know* she had stolen the caviare and the ear-rings. Momentarily forgetting Charles, she thought, oh, God, let me be wrong . . . but suppose she wasn't? If stealing was a habit with Alice, she'd need treatment. A psychiatrist. Even Cybèle mustn't know . . . not yet. Alice must be watched . . .

She jerked her head away as Charles bent to kiss her cheek. He raised his eyebrows but only said, 'I've been hoping I'd see you today. I missed you last night.'

'I went straight to the hotel and had an early night. I'm on my way there now.' Her voice was expressionless.

'Are you feeling all right, Julia?'

'Perfectly, thank you. I must be on my way.'

She raised a hand in casual farewell and drove off. In her rear-view mirror, she saw him standing on the terrace, staring after the car.

6

On the morning of Cybèle's party the villa was like an ant-hill, its quiet, sun-drenched exterior giving little hint of the activity inside.

In the kitchen, Sophie, Claire and Olivia were preparing the buffet, under Cybèle's direction. Julia was polishing glasses. She had greeted Charles with an unsmiling nod.

Christian had arrived with sacks of ice for the ice-buckets and Suzy, keeping out of his way, was helping Charles to string lights through the trellis over the terrace.

Suddenly, from the top of a ladder, he said, 'Is anything the matter with your mother?'

Draped with coloured light-bulbs, she looked up at him, frowning. 'You've noticed, too? She seemed to be off-colour when I went into La Bergerie last night, but she said there was nothing wrong.'

'She's hardly spoken to me. I'm wondering if I've offended her in some way.'

'She doesn't offend easily. I'm sure that's not it. It's probably a tummy upset or something, and if I know her, it'll only annoy her if we fuss.'

Forty people had been invited to the party, including ex-patriates and some native residents.

When he had finished threading the last lights through the grapevine, Charles sought out Cybèle to pass on a message from Klaus Fischer. 'He's asked me to say that if you'll forgive him, he'd prefer not to come to the party, since there are to be French guests.'

'What nonsense! Tell him I *insist* that he comes.'

'I did my best to persuade him, but he's very conscious of local feeling and he doesn't want to cause any embarrassment.'

'Charles, my guests are all civilized! They certainly aren't of the Sèzille persuasion. I will not allow that nice man to be left out!'

'Then you'll have to talk him into it yourself. I tried all the arguments I could think of.'

'I'll go up and see him.' She marched off to her car, her mouth a resolute line which members of her staff would have recognized.

As she drove up to the mill she thought that her scheme to separate Charles and Julia was working. She hadn't seem them speak to each other all morning, and Julia had told her that she would be going back to London immediately after the

325

festival. At the same time, she was aware of a disturbing flicker of conscience. Julia was not looking herself. She was pale and her normal ebullience had deserted her. There was something forced about her cheerfulness and when she was unaware of being watched, her face fell into lines that made her look years older. Surely it wasn't possible that she'd been serious about Charles?

She had not returned when the telephone rang in the villa. Alice set down a tray of glasses and picked up the receiver.

'Lady Meredith?'

'This is her daughter, Mrs Lynam.'

'Henry Franklin here. May I speak to Cybèle?'

'Hi, Henry. She's gone up to the mill.'

'You might be able to help, Alice. It's about our former odd-job man, Alfred Brown. Is he with you?'

After the briefest hesitation, she said, 'No. No, he isn't. Should he be?'

'He left me a note a few nights ago, saying he was on his way to see Cybèle.'

'Why, that's extraordinary! He never arrived. Maybe he changed his mind.'

'You're sure? You haven't seen him at all?'

'I'm quite sure.'

'Right. Thank you, Alice.'

'We'll see you tonight, won't we?'

It took him a moment to answer, and his voice was abstracted. 'Tonight? Yes, of course. Looking forward to it.'

He hung up. Alice put the telephone down and carried on with her work.

The guests had been invited for six-thirty, and by seven o'clock almost everyone had arrived, including Fischer, who, like most people, had found himself unable to withstand Cybèle's determination. For many, it was their first visit to the villa and they spread through the ground floor, peering at the furnishings and the portrait of Cybèle that dominated the sitting-room. They looked into the dining-room, with its tile-topped refectory table, big enough to seat ten people, and Cybèle's study, its walls lined with crowded book-shelves. They admired the extravagant bowls of flowers in every corner and invaded the kitchen to sigh over the gadgets and expensive fittings.

Waiters, hired for the evening, circulated with trays of champagne and vodka. Tables on the terrace were loaded with platters of buttered Melba toast, bread, smoked salmon and chopped eggs and slivers of raw vegetables and sliced lemon surrounding crystal bowls of caviare, each with its silver serving spoon.

The volunteers had brought a hi-fi from the mill and a Piaf tape had been set at the right volume to fill any early silences, but not too high to drown conversation.

If some guests were overawed by the splendour at first, for this was by no means a typical expatriate party, the rapid circulation of champagne soon drowned their inhibitions.

Cybèle and Suzy were the fashion stars of the evening, the older woman in a white silk-jersey dress by St Laurent ('Seven thousand if it cost a penny,' Suzy whispered to Julia) and the younger in turquoise silk harem trousers with a silver thread. A brief top in the same material left bare several inches of her smooth brown midriff.

It was just after seven when the final guests, Emily and Henry Franklin, arrived. Their car was followed by a second which contained someone who had not been invited: Jacques Millet, the policeman from La Bergerie.

Henry made purposefully for Cybèle, who was talking to Klaus, with Alice standing by. Millet hovered uneasily at the edge of the crowd.

'May we have a moment, Cybèle?' Henry said. 'Millet wants a word with you.'

She frowned. 'What does he want?'

'Rather tell you in private, if you don't mind.'

'Come into the study.' She led the way inside. Alice followed, unnoticed by Cybèle until they reached the room. Then she said, 'I don't think your presence is required, Alice.'

Millet, who spoke excellent English, said, 'If you please,

327

madame, I understand your daughter lives here with you. She could perhaps be of help.'

'If you like. But be as quick as you can, I must get back to my guests. Is there some problem?'

'It's Alfred Brown,' Henry said. 'You remember? The chap who was coming to work for you. Did Alice tell you I phoned about him today?'

Alice covered her mouth with her hand. 'How about that! I forgot!'

'It doesn't matter. Cybèle, Brown's body has been found a few miles down-river. He had been drowned.'

'Drowned?' For a moment it was as though she held her breath. 'Alfred . . . Brown?'

Alice went swiftly to her side, linked arms with her and said, 'My, that's awful! But I told you on the phone, Henry, we never saw him. I mean, he never came here, did he, Cybèle?'

Like a gramophone record on which the needle had stuck, Cybèle repeated: 'He never came here.'

'You're sure of that, madame?' Millet said.

'Oh, quite sure, aren't we, Cybèle?'

'Quite sure.'

'We believe he must have fallen into the river somewhere between La Bergerie and here. The body was found washed up on a *plage* yesterday. He had been in the water for some days and carried no identification. Only from the labels in his clothes it was known that he was an Englishman.'

'How did you find out who he was?' Alice asked.

'His description was circulated in the towns along the river: I remembered an old Englishman, looking like a tramp, who had been employed by M. Franklin.'

'I had to identify the body,' Franklin said. 'It was him, all right. Very nasty . . .'

Millet said, 'One of our taxi-drivers, Lucien Saintes, recalls having driven him here late in the evening. He had been in the Café des Arts and he was very drunk. Saintes left him at the end of the drive and said he staggered off. It is possible that he wandered towards the river, to relieve himself, perhaps, and fell in. He was carrying a bag, and it has not been found. You have not seen it?'

'No,' Alice said.

He shrugged. 'We will send his description to the police in London, but if no-one reports that he is missing, there's nothing more we can do.'

He shook hands all round, and departed. Henry followed him out.

Cybèle deliberately relaxed her hunched shoulders and straightened her spine. She looked at Alice, who was watching her expressionlessly. 'We will talk about this later,' she said.

They faced each other in the sitting-room. It was ten o'clock. Even the late stayers had long since gone and the party debris had been cleared.

For Cybèle, the hours had passed in a blur and only an effort of will had enabled her to maintain the appearance of an untroubled hostess.

Now, in the silence of the empty house, her body began to tremble.

Alice perched on the arm of a chair and said, 'You surely can be proud of yourself, Cybèle. It was a terrific party. Can I get you a cup of something? Or shall we have another little drink together, just the two of us?' She was carefree, exhilarated, nothing on her mind but the good time she'd had.

'Alice, I want to know what happened that night.'

'What night?'

'I can't believe you don't know what I'm talking about. The night Arnie Gold died.'

'Oh, that. Why, nothing happened. I guess he just fell in the water because he'd had too much to drink.'

'But how could he have been near the river? You drove him back into La Bergerie. Where did you let him out of the car?'

'I told you. Near the square. He must have decided to take a walk or something, and gone down to the river.'

'The river is half a mile from the square. He was much too drunk to walk that far.'

'I don't suppose he knew what he was doing. Oh, Cybèle. I know about drunks. Believe me, you can never tell what they're going to do.' Her face was guileless and she met Cybèle's eyes without blinking.

'If he was as drunk as that, how was it you managed to persuade him not to come back here? Alice, you told me he wouldn't be back at all. You said, "We don't have to worry about him again." *How did you know?*'

'Honey, I did happen to see him wandering off towards the river, but I didn't take too much notice. All I wanted was to get rid of him, like you told me to.'

'You haven't answered my question. How did you know he wouldn't be coming back?'

'I was only obeying what you said. "Just get rid of him." Your very words.' She slid from the arm of the chair on to the cushioned seat, slipped her shoes off and curled up with her feet under her. 'Don't let's talk about that old man. Let's talk about us instead.'

Unconsciously, Cybèle began to massage the tense muscles at the back of her neck. She was washed by horror such as she had not experienced since the dreadful night when she had cradled Dominic Stone's dead body in her arms.

Her voice was little more than a whisper. 'Alice, what did you do?'

'For Heaven's sake, I just let him go, that's all.'

'You knew he might fall into the river?'

'Oh, well, sure. He wanted to pee. Disgusting old man. It was his own fault.'

'Why didn't you call the police?'

As though she was talking to a child, Alice said patiently, 'I was doing it for you. Don't you understand? You never wanted to see him again. What was the point of calling anyone? I mean, it would have been very unpleasant, the police and all. Questions. People finding out who he was. This way, you and I are the only ones who know. I bet there's no-one in England who'll miss him. We can just forget the whole thing.'

'The police must be told.'

330

'Don't be silly, Mother.' It was the first time she had used the matronymic, and she smiled as she emphasized it. 'Are you truly going to tell them that your daughter killed her father?'

'You *killed* him?'

'Well, that's what they'll think, and maybe I sort of helped him on his way. And I'll tell you something. If you think you can call the cops and make up some story about it having been an accident, you're wrong. I'll tell them the lot, how you *ordered* me to do it because you couldn't bear to have anyone know that awful old man had fucked you and that he was probably our father. Julia's and mine. Oh, Julia's going to love that, isn't she? Her twin sister and her mother both up for murder. And I bet I'm the one who gets off, everyone will feel so sorry for me: abandoned when I was twenty-four hours old, brought up by a hooker, so happy to find my real mother that I was prepared to do anything she asked. The newspapers will love it.'

The strength drained from Cybèle's limbs and she sat down abruptly. The soft voice went on. 'But of course you wouldn't force me to do that, would you? No, you're going to tell Julia you've decided that I'm to take over your company instead of her. You'll teach me how to run it and we're going to make more and more money. Just you and me.'

Cybèle was unable to speak as her mind tried to deny the undeniable.

Hadn't the seeds of the truth already been planted? When they had talked on the night of Arnie's disappearance, Alice had said, 'I got rid of him for you . . .' Cybèle had believed this simply meant that she had talked him into leaving, because that was what she wanted to believe.

She looked at the woman sitting opposite her: quiet, helpful Alice, apparently so appreciative of all that had been done for her. With her new understanding, the face, superficially identical to Julia's, now appeared totally unlike. The scarlet mouth was twisted up on one side in a malicious smile; the eyes were opaque and hard as brown pebbles, the features were plumper and coarser and her expression could never

331

mirror Julia's generosity and charm. But Julia's expression had changed, she thought suddenly. Even at the party it had been sombre and without animation.

'So what d'you say, honey? It's just you and me from here on, isn't it?' There was no trace now of the cultivated accent she had been at pains to acquire.

Cybèle rose. Time. She needed time to think.

'I'm going to bed,' she said evenly. 'We'll talk again.'

As though reading her mind, Alice said, 'You do that. Go to bed and think about what I've said, Mother. Think all you like. It won't make any difference. You and I *need* each other. Enjoy the festival, and then we'll get together and make our plans for the future.'

Cybèle went slowly up the stairs to her bedroom, conscious of Alice's eyes following her. She locked her door behind her and lay on the bed, knowing that her churning thoughts made sleep out of the question.

What were the options?

She could defy Alice and tell the police the whole story, hoping that she could persuade a court she was telling the truth. Even worse than the consequences for herself, she could not endure the thought of the effect that situation, with its inevitable sleazy publicity, would have on Julia.

The alternative was to accept Alice's ultimatum, keep the secret of Arnie Gold's death and take her into the company.

For just one second, she considered a third option: to get rid of Alice as Alice had got rid of Arnie.

But Alice was her daughter, carrying her genes, and it was not impossible that what Alice was, she might herself have become if she had been deserted by her mother, farmed out and brought up in a world of poverty and violence in which the only morality was to survive, at whatever cost to others. Her guilt mounted as she forced herself to face the fact that her own creed had been precisely that as she had struggled to achieve her ambitions. Perhaps it had only been by luck that she had not been forced to sink to Alice's depths.

By midnight, she had reached the bleak conclusion that the second alternative was her only choice. After the festival, she would tell Alice that she had won. It was fortunate, in the circumstances, that Julia had rejected her attempts to bring her into the company.

Julia. All the doubts she had been trying to smother about her plan to separate Julia and Charles returned. Despite her preoccupation with Alice, she had watched them during the evening. Julia, looking tired and unhappy, had treated him with studied indifference and avoided him as far as possible. She had seen the hurt in his eyes as they followed her, and his manner towards herself had been abstracted. With stark clarity she understood suddenly that she had made a mistake: Charles would never marry her, even if he were to become her business partner, because he was in love with Julia.

Her breath caught in her throat. If Julia were to discover that she had lied . . . it would be distressing to lose Charles, but losing this daughter would be unbearable.

She switched on the bed-lamp and reached for her book. She had often asked for advice from her husbands, but there had been another man in her life who had perhaps been wiser than either of them. She turned to the last page . . .

7

Extract from *I am Cybèle*

I have never found it easy to lose a fight – or even an argument – but whenever I do, I seem to hear the echo of my father's voice as he talked to me before he died.

After he was bed-ridden, too ill even to be moved into his wheel-chair, I used to sit with him, listening to the roar of the circus audience in the distance.

One night, as Etta's voice was lifting the tent-top in *Musetta's Waltz Song*, he had been muttering to himself in Hungarian, into which he often lapsed now. Then his eyes opened and they were no longer vague, but sharp and bright as they had been before the accident. He focused on me and reached for my hand. In English, he said, 'I shall not be here much longer.'

'Of course you will!' Neither Etta nor I could bring ourselves to accept that his death was imminent, and to date he had never spoken of it either.

'No. You must fight your own battles from now on, my Sybil. I pray the good Lord you win most of them, but remember, when you lose, make it be with dignity and do not blame anyone but yourself.' His eyelids drooped for a moment, then he smiled. 'You will come through. You are a survivor.'

A few hours later, he was dead.

His words have remained with me, and I've tried to carry out his advice. In my terms, they are translated: 'Fight like hell for what you want as long as there's a chance. When there's no hope of winning, cut your losses and tell yourself – and everyone else – that you never wanted it anyway.'

She closed the book, put it back on the table and switched off the light. Lajos had been right, and in the present circumstances, there was only one way to retain her dignity: she must retire gracefully from the competition for Charles before it was too late. That way, there was a chance that she might retain Julia's friendship at least.

Two daughters, she thought wryly, two battles lost – but with Alice, even friendship had become impossible.

8

The first day of the festival dawned fine and hot.

Cybèle stared at herself in her dressing-room mirror. She looked ten years older, heavy-eyed and pallid, the fine lines on her face incised more deeply by her sleepless night. The flesh had sunk below gaunt cheek-bones and her silver hair was like a grey door-mat.

It was her appearance, more than anything else, that brought her back to life as she confronted a day that promised no pleasure. The festival had become something to be endured as she struggled to adjust herself to a future over which, for almost the first time in her adult life, someone else was taking control.

Detachedly, as though she was watching another woman in the glass, she saw her tired lids lift to reveal the blue eyes. She raised her head to flatten the sagging flesh under her chin, and smiled. Although it was little more than a grimace, it changed the pattern of lines, and wiped away at least a few of the added years. This was the picture she would present to the world.

She showered, washed and dried her hair, then tied it back and began to work on the blank canvas of her face. By the time she had finished, the battered, defeated Cybèle whom only she was ever allowed to see had been replaced by a flawlessly groomed woman whose age might have been anything from forty to fifty.

It had been decided that the costumes she, Julia and Alice were to wear would not be unveiled until the following day, when they would gather on the dais for the start of the relay, so she chose an olive-green skirt by Calvin Klein, with a coffee-coloured shirt and a silk Hermès scarf that picked up the colours. The simple outfit suited her, and restored her confidence.

With the rest of Le Bas-Fond's residents, she was to spend the day in La Bergerie, where the festival would be opened officially by the town's mayor at ten o'clock.

She was checking her appearance in the mirror when there was a knock on the door and the handle turned. Because she had not yet unlocked it, it did not open.

Alice's voice carolled: 'It's only me. I've brought you up some coffee and a croissant.' Her tone was as it always had been, gentle, almost apologetic. But she had never

335

before dared to come to the bedroom in the morning.

'Take it downstairs, please, Alice. I don't want any breakfast.'

'I just thought, it's nearly ten, and we're being picked up . . .'

'I'm aware of that, thank you.'

She lingered in her room until she heard a car draw up outside. When she went down, Suzy and Alice were standing beside the Volvo.

She kissed Suzy and forced herself to nod to Alice, who smiled brightly. There was no indication in her manner of any change in their relationship.

La Bergerie was *en fête*. Many of the locals were already in costume, visitors were pouring in and the streets and square were festooned with bunting. A fair had been set up in a field on the edge of town, a circus in another. There was a marquee with a motor exhibition and stalls selling everything from *crêpes* to junk jewellery and North African rugs. The market-square had been given over to entertainers, and groups of young people were making music in the side-streets.

Julia was waiting for the party from Le Bas-Fond at the hotel. There was a general discussion about where to go and what to do, a lunch rendezvous arranged before they broke up into smaller units.

Cybèle, Julia and Alice were to stay together and, to Julia's surprise, Suzy elected to join them. Chris went off with Olivia hanging on to his arm. Charles, who had persuaded a reluctant Klaus to join them, remained protectively by his side and they decided to start the day with coffee on the terrace outside the Café des Arts.

Cybèle heard Charles say softly to Julia, 'Won't you join us?'

Without looking at him, she said, 'Thank you, no. I don't feel like coffee.'

When the others had gone, Cybèle said, 'I want to have a few words with Julia. Suzy, you and Alice wait here. We won't be long.'

336

Alice looked at them suspiciously. 'Where are you going?'

'To Julia's room.' Before anything more could be said, Cybèle took Julia's arm and led her inside, conscious of Alice's narrowed eyes stabbing into her back.

As they walked up to the first floor Julia thought, she's going to try again to persuade me to join her company. She's going to tell me that when she and Charles are married, she won't be able to carry on, and there isn't anyone else.

In the bedroom, the two women faced each other.

'I want to clear up a misunderstanding,' Cybèle said briskly. 'The other day I told you that I intended to marry Charles McDonald. That was not true. There has been no discussion of marriage between us.'

Bewildered, scarcely able to believe what she had heard, Julia stared at her. 'But you said . . .'

'I know I did. It was – wishful thinking.' Hastily, she added, 'No, not wishful. I really haven't the slightest desire to take on a third husband and I know it's never entered Charles's head. It was – call it a momentary fantasy. No more than that. As soon as I'd said it, I realized how foolish it was.'

'Your loneliness? Your need for companionship?'

'Part of the fantasy. I'm not in the least lonely, especially now I've found you, and Charles is only my very good friend. No more than that.' She leant forward, kissed Julia's cheek and linked arms with her. 'Now let's go back to the others.'

'I still don't understand . . .'

'Just forgive me for my nonsense, and forget it, my dear.'

Dazedly, Julia followed her out on to the terrace and suddenly the day was brighter, people were more attractive, smiles were wider and there was a new lightness in her step.

She did not notice Alice's spiteful, jealous eyes slanting from her to Cybèle as she wondered what had been going on.

They walked into the town and despite her renewed happiness, Julia found herself watching Alice uneasily whenever they passed a stall where an object might be picked up and slipped into a pocket or hand-bag. And there were other tensions which were difficult to ignore. Suzy had clearly quarrelled with Christian and was unlike her normal self,

337

walking apart, withdrawn and silent. By contrast, Cybèle was now exhibiting a forced, uncharacteristic gaiety for which she could find no explanation.

They were standing in the square, watching a young couple performing a mime, when Julia saw Alice slip her hand through her mother's arm. Cybèle drew away and moved to Julia's side. It was an unmistakable rejection and as Julia met Alice's eyes, she was shocked at her expression.

Suddenly, it was as though she was in one of the dreams she had suffered intermittently since she was a child, when she and her unknown twin found each other. Their meetings had always been in some improbable, nightmarish location: on a mountain-top wreathed in swirling mist, in a dark tunnel, a waterless, black desert. The one constant had been her fearful recognition of her sister's hostility as they moved towards each other.

But now she was awake, had seen the bland mask slip and discovered that in reality, as in the dreams, Alice hated her.

All the colour and music of the festival faded and it seemed that she was suspended in space as she tried to understand what had happened. Alice's face had been a momentary vision of evil, the more terrifying because it had been her own face, seen in a distorting mirror.

Had her dreams been manifestations of the curious bond that was said to exist between identical twins, operating even over the thousands of miles that had separated them? Had she always *known* that her twin sister would become her enemy?

Claire had prepared a picnic and the whole party met down by the river for a late lunch. Rugs and a red-and-white-checked table-cloth were spread on the grass under a weeping willow and hampers of food and wine were opened.

Charles and Klaus were the last two to arrive, and when Klaus had been settled on a folding canvas chair, Julia went over to them. Charles turned, his expression noncommittal. She smiled up at him. 'May I join you?' He blinked, then nodded warily. She sank down on the grass beside him and slowly he began to relax. Cautiously, his hand reached out for hers and instead of drawing away, she returned the

338

pressure of his fingers and the last strain between them disappeared.

But although they talked easily and lightly, the memory of Alice's undisguised hatred remained in the back of her mind like the echo of a bad dream.

It was nearly five o'clock before the picnic-site had been cleared and plans for the evening were discussed. There was to be dancing in the square later, and most of the young people opted to stay on in town.

Alice had drunk several glasses of red wine. 'I'm gonna stay, too,' she declared. 'I'm just loving this festival. Cybèle, let's you and me spend the rest of the day together. I bet we can dance with the best of them.'

Cybèle shook her head. 'No. I've had enough. Julia, perhaps you'd give me a lift back to Le Bas-Fond?'

With relief, Julia said, 'Of course. I believe I've had enough, too.'

Alice was silent for a moment, then said defiantly, 'Not me. I'm celebrating.'

'Something special?' James asked idly. 'Your birthday?'

'No, no. Just – things. Being here. The future. I'm a very lucky girl.'

She looked around the circle as though challenging anyone to argue. Julia kept her eyes lowered and noticed that Cybèle's hands were clenched by her sides.

In the end, it was decided that Julia and Cybèle would go back to the mill with Klaus and Charles, while the rest of the party stayed in town. At first Suzy said she would join the home-goers, but Rob and Arthur insisted that she should stay. Olivia drew Chris away towards the river, whispering to him. He looked towards Suzy, but she pretended not to see. Alice went off with the two actors.

The quiet of the mill was soothing and for Julia it was a relief to be free of Alice's disturbing presence.

Cybèle, too, was more relaxed, although her eyes were tired and her skin papery in the late afternoon sunlight.

After an early supper, Klaus excused himself and went up to bed. Soon afterwards, Charles drove Cybèle down to the

339

villa. She hardly spoke, and hurried inside with a brief good night.

Back at the mill, Julia was waiting for him in the kitchen. He held out his arms and she went into them without hesitation.

'What's been wrong?' he said softly.

'Nothing. A misunderstanding. I'll tell you about it some time. Not now. Please.'

'Are you sure that's all?'

'Yes, I'm sure.'

'Then we should make the most of having the place to ourselves.' This time he offered no restrained caress, but a passionate, demanding kiss that set alight all the emotions she had been damping down since his first embrace by the stream.

When he released her, they both knew that the time for prevarication had ended. He stood back, took a deep breath and said: 'Julia Leander, will you marry me?'

Dizzily aware that all her doubts had been swept away, she said. 'Yes, I do believe I will.'

He lifted her hand and kissed it. 'In that case, will you come to bed with me? I want to make love to you and I want to talk to you. We have a great deal to find out about each other.'

She reached up and kissed him again, more gently. 'I want to sleep with you, spend the night – all the nights – with you. But not here and now. I couldn't bear to come down in the morning to nudges and knowing winks from the young – especially my own daughter.'

'You're right, of course,' he said regretfully. 'I'd hate it, too.'

'When then?'

'After the festival. We'll make the announcement, get it all into the open. Tell Cybèle and Suzy first, hopefully receive their blessings.' He felt a momentary *frisson* as he wondered how Cybèle would take the news. 'Get married as soon as possible after that.'

'Perhaps we don't need to wait that long before we get together?' she said hopefully.

'You're an immoral woman – but I was thinking that when

340

the news is out, we might go away together. I have a friend who rents his house near Grasse during the summer. We could take it for a couple of weeks.'

'And find out whether we can stand each other for twenty-four hours a day? Good idea.'

'Find out whether *you* can stand *me*. I already know my feelings . . .'

They were beaming at each other idiotically, when they heard the sound of cars.

'Shit!' he said. 'I hoped we'd have a bit more time. But, my love, soon we won't need to pretend any longer.'

When the volunteers poured in, they were sitting sedately on opposite sides of the kitchen table, drinking coffee.

There was an outburst of chatter about the day. Alice had been driven back to the villa, alcoholically tearful and talking endlessly about her poor Hank and his tragic death. Suzy had been elected Queen of the Dance-Floor in an impromptu competition and been virtually mobbed by men determined to dance with her. One of Paul Sézille's friends, drunk, had driven his motor-bike into the river. Jacques Millèt had arrested two English louts who were harassing the local girls.

Charles and Julia sat quietly, hardly hearing the talk, and after half an hour or so, the young people started to drift off to bed.

Olivia had been one of the first to move.

Upstairs, out of sight of the others, she went past the room she shared with Suzy. She'd had Christian to herself all day and she had no intention of allowing him to escape her now.

She opened his door, went through and closed it behind her. She switched on a bed-lamp and looked around. The room was tidy, the single bed neatly made, his denim bomber-jacket hanging over the back of the chair, rope-soled espadrilles side by side in a corner, piles of paper on the table beside his little Canon Typestar.

Cybèle's book was there, too, with some typed sheets protruding between the pages. His article about Le Bas-Fond? Would she be in it? Inquisitively, she pulled them out and glanced at the front page. Like everyone else at the mill, she had read *I am Cybèle* and she remembered the story of Marie Masson. The first words were intriguing, but for the moment she was too excited by what was to come when Chris returned to read on. She would ask him later about this so-called 'truth'. Now they had better things to do.

She put the book down, moved to the open window, which overlooked the terrace, and saw that everyone had gone. He would be up any minute.

She took off her clothes and slid between his sheets. There was sexual stimulation in fitting her body into the groove his heavy form had made in the mattress and she lay on her back, arms behind her head, and waited.

A few minutes later, she heard voices on the terrace. Naked, she switched off the bed-lamp, crept to the window and looked down on the two people below her.

As usual, Julia had insisted on returning to the hotel and when Charles and Suzy came back after seeing her off, there was no-one on the terrace.

Suzy said, 'Charles, I don't feel like going up yet. I'm going to sit out here for a while.'

Aware that all was not right between her and Chris, he sensed that she would rather be alone and said good night.

She sat on the parapet by the mill-wheel and looked down into the dark water. She had hated every moment of the day and the wine she had drunk in an effort to cheer herself up had only increased her depression. Everywhere she had been, she seemed to have run into Christian Morel, with Olivia plastered to him like a fly to a wall, reaching up to ruffle his hair, patting his cheek, brushing invisible specks off his shirt.

She had just come to the conclusion that she hated them both when she heard footsteps and Christian emerged from the hall.

She stood up and said, 'I thought you'd gone to bed.'

'I was in Charles's study. I've been waiting for you.'

'Why?'

'I want to talk.'

'We have nothing to talk about.'

'Yes, we have.' He was holding a glass of whisky. 'Would you like a drink?'

'No, thank you. I'm going up to my room.'

He grasped her wrist. 'You're going to listen to me. Then you can go.'

She realized that if she tried to leave, he would not hesitate to keep her by force and made herself speak calmly. 'You're hurting me. Let me go, then say what you want to.'

'Sit down. This won't take long.'

She perched on the edge of the parapet like a bird lighting on a branch, ready to fly at the slightest sign of trouble. He sat beside her.

Neither was aware of the naked listener at the window above.

'I'm not going to use that story about Cybèle and Marie,' he said.

Her head jerked towards him. 'Do you mean that? Or is it just a ploy?'

'A ploy? You mean, to bring you back to me? No. Well, not entirely. Maybe it's too late, anyway . . . after what you said the other night. I've thought about it – Christ, I haven't thought about anything else! – and even if it doesn't make any difference to – to us, I can't do it. As you said . . . what right have I to humiliate that woman, maybe ruin the rest of her life for something that happened so long ago?' He paused. 'There's another thing: I never expected to, but I like Cybèle. She's a fighter. She's tough and ruthless, all the things I thought she was, but I can't help respecting her. I've been re-reading her book in bed at night . . .' His teeth flashed in a brief smile. '. . . There hasn't been anything else to do. The first time I read it, I was only concerned with the part that dealt with my mother. I hardly registered the rest. Now I realize that she's an extraordinary woman and you were right, she doesn't deserve to be pilloried by someone who wasn't even born when she was risking her life.' He drained the last of his whisky. 'That's all I have to say. Thank you for listening.'

'Thank you for telling me.' The words were so formal that his heart sank. So it had been too late.

Then she said, 'There's something I have to ask.'

'Yes?'

'Have you been sleeping with Olivia?'

The question was so unexpected that it took a moment to sink in. Then, out of sheer relief, he laughed. 'My God, no! She has been driving me mad. Nothing would get rid of her. She believed that with you out of the way, I became her possession, but I would rather sleep with – with your Aunt Alice than with her.'

She went to him, as a short time ago her mother had gone to Charles, and her voice was muffled against his chest as she said, 'I've been so bloody miserable! I'd just decided that I was giving up men for ever.'

'I approve of that. From now on, you do give them up, all except one. You understand?' He kissed her. 'So now we will go upstairs and take up where we left off.'

As they went towards the french windows she said: 'Chris, you will destroy your notes about Cybèle, won't you? If she ever found out what you'd intended to write, she'd do her damnedest to separate us.'

'She would not succeed, but I assure you I do not wish to antagonize my future grandmother-in-law. I'll burn them.'

Olivia was shivering with rage and humiliation. He would rather sleep with Alice than her, would he? And all the past days, while he'd been leading her on, he'd only been thinking about that red-headed tart.

She collected her clothes, quickly smoothed his bed and made for the door. Passing the typing table, she pulled his notes out of Cybèle's book. When she reached her room, she read them.

9

One of Le Bas-Fond's important daily rituals was the morning postal delivery.

Normally there was a rush to collect the letters, which were then taken into the kitchen and distributed.

On the day of the relay race, only Klaus was at home when the yellow PTT van was due to arrive. Everyone else had gone into town to watch the pageant which would precede the race.

Charles had tried to persuade him to accompany them, but he had refused, making the excuse that the amount of walking he had done the previous day had tired him. In fact, despite having enjoyed himself, he had been conscious of unease and had been constantly watchful for signs of aggression from the locals. He had seen young Sézille and his friends in the distance, but they had kept well away from the mill party. Nevertheless, he decided not to push his luck a second day. With the relay coming up, sufficient antagonism had already been generated between the rival teams. His presence, supporting France's other historic enemy, would only be an irritant.

He intended to watch the race from a comfortable chair on the terrace, which gave him a view of the field from which it would start, and the finishing post.

He looked out across the scene. Deserted now, it seemed to be suspended in time, awaiting the people who would bring it to life. Just over the stream was the dais where Cybèle and her daughters would sit with local dignitaries. Above their chairs a blue and white striped awning had been stretched, with flag-poles at each corner from which fluttered rainbow banners. There were grand-stands on either side for special guests. The starting and finishing posts were below the dais.

He could see the first obstacle, ropes hanging from the branches of an oak above one of the stream's deep pools. The first two competitors would swing across and, if either landed in the water, he would have to keep trying until he managed to drop on to the opposite bank. The second obstacle was a row of wine barrels, their bases removed, through which the men would wriggle. After negotiating them, they would disappear from view as the course circled towards La Bergerie, around the town, and back. The last two runners would scale a high brick wall and race the last stretch to the finish.

Later in the morning, Charles and the other senior members of the teams were going to drive over the course to make sure all the obstacles were safe.

Klaus thought how much he would miss this place and his new friends when he returned to his lonely house on the Wannsee.

He would miss cheerful little Claire and her excellent cooking; Olivia and the amusement of watching her relentless pursuit of Christian Morel; Christian himself, intelligent, thoughtful, recently disturbed about his relationship with Suzy, but ebullient today, indicating that they had settled their difficulties; the actors, whose sexual habits intruded no more on the company than those of a normal married couple; Rob, with the hands which were equally skilled binding wounds or making furniture; Arthur, abrasive, reticent and efficient; Charles, whose friendship was the thing he valued most from the past weeks. And Julia and Suzy, whom he had come to love.

He didn't realize, as his thoughts drifted on, that he had excluded Alice.

And Cybèle. He could hardly believe that it was she who had altered the course of his life, who had dominated his thoughts, to whom he had imagined himself making love when he lay with his wife. Still, he would miss her, too, because she had received him kindly and was part of Le Bas-Fond.

His musing was interrupted by the rattle of the PTT van along the drive.

By the time he reached the front door, it was already disappearing, and there was a pile of mail on the table.

He riffled through it and at last found the letter from Neil Simmonds for which he had been waiting.

He tore open the envelope and began to read.

My dear Klaus,

I was delighted to hear from you again and to have a chance to tell you how much I enjoyed seeing you during your recent visit to New York.

Your commission was decidedly off-beat for one who normally spends his time foraging in libraries and newspaper morgues. I must say, though, I have enjoyed it, and you might well have started me on a new career as a private eye.

As you suggested, I began my investigation by contacting Alice Lynam's friend, Bibi Jackson.

She is a somewhat drab unmarried lady in her late forties who lives alone in a walk-up apartment in Brooklyn. She is a book-keeper in the menswear store of Nathan Weitz on Seventh Avenue, which is where she met the women then known as Alice Bukowsky. Hank Lynam, who became Alice's husband, also worked there before diabetes caused him to give up gainful employment.

I telephoned her, saying I wanted to have a chat about Mrs Lynam, and was immediately invited to her apartment.

We fenced a bit at first. She asked me politely what news I had of Alice and said wasn't it great the way she'd fallen on her feet with this famous British writer who had turned out to be her mother. However, I sensed a distinct lack of enthusiasm and eventually I decided to tell her the truth: that I had been asked to find out something about Alice's background and character on behalf of friends of Lady Meredith.

That opened the flood-gates, and I'll try to set down verbatim the significant parts of our conversation.

'Well, Mr Simmonds,' she said, 'I'm glad *someone* hasn't been taken in by that woman! I mean, the impression she gives, of being so sweet, and all, she isn't really like that. I could tell you . . .'

'I wish you would, Ms Jackson.'

'Well, then, I liked her well enough at the beginning. We used to go out at lunchtime, and I guess she told me more about herself than most people. She didn't have many friends, especially because she never much liked women. She always thought of them as competitors, sort of.' Here she paused and then said sadly, 'I guess I didn't count that way.

'Then I got to know her and I found out things, like how she was sleeping with Nathan Weitz, and being paid for it. She used to tell me what they did in bed. In the middle of the day! It was disgusting.

'She was such a hypocrite! She always said how much she hated Hank Lynam. Then after he died – and that was a peculiar thing, I'll tell you about it in a minute – she carried on about what a good man he'd been and how much she'd loved him. Once I said, but you hated him, Alice, and she said how could I say such a terrible thing when I knew she'd always adored him. Bullshit!

'About Hank's death. He fell down the stairs and she told everyone it was because he was drunk. But it happened so conveniently, I've always wondered if there wasn't something funny about it.

'We'd seen a picture of this writer, Lady Meredith, in a book-shop and I'd said Alice looked like her. She liked that, and she bought Lady Meredith's book. I think that right away she decided that she was going to France to find her and see if they were related. Apparently there was something in the book that had given her a hint.

'Hank would never have let her go, but that's when he died. Just the right time for her to be able to go away by herself. Now wasn't that a bit too convenient?'

'Are you saying that Alice might have . . . helped him down those stairs?'

'I wouldn't be at all surprised. She did some very funny things. Once when she and Nathan had had a row she took a pair of scissors and that night she stayed late at the shop and cut up a whole rack of new season's jackets.'

'She told you she'd done it?'

'She said it must have been vandals who'd broken in. But I saw her smiling when Nathan found out and I *knew* it was her. Another time when he wanted to break off their relationship, she said – I heard them talking in his office – that if he did, she wouldn't only let his wife know what had been going on, but she'd get in touch with the IRS and tell them about how he'd been cheating on his taxes. That wasn't very nice, was it?'

'Was anyone else suspicious about the way Hank died?'

'I don't know. You'd better ask the other people in the house where she lived. I can give you the address if you like.'

I accepted the offer, then she told me about the letters Alice had written after she reached France, which were enthusiastic reports of how Lady Meredith was, indeed, her mother, had welcomed her with open arms and she was now living in the lap of luxury.

She also described meeting her long-lost twin sister, who has an unfortunate background, having been adopted by a prostitute, and said how different this had been from her own happy childhood, brought up in a big house in a park, where she even had her own pony.

'Well, really!' Bibi said. 'She must have forgotten she'd told me years ago that *she* was the one whose Mom was the hooker! They lived in Boston and the only money they ever had was what her Mom got from men. Not only that, but she'd stabbed some guy she'd been living with, and had gone to prison. Alice made a real tragic story out of it.'

Next I went to the address she gave me in the Bronx, where the Lynams had lived. It's a run-down apartment house but the residents are mostly respectable black folk. I was lucky enough to find a couple who live on the ground floor and knew the Lynams well.

Ella-May Doonan is a lovely, large, exuberant lady who has a great admiration for Alice. I talked to her before her husband, Johnny, came home from work. He's a storeman

349

in a cardboard-box factory nearby and Ella-May is an office cleaner.

She was proud because Alice had trusted her enough to let her look after some new clothes she had bought to go on vacation with Hank.

Ella-May said, 'He died the very night she'd taken all those beautiful things upstairs to give him a surprise. That Hank, he'd been down to Casey's Bar and got drunk. When he came home, he made an awful noise going up the stairs. He got to the top and there was this shout, scream more like, and this crash, an' Johnny and me rushed out and there was Hank lyin' with his head all twisted on one side. Dead. Then poor Alice opened the apartment door and rushed down and fell on the floor beside him. I swear, she really loved that man!'

Johnny came in while she was talking, a neat, quiet man about half Ella-May's girth. He listened without saying anything and when she stopped, he suggested she should make us a cup of coffee and bring in a plate of her brownies.

When she'd gone, he said, 'Sir, I don't want Ella-May to know what I have to say, because she loves everyone, my Ella-May, and it'd be a shame for her to find out how wrong she is about Alice Lynam. You understand me?'

I said I did.

'It's like this, there was something real strange about Hank Lynam's falling that night, and I reckon I know what it was. Alice wasn't the love-bird Ella-May thought. I used to meet Hank sometimes in Casey's and he told me she'd taken a knife to him more than once, really meant to kill him, only he was a lot bigger than her and he managed to get it away from her. You'd never think she could do such a thing, so nice and always smiling.'

'Why did he stay with her?' I asked.

'He had this diabetics so he couldn't work, and he depended on her. I always thought that eventually, when it suited Alice, she'd be the one to leave, never mind what happened to him.' He shuddered. 'Sometimes she had this

350

look in her eyes, when she didn't know anyone was watching, like she hated the whole world.'

'Johnny, you said you know what happened the night of Hank's death . . . ?'

'You remember Ella-May told you we were in bed when he came home? It was around midnight. He started upstairs, singing all the while. What Ella-May didn't say, because I guess after what happened, she forgot all about it and I didn't think about it again myself until later, was that when he reached his landing, a door opened and right about the moment he fell, it closed again.'

He could see that I didn't understand what he was getting at. 'Sir, we was the first persons into the hallway to see what'd happened. I turned on the light. The Lynams' door at the top of the stairs was closed, then Alice opened it and came running out. All the other apartments' doors were closed, too, so you tell me: which was that door I'd heard open and close as Hank fell? I got good ears, and I reckon it was the Lynams'. I think she shoved him down those stairs.'

I said, 'Did you tell the police this?'

'No, man! I don't get mixed up in no police business. Never have and I didn't aim to start on account of the Lynams. Hank was dead, couldn't have done him no good. And soon after that, Alice left.'

'So why have you told me?'

'You ain't police. All these months, I been wanting to get it off my chest. Couldn't talk about it to Ella-May, she's too emotional and she wouldn't have believed me anyway. When she likes someone like she does Alice, she won't hear a word against them.'

I have to tell you, Klaus, that Johnny Doonan is a man I would trust absolutely. He is honest, intelligent and not one to jump to hasty conclusions. But you must, of course, decide for yourself whether you go along with his opinion.

You will remember that Bibi told me Alice's foster-mother had been imprisoned for stabbing one of her lovers, so I reckoned a trip to Boston might be productive.

My first stop there was at a newspaper morgue and I struck lucky. The case in 1957 had been given full coverage.

Mavis Bukowsky had been living with a man named Duke Raymond, a rough character who worked as bouncer in a night-club.

One night, according to what Alice told the police, she was lying in her bed (it was actually the sofa in their living-room, because their apartment only had two rooms) listening to a terrible row going on next door. Duke and Mavis were yelling at each other, and fighting. She huddled under the blankets blocking her ears, and next thing she knew, Duke came in. He dragged off her covers and grabbed her, clearly intending rape, she said. She screamed and Mavis rushed in, holding a knife. As Duke was lying on top of Alice, she plunged it into his back. He was dead a few minutes later.

Mavis was arrested and charged with murder. Then came the twist: *she* claimed that it was Alice who had knifed Duke. Her version was that as they were fighting, Alice had come into the bedroom with a kitchen-knife. She shouted, "You're keeping me awake!" and stabbed him.

He had managed to stagger into the living-room and collapsed near the sofa, which was where the police found him.

It became something of a *cause célèbre* and the jury had to decide whether they believed the mother or the daughter.

Alice, a sweet-faced, innocent teenager who shivered and cried when she told the squalid story and was declared a virgin after medical examination, won out. Mavis, the known prostitute, was found guilty, and went to jail protesting her innocence. She served three years, then was found dead in her cell after slicing her wrists with a pair of scissors.

My final call was on a woman named Sadie Lewis, who had shared Mavis's cell during the first year of her imprisonment and is now living in an old persons' home near Boston.

She couldn't tell me much I didn't already know, but of

one thing she is absolutely certain: Mavis did not kill Duke. Sadie said she talked compulsively about Alice, claiming that she was a pathological liar, an accomplished shop-lifter and that since she was a child had been given to sudden violent rages. She swore on everything she held sacred that Alice had killed Duke.

That about wraps it up. I've tried to remain objective and simply report the words of my informants. Now it's over to you. If there is anything further you'd like to know, don't hesitate to get in touch.

As he finished reading, Klaus knew that the problem which he and Charles had hoped Simmonds's investigations would solve was more serious than they could ever have imagined.

10

After an over-long official lunch with the Mayor in La Bergerie, Cybèle was listlessly changing into the golden dress which had given her such pleasure a few days ago.

It was a hot day, with unclouded skies. The temperature had climbed into the mid-twenties, with high humidity. Her brocade train dragged at her shoulders as she went down the stairs, thinking that the only bright spot in her life during the past few days had been the characteristic generosity with which Julia had received her confession. She had been pleased to see that her friendship with Charles was back on course.

Alice was waiting in the hall, her cheeks bright pink, for she had again been tippling enthusiastically during lunch and her costume was heavy. But she appeared to be in high spirits and swept a slightly uncertain curtsey.

'Isn't this the greatest?' Her eyes were blinking excitedly and her words were slurred. 'You and me, the queen and the princess! Gee, I never expected anything like this when I left the Bronx! I mean, gorgeous clothes make you feel a different person, and when I take over the company, I'll be able to get anything I want for free from our shops, won't I?' When Cybèle said nothing, her eyes narrowed. 'You know what, I think we should make our announcement this very afternoon. How 'bout that?'

It was an obvious challenge. Coldly, Cybèle said, 'No. Not today.'

'When, then?' Her voice became softer. 'Not thinking of changing your mind, I hope, Mom?'

'I haven't decided anything yet. Leave me alone, Alice.' She walked outside as Julia, also in costume, arrived in her car.

Alice watched her. Hadn't decided? What made her think she had any choice? Mother Cybèle needed to be taught a lesson.

She went into the kitchen and drew from the drawer a sharp-pointed steak knife with a serrated edge.

As she returned to the sitting-room, she heard Julia calling her from outside.

Her voice was honey-sweet. 'I'll be right there, dear.'

She turned towards the portrait that hung on the wall, stabbed the knife between Cybèle's eyes, and slashed down through the canvas, slicing the painted face in half.

Smiling, she slipped the knife into her little reticule, and joined her mother and sister.

They drove together to the dais from which Cybèle would start the relay.

The crowds had already gathered. Many people were in costume and the majority of them had at least tried to create an historical effect, even if they had paid little regard to period: the men in everything from tights and pantaloons to Roman togas, some women in wimples and robes cut low at the neckline so they looked like debauched nuns, others in crinolines, ruffs, bustles, wearing feathered hats, flirting fans, befrilled, bedizened, bejewelled.

The only dark notes in the gaudy scene were provided by a scattering of motor-cyclists near the dais. Despite the heat, they were dressed in black leathers and helmets, their eyes covered by goggles. They stood, grim figures, moving only their heads as they looked around. Instinctively, people gave them a wide berth. A *gendarme* imported from Bergerac to control the crowd kept his eye on them and was relieved when they moved away from his patch.

By now, all the local people had heard the romantic story of the Englishwoman's reunion with her twin daughters, and their arrival on the stand brought an admiring gasp from the crowd followed by a burst of applause. They were a spectacular trio: the tall, graceful central figure in her gold dress and train, flanked by the two shorter women with their uncannily identical features.

At three o'clock the first members of the rival relay teams were at the starting-post. Arthur was running for the expatriates, self-conscious in blue tights, puffed pantaloons and a kind of medieval t-shirt in red with silver trimmings. The French runner was a young farmer wearing a green costume that made him look like an oak-tree in full leaf. They would have to swing over the stream, then scramble through the line of wine-barrels. Arthur was carrying a blue pennant which he would hand on to the second member of the team, the farmer a red one.

Reports were to be broadcast through loudspeakers from different points along the route to keep the crowds in touch with the competitors' progress.

Excitement mounted as the race's start was announced.

Cybèle moved to a position where both men could see her. She paused for a moment with her arm upraised, holding a red and gold banner, then swept it down. There was a roar as they raced off.

They reached the stream simultaneously, then both, clinging to their ropes like monkeys, swung safely over. The thinner of the two, Arthur snaked through the barrels more quickly and, by the time they ran out of sight, he was well ahead.

Clapping her hands, her problems momentarily forgotten, Julia turned to share the excitement with Alice and her mother. She instantly sobered. Alice was leaning back in her canvas chair. Her face was puce and sweat was pouring down her forehead.

'Alice . . . what's the matter?'

'I don't feel . . . it's the heat . . . oh, God . . .' She jumped down from the dais and began to retch. The other dignitaries glanced around, then politely averted their eyes.

Appalled, Julia whispered to Cybèle, 'I must get her away.'

Cybèle's lip curled with distaste. 'Yes, do. It isn't the heat. She had too much to drink at lunch-time.'

Alice was leaning against the dais with her eyes closed. Julia said gently, 'Listen, dear, I'm going to take you up to the mill where you can lie down.'

Alice's eyelids flew up. 'I don't need you!' she gasped. 'I'm all right. Go away!'

'The race won't be over for ages. There's time for you to have a rest, and be back for the finish if you feel well enough.'

'Leave me alone! I'll go to the mill by myself. I don't need you along.' She glared at Julia, her expression a mixture of humiliation and hatred.

'I'd like to help you . . .'

'Don't you understand? I don't want you!' Her chest heaved. Then, while Julia watched helplessly, she made her way unsteadily towards the little bridge that crossed the stream on to the path which led up to the mill.

Klaus Fischer was watching from the terrace, enjoying the scene less than he might have because of the letter in his pocket. He'd also had a moment of unease when a biker had turned his head towards him. There was something undeniably sinister about the black figure with its goggles like eyeless sockets, and he'd had to force himself to look away. A few minutes later, when he glanced back, the man had gone.

He might have been gazing at a Breughel painting, he thought, with its multitude of figures, all set on enjoying themselves in the rural setting. Many would be drunk by the end of the day, others bloated from overeating. Some, roused by the heat and excitement, would seek private places for open-air love-making. He had a moment of wistfulness. His single-minded, life-long obsession with Cybèle had spoiled any pleasure he might otherwise have taken in such primitive amusements.

His eyes moved across the field to the blue and white dais, with Cybèle, Julia and Alice sitting in the centre of the more soberly clad local burgesses. Beyond them was the final obstacle, the newly built brick wall, nearly five metres high. Christian Morel, as the strongest of the Blue competitors, was to run the last leg and would have to scale it with the aid of a rope, slide down the other side then dash a hundred metres to the finishing-post.

Suzy, in her capacity as one of the stewards who were on duty at each obstacle to ensure there was no cheating, was lolling against a tree near the wall.

She had opted out of wearing costume, saying that years spent posing in bizarre clothes for the camera had turned her off fancy-dress for ever. In her brief denim skirt and scarlet vest, her copper hair loose and gleaming in the sun, Klaus guessed that she would turn more heads than any of the other women in their elaborate gowns.

He was about to settle back in his chair after the race started when he saw Alice break away from the crowd and walk towards the bridge. Realizing that she was making for the mill, his hand went instinctively to Simmonds' letter.

Charles had appeared only briefly after lunch to change into his costume for the race, and there had been no opportunity for him to see it.

Alice reached the steps that led up on to the terrace and paused as she saw him.

Her face brightened. 'Well, this is nice. I forgot you'd be here! I've been feeling so bad in all this heat, and my head's just splitting. I had to get away from the crowds.'

'May I get you something? A glass of water?'

'It's OK. The walk has made me feel better. Let's sit down together for a few minutes.' A flirtatious smile lifted the corners of her mouth.

He looked at her, seeing not the daughter who might be his, but a scheming, lying woman who lacked any sense of right or wrong. A woman who he now believed had murdered two men. A psychopath from whom Julia and Cybèle must be protected.

She sat, looking up at him as he leant on his stick, then pulled another chair close to hers and patted it invitingly.

He said, 'Alice, it is time you went back to New York.'

She shook her head. 'Oh, no, I'm not going back. Not ever. Didn't you know? I'm going to live with Cybèle. She's asked me to take over as head of her company.' There was triumph in her smile.

'I think not,' he said quietly, and held up his letter. 'I know about Hank's death, and Duke Raymond.'

Her smile vanished. 'And just what the hell does that mean?'

'It means that I have had some enquiries made about you. Today, I received a letter from my investigator in New York. He has spoken to people who believe that you were responsible for your husband's death. He has been to Boston and talked to a woman who shared a cell with Mavis Bukowsky. She is convinced that the story Mavis told in court was the true one and that you killed Duke Raymond.'

She surged upright and reached out her hand. 'Give me that letter! Who's been writing those lies?'

'No-one you know. Alice, it wouldn't be easy to prove his allegations, but I'm sure it could be done. I propose to give you a chance: I want you to go away and never contact Cybèle or Julia again. If you agree to do that, I will keep this information to myself. If you do not, I propose to hand the letter to Cybèle.'

She felt the blood pounding in her head like hammer-blows and her voice was low and vicious. 'You old fool! D'you think I'd let you do that? I'll kill you first. Give it to me!'

They were standing in the middle of the wide terrace, so intent on each other that neither registered the sound of motor-cycle engines until the noise became deafening. Three machines swept around the terrace from the front of the mill. Helmeted riders crouched over the handle-bars.

The bikes circled them. They began to make patterns,

figures-of-eight around the tables and chairs, coming within inches of Klaus so that his white hair lifted in the wind of their passing.

The instinct for self-preservation made him momentarily forget Alice. The louts couldn't be intending to injure him. This was no more than harassment. If he stood quite still, he would be safe.

Then he felt hands against his back. One of the riders was making for him, ready to swerve past. The hands pushed him violently and his stick flew up so he lost his balance and fell directly into the motor-cycle's path. He heard an agonized shout and did not know whether it came from himself or the rider. A fraction of a second later, he felt a burning pain as the cycle's tyre scraped his outstretched arm.

The engine-notes changed, quietened. He looked up. The three riders had pulled up their machines in a row and were staring down at him. He heard one of them say: '*Merde! She pushed him! I saw her. She tried to push him under the bike!*'

Another said, 'Let's get out of here!'

They revved their engines, each made a tight circle, and they were gone.

Painfully, he began to climb to his feet. His stick was lying near the parapet that surrounded the mill-wheel.

Alice was facing him, her face contorted. 'Give me that letter!' she hissed.

It was crumpled in his hand. He shook his head, incapable of speech, conscious of the pain in his scorched arm.

She advanced towards him and she was holding a shining knife in her right hand. He backed away, and she followed.

Step by step, they moved across the terrace, until he came up against the parapet and could go no further.

She raised the knife. With her left hand, she reached out to grab the letter.

At that moment, he heard a scream and running footsteps. Alice half-turned, the knife held high, then she continued her plunge forward. But in her moment of inattention, he had managed to jerk his body sideways. As she twisted towards

359

him, her foot landed on his walking-stick. It rolled, she lost her balance and jack-knifed over the low parapet.

For the rest of his life, he would remember the scene in slow motion and hear the sounds: Alice's heavy robes flying up as she somersaulted into one of the mill-wheel's wooden buckets; the creaking of the planks, which had been rotting in the weather for more than a hundred years; the snapping of the old ropes which had prevented the wheel from moving, then the groaning as her weight began to turn it, faster and faster, carrying her down towards the deep, muddy pool.

Only half aware that someone was beside him, he stretched over the parapet to grasp her, but she was out of reach and there was no way he could stop the wheel. The bucket sank inexorably until the bright bundle of clothing was carried into the water. There was no counter-weight to bring it up again. It stopped when it reached the bottom of its revolution and Alice was held fast below the surface.

The relay was reaching its climax. Through the loud-speakers, the audience gathered at the finish had been able to follow its progress as first one team, then the other had gone into the lead.

Among the six older men, who ran in the middle of the field, the French team had drawn ahead. Charles had kept up with his opposite number, Victor Sézille, but Henry Franklin and Frank Dunnett fell back against the butcher, Maurice Simon, and the burly lawyer, Louis Prévert, who were both a few years their junior. Fourteen-year-old Anthony Franklin, Henry's grandson, lessened the gap, and so did the other Blues, so that when Rob handed over his pennant to Christian, he took off level with the French anchor-man.

When they came within sight of the finish, Suzy had taken up her position at the side of the last obstacle. She had time to note that Chris, tall, tanned, and well-built in the short, sleeveless brocade tunic the girls had made, looked less ridiculous than most of the other men in their curious versions of medieval costume. Then, like the rest of the spectators, she was overtaken by the excitement of the finish.

The two men were pounding over the field, neck and neck. Both had negotiated their first obstacle, a series of planks a few inches wide, suspended over trestles. Each had fallen once and had to go back to the start.

Now, as they came towards the brick wall, Suzy looked up and caught a flash of sunlight reflected from the top of it, where Chris's rope was attached. Puzzled, she stepped back on to a little rise from which she was able to see it more clearly.

She still couldn't make out what it was, but a man beside her was holding binoculars. With a hasty word of apology, she took them from him and saw that the glinting object was one of several slivers of broken bottle-glass scattered at the point where Chris would grasp the wall to pull himself over.

She shouted, but her voice was drowned by the crowd. He was hauling himself up the rope, neck and neck with his rival. One hand reached for the summit of the wall and simultaneously he released the rope and threw up his other hand.

There was a sudden hush as he yelled with pain, then fell back and landed in a heap on the ground. He came to his feet, looking unbelievingly at the blood pouring from his hands, staining the front of his tunic.

His opponent was already racing for the finish.

It was during that hush that cries were heard coming from the mill's terrace and a woman appeared, waving frantically.

Charles, on his way back to the dais, was the first to react. Unaware of what had happened to Christian, he realized that the woman was Julia, and she was in trouble. He ran towards the bridge.

Like spectators at a tennis-match, heads swivelled from the terrace back to the bleeding man and the girl beside him, who was shouting for a doctor and bandages.

11

Among people who had gathered for *le pique-nique*, few were aware of the drama that had been enacted at the mill as police, summoned from their duties along the relay route, worked frantically to release Alice from the wheel. But by the time they had cut through her heavy, water-logged draperies, which were inextricably wound around its shaft, she was already dead.

When Charles reached Julia, she had splashed into the stream and was vainly attempting to pull the body free.

Struggling to comprehend the extent of the tragedy, it was some time before she was able to explain that she had left the relay because she had been worried about Alice, who had looked so ill. As she reached the terrace, she was appalled to see her trip and fall over the wall and had rushed to help Klaus in his efforts to halt the wheel.

'Before that . . .' she stopped.

'What, my darling?' Charles's arms were wrapped around her.

She shook her head. She still couldn't believe the evidence of her eyes: the woman who had been only momentarily distracted by her own appearance, apparently about to plunge a knife into the heart of the old man, who was pressed back against the wall, his face a terrified mask. Until she had talked to him, she would not mention it, even to Charles.

The incident about which the picnickers were talking as they drank red wine and watched the carcases of lambs and pigs slowly turning on spits over the barbecue fires was the sabotage of the foreigners' relay team.

It had been deliberate, because the shards of glass had been cemented in place. It had also clearly been specifically intended to injure Christian Morel, the Frenchman who had defected to the British.

Bleeding profusely, almost incoherent with pain and anger, he had been rushed to the hospital in La Bergerie by Suzy and a doctor who had emerged from the crowd. There the deep cuts on his palms had been stitched and bandaged.

Rob had looked after Klaus at the mill. His scorched arm, though painful, needed only soothing ointment and a light bandage.

He described to a grim-faced Jacques Millet the motor-cyclists' assault, but said nothing about the push that had sent him sprawling in front of one of them. Neither, like Julia, did he mention Alice's attack. Each of them wanted to talk to the other, but the attentions to which they were subject gave them no immediate opportunity.

It was Charles who, when Julia was calmer, volunteered to break the news of Alice's death to Cybèle.

He found her still down in the field, unaware of what had happened. She was surrounded by officials and police who were trying to establish how the brick wall had been sabotaged – and by whom.

Prevented from speaking to her by a hail of questions, he described as briefly as possible how he and Sézille had checked the obstacles before the race, but admitted that it had not occurred to either of them to do more than make sure the climbing-ropes were securely fastened to the wall. The glass was invisible from ground level and could, therefore, have been set in place at any time after the wall was built, probably at night.

Victor Sézille, looking old and ill, took little part in the discussion.

Charles was still trying to draw Cybèle away when the talk turned to the result of the race, and what should be done about a prize-giving. It was then that Sézille rose and, with a certain bull-like dignity, said heavily: 'There will be no prizes. On behalf of our team, and all the people of La Bergerie, madame, I offer a public apology for this appalling act.'

Finally, Charles and Cybèle were able to leave. Julia's car

was nearby, and as they sat in it, he told her gently that Alice had died in a tragic accident at the mill.

'Is Julia all right?' she said sharply.

'She's very distressed. She tried to save Alice, but it was impossible. I'm so sorry, Cybèle.'

'Tell me about it.'

Her face was expressionless; only her thin hands, gripping each other, betrayed tension.

When he had finished, she said quietly, 'Let's go to Julia.'

That evening, there was a subdued gathering in the mill's kitchen.

It was late before the police finally departed and Alice's body was removed. As the news spread, the Franklins and other friends called in to express their shock and sympathy.

When the last outsider had gone and the barbecue fires in the field had burned down into glowing ashes, Cybèle asked Charles to drive her home. She rejected all offers to keep her company overnight.

When they reached the villa, she did not invite him in, so she was alone when she discovered the mutilation of her portrait.

She stood looking at it for some minutes, then took it down and turned its face to the wall. As she walked slowly up to her bedroom, she realized that she would no longer have to lock her door, and it was as though a weight had been lifted from her shoulders.

By the time Charles got back to the mill, Claire had produced some cold meats and salad, but no-one felt much like eating.

Klaus and Julia, subdued and silent, had retired. Julia had given in to Charles's insistence that she should not return to the hotel and taken over his attic room. He would, he had assured her, sleep comfortably on the sofa in his office.

The volunteers, changed from their garish costumes into normal clothes, drifted in one by one. Chris's hands were heavily bandaged and Suzy sat beside him to cut up his food and lift his wine-glass to his lips.

At first, as though still in the presence of death, voices were hushed, but gradually wine banished inhibitions and, inevitably, the talk concentrated on Alice's death. Neither Klaus nor Julia had offered any further details of what had happened on the terrace and it was assumed that she had either tripped or had been sitting on the low wall and lost her balance. This was the more popular theory, since it was generally known that she had drunk too much wine at lunch-time.

It wasn't until after nine o'clock that Arthur said suddenly, 'Anybody seen Olivia?'

It appeared that she had not been sighted since she had gone off to take up her steward's position at one of the obstacles near La Bergerie.

'I haven't been into our room. Maybe she came back and went to sleep. I'll go and see,' Suzy said.

She was back within a few seconds. 'She isn't there! All her clothes have gone!'

Charles rubbed a hand wearily over his forehead. 'Jesus, what next? Did she tell anyone she was leaving?'

Heads were shaken, then after a moment Suzy said hesitantly, 'She's been a bit – irritable for the past couple of days. I've a feeling it might have been something to do with me.' She slanted a glance towards Chris.

'And me,' he said grimly. 'You might as well know, Olivia thought she and I were . . . had . . . and then Suzy . . . This is very embarrassing!'

'Suzy took you over,' Claire said calmly. 'As if we didn't know. Then you two had a row, didn't you? And Olivia thought she was back in the running, only you made it up and this morning you were like a couple of mating budgerigars. I bet that's why she's taken off.'

'Didn't she even give you a hint, Charles?' Tim said. 'I call that bloody bad manners.'

'Not a hint . . . wait a minute!' He left the table. When he came back, he was holding a letter. 'I remembered noticing an envelope on my desk but in all the chaos, I didn't open it. It's from Olivia, says she's discovered she doesn't really enjoy the work here and she's going home. Thanks for having her, and all that.'

A little while later, he went upstairs to see if Julia was awake. There was no response to his knock. He opened the door and peered in. The room was empty. He had a sudden, irrational fear that she, too, had fled. Then he heard low voices coming from along the corridor.

Julia had undressed, but been unable to sleep, haunted by the vision of Alice's hand clutching a knife, then the dead face, so like her own, but with its contours distorted under the brown, oily water.

Eventually, she put on Charles's dressing-gown and went to Klaus's room.

He was sitting up in bed, a book, unread, lying face-down on his knees. His eyes were heavy, his Roman-coin face sad and old, but it lightened when he saw her. 'My dear girl, I was hoping it might be you. We must talk, yes?'

She sat on his bed and said without preamble. 'What happened before Alice fell?'

'How much did you see?'

'I saw her standing. The knife. As though she was going to . . .'

'To kill me. That is what she would have done. She had already attempted to push me under one of the motor-cycles.'

She was staring at him, speechless, when they heard a tap on the door. Charles came in and relief spread over his face.

'For a moment I was afraid . . .' He stopped. 'Klaus, what's my girl doing in your room at ten o'clock at night?'

Klaus managed a smile. 'I am flattered that you would ask such a question. I have things to tell Julia, Charles, and I believe you should hear them, too.' He reached out to his bedside table and picked up some crumpled sheets of paper. 'This is a letter I received today. I wanted to show it to you at once, but there was no chance. You may read it later, but I will tell you briefly what it contains.'

His voice was tired as he unfolded the story of Alice Lynam's past, and then described what had happened on the

366

terrace. Halfway through, Charles reached for Julia's hand and held it tightly.

'. . . So you see why she wanted to kill me. If Cybèle had discovered what she was, there would have been no future for her here. I was always going to be a threat. That knife . . .' He shivered. 'There is no doubt she would have used it. You were right about her, Charles.'

Julia said sharply. 'You suspected? Why didn't you tell me?'

'I wish I had! I recognized certain signs. I've met psychopaths before, but I couldn't be sure. It seemed too bizarre.' He frowned. 'Does Cybèle know what's in the letter?'

'No. And I do not think she should be told. Why should she suffer further distress?'

'There's no need for anyone else to know, not even Suzy,' Julia said decisively.

'So you will carry this secret by yourself?' Klaus said. 'It will be distressing for you, I think, Julia.'

'Not by myself. I have you and Charles to share it with. And there's something else . . .' She told them about the shop-lifting incidents in Bordeaux and La Bergerie. Then she said, 'I often dreamed of finding my twin sister, but in my dreams she always hated me. When we did meet, at first it was wonderful, but then . . . we never became close. I felt that she resented me and it was as though the dreams were coming true. It worried me. I thought it was something lacking in *me*. In a way, knowing the truth about her makes me feel better, although the – the enormity of what she did probably hasn't sunk in yet.' Her voice broke. 'I do wish, for Cybèle's sake, that she had been different . . .'

'Cybèle has you,' Klaus said quietly. 'She is a very lucky woman.'

12

Julia came early to the villa the morning after Alice's death.

Downstairs, Sophie was moving quietly in her espadrilles, her normally cheerful face self-consciously solemn as befitted a house struck by tragedy.

She pointed upstairs and whispered: 'Madame is in the room of Madame Lynam.'

Alice's door was closed and Julia tapped gently. A voice said, 'I don't want to be disturbed, Sophie.'

'It's me.'

She opened the door on chaos. Drawers were pulled out and clothes lay in piles on the floor: glittering pink sequins, garish satins, underwear and newer garments of restrained good taste. There was an overflowing ashtray on the dressing-table, and a smell of old cigarette-butts.

Cybèle was standing in front of an open cupboard, looking at a shelf crowded with knick-knacks.

Julia said, 'You shouldn't be doing this. Leave it to me.'

Without turning her head, Cybèle said, 'I want to get rid of this stuff as quickly as possible. I can't stand knowing – knowing part of her is still here.'

'Then I'll help you. Shall I clear the shelf?'

'If you like. I'm going to send the clothes to a charity in Bergerac or Bordeaux.' She began to cram the piles into black polythene sacks.

The dead woman's personality was all around them. Julia could almost see, hanging in the air like the Cheshire cat, the round face, its eternal smile hardened by scarlet lipstick, the heavily powdered skin, and the brown-marble eyes, hate-filled as they were the last time she had seen Alice alive.

She picked up a polythene bag and began moving objects into it from the shelf. It was a curious collection of chain-store junk: ear-rings still attached to their cards, cheap bracelets, necklaces, ash-trays, glass and china animals, a rubber bath-duck, cosmetics, bars of chocolate and packets of sweets, ornaments ranging from a crudely painted wooden donkey to a small gilded basket containing pink plastic roses. And at one side, unopened, a white opaque-glass pot of caviare.

· A voice spoke behind her: 'I think she stole those things, Julia. I never saw her buy any of them.'

'Yes.'

'You knew?'

'I – wondered.'

'It never occurred to me that she was a thief.'

'I wish – I wish we could have helped her.'

'If I hadn't abandoned her – abandoned you both . . . It's taken me nearly fifty years to feel guilty about what I did, but I'll live with it for the rest of my life.'

Assuming that her distress was focused on the thefts, Julia said gently, 'We found each other in the end. Alice had an – illness, but she loved you, and her accident was nobody's fault.'

'No.' The previous night Cybèle had gone over and over the events which had preceded the festival and had come to the conclusion that nothing would be gained by disclosing the part Alice had played in Arnie Gold's death. Nor, indeed, by identifying 'Alfred Brown'. Arnie and Alice were dead, let them rest in peace. And if Julia liked to believe that Alice had felt some affection for her mother, no need to disillusion her. Eventually the vandalized portrait would be burned so no-one would ever see the destruction that had revealed her true feelings.

As Julia cleared the shelf, she was thinking about her conversation with Charles the previous night. After leaving Klaus's room, they had sat together for hours, discussing the revelations in Neil Simmonds's letter, and Charles had surprised her by confessing his psychiatric background.

At one point, she said, 'You say Alice was a psychopath. Is there any treatment she could have had?'

'I'm pretty certain the condition stemmed from her rejected

childhood,' he said. 'She was striking back at anyone who got in her way, believing that the world owed her a living. Nobody knows precisely what makes a psychopath. There are millions of people who survive environments as bad as or worse than Alice's without going off the rails, but I'm afraid that by the time we met her, she was beyond help. Children can be helped sometimes by changing their environment, but therapy is rarely wholly successful with adults. The problem is that a psychopath has to be forced to feel guilt and shame for his actions. That can be a hell of a lot harder than relieving the same symptoms in other patients.'

The two women worked on, and neither knew that the other was guarding knowledge which, to protect each other, they would never share.

By the end of the afternoon, all traces of Alice had been removed from the villa.

13

Normal life was slowly resumed at Le Bas-Fond after Alice's funeral.

Julia had moved permanently into the mill and was sharing Suzy's room. Cybèle had hardly emerged from the villa and Julia, who visited her every day, was the only person to see her regularly. She reported that she was as perfectly groomed and self-possessed as ever. At the same time, she was uncharacteristically inclined to sit, inactive and staring into space, for minutes at a time. They rarely spoke of Alice.

'One curious thing,' Julia said to Charles. 'Her portrait has gone. When I asked her about it she said that she was tired of the past intruding on her life and she'd got rid of it.'

'She hasn't mentioned you working with her again?'

'Not yet. Charles, we must tell her soon.'

'Give her a few more days.' He recognized that there was more than a touch of cowardice in the postponement. Having made up his mind to reject Cybèle's offer of a partnership, he had already hardened himself to the knowledge that his days at Le Bas-Fond were numbered. But even more, he dreaded the confrontation when she learned that he was going to marry Julia. Although he was not a vain man, her hints about a closer personal relationship had been unmistakable, and Cybèle was not one to tolerate a rival.

Knowing nothing of this, Julia said, 'You must decide when she's ready to cope with another shock. You're the one who understands people's minds.'

'Not well enough,' he said, and she knew that he was thinking, not only of Alice, but of Laura.

After the funeral, he had told her about his marriage and his wife's murder. In return, she had talked about Alex, whose death had been no less agonizing than Laura's. They had sat for hours in his office, ignoring the world outside, as they relived the past. In the end, both felt as though they had gone through a catharsis which had brought them even closer together.

Less emotionally touched by Alice's death than her mother and grandmother, Suzy's post-festival nightmare was the memory of blood pouring from Chris's hands, staining his tunic and legs, dripping on to the green grass. At the hospital, it had been some time before she could be convinced that he was not going to die from his wounds, which had, in fact, missed the veins in his wrists by an inch.

A few days after the funeral, she was working in the vine-yard when he hurried towards her. His hands and forearms were still heavily bandaged.

She frowned at the expression on his face. 'Is something wrong?'

'My notes have gone.'

'Notes?'

'The notes about Cybèle and my mother. Did you take them?'

371

'Of course I didn't! You told me you were going to destroy them.'

As always under stress, his French accent, normally hardly noticeable, thickened. 'They were folded in my copy of her book. I was going to ask you to light the matches for me so we could burn them, but they are not now there.'

'Who on earth would take them? And why?'

'I do not know. It could not be Cybèle herself, she has never been into my room. Charles? Klaus? The other volunteers? Not possible!'

'Who else is there?' Then she said, 'Olivia! Could it have been Olivia?'

'She has not either been in my room – *mon Dieu!*'

'What?'

'The night you and I talked on the terrace, when I told you I would not write that story . . . we went upstairs together. You remember?'

'I could hardly forget.'

'When we were in bed, I said to you, what is that perfume you are wearing, and you said you were not wearing any. But there was a strong scent on the pillow. I took no notice at the time . . . there were other things on my mind . . .'

'I smelt it too. I thought it was your after-shave.'

'I do not use after-shave that smells like *muguet*. Olivia went upstairs before me. She had been very – clinging. I wished her good night, and I remember she said dramatically, "We only part to meet again." That is a famous quotation in English?'

'I don't know it. Do you think . . . ?'

'At the time, if I *had* thought about it, I'd have assumed that she meant the next morning. But suppose she went to my room to wait for me, and picked up the book? The window was open . . .'

'. . . So she could have heard us talking on the terrace. That would explain why she was cross afterwards, and why she decided to leave.'

'We spoke about the notes. I remember you said, "If Cybèle found out, she would try to separate us." *Merde!* Olivia *must* have taken them. Perhaps to publish? Because she was angry with us and knew it would cause trouble?'

'What are we going to do?'

'I must see Cybèle before anything happens.'

'I'll come with you.'

The villa was silent, but the front door was open and as they drove up, Cybèle appeared at the top of the steps, elegant as always in cream trousers and a pink polo-shirt. Suzy wondered whether any living person had seen her looking dishevelled.

She watched them silently as they came towards her. She did not stand aside to let them in, simply stood, unsmiling.

'Madame, we wish to talk to you,' Chris said haltingly.

'I presume it is to do with this extraordinary story you sent me about Marie Masson.'

'You have it? How did you get it?'

'It was sent down to me with my mail the day after Alice died.' He and Suzy looked at each other and he nodded as her mouth shaped the word Olivia. 'I notice you aren't denying that you wrote it.'

'No. I wrote it,' he said unhappily. 'But I would like to explain.'

'You read my book, you know the story of my relationship with Marie Masson. Did you make up that version hoping to sell it to *France Dimanche* or *News of the World*?'

'Cybèle, it wasn't like that!' Suzy said. 'Look, we can't go on talking on the door-step. Mayn't we come in?'

She shrugged. 'I suppose so. I have, in fact, been considering what to do about this.'

They followed her into the living-room. She sat down in a cane chair. Hands on its arms, her head arrogantly high, she looked like a queen receiving unwelcome supplicants, but Chris refused to be cowed. He sat at one end of the sofa and Suzy settled next to him.

Cybèle wasted no words. 'What I wish to know is why you chose Marie Masson as the subject for your fiction. There were other people who might have been more rewarding if you were looking for scandal.'

'I'm her son,' he said.

For the first time, they saw her lose her poise. Her mouth sagged open and her body curved forward as the careful rigidity of her spine collapsed. 'Marie? Your mother?'

Now that the moment of confrontation had arrived, his face hardened. 'Everything in those notes was what she told me. I watched her live a miserable life, constantly in pain, and die a lonely death. I was shocked when I read your version of what happened and how you accused her of having betrayed you. I was going to set the record straight.'

'I don't understand why you bothered to come to Le Bas-Fond. You could have published that nonsense without leaving Paris.'

'I wanted to see the kind of woman you really are, and your reaction when I told you I knew the truth.'

With an obvious effort, she regained her equilibrium. 'But you were too much of a coward to face me with it yourself.'

'I didn't send that manuscript. Suzy and I believe that Olivia did – it doesn't matter why. In fact, I had decided to destroy it.'

'Are you telling me you've changed your mind about publishing? Why?'

'Because you're Suzy's grandmother, and I'm going to marry Suzy.'

'Ah.' She shot a glance at Suzy and said acidly, 'I cannot admire your taste in men. So it was not because you realized the story was untrue?'

He shook his head. 'No. But there's another reason. I've found that I – admire you, and I don't want you to be humiliated.'

'Thank you, but I'm afraid the humiliation would have been yours. There isn't a word of truth in your mother's story. I never told the Gestapo about her. Raoul, who was one of our Resistance colleagues, warned me that she had been picked up and would probably be forced to talk. When the Gestapo arrived at my apartment, I knew he had been right.'

'He was wrong! They did everything they could to make

374

her talk. In the end they threw her down on a concrete floor. *But she never talked!'*

His vehemence was impressive. She leant forward. 'Then how did they know about me? There was no other way.'

'How did they find out about *her?*'

She began to nibble at her lower lip and her eyes seemed to focus on a scene neither Chris nor Suzy could see. Finally she said slowly, 'Perhaps there was a way. I used to pass information to Marie in the street whcn we pretended to bump into each other accidentally. I had been the . . . friend of a Gestapo officer named Fritz Bauch. He liked to talk about his work, so he was useful to us. But he was arrogant and pathologically jealous. After a few months, I began to avoid him. He accused me of seeing other men. We had a row and I told him I never wanted to see him again. I knew I was taking a risk, but I didn't care.'

'That wasn't in your book.'

'In the context of my escape, he was unimportant, or so I thought.' She raised an eyebrow. 'And I did not feel it necessary to record *all* my lovers.

'During my last week in Paris I had to meet Marie three times to pass on written messages.' The words came more quickly. 'It could be that Fritz had me followed – or even followed me himself – to see whether I was meeting another man. It would have been in character. He was no fool . . . he would have registered the pattern: how during each walk, in different areas, I bumped into the same woman. Marie was quite noticeable: big, with that bush of black hair. Isn't it possible that he had her followed, raided her apartment and found the transmitter? Then he would have known what I was doing. They probably told her that I was a traitor to persuade her that there was no point in not answering their questions. When she still wouldn't talk, and they found that I'd already escaped, they tortured her in an attempt to make her reveal the names of other Resistance members.'

There was silence for a moment, then Chris said reluctantly, 'It could have happened that way.'

'I'm sure it did! My life was so chaotic after that, escaping, being passed from hand to hand down through France, walking across the Pyrenees into Spain, that it didn't occur to me to doubt that Raoul was right and Marie had given me away to save herself. I could never understand it, because I had admired her dedication.'

'She was always convinced it was you.'

'Marie and I were never close friends. We were too different and she disapproved of the way I worked. It hurt her to use information I provided, knowing how I'd obtained it. But I would never have let her down.' She rose and faced him. 'I was wrong about her and I'll put the record straight myself. It's too late to do anything about the first edition of my book, but they're planning a second printing, and I'll see that the section is altered. I'll talk to Klaus Fischer and I can rewrite it for the German edition, and the French.'

She held out her hand. He raised it to his lips and said quietly, 'Thank you, madame.'

The full force of her charm reached out to him as she smiled. 'Your loyalty to your mother is impressive, my dear boy. Maybe my grand-daughter's taste in men isn't so bad after all.'

14

The night before Klaus Fischer was due to return to Berlin, Cybèle arranged a small farewell dinner-party for him.

In the early evening he was packing when Charles tapped on his door. He was carrying a bottle of Scotch and two glasses. 'I thought we'd have a last quiet drink together before we go out. Did you know that the young people have decided that we're going to the airport *en masse* to see you off?'

'I'm honoured. It will be hard to say goodbye to them.' They lifted their glasses in a silent toast. 'I am not good at speeches, Charles, but I thank you for everything.'

'Everything? Since you came here, you've been insulted, attacked by thugs and nearly killed by a psychopath. You haven't much to thank me for.'

'Believe me, I have. I won't go into details, because there's something else I wish to talk to you about, and there isn't much time.' He closed his suitcase and sat on the bed. 'Not long after I arrived here, you honoured me with your confidence about the death of your wife. Now I want you to know the real reason why I came to Le Bas-Fond.'

'The real reason? Other than editing Cybèle's book?'

'It didn't need editing. That was an excuse. How well do you recall the book?'

'Pretty well.'

'Do you remember a man she called only "the German"? A very young officer she met when she was with the circus, just as the war broke out.'

Charles didn't answer for a moment, then he said, 'I remember. It was you?'

'Yes. Losing that girl changed my life. I was very young, very naive, very much in love. Then . . . she was gone. For years after the war, I searched Europe for her. Even during my marriage, I couldn't forget. Work was the only thing that took my mind off her.

'Nearly fifty years later, I read this book, *I am Cybèle*, which we were going to publish, and I knew I'd found her. But the most important thing was that she'd borne twins and did not know whether they were from her step-father or from "the German". I always wanted children, Charles, but my poor wife could not give me any.

'I decided to come and see Cybèle, without telling her who I was. Fortunately, my name is a common one and I now look very different. I wanted to find out whether there was any possibility that she knew more about what had happened to the twins than she had admitted in the book. I also wondered – of course I wondered! – whether there might not be a chance . . .' He shrugged. 'When I met her, I knew at once that there wasn't. She was not the girl I'd known, and I wasn't any longer that silly young man.'

Charles shook his head bemusedly. 'Life lately has been one surprise after another. It never occurred to me . . . Klaus, thank you for telling me this, but I wonder why you have?'

The old man gave one of his rare, youthful smiles. 'Because it gives me pleasure to think that when you marry Julia, as I imagine you intend, it is just possible that you will be my son-in-law and I wanted to give you my official blessing. No, I make a joke. It is because I wish for your advice.' He took a deep breath. 'I do not know whether I should come out of my cupboard – closet? – and admit my identity. To you, I have, because I know you'll respect my confidence.

'I have thought about this a great deal. Of course I would like Julia to know that there is a possibility that I am her father. But Cybèle? Do I have the right to reopen the past, especially after what she has gone through with Alice? The mere fact of telling her who I am must make her suspicious of my motives. Perhaps she would even wonder whether I am threatening her relationship with Julia. What do you think?'

'I think you've already made up your mind what you're going to do,' Charles said. 'And I agree with you.'

'So I stay as I am, *ja*? The family friend. But one who will, I hope, be allowed by her future husband to see occasionally the lady whom I will always think of as my daughter?'

'We'll insist on it. And let's leave the options open. Some time in the future, we might feel we can tell Julia – and I'm sure that nothing would give her greater pleasure than to find out even that you *might* be her father.' He paused, then said suddenly, 'Have you a copy of Cybèle's book handy?'

'It's in the top of my suitcase.'

'May I look at it?'

Klaus unlocked the case and handed him the book. He turned the pages until, near the front, he found what he wanted. 'I thought so! Listen, this is her description of Arnie Gold: "a sleek, agile young man with a beaked nose, pencil moustache and roving blue eyes."'

'So? I remember that. It means something?'

'Well, I'm no geneticist, but I do know that it's very unlikely, if not impossible, that two blue-eyed people could produce brown-eyed children. Cybèle and Gold both have blue eyes. Yours are dark brown, and so are Julia's.'

Klaus turned to the mirror that hung near the door as though to make sure the eyes that looked back at him were indeed brown. Then he said, 'I think you have given me the best news I could have hoped for.'

For the first time in weeks, Cybèle was not displeased with her mirrored image as she dressed for dinner. The deep lines of strain on her face had softened and the skin stretched over her cheek-bones was firm and smooth.

During the days she had sat alone in the villa, she had tried to come to terms with her guilt.

She had told no-one how often the spectres of Alice and Arnie Gold returned to haunt her dreams. She clung to the hope that time and hard work would blur the memories and, as she often had before, found comfort in the memory of her father's words so long ago: 'You're a survivor.'

She drew a dark line under her lower eyelashes, then another along the rim of her upper lids. As she picked up a brush to apply blue eye-shadow, her thoughts went back to the book she had written, for no other reason than personal aggrandizement. If she hadn't written it, none of the horrible events of the past weeks would have occurred. It had brought her chickens home to roost with a vengeance – and some of them had turned out to be vultures.

But equally, if she hadn't written it, she wouldn't have found Julia and Suzy.

My God, she thought, if that girl has children, I could be a great-grandmother before I'm seventy! She examined the prospect, and to her surprise, did not find it unpleasant. At this rate, she might soon find herself *boasting* about her age.

Not yet, though. Tonight, she intended to impart to her guests her plans for the future, which did not include woolly shawls and felt slippers.

She went downstairs where Sophie, who had turned out to be an excellent cook, was preparing dinner. The dining-table was set inside, because a wind was whipping over the terrace. She approved the shining crystal and silver, the fine linen mats and napkins, the centrepiece of full-blown red and yellow roses. There were places for six: Julia and Charles, Suzy and Christian, Klaus Fischer and herself. A nice man, Klaus, she thought casually. Reserved, a little stiff, inclined to be over-formal with his bowing and heel-clicking, but good company when he relaxed. Not the kind of man to whom she had ever been attracted, though.

They had reached the final course, a pyramid of light-as-air *profiteroles* filled with cream and smothered in caramel sauce, when she made her announcement.

Without any fanfare, she took advantage of a pause in the conversation to say casually, 'I must tell you all that I'm going to get rid of Le Bas-Fond.'

The silence extended. Julia reached out to take Charles's hand. After a moment, he said, 'This is sudden, Cybèle.'

'Not really. I've been thinking about it for some weeks and I've decided against going into the wine business. It isn't my scene and at my age . . .' (It was the first time anyone had heard her use the phrase.) '. . . I've decided I'd better stick to what I know.'

'I thought you'd retired from that,' Suzy said.

'Only semi, when I was writing my book. But leisure doesn't suit me, and things get slack at the magazine and in the shops if I'm not around to frighten the staff.' They were not to know that one reason for her anticipatory smile was the prospect of Max Harrison's annoyance when he discovered that his ambitions would have to be returned to the shelf. 'I believe I'll go to Australia and open a branch of Cybèle in Melbourne, then investigate possibilities in the Far East. It'd be foolish to keep this place when I'll have hardly any time to spend here.'

'When are you putting it on the market?' Charles's voice was strained.

'I didn't say anything about putting it on the market. I'm giving it to you and Julia as a wedding-present.'

He gaped at her. 'That's impossible! Anyway, how do you know we're getting married?'

She had no intention of telling them about Alice's malicious report. 'Any fool could see which way the wind was blowing. What is impossible?'

'For you to give away Le Bas-Fond. It's a going concern now. With all the improvements we've made, it's worth much more than you paid for it.'

'I can do what I like with it!' she snapped, sounding more like the woman he had come to know. 'And now, we will drink to your future, and to Chris and Suzy.'

They raised their glasses, then Charles leant over and kissed her. Feeling the firm lips on her cheek, she had a moment of regret for a lost opportunity. But she knew that she did not really want to share her life again. After Alice's death she had rediscovered the pleasure of solitude – solitude as distinct from loneliness. Looking around the table, she thought that loneliness was no longer the threat it had been.

THE END

SEX IN THE AFTERNOON
by June Flaum Singer

She was the most beautiful and alluring woman he had ever seen. She was also the most elusive. But Jonathan West was a millionaire and knew how to get what he wanted. And he wanted her – the mysterious woman in the luxury suite on the *QE2*. He set his vast organization to find out who she was, where she came from, but even as he tried to subdue her, possess her, claim her as yet another of his conquests, he found himself drawn into a web of sexuality and mystery. All he could discover was her name – Andrianna DeArte.

As their devious and curious relationship grew, the secrets grew stranger. For Andrianna DeArte had many names and many lives. And no-one knew the real life, the life that had begun as the daughter of a Mexican girl and the ruthless man who had bought her, the life that had shattered into violence, lies, and passionate sexual betrayal until there was no man she trusted, no man she would not use.

Between her and Jonathan West exploded a raw sexual hunger, a passionate obsession that threatened to shatter both their lives.

0 552 13503 8

THE NAKED HEART
by Jacqueline Briskin

Their friendship began in the Paris of 1941 – a Paris held in the double grip of an icy winter and the Nazi occupation. But for Gilberte – the daughter of aristocratic French parents – and Anne, vibrant, generous and American, it was the beginning of a lifetime of friendship, betrayal, love and hate. It was the time that they both fell in love with Quentin Dejong, handsome, brave, and a member of the Resistance – Quent, who was to prove the catalyst in both their lives.

As the frightening shadow of the Gestapo moved closer, touching first Anne, then Gilberte, their lifetime pattern was set. Gilberte, whose experiences turned her into a survivor, a collaborator, and a cold ruthless planner, was to become obsessed with seeking vengeance. Anne – forced to grow up almost overnight – made a daring escape over the Alps and then waited for Quent to come back to her.

It was not until the Liberation that the three met again – and by then the terrible secrets of the past began to dominate their lives and the lives of those who loved them.

0 552 13395 7

A SELECTED LIST OF FINE TITLES
FROM CORGI BOOKS

THE PRICES SHOWN BELOW WERE CORRECT AT THE TIME OF GOING TO PRESS.
HOWEVER TRANSWORLD PUBLISHERS RESERVE THE RIGHT TO SHOW NEW
RETAIL PRICES ON COVERS WHICH MAY DIFFER FROM THOSE PREVIOUSLY
ADVERTISED IN THE TEXT OR ELSEWHERE.

All Corgi/Bantam Books are available at your bookshop or newsagent, or can
be ordered from the following address:
Corgi/Bantam Books,
Cash Sales Department,
P.O. Box 11, Falmouth, Cornwall TR10 9EN

UK and B.F.P.O. customers please send a cheque or postal order (no currency)
and allow £1.00 for postage and packing for the first book plus 50p for the
second book and 30p for each additional book to a maximum charge of £3.00
(7 books plus).

Overseas customers, including Eire, please allow £2.00 for postage and
packing for the first book plus £1.00 for the second book and 50p for each
subsequent title ordered.

NAME (Block Letters) ....

ADDRESS ....

....